WINDBURN
WHIPLASH

MATT WEBER

COBBLER & BARD PRESS

For Kira,
who hasn't gotten a book yet

CHAPTER 1

DRAGON. *Also "*WYRM*";* AFFECTIONATELY, *"cargo parrot," "death chicken." In Yemareir and the surrounding area, a hollow-boned, winged, feathered, flying, fire-breathing reptile. Sociable and intelligent; innumerable species breed and live within the city limits. Named by analogy to a species of featherless reptiles (also with the fire breath, long extinct) used by the Empire of Mlinivoun to assert dominance over their territories, back when they had territories. The historical record indicates that the Mrineen who settled Yemareir had dreams of using the native wyrm population to resume their colonial bullshit, but—*

(We invite the reader to interpolate six eruditely referenced paragraphs of fulminating deletia on Mrineen colonialism. Please see Dr. Agama's widely praised articles, "Ectothermic Bastards of the Dragon Princes" and "Face-First Into the Conflagration," for more detail. —Ed.)

The main things for you, tourist, are these:

> 1. *Stay out of the precincts where breeding season is occurring. If you're in an area that doesn't look blighted, but the streets are empty, get out. If, in getting out, you run into a giant tower of obsidian and basalt that looks like the world's most evil termite mound, TURN AROUND.*

2. Unless you want a pushy best friend with big teeth and no boundaries, do not feed these things.

I'm not guaranteeing you won't get roasted and eaten if you follow these guidelines, but the probability will be much closer to whatever it is wherever you're from.

SEE ALSO: Brimstone Slipstream; Broodspire; Dragons, Common; Dragons, Rare.

—From "A Visitor's Handbook for Yemareir," by Shenireen Agama

***

THERE WERE A FEW ways to get hotter on dragonback than Zaya was in her third hour coasting over the Emerald Dunes—a direct hit from a geyser in the Mariposa Annulus, for one, or fifteen seconds coursing through the Devil's Tureen at an hour past noon. But when you were racing, there were other things on your mind, whether it was fending off the wyrm behind you or overtaking the one in front, and the rush of parting air keening a high white song the whole time. Out here, well—in theory, she was deeply absorbed in guarding the safety of the camel caravan below, stuffed with durable goods from Nistrium and the northern Ililuë convivencies. In theory, she was scanning for threats from all sides and triple-checking any shifty-looking clouds. In practice, all this vigilance occupied some small sliver of brain tissue deep in the back of her skull, leaving the rest of it free to dwell on every muscle moaning with the ache of spending hours clinging to a fire-breathing feathered lizard the size of an elephant.

She looked ahead at Vrinzhoon and Zrileen, sitting upright on blue-and-grey Dusk Stalker wyrms, and thought idly about whether she could shake them in a chase, and how long it would take. A wide-open course like this didn't reward agility; it would be purely an efficiency play. It wouldn't be hard to get them to waste their wyrms' blood sugar on extravagant sprints, pile up lactic acid in the muscles of their shoulders to slow them down. She could take this Dawn Wyrm anywhere and never get caught.

Or, anywhere except where the caravan was going to begin with: Back to Yemareir, to the house in Lilac Precinct, and to the purse of cash her family was waiting on. If they could afford to lose that, she wouldn't be here in the first place.

At the edge of Zaya's mind, she noticed the Dawn Wyrm notice a flutter of some kind in the corner of its eye, far above them.

"Don't chase buzzards," she said. "They're not good eating."

Too fast, the wyrm's mind responded. *Too big, too close.*

"How many?" Zaya asked. "What kind? Don't look up."

The wyrm waited several seconds, watching from the corner of its eye and tallying. *Maybe three.* The smell-image of the stalkers was thin, sharp, cold, the feather-pattern image grey-brown, the sense of size and mass substantial. Zaya put an image of a Greater Gyrdrake into the Dawn Wyrm's mind and got back a buzz of confirmation. *Your sense of smell is terrible.*

"Learn to add single-digit numbers and you can drag me," said Zaya.

The trajectories sharpened in her mind as they did in the Dawn's: Wide circular arcs, but moving forward, like a child drawing loops in a line, to keep up with the caravan, high enough that the clouds provided cover. Zaya slipped her goggles on and reached into her jacket to loosen the knife in the sheath against her ribs. "We're about to get hit." She imaged what she meant: Dragons plummeting from the clouds to crash into them with fire and talons, rag-clad bandits laying about with rusted bolos and machetes. "How would you get above a Greater Gyrdrake?"

Wait for it to kill another wyrm and land to eat it.

"Not an option."

Run away from it, go higher when it's out of sight.

"You're a shit tactician."

I don't eat Greater Gyrdrakes. I think maybe your friend there does though?

Vrinzhoon had his saber out and was pointing up at the sky; he shouted something to Zrileen, too far away for Zaya to hear. They peeled off and began to surge upward, broad wings and huge shoulders hauling them upward faster than anything that large had a right to move. The late morning sun caught them in stark shadows; they were beautiful sights, Zaya had to admit, tall, pale warriors with flashing blades, climbing upward through the sky on lithe, bright-feathered wyrms—their dorsal feathers straw-colored like the veldt, their bellies the color of the sky.

They're going to die, the Dawn Wyrm remarked in awe.

"Here's what we're going to do," said Zaya, and made an image of it for the dragon.

That's stupid, it said. *That's the kind of thing that gets you eaten.*

The gyrdrakes had stopped looping and begun to lose a little height, pulling slightly closer to Vrinzhoon and Zrileen. "Regret to inform that we are getting eaten one way or another if we lose this thing," said Zaya.

Not if we run away.

As one, the gyrdrakes fell into a stoop, gaping mouths belching cadmium-and-cerulean fire, plunging like knives down at the two climbing Dusk Stalkers—and at Zaya and the Dawn.

Its mind seized, frozen by the vision of the coming impact: flame stripping flesh from its face, talons and teeth parting feathers and flesh, blood bursting forth in rivers.

"It's OK," Zaya said, and *reached.*

In her mind, her own limbs doubled; she felt her own weight on her back, the push of massed air under her wings; her senses were overlaid with keen smell, dull hearing, a veil of slightly-off colors and contours in fine, swarming detail. She lashed her tail and hauled against the air, and the Dawn corkscrewed out and up, the gyrdrake missing them by inches.

The gyrdrake spread its wings to stop the fall, but Zaya had pulled the Dawn into its own stoop; and, before her wyrm could seize its muscles back from her control, it was on the gyrdrake's back, claws sinking into the grey feathers and then into skin, jaws locked around the joint where long neck met skull for control. Copper blood-savor filled the Dawn Wyrm's mouth, and Zaya's.

It wasn't enough to drown out Vrinzhoon and Zrileen's screams. She did not need to see the scene to know how it had gone; wyrm-fire had seared them to death, and the sheer force of the stoop had given the massive gyrdrakes every advantage, knocking the wind from the Dusk Stalkers and pitting them against a larger, more savage enemy face to face and from below. Whether they died valiantly or ran away would not matter much; in fact, a bandit of any sense would give them the opportunity to run, because—

—an odd sensation, referred from the Dawn Wyrm's belly: A tickling, almost, a scrabbling. The gyrdrake's rider, climbing from his own wyrm to hers.

Zaya's Dawn and the gyrdrake were plummeting toward the ground; the Dawn, at her urging, had pulled its own wings in, forcing the larger wyrm to do the work of slowing their descent. The Dawn's pink, blue, and violet feathers shone against the gyrdrake's dull grey; the bright red blood of the gyrdrake welled into a ruby bridge between granite-grey neck and magenta jaw; the gyrdrake's tongue lashed against the air as it bellowed its rage and terror. But the rider was coming, and they would be larger and stronger than her, and they would be better at clambering over dragons in midair than her, and better with a knife.

They hoisted themself onto the Dawn's back with a grace entirely out of place on this terrible plunge. They'd done this before. Zaya felt their body shift, felt the pain of their hand gripping her feathers—not hers, the Dawn's feathers—to steady themself while they drew a knife. She realized she had no idea what they looked like, save that their body was long-limbed and starved lean, and they were right-handed; she knew them only from the Dawn's referred sensations, not her eyes. They did not know she knew they were there. With a painful surge of will, she made herself not look as she felt them creep toward her.

"If this doesn't work," Zaya said quietly, "I'm going to need you to roast the gyrdrake's head."

If I do that, we're going to fall a lot faster.

"If you do that, you can let go of it and we can fly."

Why didn't we do that before this other human got up on my back?

"You're the one with its neck in your teeth! I can't do all the thinking around here!"

The gyrdrake's rider was in arm's reach of Zaya now. She *reached* for the Dawn, but didn't move it.

I don't like this. I don't like you in my head.

"You're alive because of me in your head."

The bandit's weight came forward on their feet, and Zaya lashed at them with the Dawn's tail.

It was not long or strong enough to knock them off—but the long orange feathers of the Dawn's tail-tip blinded them for a moment, and Zaya drew her knife and wheeled to stab them in the meat of their thigh.

It was an awkward stroke, without much strength in it, and it glanced off a strut of some hard substance sewn into the bandit's pants. She looked up into their eyes for a moment. The bandit was a Mrineen man, with the awkward tan of a human who's spent a long time outside in a climate his complexion hadn't evolved for. He was too thin, his teeth poor and partial, his hair weirdly well-kept. She felt his weight shift forward again, ready to swing, and thrust the Dawn's tail between his legs.

He buckled his knees in for protection, but she wasn't after the jewels. She switched the tail back as hard as she—the Dawn—could, swept him half off his feet.

She tucked her knife into her armpit, grabbed a handful of feathers with all the strength she could muster, and *reached* to release the flame from the Dawn's mouth.

The gyrdrake shrieked in agony and belched its own jet of fire, but its wings went slack before its voice gave out. The rush of air redoubled, and the half-pried-off bandit skirled off into the air.

"Letgoletgoletgoletgo," Zaya shouted, and after a moment's confusion the Dawn did, using its wings to catch the air and stop, at last, the roar of careering sky that would have spelled their deaths.

"Slayer of the Beasts that Haunt the Night," Zaya breathed, and before she could thank the god for their intercession, her sight went black with an impact that hit her like a brick house collapsing.

When her senses came back, she was falling, wedged between the Dawn's shoulder and its wing. Her arm burned with effort—not her own arm, but the Dawn's wing, which was pushing up in ways it wasn't built to do, keeping her just barely balanced on its back. The Dawn was snapping and shooting fire at a gyrdrake that had come at them from above, weaving back and forth to keep the bigger wyrm from gaining any more purchase. She felt the gyrdrake's talon graze her thigh.

She wrestled herself back up onto the Dawn's back, then felt something disengage from her jacket and fall away. She caught it by reflex; sharp steel bit her palm. She had not lost the knife.

The gyrdrake's talon was inches away from her. It could gut her with a twitch. Zaya grabbed its feathers anyway, pulled herself over the wing like a half-lamed sloth, felt the whistle of a blade lash past her shoulder blades, and severed the thong on the wyrm's saddle with a single stroke. She darted out of the Dawn's mind and into the gyrdrake's just in time to amplify the frequency range of the human voice: The bandit's plummeting shout echoed louder in the gyrdrake's brain than it had any right to do. The gyrdrake pushed off the Dawn like a hawk off a branch, following its rider.

Its talon snagged her jacket as it left. For a brief moment, it dragged her with it off the Dawn. Then she fell away.

Between her and the gleaming green sands there was nothing but air.

She knew she was falling, heard the slipstream roaring in her ears and tearing at her skin, but all she felt was a deep, suffusing stillness. There was nothing she could do.

What peace there was in that.

Her jacket jerked upward, the leather cutting into her armpits; weightlessness became weight, and her heart crashed against the cage of her ribs. The air stank of rotten eggs, and she heard the Dawn pant from above her: It had seized her jacket in its teeth. She laughed, high and hooting, tears steaming from her eyes. "Fseni-vain!" she said, *reaching* into the wyrm's mind as she said it.

What?

Zaya imaged Fsenivain and the Ranger Wyrm; she felt the Dawn twist its head to look up.

She's fine. The other wyrm is running away.

"You saved me."

The wyrm's mind acknowledged this, but seemed to feel no need to reply to it. Zaya looked down on the still-onrushing sands. Two bodies sprawled like dropped dolls; when she looked up to the horizon, she saw the dwindling forms of two gyrdrakes, headed west.

"They could have killed us."

Probably. But why?

"I feel like you're saying you wouldn't avenge my death."

I wouldn't avenge your death.

"My old dragon would have."

I can't keep flying with you in my mouth. I need to land.

"I know."

The caravan and the curves of the dunes grew as they descended, and the Dawn's hot breath stank, and the leather of Zaya's jacket cut into her armpits. She couldn't wipe the sweat from her brow for fear of slipping out of the jacket, so she let the drops form, swell, and fall, evaporating in the desert air before they hit the sand.

Chapter 2

ETHNICITIES. *As of this writing, there are three main ethnicities occupying the city: The Mrineen, who fucked off from Mlinivoun so they could live around dragons again; the Kayalim, who fled here to escape the anti-psionic putsches in Kayazē a few decades after the Mrineen made landfall; and the Ililuë, who've lived here literally forever. There's much to be said about the politics of all this, but I've received editorial feedback that my charismatic authorial voice is prone to off-putting compound tangents, so let's stick to Actionable Intelligence For Tourists With Good Taste in Guidebooks:*

Yemareir is a profoundly unequal city, and if you're just sightseeing in the relatively affluent areas you'll probably run into mostly Mrineen. Don't dump on dragons or talk politics and you'll be fine. With Kayalim: Don't assume they don't speak Mlin (they do), don't default to "they" if you don't know gender (ask for pronouns, it's fine), and don't ask them to make animals do tricks (SO RUDE). With Ililuë: Don't assume that they are struggling if they are unhoused (a lot of them are well-resourced transients from outlying communities) and, for the love of all you hold dear, don't assume that they're forest spirits or like mammal-plant hybrids just because they've got some green in their skin or the whites of their eyes. It's diet. Don't get creative.

SEE ALSO: Amalgam (Ililuë); Church of the Wyrm Immanent; Conurbation (Ililuë); Dragon; Precinct; Psionics.

—From "A Visitor's Handbook for Yemareir," by Shenireen Agama

***

ZAYA STUMBLED AND NEARLY fell on her face when she dismounted from the wyrm to check back in with the caravan, but after a swift debrief, she and Fsenivain were back in the air: The first thing to be done was put some distance between the caravan and the site of the attack, in case the bandits had friends who'd come looking. She spent the flight aching, sweating, trembling, and revising hate-filled monologues aimed at the head of the expedition—who had unquestionably made the right call in moving on, but Zaya needed something to take her mind off her mutinous body. She wanted to pour herself into the Dawn's mind, but didn't dare. It wasn't exhaustion that had made her fall when they had landed; she'd gone too deep into the Dawn's mind during the dogfight, and her brain had begun to forget her own body plan.

The caravan moved at a forced-march pace, and by the time they landed, they were ahead of schedule for the day. At that point came the questions, the stories, the tears. There was extra food because the cook forgot that Vrinzhoon and Zrileen were dead; there was extra drinking in their memory. The expedition head, Anzoun Rinkhal, took one sip of arrack to thank them and left the rest of the crew to the valediction. Zaya did her part, roasting Vrinzhoon for his unearned pride in his wyrm-handling and Zrileen for her awkward crush on one of the camel-drivers, then blunting the barbs by recounting times they had displayed basic humanity, the sort of story that draws praise and weeping only when it is told about the dead. She would sooner have done a haka, where the fixed forms of the funeral words gained new meaning from the memories of the mourned souls; but there weren't any other Kayalim on the expedition, and she wasn't in the mood for teaching.

When Zaya stumbled away from the campfire, duty done, light was still bleeding through Anzoun Rinkhal's tent-flap. She peeled it aside to spy him at his writing desk, bent over a letter. It would go to Vrinzhoon or Zrileen's family. Maybe it would have some of the stories from their campfire wake. When she put her head down, she thought as hard as she could about Kiriki, hoping to dream of her. But sleep came fast, black, and heavy; and if she dreamed, the dream did not stay.

***

"What do you think Rinkhal was after in the souk?" Zaya asked Fsenivain as they doffed their uniforms in the locker room at the depot. Weeks on dragonback had given Fsenivain a farmer's tan on face, neck, and forearms; the latter were smooth, but her chest and legs were thick with brown hair. It seemed she'd only bothered to shave the skin that showed when she was in uniform.

They had come through the Amber Gate late in the afternoon, the sun in their faces as it slid down closer to the city. Customs took longer when you'd lost people, although in truth the customs officers spent less time on Vrinzhoon and Zrileen than the investigator from Transdesert Corporation spent on the loss of their wyrms. But Zaya and Fsenivain had had to talk to both. Then Anzoun Rinkhal kept them waiting in the Souk of All Worlds while he made a rendezvous. By the time they made it to the depot, the sun was down and stars were coming out.

"He had that sack of emeralds," Fsenivain said. "The one we dipped south to go pick up."

Zaya remembered the sack, a rectangle about the size of a paperback in tan raffia velvet. "Is that why spent the night at that convivency?"

Fsenivain paused her shaving to shrug. "We didn't have it before, we had it after."

Zaya sighed and took out her own razor. She pulled the hair back from her forehead and began cutting a bit above the roots, doing her best to keep the azure locks from getting everywhere.

Fsenivain met her eyes in the mirror. "Scared straight?" she asked—enough singsong in her voice to make it plausibly a joke, enough depth in her gaze to invite an honest answer.

"What's it to you?" Zaya asked, putting more warmth behind her smile than she was feeling.

"I liked your hair. But, look, if your near-death experience in the desert made you realize you want to settle down with a nice man and squeeze out a million babies, far be it from me to stand between you and happiness."

"This isn't about settling down with a nice man," Zaya said, continuing to work back over her scalp. "I killed a man and a wyrm out there. This is in memory of that. That's where the hair-cropping custom comes from. In Kayazē, warriors would shave their heads when they made a kill. About a generation after we came here, we decided everyone who'd survived that long was a warrior." She was almost halfway back on her scalp by now; a scraggly fuzz of blue remained. She'd forgotten how much she hated the shape of her naked head. "About a generation after that, those of us who'd gotten kicked out of their families for kissing the wrong people decided we didn't want to identify as killers. And then we spent five hundred years living in a city where most of us shaved their heads all the time and never killed anyone, so most people forgot what it used to mean."

"Things they never teach you in school," Fsenivain sighed. *Ask yourself why that is,* Zaya did not say. "So what does coloring your hair mean?"

"Whatever it would mean if you did it. Not everything's about history." This wasn't really true, but it was close enough. She was on the back of her head now, groping for the last few strands of longer hair.

"Well, in any case, let me know if you need some help cleaning up back there."

Zaya appraised her no-longer-colleague with the eye of a thirsty woman appraising a cold beer. Fsenivain wasn't her type... but that might be better than it was bad, all things considered. And the family wasn't expecting her home at any particular time. Then again, any drink looks good when you're thirsty, even if you know you'll regret it later.

"I'll be all right. Thanks for the offer."

Fsenivain shrugged and turned to her ablutions. Zaya was still shaving when she left. Regret nipped at her, but lightly. In any case, Fsenivain had left a calling card in Zaya's locker: A smooth, black bead. She pocketed it.

She went to the mailroom to drop off a figurine she'd picked up in a covered market in Kerkakan: A pair of little owls carved from elephant ivory, a larger one wrapping its wings around an owlet so expertly done that each time Zaya touched it she expected to feel the fuzz of down. No one was there, so she wrote "for Kanireen in the routing office," then turned to leave.

The stable at the depot was in the opposite direction of the exit, but still, she made the detour. The smell of ham was in the air; dinner for the wyrms was quarter-pigs tonight. She found the Dawn, which was eating a seared carcass with more than a little enthusiasm. She felt its mind *reach* out tentatively to her own.

"I just wanted to thank you," she said. "For not getting me killed."

It understood the sentiment, she thought, but did not have much of a repertoire for responding. That was all right. "That's all," she said. "Enjoy your dinner."

I liked flying with you, the wyrm said.

Zaya smiled. "Maybe we'll do it again one day."

I don't think so.

"Me neither. But we humans like to tell stories about nice things that won't happen."

The wyrm's mind showed no particular appreciation of the telling of stories about nice things that won't happen. Zaya took the hint and left.

***

THE DEPOT WAS IN Madder Precinct. Zaya thought about renting a rickshaw, but compromised on a bike, taking the long way through the Boulevard of Parfumiers, which was wide and well lit. A Ranger Wyrm and an Eyrie Shrike screamed over her as she pedaled down the boulevard, the Ranger struggling to overtake but never quite managing; the Shrike's rider was too good, anticipating the Ranger's moves and generally making a nuisance of occupying the best lanes for passing. They disappeared into an alley in the direction of the shore. The Glimmerblind, then—if they were 'streamers at all, and not just a pair of wyrm-riders with something to prove. Zaya looked behind her to see if any other wyrms were flying the course that night, but saw none. She breathed the scent of sulphur, hanging in the wyrms' wake; her legs felt strong on the pedals, her balance on the two wheels unshakable. The walkers on the Boulevard pointed at where the racing wyrms had gone, laughing, complimenting, analyzing.

She left the bike on a corner a few streets from the house, then walked the rest of the way. She waved at the waitron in the mate shop, then to the kids sitting out on the rim of the fountain in the square when they should have been studying, then walked down Laurel Street, unlocked the gate in the low glass-crowned wall around the tenement, and ducked in to take the stairs, which smelled of the cedar planks they were clad in. It had been three years since she'd smelled that staircase. House Shearwater had moved back in from the co-domiciled flat in Celadon Precinct while she'd been gone. The last time she'd walked up these stairs, Jaliki's legs had been as stubby as sausages; Taavi and Gilthiniel had been shorter than her; Eäril had been a baby, Enwë had not been born yet, Vnaleen had not died, and Vanako had not joined the family. She paused outside the door to take one extra breath, then, for the first time in six weeks, entered her home.

Minshoon was at the table, of course. He'd taken over half of it with stacks of paper, half of it house finances and half mathematical enthusiasms (Zaya had long given up on telling which was which). His smile was as broad as his shoulders and as quick as his legs; he closed the distance and scooped her up before she could say hello. She felt a knot loosen inside her as she squeezed his ribs.

When he set her down, his smile was mostly gone. "We missed you," he said.

She chuckled. "You and who exactly?"

"Everyone. Even Vani misses your potatoes in chili sauce. I tried to make it once, but it never comes out the way they like it. What did you do to your hair?" He looked at her as though seeing her for the first time. "Oh, Zaya."

She ran a hand over the new stubble on her scalp. "It's all right. Couple of bandits on gyrdrakes. We lost some guards."

"More than one?"

"Two." She knew what he'd ask next. "There were four of us."

"Hey," came a quiet voice from the hallway: Kirono had come out, broad as always and no taller than Zaya but a little more gaunt than he had been, the circles under his eyes a little darker. His hair was pale violet and slicked back.

"New hair," said Zaya, walking over to embrace him; he smelled of copper and gunpowder. "It looks good."

"Yours not so much," he said. "I caught the story. I'm glad you're OK."

"I'm definitely dead, I just haven't realized it yet. I'm going to say hi to the kids and then collapse. You can wake me in autumn."

"No way," said Minshoon. "You don't get to spend six weeks in the desert and then sleep all summer. And you don't get to just sneak out of this conversation about almost getting killed on the job."

"The wyrms are very well trained." Zaya gave him a look that was supposed to communicate *And so's your girl, by the way,* but it was hard to summon the steel of a gimlet gaze when her eyes wouldn't focus from fatigue. "And it's the last haul of the season.

I'm going to be here all summer. I couldn't sneak away from you if I wanted to."

"Good," said Minshoon, returning to the table and his papers. "You're going to want to."

"He who needs his kith to make potatoes with chili sauce should be careful about getting salty with the cook."

"All right."

"I can take care of myself in the air, Minshoon."

"I know." He put a hand up in conciliation. "I do, actually, know. Go kiss your children, they miss you. Or at least your potatoes."

"You watered the irises, right?"

"I watered the irises."

Zaya turned to enter the hallway, and Kirono turned with her, headed back to his room. "Hey," he said. "Be gentle with Vani, all right?"

"What happened?"

"I don't know. Not nothing. She's been stroppy for days. Worse than usual, I mean," he added before Zaya could say the obvious thing. "She's been snapping at Jaliki, even."

"And all you've got is 'not nothing'?"

"I'm on the edge of a breakthrough, and if we don't publish it soon then Keneftheen Ferdelance will."

"What breakthrough?"

"A new configuration for steel injection molding that'll improve efficiency by—"

"Forget I asked."

"She's been out late a lot on the nights when she's at her apprenticeship," Kirono said. "That's all I've seen. Normally Cer would just spy on her, but Enwë takes up all her time, so Minshoon's basically been the only parent for the rest of them, and with Jaliki's attack—"

"Jaliki had an attack?"

"Not that bad. Nipped him in the calf, it was over in a minute, he was only down for a day or two. But Minshoon's been off his game since. I think he's been just kind of getting through the days until you got back."

Zaya took a deep breath through her nose, then touched the wall and looked up at the ceiling. "Maybe one of these days, a party when I get back? Instead of throwing me directly into the garbage fire?"

"You can go to bed if you want," said Kirono. "The garbage will still be on fire in the morning."

Zaya shook her head. "I've missed them for too long already."

"I'm glad you're OK." Kirono jerked his head toward his room. "I've got to get back to work."

Zaya nodded, and he slipped through his door, releasing a gust of odors she didn't want to think too hard about. She looked at the doors off the hallway one by one and chose.

CHAPTER 3

KEROSTASIA. *THE STATE OF being preyed on by a ker. Colloquially,
"hunted."*

SEE ALSO: Ker.

—From "A Visitor's Handbook for Yemareir," by Shenireen Agama

***

THE FIRST ROOM WAS Taavi and Gilthiniel's—the one they'd chosen to
stay in together, even as the oldest children in the house. Taavi was
studying a diagram Zaya half-recognized as a schematic of some
organic process, iterated panels showing a cluster of colored balls
docking at a conveniently shaped aperture on a large tube, which
opened at their attachment. Gilthiniel was scribbling equations
and cursing. The room smelled a bit like boy, but forgivably so.
They turned a hair too quickly when she opened the door, then
regained their cool; Zaya had to claim her hugs. She went for Gilthiniel first, throwing her arms around his neck from behind. "New
beard," she said. "It looks good on you."

He rubbed her head, cringing from her kiss on his cheek only enough to be able to say he'd done it. "I guess I'm making up for you?"

"When mine grows back, will you shave yours?"

Gilthiniel's look was as dire as the grave.

"Then you're not making up for anything." Taavi had gotten up; Zaya had to reach up for her embrace. "Cerminir put fertilizer in the tagine again, didn't she?"

"Please, Mom, I've been taller than you since forever?" She gave Zaya the same look Minshoon had. "What happened?"

"A couple of bandits. Nothing we couldn't scare off once they realized we could—once they took a loss."

"And you gave it to them?" Taavi nodded in cool appraisal. "Pretty hard, Mom?"

Zaya sat down on Taavi's bed. "There's a reason you're not allowed to leave the house until facts are piling up on your desk from pouring out your ears, and it's so you don't end up like your mother. How's studying going?" Taavi would be reading entrance exams in natural philosophy, Gilthiniel in engineering.

"Written should be fine?"

Zaya closed her eyes against the sight of Taavi for a moment. She and her twin had always been beautiful, long and slim with rosewood skin and soft curls that Taavi wore short and azure and Gilthiniel wore long and undyed. Zaya had never been within wyrm-flame range of a university examination room, but she knew who the examiners would be, and how they would look on Taavi's skin, her hair, her bright, loose Kayalim clothes. "Oral will be fine too."

Taavi was clearly not so sure, and just as clearly afraid to express her doubt; Zaya's heart twitched in sympathy. "You looked at me like that when I asked you if you wanted to live with us," Zaya said. "Just like that—you didn't want to say yes, but you were too afraid to admit you didn't want to say yes." She got up from the bed and touched Taavi's cheek, then tousled Gilthiniel's tight-kinked hair. "But you made the right call. You're good at thinking on your feet. Both of you."

"You don't always have to shower us with wisdom when you come back," said Gilthiniel, not looking up from the double integral he was chewing on. "We're not kids. We know why you have to go."

"Showering you with wisdom reinforces my place in the dominance hierarchy," said Zaya. "Which is especially important when adolescent males in the troop start doing insubordinate things like killing it on university entrance exams. Hey, your fathers told me Vani's been acting strange. Is there anything you can share?"

At that, Gilthiniel did look up; he and Taavi shared a glance. "She's been out late at her apprenticeship a lot," said Gilthiniel. "I guess the architect is kind of a hardass, makes her redo a lot of work."

He looked at Zaya; Taavi looked at him; he looked at Taavi; Taavi looked at Zaya. "I saw her come back to the square the wrong way one night?" Taavi said. "She came in going north from Orange Street instead of west from Goosefoot Street? But her apprenticeship is in north Viridian?" North Viridian was well northeast of House Shearwater; there was no reason to come back from the south.

"That doesn't prove anything," said Gilthiniel. "Maybe she was getting food."

"There's nothing there but houses and schools?"

"Maybe she was dropping someone off."

"Taavi knows it doesn't prove anything," said Zaya. "Vani's not in trouble. But I've been gone six weeks. I just want to know everything's all right."

"Reinforcing your place in the dominance hierarchy," said Gilthiniel. It didn't sound as funny when he said it.

"It's good to see you," Zaya said. "Thank you. Don't study too hard."

"You sure?" said Gilthiniel.

"Good point. Study too hard, please. I love you."

"Love you," they said in one voice, and Zaya left, closing the door gently behind her.

***

VANAKO WAS NEXT OLDEST, and had the next visit by right, but Zaya skipped her room. No one, she knew with a certainty not unmixed with guilt, would question the decision to see Jaliki next.

He was in bed, propped up on an elbow, reading by moonlight—or, rather, scrambling to hide the book and close his eyes, which he hadn't quite managed by the time Zaya had slipped into the room. She let him finish, let the eyes close and the breath deepen and the book flash under his pillow, then gave him a moment to open his eyes again.

When he didn't, she flashed a glance around the room. Her eyes came to rest on a sleek brown hound under the desk, its eyes peacefully shut, its chin resting on crossed forepaws. She took two silent steps toward it and kicked out as hard as she could. Its ribs shifted satisfyingly under her boot-toe; its eyes snapped open, wide and liquid and soulful. They met hers for a moment, and the hound vanished.

"And stay out," Zaya whispered, knowing it neither would nor could. She sat beside Jaliki and rested a hand on his hip, which was as bony as the rest of him. "No sale, little man," she said in her low, don't-wake-the-children voice. "Come give your mother a hug."

He bolted up, threw strong skinny arms around her, and the world was hers: the weight in her lap, the sharp angles of his shoulder blades, the smell of his hair. She kissed him on the scalp and the shoulder and on the thick bone behind his ear. Her fingers drifted down to his calf and felt the linen of the bandage.

He pulled away to look at her, and she regretted looking for the wound. "It's OK," he said. "It wasn't that bad. Just one bite, and he didn't go for the center of my body. That's better, right?"

Her right hand found his left, where the middle and ring fingers were missing past the third joint. Immediately she regretted it, but he didn't say anything. "It's better," she said. "Papa Minshoon said you were only down for two days. That's good. How's your walking?"

"Little slow. It hurts to put too much weight on it. Dr. ze-Jashi says I should be back to normal in a month or two."

Tears sprang forth; Zaya fought the urge to wipe them. "When did it happen?"

"I don't really want to talk about it."

That was new. "I won't make you," Zaya said. "But I'd feel better if I knew."

Jaliki shifted his weight as if he had to pee and made a dissatisfied grunting noise, which was generally a sign that she should drop the subject. But then he spoke.

"It was about a month ago, at dinner. He knocked me back in my chair and started biting. He just appeared out of thin air, we thought he was in here. Gil and Papa Minshoon and Mom Cerminir all got hands on him, but..." Jaliki shrugged. "At least he didn't want too much this time"

"Oh, breath of mine." By now it was pointless to pretend the tears weren't there. "Enwë and Eäril saw?"

"They're pretty scared of him now."

They can get in line, she did not say. "Have you and Minshoon been doing the rituals?" she said.

"Yeah," he said, with a look off to the side that said not as often as the doctor prescribed.

"Of course," she repeated. "School?"

"I can't," said Jaliki. "The schools in Lilac don't want the ker there. They say they don't have room for it. But I think they're worried it'll attack me again in class. Papa Minshoon is looking for something," he said hastily, and Zaya realized she had drawn in a great draught of air without plans for what to do with it. She let it out with as quiet a sigh as she could.

She squeezed Jaliki around the chest; he tucked his head in the crook of her neck. "I missed you," she said. "Do you remember anything about this house?"

"A little," he said. "I remember the murals on the ceiling. I remember how you slept with your feet at the head of your bed so the sun wouldn't shine on your face. Why didn't you just move your bed?"

"Mama Kiriki and I had the bed that way," said Zaya. "She liked to wake up early."

"Why?"

Memories of those early mornings blazed through Zaya's blood like strong coffee—bruised lips, aching tongues, sweat drying under dawn light. She kissed Jaliki's head, lifted her arm and got up; it felt wrong to hold a child with her mind wrapped up in those thoughts. "She and I were different that way," she said. "Anyway, that's the bed you were born in, and that's where it was when you were born. How could I change that?"

Sometimes those little stories would make Jaliki ask for a bigger story, something from the weeks that Kiriki had had with him before Ashen Precinct took her. Zaya didn't realize that's what she'd been hoping for until he didn't ask for it. "Good night, heart of mine," she said. "I'll see you in the morning."

"Good night."

The ker had reappeared under the desk. Zaya kicked at it again in passing. It yelped and whined, but it looked her in the eye and did not leave.

"Mom, don't."

She turned to look at Jaliki, conscious to make sure she wasn't wheeling around in attack. The words came to her mind as though they'd been there waiting to surge forth:

I know it'll never leave, not until it takes you from me. I know I can't stop its teeth from finding your flesh, your bones, your heart. But I can make it suffer. You can't take that from me. It's all I have.

But it was not all she had; and she smoothed every tremor from her voice as she looked him steadily in the eye and said, "All right, breath of mine. For you, I'll stop."

***

CERMINIR HAD TAKEN WHAT Zaya still thought of as Yyrreen's old room, around the bend in the hallway, and the younger children slept with her, Eäril in her own bed and Enwë in Cerminir's, the bassinet a formality. The room was thick-curtained and dark, and close with the musty-sweet smell of baby. Eäril was asleep; Zaya planted a kiss in her eyrie of soft curls and let her be. Enwë was latched on her mother's breast, and Zaya kissed them both on the crowns of their heads as well. Cerminir stirred and whispered, "Welcome home."

"Hi, Cer. It's good to see you. Enwë's so big."

Enwë fussed, mewled and pawed at Cerminir's breast, then fell to sucking. "She puts on this performance every night," Cerminir whispered. "She'd better be fucking growing. Get out of here before you wake them, otherwise they'll be insufferable in the morning. I'll see you when I'm decent."

Zaya closed the door as gently as she could, then looked up and down the hall. Her own room was next door, at the point on the corridor of bedrooms farthest from the common room, just behind the kitchen. Then there was Kirono's, then Minshoon's, and then Vanako's.

The pull of bed was strong, just then: If Kirono thought "not nothing" was going on with Vanako, then any conversation with her was going to be long, one-sided, and exhausting, with a strong chance of an explosion. But if it happened now, they could go to sleep afterward, and maybe it would only ruin the evening instead of an entire day. Zaya drew in a long breath, held it for a moment, and knocked.

"Hey, Vani, It's me," she said. "I just wanted to say hi before I went to bed."

Nothing.

"Minshoon," Zaya called from the hallway. "You said she was here, right?"

"She's not here?"

"I don't know. Vani," she called, "I'm opening the door on three unless I hear something. One, two, three."

A bitter, acrid scent nagged at Zaya's nostrils when she opened the door. It wasn't easy to be sure Vanako wasn't there; books, clothes, soft toys, pillows, blankets, and papers covered in paintings and sketches piled up in drifts, any number of which could have concealed a person. But of people it was empty.

Minshoon looked over Zaya's shoulder. "Vani? Did she go out the window?"

Zaya sniffed once, then again, then laughed. "Smell that?"

"What?"

"Mastic and Dusk Stalker feather. She used a stealth charm. Sneaked right by you."

"Or maybe right by you."

"No way. I'd pick up that smell in a second." Zaya briefly auditioned a few swears, then settled on "Shit."

"What do you think we should do?" said Minshoon.

Zaya made herself breathe in and out: Once, twice. "I've been gone for six weeks," she said. "The only context I have for the disappearance of this entire problem child is that you and Kirono think possibly 'not nothing' might be going on with her and, now, that she's learned enough petty sorcery to catch you napping. Six weeks ago, the only sorcery she knew was how to say 'Fuck you, mom,' in a voice that scraped the inside of my skull like a grapefruit spoon and when I asked anyone where she was, I got the right answer!" The last word came out loud enough to ring from the close walls of the hallway. She held a single finger up, breathed deeply into her nose, and blew a thin stream of air out through her mouth. "This isn't your fault. She's old enough to be responsible for herself. But you've actually been here for the past six weeks, and I need more from you than I'm getting. Like, for example, where could she be, and what could she be doing?"

"I don't know."

"Minshoon. *Try.*"

Minshoon ran a hand through his hair; his face looked like he'd eaten something that was just starting to go sour in his stomach. "She doesn't say much about school other than she hates it. She found an apprenticeship with a draughtsman twice a week in Viridian, right across the border from the school. I've seen her walking back from those with a Kayalim girl, she said her name was Eneki. I've seen her in the courtyard with a few kids from the project, the only ones whose names I know are Vayali and Berilien—"

"That girl's name isn't Eneki."

Jaliki had walked down the hall to Vanako's open door. The ker was panting from between his legs, smiling for all the world as though it were a normal dog.

"Hey, Jali," said Minshoon, squatting down and reaching out to touch his cheek. "Why didn't you say something?"

"I didn't know she told you her name was Eneki. It's Zayeni. We met up with her a couple times when we went over to Dr. Snow's for shaved ice."

"Are they courting?"

"I don't know. I saw Zayeni count out money and give some to Vani, though. I thought I had to go to the bathroom but I tried and I didn't have to go, so—"

"Why not the Sweet Soldier?"

"I *know*," said Jaliki, growing very serious. "Sweet Soldier has the *best* lemon cloudberry ice and Dr. Snow's doesn't even *have* cloudberry and their lemon is way too sweet and they have the crappy ice that's all pebbly—"

"Don't say crappy," said Minshoon, relieved to be on familiar ground.

"And it's across the entire precinct from the border with Viridian," said Zaya. "Right by the Chartreuse border." Zaya mulled this for a moment, then shoved the ker out of the way to give Jaliki a quick hug and a kiss on the temple. "Thank you, Jali. Go to sleep."

"What about Vani?" he asked. The ker whined as if in echo.

"I'll find her."

"Where?" said Minshoon.

Zaya's eyes flickered over to Jaliki, but fuck it: This was his sister, he should know who she was. "There are three bars in east Chartreuse that are open at this hour," said Zaya. "Even Vanako's friend Zayeni wouldn't be dumb enough to set foot in the Blind Beggar without a crew. That leaves Jizeki's and the Vat. If I don't find her in one of those places, I'll be back inside an hour."

"How do you know which bars are open in the middle of the night?" said Jaliki.

"We'll talk about it when you're older."

"I'm older than I've ever been!"

"What if you do find her?" asked Minshoon.

"That depends," said Zaya, "on how long it takes me to skin and gut her before I drag her home."

"*Mom*," said Jaliki—half in admonition, half impressed. The ker yipped with excitement, and Zaya probably would have kicked the teeth out of its shitty face if she'd been in range, but she was already out the door.

Chapter 4

KER. *"The terminal instar of certain teratopneumic entities. Like most other pneumic entities, kers engage in protective mimicry, usually manifesting as intelligent social animals such as mammals and birds." I read this in Tgarain Amphisbaena's* Nosomimetic Curses; *the whole thing is like this.* **Translation for humans:** *A ker is a baby demon cosplaying as an animal, who even knows why.*

Amphisbaena again: "The metamorphosis to adulthood requires the ker to bond with, alter, and ultimately consume the ba *of an intelligent animal. A ker's method of stalking is reminiscent of the ora or land crocodile, with long bouts of leisurely and even amicable society punctuated by probing attacks that escalate in ferocity until the final, fatal strike."* **Again for the humans:** *Kers fuel their final metamorphosis by persistence hunting humans and tearing hunks off their bodies and souls over the course of months and years.*

Why put this grim shit in a guide for tourists? Well, Reader, this affliction is pretty common in Yemareir, and you'll probably see some folks in the streets being followed by vultures or hyenas or massive monitor lizards and you could be forgiven for thinking, hey, this city is full of Kayalim empaths, doesn't it kind of rock that these people have tamed all these dangerous pets? And you should know that they're not pets, they're not tame, they're eventually going to eat those people they're following, and there's nothing anybody can do to stop it.

SEE ALSO: Empathy, Psionic; Goety; Magic.

—From "A Visitor's Handbook for Yemareir," by Shenireen Agama

***

HOUSE SHEARWATER WAS ON the northeast side of Lilac Precinct—high-towered, clean-streeted, well lit even at this waning hour. The bicycle Zaya had ridden earlier was where she'd left it, and she wheeled onto one of the broad, smooth thoroughfares that radiated like spokes through the precinct from the broodspire.

A broodspire was the heart of its precinct, and the architecture always converged on the approach to it—windows grew smaller, heights shorter, and stones rougher, while draconic friezes, mosaics, and gargoyles became a noticeable theme and then a frantic, all-encrusting obsession. In Lilac Precinct, even the streetlights were dragons, globe gas-lamps resting teeth-rimmed in hyperextended jaws.

The broodspire itself arose from a circular plaza, with a low wall of thousand-year-old slate forming the inner edge of a ring road. The spire was not the tallest structure in Lilac Precinct, still less in Yemareir, but it was the tallest by far in the plaza, where the entirety of the architecture was proto-Yemari, squat and wyrm-festooned. It was built much like its perimeter wall, of stacked slates and much-patched mortar, a soaring stone needle shot through with warrens and bowers in which, when the season came, Dawn Wyrms would meet and mate. In midsummer afternoons the stench of guano and carrion would pour off it like a waterfall. The spire's hugeness seemed to bow the city itself in toward it; Zaya felt her body slant dangerously inward as she whipped around the ring road, to emerge on the opposite side.

Sweat and cool night air cleansed Zaya's mind, the burn of her lungs and the ache in her legs cleared it; but the streets on a bicycle felt ponderous and interminable, and with the torque of her turn on the ring road she recognized—not for the first time—that she had been straining to push the bike to wyrmspeed. She let herself ease off on the pedals, swallowing the slow creep of the streets like a dry scrap of bread, and thought forward. She would take Jizeki's first; the barmaster knew her and, since she'd started coming without her fathers, had even grown to like her. The Vat's owner was a self-hating Kayalim—which wasn't to say she wouldn't take two young Kayalim girls' money, but she'd surely take any excuse to get them out as fast as she could manage it. Which meant they were probably at Jizeki's.

The Vat was also nearer the Blind Beggar—which, in spite of her reassurances to Minshoon, Zaya was not at all sure Vanako was smart enough to avoid.

Zaya didn't remember the day they'd first interviewed Vanako, three seasons ago in Celadon Precinct, because she hadn't been there; she'd been on a months-long haul, shepherding a shipful of teak and argan oil halfway across the inner sea on one of two logy Tephratic Wyrms, which belched clots of burning phlegm that could burn holes in the sails and boards of ships. The captain had insisted that they sleep on a purpose-built raft far from the ship, and she'd joined them in solidarity, feeding them nips of her rum ration and encouraging them to attempt target practice on far-away flotsam. When she'd gotten home, flush with cash, she'd heard about this orphaned girl, a daughter of a cousin of Kirono's colleague who'd end up on a work crew for selling datura and stealing unless a family could take her off the dole. She'd been upset at how fast things had moved without her—but she understood it; the girl needed a family, Zaya had been gone and out of contact. Life didn't wait. "She's a little rough around the edges," Minshoon had said. "Really rough," he'd amended, when Cerminir shot him a jagged-knapped obsidian glare.

"Sharkskin rough," Cerminir had said. "Rough enough to rip your face off."

"But Jaliki loves her."

It had all been true.

The gradient of architecture from modern to ancient reversed itself along Temnodont Street west of the Lilac broodspire—but it reversed itself into a different version of modernity, one more slapdash and stunted than the East Lilac of House Shearwater. It was not a glaring difference—Lilac was still Lilac, a community of respectable Kayalim who tithed for schools, apprenticeships, and public art—but there were more open storefronts, more dead streetlamps, light creeping through more barred and curtained first-floor windows.

The Lilac-Chartreuse border, on the other hand, might as well have been a canyon. More stores were closed than open, more street signs missing than in place; high-rise tenements on either side, built at the same time in the same style, faced each other like cautionary tales of the ravages of time, the Chartreuse buildings pitted with weather damage and gaping with shattered windows.

Zaya's heart rose in her throat, but she felt her shoulders loosen. Her daughter was here. She was lost. She wasn't safe. It was time to take her home.

***

JIZEKI'S HELD A FREE shot of lemon arrack and the beginnings of a deep conversation about the bartender's health that Zaya felt gutted for cutting short... but no Vanako.

The Vat held a smoky-eyed young woman whose escort Zaya almost goaded into starting a brawl that would have flattened the place... but no Vanako.

***

BLOOD HUMMING WITH QUASHED thirst and lemon arrack, Zaya opened the door of the Blind Beggar. She scanned the bar, under the glowing ceiling-mural of a feathered snake, for familiar faces, and got a nod back from Shaiyo Kingfisher and Peacemaker Alwë; that would have to do. In the corner of her eye she saw heads lean toward one another, whispers leap from lips to ears. That she had associates here had been noticed, as she'd hoped.

The booths opposite the bar were shadow-cauled; the marching elephants above them had never lit up, at least in Zaya's memory, or Papa Zinji's either. She breezed past them, as if beelining to the game room at the back, then caught sight of Vanako alone in the corner of her eye and smoothly slipped into the next booth as if she'd been headed there all along.

If Vanako had noticed her passing by, she gave no sign of it—one thing to thank her new-bald head for, maybe. She pressed her back against the back of the booth and ordered a beer from a sullen waitron. She wanted to pick Vanako up and carry her out of the Blind Beggar like a baby, arms and legs wrapped around her like a sloth cub; she wanted to seize her by the ear and drag her out, shrieking. But what she needed was to know what was going on—and also to show her idiot daughter that bullshit shenanigans would invariably scuttle on the shoals of Zaya Shearwater, which admittedly might have been the lemon arrack and/or quashed thirst talking. She heard feet tap, weight shift, the sharp ring of a thick-bottomed glass. She wondered, half-darkly and half with genuine curiosity, what Vanako was drinking.

At last, someone sat in the booth behind her. Then another person joined. Zaya felt the booth move under the weight of the second, felt him contort himself to fit. A long face poked into Zaya's booth—a mandrill, she realized after a moment's surprise. She shrugged and took a long pull of beer; the ape face receded. "Hi Zayeni," said Vanako. "Who's your friend?"

Zaya risked leaning out of the booth, just far enough to get a look at the bar. Shaiyo Kingfisher made a small shrugging motion and turned back to his drink. "Screw you too, Shaiyo," she muttered to herself.

"My name's Tjaroon," said the voice that was not Zayeni's, a nice tenor with the accent of a working-class Mrineen. "I'm sorry we had to meet under these circumstances."

"You *told?*" said Vanako, shriller than she could have meant to be. "Zayeni, you *promised*—"

"I promised I'd hold off as long as I could," said Zayeni.

Tjaroon laughed—silently, but Zaya felt it through the booth. "Did you, now? We'll have to talk about that later. I'll get to the point, Vanako—we have some very concerned clients waiting for the product you're, I guess we're saying, unable to account for. What do you expect me to say to them?"

"You don't have to say anything. I explained it to all of them."

"You should have explained it to me." Vanako gasped quietly; Zaya felt her body stiffen through the thin wood of the booth. Her mind *reached* out to the mandrill's. It had something soft in its fist: a hank of brilliant purple hair. "When a member of my operation gets robbed, I have concerns. For their own well-being first, of course. Thankfully, you look well." These last four words were as dry as sand-scoured bones. "Then there are concerns over the fate of the product, and any understandings we might have to achieve with competitors. In these areas, Vanako, there is residual uncertainty."

"I can't help you. I didn't see him, he didn't say anything. I didn't smell him. I don't have anything for you."

"The thing is, though, Vanako." *Stop repeating her name,* Zaya thought. "No one's set up shop, no one's fenced the product."

"Isn't that good?"

"No one's talked about an operation like this, no one's set up the relationships. There's a particular mix of dumbness, hope, and desperation that you need to execute a smash-and-grab like this with no plan to realize a return—and there are people who have it, but none of them were on Cicada Street in Maroon Precinct between the kebab cart and the Red Fountain at three hours past noon on the fifth of last week. So, Vanako, I have to ask you—"

Zaya didn't have to feel the tension in the mandrill's arm to know what was next; the rhythm was built into the script. She stepped out of the booth and elbowed Tjaroon aside to claim the space beside him.

Things happened all at once. The mandrill nearly leaped across the table, but Zaya was already touching its mind, and it was nothing to scramble its brain's instructions to its limbs; it collapsed in front of Vanako, then reared back, baring its fangs. Zayeni, a pretty Kayalim girl of maybe eighteen, fumbled for something between her breasts but seemed to have trouble finding it; Zaya heard something bounce from the seat of the booth to the floor, presumably a knife. Tjaroon collared Zaya and raised a fist, but Zaya sent the mandrill to roar in his face, and he dropped her and scrambled back; and Vanako covered her face in her hands and moaned "Mom, *no*."

"Good evening," Zaya said to Tjaroon. "I'm a much better empath than you, so that handsome monkey is now a much bigger danger to you than he is to me. Mandrills are about four times stronger than humans pound for pound, so if it's you and maybe young Zayeni against the rest of us, I don't like your chances. Lucky for you, I'm just here to talk." Her heart was beating so fast it felt like she was shaking, but each word came out steady.

Tjaroon let the silence hang for a breath, as if ensuring he wouldn't miss anything else. Then he rested his back against the back of the booth and placed his hands palm-down on the table. "With whom do I have the sudden and unexpected pleasure of speaking?"

"Vanako's mother," said Zaya.

"Shearwater-*cha*," whispered Zayeni.

Tjaroon looked from Zaya to Vanako and back again.

"Vanako joined my family a year and change ago, in Celadon Precinct," Zaya said. "Yes, I'm obviously too young to have given birth to her. What you care about is that I have money. Vanako owes you for some lost product. That's a financial matter, and we'll settle it like a financial transaction."

"All respect, Shearwater-*cha*, if she's setting up as a competitor—"

"Look into her mother's eyes," said Zaya, "and tell me you're seeing someone who's going to let her daughter continue selling drugs on the black market for one hot second longer. All she's going to be 'setting up' as is an unbelievably diligent scrubber of dishes and floors for the foreseeable future."

"If there's product on the street that isn't ours, we'll know."

"Of course it's not yours. We're buying it."

"You're not buying it."

"Yes we are. Whoever mugged Vanako is stealing from us, not you."

"You don't have the cash."

"We will."

"Bullshit."

"You know where we live. I can come up with the money."

Tjaroon raised an eyebrow. "Lilac Precinct is perfectly respectable, but—"

"I have a house. I know you, not an idiot, didn't give this girl enough 'product' that she could buy a house with it."

Tjaroon looked over at Vanako; laugh lines deepened around his eyes, bringing a strange warmth to his expression. "Mom doesn't pull punches, does she?" Vanako rolled her eyes. The laugh lines disappeared; Tjaroon's thick features darkened. "But this isn't just about money. It's about respect—"

"Yeah, no."

Tjaroon looked at Zaya as though she'd spat in his beer. "Speaking of which—"

"No," Zaya cut in. "Let me explain. Taking the payout feels wrong to you because you want to punish my daughter for being a bad daughter *to you*, and you want to do that because shame and pain are how you build your family. But she's not your example to shame other dealers into performing, she's not your redemption story to show bad kids how to get back in your good books, she's not going to be the good soldier you scared straight. She's just gone. We're just settling her debt."

Tjaroon gave her a frankly dark look. "You're making this sound like a bad deal for me."

"If you think you can get a better one, I've got a mandrill that'll tell you differently, as soon as it's done picking shreds of your face out of its teeth with splinters of your finger bones."

"Holy shit," Zayeni whispered, leaning into Vanako.

"Twelve slabs," said Tjaroon.

Zaya's chest felt like it was full of sand.

"Any less and you can send that monkey at me," he continued. "But you know I'm not at the top of this operation."

Zaya looked at Vanako, making her stomach into a ball of steel. "Does that check out?"

"I was going to pull in about eleven," she said.

"The extra slab's for my trouble," Tjaroon put in.

"Fine, you baby," said Zaya. "We'll have the first two slabs to you in two weeks. Here?"

"Here's just fine," said Tjaroon. "Pleasure doing business, Shearwater-*cha*."

"The pleasure's all yours," said Zaya, standing. She fixed a steel stare on Zayeni and jerked her head; the girl scrambled out of the booth to make way for Vanako—who took her sweet time clambering out. "After you," Zaya said.

"Please," said Vanako, "after *you*."

"If you think I'm taking my eyes off you before I can confirm you're in your bedroom under a blanket, I've got a surprise for you."

Vanako's face made it clear that she'd love to answer that with a cutting riposte, but her tongue wouldn't deliver. She settled for a dramatic turn, making sure each footfall landed as loudly as it could.

***

THE NIGHT AIR WAS a benediction; Zaya sank into a squat with a shuddering sigh, covering her face with her hands—but not for long; when she drew breath again, she looked up at Vanako, who was just beginning to turn. "Vani," she said, "what did you do?"

Vanako looked away and shrugged. "I'm not smart like the twins. I was doing what I know how to do. To make some money. Support myself."

"Vanako. I just got back from eight weeks where I was on top of a dragon in the searing heat for more than half a day at a stretch. I do that so you don't have to support yourself. We told you this when you joined, because saving children from criminals with knives and monkeys is *exactly what I don't want to do with my evenings.*"

"I don't need you to decide whether I should have my own money. And I didn't need you to save me."

"You do, and you did. Who robbed you?"

"You think I was hiding it from Tjaroon? Trust me, if I ever find out who it is, I'll sic Tjaroon and that monkey on him before I say a thing to you. He didn't hurt me too bad, though, thanks for asking."

"If he had, your other parents might have noticed, and we wouldn't be here."

"Great. So instead of this dumb scene playing out in the planet's worst dive bar, Tjaroon and his monkey come knocking around the house. Little kids live there, maybe you remember?"

The grit of a long day's travel felt like raw rice in Zaya's eyes; the tension in her forehead became, or revealed itself to be, a pounding.

Vani was wrong about everything else, but she was right about that. Zaya pinched the bridge of her nose and squeezed her eyes shut.

"I'm right," said Vanako, smirking, "and you hate it."

"I'm on the hook to a violent criminal for twelve slabs is what I hate. What were you even selling?" Zaya held out a hand to stop her before she started. "I don't even want to know right now. We'll talk tomorrow."

***

ZAYA WASN'T ABOUT TO let Vanako get on a bike, so they walked the half-hour home without speaking. With each step, Zaya thought of the same thing: The tiny breath Vanako had drawn when Zaya had asked what she'd been selling. Just before her mother had said "I don't even want to know."

Actually, I do want to know. It would not have been hard to say. But she thought of the ways Vanako might reply, the deep, quick cuts her words could make, and couldn't say it.

Zaya's room was as she'd left it, plus a couple of books on the unmade bed; Jaliki sometimes used it when she was gone. She opened the shutters to check the window box. The irises looked healthy enough—the leaves unwithered, the blue and magenta of the petals untouched by brown. The soil was damp. Minshoon had probably watered them while she'd been out finding Vanako.

"My breath," Zaya said. "I don't know what I'm going to do with this family."

A tongue of blue-and-yellow flame licked out in the night: A Merlin wyrm, most likely, chasing a monkey or a nightjar.

"'Burn it all' was not really the answer I was hoping for." Zaya closed the shutters and cleared the bed. Her mind reeled and spun in the thick dark; but sleep came quickly.

43

CHAPTER 5

FAMILY, AGGLOMERATIVE. THIS FAMILY structure describes, to a lesser or greater extent, all the Great Houses of Yemareir and a large fraction of the households: Rather than a small, fixed cluster of genetically related individuals, the House or household is a dynamic entity that actively recruits members who might fit its tjerimar.

"Tjerimar" is an ancient Mlin word popularly translated as "house-way." The tjerimars of the great Houses are volumes of stipulations, guidelines, heuristics, and tests, continually revised and evaluated for the times. Most of their leadership is recruited as children rather than born into the House.

Outside the peerage, we are strapped for time, and our "house-ways" tend to boil down to "can they pay their share of rent?" But occasionally you do find a household that has a proper tjerimar—whether they call it that or not, whether it's written down or not. For me, at least, I usually feel a mix of envy and relief: Envy that I didn't grow up with my mind trained on that kind of purpose, and relief that I didn't have it forced on me.

The word means "bridle," by the way.

SEE ALSO: Government.

—From "A Visitor's Handbook for Yemareir," by Shenireen Agama

***

"ABOUT TWO SLABS IN cash," said Minshoon. "Maybe another two we could easily borrow against the house, plus a quarter from debts we could try to call in. Why?"

Zaya turned to Vanako, whom she'd forced out of bed as soon as she herself had woken up. "You tell him."

Vanako did. Zaya went to make a cup of mate and watched his hands. Minshoon had a flawless poker face, but his hands were the valve for his emotions; if he was bored, they might move loosely, and they stayed as still as a stalking cat if he was anticipating good news, but it was a sign of tremendous stress if he sank the nail of his thumb into the knuckle of the same hand's forefinger.

It didn't take long for thumbnail to meet knucklebone.

"I've never even heard of worldvine tar," said Minshoon when Zaya sat back down. "We're sure that's a real thing?"

"I've never heard of it here," said Zaya. "I've seen it out east, in Zaqzuq and Tzadiscari. They pulp it and then slow-cook it. It's not any more potent, but you come up faster and stay up longer."

Vanako shrugged. "All I know is you can carry eleven slabs of it under your arm."

"And because of that, we're going to be broke and in crushing debt just to make the two-week deadline," Zaya said to Minshoon. "Did I math that right?"

"That is about the size of it," said Minshoon. "Maybe we can do a little better—if Kirono can get an advance on his salary, or if we can get help from Yyrreen? Vani, if you've got a secret bank account or something, now would be the time to let me know."

"The Shaved Ice For Jaliki Fund has three sherds and eleven flinders in it, you can have that if you want."

Zaya's head snapped around to Vanako so hard her spine let out a *crack*. "If half your shipment was worth eleven slabs, and you've delivered at least one full one since you moved back here, that means you've moved dozens of slabs of product. I don't care how small your cut is—"

"Moved *here*."

"What?"

"You moved back here," Vanako said. "I never lived here. I moved here."

"What did you spend the money on, Vani?" said Zaya, resolving to be proud of the scant calm she managed to muster.

"Arrack, boys, and shaved ice," she recited. "Oh, and stealth charms."

Zaya stood up fast enough to push the chair several inches out behind her. "Give me a solitary reason not to search your room right now."

"Mom," Vanako said, softly but clearly.

Zaya looked down at her with a raised eyebrow.

"You won't find anything."

Vanako's eyes were open, earnest; she had not moved to get up. She would let Zaya do it if she chose. Was that a note of *pity* in her voice?

Zaya drew breath to speak—disastrously, she knew, reaching blindly into a basket of words and choosing the ones that worst cut her fingers—but the morning quiet shattered around her with the dish-rattling thumps of tiny feet and squeals of "Mama! Mama! Mama!" as Eäril tore out of her room and wrapped soft arms in a bear hug around Zaya's thighs. She picked the girl up and buried her face in her ringlets, drawing out ringing laughs with growls into the base of her neck. "Heart of mine," she said, "I missed you." She put Eäril down just in time for a slobbering hug from Enwë, who was not old enough to run. "And hello to you too, Little Green." Enwë put a hand up to her own tight curls, which were the same green-black as Cerminir's. Zaya felt Vanako's stare on the base of her neck, like hot lead, and sighed as she stood. "We'll talk later," she said, with a look at Vanako. "I guess we have some schools to visit. I'll take the little ones out," she said to Minshoon, "and then I'll talk to Yyrreen."

***

Taavi, Gilthiniel, and Vanako all studied at the lyceum on Fig Street; Eäril spent the first half of the day at the nursery, then came home to play or do lessons with Minshoon. Cerminir took Enwë and walked with the group. Zaya had never really thought about how the nursery and the lyceum were both east of the broodspire; you could see the border with Viridian from either. She had also never noticed the looks she got from parents of the nursery until she saw them, amplified, in the students at the lyceum. Zaya was used to Mrineen looking at her like a broken window or a questionable animal, but she'd never gotten used to it from her people. She wished for her hair back, so she'd not look like she was passing; she felt and fought the ludicrous urge to say "She's not my wife." *If my wife were here, I'd kiss her in front of you just to watch your faces. With tongue and everything.*

When the children were where they needed to be, Zaya and Cerminir crossed into Viridian to an Ililuë coffeehouse, and Zaya laid out the situation with Vanako over steaming earthenware bowls while Enwë played with another baby in a corner. Cerminir laughed at inappropriate places and asked pointless questions ("Was it a Medinior mandrill or a Tanrë mandrill, do you think?"), and between that and the coffee, Zaya felt her stomach settle and her heart slow. She was sitting in a cafe sipping coffee with Cerminir on a beautiful summer morning. How bad could it be?

Then Cerminir, after spending some time examining a walking-stick insect that had somehow gotten inside the cafe, said "Cut her loose."

"What?"

"Let her go. She said she doesn't want to be part of the family. Grant her wish and let her handle her debt. She's not worth losing the house for, and I don't see a way out of it where we don't lose the house."

"Are you out of your too-tall gourd?" Zaya said. "If I'd wanted to cut her loose, I'd have left her with that idiot Tjaroon and his mandrill, whatever species it is. That's not how it works."

"Medinior and Tanrë aren't *species*—"

"That's not how it works, Cer."

"All I'm saying is an Ililuë amalgam would have taken her at her word."

"If she were in an Ililuë amalgam, she wouldn't have said it." Zaya noticed that Cerminir's wide eyes were moving rapidly, focusing on a succession of points on her face. She rolled her eyes. "Is this some kind of Cerminir test?"

Cerminir looked over at Enwë; she'd never admit it, maybe didn't even know it, but that was as strong a signal as any that Zaya was right. "I barely know her," Cerminir said. "You adopted her when I was about to burst with Enwë, and since I've been able to think straight, I haven't seen much I like. So I want to know: Do you think she's worth saving?" She shrugged. "Seems like you do."

"We don't leave each other behind. That's how we got as far as we've come."

"Crushed under an unpayable mountain of debt thanks to one feckless teenager?"

Zaya gave Cerminir her shadiest glare over a sip from the coffee bowl. "You might as well say, 'saddled with a terminally ill kid who's a drag on everyone's time and money.'"

"I would never," said Cerminir, "because I don't want to have my skull crushed by a brick in my sleep. And, more importantly, because It's not Jaliki's fault he's hunted."

"It's not Vani's fault she's a garbage fire."

"Yes it is."

"It is and it isn't."

"You can't say 'it is and it isn't,' that violates the law of the excluded middle."

"If the law of the excluded middle were a real thing, we'd all be living in the gutters begging Mrineen lordlings to let us give them handjobs for flinders, because Minshoon couldn't run his arbitrage magic on the betting markets."

"That's—" Cerminir came up short. "That's kind of a shockingly insightful way to think about arbitrage."

"I'm not as dumb as all you nerds think I am."

Cerminir reached a long-fingered hand across the table and wrapped it around one of Zaya's, intoning, with the utmost sincerity, "Of course you're not."

Zaya chuckled weakly and looked at Enwë, who was building a tower out of books. "Thanks, Cer."

"So you don't want to cut Vani loose, and the numbers don't work. What are you going to do?"

"Talk to Yyrreen."

"That isn't what I'd do first."

"Yeah, but I don't smoke up."

"Rude."

"You have any better ideas?" Zaya asked.

"You said something about handjobs before—"

"I'll take my chances with Yyrreen."

"What about your sister?"

Zaya's lip curled. "She's not my sister."

"O-kay. What about the 'stream?"

Zaya felt herself deflate as she rested her forehead on the heel of her hand. "I suppose someone was always going to ask me about that, and if someone was going to ask me about it it was going to be you."

"What's that supposed to mean?" Cerminir said, blank-faced.

"Cer—"

Cerminir flashed a strange grin. "Just kidding, I know exactly what it's supposed to mean. It's my job to be the one who doesn't know any better than to say what everyone else stops at thinking. That's fine, I'm good at it. So what about it?"

"I can't do that again."

"It's been six years."

"I can't do that again."

"All right," said Cerminir. She quaffed the rest of the bowl in a long pull and then stood up. "But you know what the alternative is. You don't want to cut Vani loose, fine. You don't want to get back in the 'stream, fine. You don't want to lose the house, fine. But I think you get two out of three, maybe."

Zaya tried to swill the rest of her own coffee, but it was blazing hot still; she took as long a sip as she could, then bade a wistful good-bye to the rest. "It's less than a day since I've been back," she said. "It took me more than a day to find money for the insane diet you insisted on leading up to the Mariposa Annulus, but I did it. It took more than a day to get Saavero to rent the stable for free until we could pay, but I did it. The difference between me and a guttersnipe handjobbing for flinders is doing hard things that take more than a day to figure out."

"There's a lot riding on this one," said Cerminir, picking up a squealing Enwë.

Zaya walked up to Cerminir and offered Enwë a finger, which she gleefully yanked and squeezed. "There's always been a lot riding on who we let into House Shearwater," she said. "You just didn't get it until now."

Cerminir shrugged, then swung Enwë up on her shoulders. "Math checks out."

***

"PAY ME," SAID YYRREEN.

They were in her office in Incarnadine Precinct; every wall was covered in maps, which were covered in notes, pins, scrawled circles and stars, and occasional constellations of long slits that looked like knife-cuts. Yyrreen sat across a round table from Zaya, dressed head to toe in form-fitting indigo whose cooling field occasionally brushed, feather-light, on Zaya's forearm. She'd ceased to write on the papers she'd been working with, but her eyes drifted down to them from time to time.

"That's not what this is about."

"The hell it isn't. You'd rather pay some thug with a monkey than me."

"I have to pay for the drugs that my idiot drug-pusher child got mugged out of."

"Sitting right here," Vanako said, rolling her eyes.

"Or what?"

"Or she'll die! Or be sold into slavery! Or Tjaroon's mandrill will use her as a bucket! You of all people know what a thug with a monkey would do, you were fucking Zaako Saarizen for a year and a half!"

"Was he the thug or the monkey?" Vanako asked.

Yyrreen rolled her eyes. "He was a little rough around the edges—"

"He ate datura for breakfast," Zaya said. "He put a bomb inside a capybara carcass and dropped it between two alligators."

"The groundskeeper at my school is named Zaako," said Vanako. "He's deaf."

"That capybara blew a hole in the Scarlet-Celadon bridge," Yyrreen said, her eyes fond and far away.

"Your aunt had no idea he was deaf for a week," Zaya said to Vanako, "because he was so dissociated all the time anyway—"

"Don't," said Yyrreen.

"Come on," said Zaya, "you can't possibly make me believe you had it that bad for Zaako—"

"That's because you've never believed we could really care for anyone outside 'House Shearwater,'" said Yyrreen. "But you can believe what you like. I mean, don't call me your daughter's aunt. I'm not your sister. And your daughter's not going to die. Or be a bucket or whatever you said."

"Yay, immortality," said Vanako, twirling a finger.

"You don't have to call yourself my sister, but at least don't let whatever fond memories I never knew you had of Zaako Saarizen blind you to—"

"I don't give a shit about Zaako Saarizen. I'm saying you can stop your big bad man and his big bad monkey, right now, without my help."

Zaya raised an eyebrow. "Elaborate."

"You've got a beautiful Lilac Precinct apartment—"

"Do *not*—"

"—co-domiciled with a perfectly serviceable flat in Celadon. I'd be shocked if that doesn't cover your debts, but if it doesn't, I'll make up the rest."

"That's my house."

"That's your daughter."

Zaya looked at Yyrreen for a long time. Yyrreen stared calmly back, eyes smooth as wave-worn glass. "You're loving this," she said flatly.

"I'm feeling a lot of things," Yyrreen said, "but it's safe to say I'm not hating this."

"You can't get what you think you're owed, so you want it to go to the mob instead."

"At least the mob doesn't lie about why they take your money."

"They actually do!" said Zaya. "They actually lie all the time! About everything! To everyone! If they just went around telling the truth about all their shit, they'd all be dead! Or in jail! And I never lied about the money! I used it exactly how I said I would when you agreed to pay in—to build something, for us, as a family that you used to say you were a part of. Buying people out was never part of the deal."

"You built something you couldn't afford," said Yyrreen.

"I built something that three out of five Mrineen in this city are born into, and maybe one in fifty Kayalim ever see."

"And you chained us to it."

"Money doesn't work like that," said Vanako.

"One hundred percent of what I know about you is that you were too dumb to watch your own back while you were carrying eleven slabs of product," said Yyrreen.

"You think that just because you put money into a thing, you should be able to turn it back into money when you feel like it," said Vanako. "If that worked, I wouldn't be out the cash I spent on snake oil ker repellent for my mom. You pay your money and you take your chances. That's how the world works."

"Please, child who got bushwhacked out of eleven slabs of someone else's drugs, tell me more about how the world works."

"In my experience," said Vanako, "some chucklehead robs you, you're on the hook for the loss, and when you ask for help, some asshole says you deserve to be homeless."

Yyrreen laughed bitterly. "And how often does that little speech work on 'some asshole,' in your experience?"

"I don't care? My mom brought me here because she thought it might shame you into helping if you laid eyes on the person you were screwing over. She obviously thinks way too highly of you. You care more about your little *atelier* in Incarnadine Precinct than you do about your family."

"Get out," Yyrreen said, "or I will call the police."

"Pale stuck-up thing like you," said Vanako, "what else could you do?"

Zaya had her by the elbow at this point; Vanako allowed herself to be hauled out of the chair. Apologies to Yyrreen and disbelieving reprimands to Vanako scuffled for control of her tongue; Vanako, for her part, was happy enough to put up only a token resistance to being bustled out the door, slowing Zaya just long enough to shout "Come at me, if your dick's hard enough!" before Zaya could get her past the front desk.

***

WHEN THEY WERE OUTSIDE, Vanako practically jackknifed with laughter. "Did you see her eyes go wide?" she howled. "'Tell me more about how the world works.' She got her answer, didn't she?"

"Get yourself together," Zaya hissed. "People are watching."

It was true; a number of passersby had stopped to stare, all Mrineen as well-dressed as you might expect for a street full of architecture studios and real estate brokers, as well as a grey-feathered Merlin Wyrm tearing at a pigeon. Zaya felt the laughter drain from Vanako's body as she straightened up. Zaya started walking to the square at the south end of the street, and Vanako followed.

At the center of the square was a fountain, tiled in red with white accents. Zaya sat on its lip, and Vanako joined her. "I guess this is when you ream me out for telling the truth," said Vanako.

"Just because you saw it coming doesn't mean it's not happening."

Vanako looked at the cobblestones of the square. "What if I just admitted I really didn't want to get yelled at?"

"Vulnerable definitely beats shitty teenage know-it-all in terms of not getting yelled at."

"Cool, I'll file that one away then."

"That was a bad move, Vani."

"She wasn't going to help."

"Not today."

Vanako picked up a chip of red tile and threw it in the fountain.

"I know what it's like," said Zaya. "Slide the knife in while you can, because who knows—"

"That's not me," said Vanako. "I know how to think long-term. But I said what she needed to hear."

"And how exactly does hearing that, from you, help her?"

Vanako's fingers searched for another chip of tile, but didn't find one. Zaya let her look for a while.

"My Papa Kaalo died not long after Kiriki," Zaya said at last. "We always thought he'd take too much datura or drink himself to death one day, but it wasn't that. It was more like, it had just all worn him out, and everything just slowly stopped working." She paused, mulling over whether to say what was in her mind. "That makes it sound more graceful than it was. Shortness of breath is all very civilized for a couple of hours, until you try to get to the toilet and can't make it in time. When your stomach can't take food, it tosses it back out. I was a new widow and a new mother, and everyone else in the house was sick with grief for Kiriki and no one had raised a child before, and Jaliki was going insane with missing his mother—we were paying a wet nurse but he wouldn't eat, he was up all night howling because he was hungry and Kiriki wasn't there. You could hear him getting weaker by the night. I never felt less like his mother than I did right after Kiriki was gone, when I thought he was going to starve while I watched. Papa Kaalo was the one person Jali would take a bottle from, and now he couldn't feed him any more, and my father and my son were both dying right in front of everyone else who was relying on me to keep the family going. Papa Zinji couldn't take it—he'd disappear for hours and days and come back completely out of his mind, sometimes with things to feed Papa Kaalo that I was never sure if I should just let him have or not..." The smell of the things that had come from inside Kaalo's body was like nothing she had ever smelled before or since; there were all the smells of the latrine, because how not, but it was all a layer over something old, a core of ancient decay and corruption, brimstone and peat and the gas that bloats a long-drowned corpse. That, Zaya did not share with her daughter.

"If this is a way of telling me not to do drugs—"

"On that score I actually trust you. You came up in the trade but you didn't get mixed up with the product. That says a lot. But with that history, you must know someone who got used to being let down really badly when she was young. Who's gotten punished for her trust. The kind of person who'll swim out to help you out of the riptide—but you can feel, in her hands, she's ready to let you go if the current gets bad enough. That's not you, I don't think, but you know a girl like that."

Vanako nodded with the kind of weight to the movement that showed she had somebody in mind.

"That's Yyrreen. She saw Kiriki and the Mule dead, Jaliki and Papa Kaalo dying, me losing my mind, Cer and Minshoon and Kirono completely panicked, and after being our rock for two years, she felt the current get bad. No one had a job, we were living off savings—I can't even talk about how much we were afraid of losing races back then, or of one of us dying in a race, even while we were living our lives as if we'd already won. Yyrreen wanted us to sell the house, and it made total sense. We could buy everyone out with whatever was left after we'd made the late payments on the house, which would still be a good chunk of money, and anyone who wanted to could go in on, say, a flat in Damask Precinct, which probably any two of us could have managed with the takings, and anyone who just wanted out would just be out.

"Two weeks later, Kaalo would have been buried and Jaliki would have been eating and we might have just sat down and done the math. A month later, we wouldn't have had to. I was finally digging my way up out of my grief, the house didn't smell like dead old person any more, Kirono and Minshoon were working enough to keep us afloat, I was a couple weeks away from finding my first job as a long-hauler. We were out of the riptide."

"She might still have cut loose," Vanako said.

"Maybe. But anyway, when you have your eye on the door and you decide it's time to go, you don't wait around. So she hits us with this plan right after Papa Kaalo's died. In the middle of the soul-vigil."

"*Bitch*," Vanako breathed.

"She was scared," said Zaya, "in a way she didn't know how to explain. And we wouldn't have understood her if she had. It took the four of us a lot of late nights and a lot of beer to even start figuring out what happened." Zaya shook her head. "Her folks didn't observe the rites—her dad was some Mrineen cop, not in the picture, and her mom was in the Church of the Wyrm Immanent. She didn't understand how important it was. She came to Minshoon on his break from the vigil and tried to sell him on it, I guess because he's Mrineen and she figured he didn't really take it seriously, and it didn't take much for him to snap, and I heard them talking and stormed in absolutely fucking livid that anyone was socializing during my father's soul-vigil, and once I found out what was under discussion... you can imagine how the rest of it went." Zaya shivered in the heat. "I said a lot of things she deserved to hear, and a lot she didn't. It was one of the shittiest things anyone's ever done to me. But she was as gutted and scared as the rest of us."

"Fuck her. You don't need her." Zaya could see Vanako breathe in, then, for the smallest moment, hesitate; her eyes wavered, widened, tightened. "I'll race with you."

"You're sweet," Zaya said, putting a hand around her shoulder, leaning in to touch her temple to Vanako's.

Vanako squirmed away to gain enough space to turn, then looked Zaya in the eye, half disgusted and half furious. "I'm serious."

My breath, my sweet fierce girl. I love you, but Yyrreen was one of the pillars that held up my heart; and my heart's name was Kiriki. You can't replace them. Zaya knew better than to say it. Instead she said, "I don't have a dragon. And if I did," she said into the breath that would make the words she knew were coming, "and I put you on it, Minshoon would throw me out a window."

"If you had a dragon, you wouldn't have to worry about being thrown out a window."

"When we figure this out," Zaya said. "When your debts are paid off. Then I'll fly with you."

"I don't want to, like, thrill to the wyrm's muscles rippling beneath my loins," said Vanako. "I want to race with you to win enough money to pay off Tjaroon."

"It doesn't work that way."

"Why?"

"Because Minshoon is basically banned from gambling on the 'stream any more. We didn't even complete the Bisai because our wyrm and half our team got eaten, and he *still* won a little bit. Everyone is too scared to take any side of a bet with Minshoon. Meanwhile, I can't just go pull a dragon from the bay and start winning races—those things are wild animals, they need months of training and an optimized diet just to place—"

"Please, you didn't have all that when you were coming up—"

"We did, though. We had one thing, and that was time, and we used it. We have more things now, but we don't have time."

"We need to do something."

"Yeah," Zaya said quietly. "That's why we came to Yyrreen today. That was something."

Vanako's face twisted with the bitter-taste look Zaya recognized from any number of arguments with children: *I know you're wrong, but I can't say how.*

"We'll figure something out," Zaya said. "But jumping into the 'stream on a random Dawn Wyrm isn't it."

CHAPTER 6

EMPATHY, PSIONIC. Sᴇᴇ, *I did "noun comma adjective" this time. Just like a real lexicographer!*

What psionic empathy is is just the ability to communicate mentally with other animals. You don't see much of this wherever you're from because there's a risk of overwriting parts of your own brain when you do it, which is why people who develop the talent spontaneously tend to go feral or, every so often, asphyxiate because they've clobbered the motor commands for breathing. Over thousands of years, the Kayalim of Kayazē developed a highly refined set of safeguards that allowed them to make psionic empathy into a sacred art and science. About three quarters of a millennium ago, a psionic assassin sent an eyelash viper to kill Emperor Jivaki, he tried to purge all the empaths, and a bunch of them fled here, where local exigencies channeled their psionic talents into manhandling elephants and gorillas to support the construction boom.

So you, tourist, can expect to see some large animals and apes on construction crews, and you shouldn't worry about it; stampedes are rare. You will also find some shows featuring smaller animals, most of which are adapted from old Kayalim rituals originally involving the feathered serpents they have over there. For more, please consult my book, The Tusk-Mad, *whose title I will not explain so you actually have a reason to buy it. (Buy it! —Ed.)*

SEE ALSO: Ethnicities, Psionics.

—From "A Visitor's Handbook for Yemareir," by Shenireen Agama

***

THE DEPOT AT MIDNIGHT had come alive: Shouts rang up and down the corridors, and beams of light from torch-charms played through the small windows, making odd tessellated patterns through the glass, which was reinforced with hexagonal wire. Zaya forced herself to look away, toward the wyrm-pen. The spring night's cool brought that feathered tension that's not quite a shiver to her chest and arms, and she breathed shallowly. A familiar Dawn Wyrm met her eyes and *reached* out with its mind. *Why are you here?*

Zaya's mind, cut into rags with fear and the pulse of hot blood in her veins, searched for an answer.

* * *

Because my son is dying:

The afternoon after her meeting with Yyrreen, Zaya took Jaliki out to the dunes to watch the Yemareir Air Guard drill.

No race or dogfight in Zaya's memory had ever benefited from precision maneuvers in formation, but she'd learned to keep that to herself around her son. The Air Guard's drills were more for the audience than the pilots, and it was no coincidence who the audience was: Foreign dignitaries in charm-cooled boxes, visiting from Jaidar and Kerkakan and the Ililuë conurbations in the south and center of the continent; and children from the outlying precincts, who got discounted rates on transport to these pageants twice a year. This, too, Zaya kept to herself: *Ask yourself, son of mine, why our*

House of the Stars would pay to show poor kids the power of our armed forces. If he lived to see his tenth year, she would ask it then.

In keeping with the showmanship of the thing, the Air Guard went in order of the rarity of the wyrms, although Zaya knew the "elite" riders of the rarest dragons would never see combat except in the most desperate of circumstances. The Dawns flew in pink-and-blue sheets that split up into ribbons and then into interlocking rings, reminiscent of the loose loops they made on thermals hunting fish over the bay; the Ranger Wyrms terrified everyone with low strafes, and the Dusk Stalkers dropped like grey-and-black stones nearly on top of one another, only to peel out to either side and loop around again in a sideways figure eight. But Jaliki's great love was reserved for the Argent Swordwings, gleaming behemoths whose immense pinions were as long and sharp as chef's knives. There were only three in the Air Guard; they were difficult to tame and rare, enough so that there had been no good estimate of their brooding period (thirty-seven years) for the first several centuries of Yemareir's history, because several cohorts passed in which no Swordwings hatched. "That's Kanivain Goanna," said Jaliki, pointing to the middle rider. The middle rider was always Kanivain Goanna. "She's the best rider dragonkind has ever seen, except maybe you and Mama-*taki*, because no one has ever seen the two of you fly, side by side." This was a ritual incantation, because Cerminir, of all people, had once lectured him about respecting his mothers' legacy.

"Give Bristling Son some credit." This, too, was a ritual incantation, a reminder that a rider was nothing without a wyrm.

"A second-cohort Argent Swordwing would always beat a second-cohort Ranger Wyrm in a fight, even though Rangers can grow big enough to eat rhinos. Know why?"

Zaya knew why. "Why?"

"Because a second-cohort Argent Swordwing is at least thirty-seven years old and a second-cohort Ranger Wyrm is less than twenty-six! Rangers don't start getting super big until they are third- or fourth-cohort. Also the Swordwing will cut the Ranger up with its wings."

"If it can get close enough," said Zaya. "Rangers breathe fire too, you know."

"But Swordwings are the most agile, and according to pilots, they are the smartest."

Zaya smiled and said nothing.

"But you don't think they're the smartest." Jaliki smiled as well; he didn't need an answer. "The next Swordwing brood is in five years."

"Is that right?" said Zaya. "Better tell the good men and women of Argent Precinct; they'll need that long just to pack their trunks."

"Do you think I'll see it?"

The ker, about which Zaya had forgotten, opened its eyes and looked inquiringly at her. She felt black curses and burning tears block her throat like ambergris, foul and solid. *I can't promise you that, breath of mine,* she thought. *Even if you did live, who's to say we'd see it? Could we even go to Argent Precinct and still walk out with our freedom? Do we even know any of the Swordwings will breed this year? There's nothing I'd love more than to see it with you, breath of mine, I just don't want to make a promise I can't keep and then leave you disappointed.*

"I think you'll see it," she said, looking the ker straight in the eye. It closed its eyes and rested its chin on its paws.

***

BECAUSE I DON'T KNOW *how to save him, I only know how to destroy everything else:*

Two days after Zaya came back, in the evening when the light from the ceiling-murals began to glow more yellow to aid sleep, Zaya stopped by Vanako's room. It was pristine now; there was nowhere for her to hide the traces of charm-working, and the door was gone. These had not been punishments set in anger. Zaya, Vanako, and Minshoon had negotiated them in comparative calm, in consideration of what was reasonable and what would set minds at ease, and although Vanako had bridled at the conditions she had ultimately accepted them—but she looked no more at home in the beautifully bare chamber than a jellyfish in a terrarium.

"Vani, breath of mine," Zaya said, "I need to know why you were dealing."

Vanako sneered. "You want me to say it's because I don't feel like I *belong* here," she said. "Because I'm afraid you all won't want me any more. So you can tell me that your love is unconditional and I'll always have a home here and remind me why I should be grateful for everything you've done."

Zaya smiled and took a seat on the edge of her bed. "Our love is unconditional. And, yeah, you should be grateful to us for taking you in—which doesn't mean you have to show it all the time. We're grateful for what you've brought us too."

Vanako snorted. "Like what?"

"You're the only person in this house who can draw to save their life. That's an inspiration for everyone—and I personally appreciate it, because sometimes this house fills up so high with math and biology that I can't breathe. Jaliki loves you to death, and with me gone so much I'm glad he has you. You're uncompromising, which is mostly a terrible thing you need to work on... but also a reminder that people who know what's important to them aren't always easy to live with."

"I'm supposed to notice that you didn't say I'd always have a home."

Zaya curled up her legs, perching her heels on the edge of the bed. "Love is unconditional. Sharing space is more complicated. No one's guaranteed a place here, including me."

"Sure. Good to know I'm only in the family as long as you like me."

"Would you feel safe in a house where someone was allowed to stay no matter what they did? Even if they'd done something terrible to you, personally?" Zaya tried to catch Vanako's eye, but couldn't. "You've lived in a house like that, haven't you? I have."

Vanako shrugged. "We all came from the dole-flats, and we turned out all right."

"Not Jaliki. He was born in this house. There's a rug stained with his birth-blood rolled up in a chest somewhere. Cerminir lived on the street because she couldn't stand it in the dole-flats. Too many people, too close, too loud. Enwë was born here too; Eäril wasn't, but she won't remember anything else. And you didn't turn out all right, and neither did I. I need to know why you were dealing, and what it'll take to stop it, because that choice has put all those people's lives at risk."

Vanako looked at Zaya, then down to the sketch on her desk. It was just a drawing of the room, distorted as though seen through the bottom of a glass; when Zaya looked closer she could see a thicket of three-petaled flowers growing in the closet. The silence lengthened, and Zaya's heart sagged in her chest. She tried to tell herself that it was all right, that Vanako was allowed to take time to choose her words, that there were times some of her dearest friends could barely summon words at all and it didn't mean they were lying. But that had never been Vanako. She said what she thought, sometimes before she thought it.

"For Jaliki," Vanako finally said. "I wanted to be able to get him a few nice things."

"You tried that one already. I know this didn't all go to shaved ice."

Vanako turned away. "I didn't keep receipts."

"I'm not questioning your love for your brother. I know you do more for him than I do, some days." Never mind how that hurt to say; life was long, maybe it had been true once or twice. "But if you're hiding where the money went, you're setting me up for a surprise. And if it's another surprise like an empath with a monkey and a knife shaking you down in a bar... we're lucky we walked away from that surprise, Vani."

"Shaved ice, horchata, candy, noodle bowl. You would actually be surprised at how much that kid can eat." Vanako saw Zaya's warning look and shook her head. "We went to a few plays and concerts. And I was saving up for a book. There's a bookshop in Viridian that has a three-volume illustrated Wing Windtwister that's just beautiful. Leather cover, gold lettering, good paper... you know how the libraries never have the whole set? You know how he and Eäril will sit in the corner, like in that little space between the blue couch and the wall, even if no one's on the couch? And he'll read to her? I know he'd have loved that book, and it would be something for her..."

Vanako's eyes were bright, and Zaya felt her own throat swell. "To remember him by," she said, careful to keep the tear-rasp out of her voice.

"Yeah," Vanako said, not careful.

"Vani, what happened to the money?"

"No one ever asked me if I lost anything of my own when I got robbed."

Zaya ran a hand over her scalp—her hair had grown just long enough to feel soft, still not long enough to pay to color. "You've done this before," she said.

"I feel like you say that a lot."

"Papa Zinji and Papa Kaalo were in the trade. They were a lot sloppier than you, but they knew not to carry—"

"Can you please go now," Vanako said softly, without a trace of a question mark.

"No." Zaya put all the iron in her voice that she could find. "Are you kidding? No. You put this family at risk. You don't just quit when there's a question you don't feel like answering."

"I'll tell you if you go out that door."

Zaya bit back the urge to point out there was no door. "You know, I might have a follow-up."

"Fine. Just get off my bed."

The anger rose, and words with it—*this is your fault, ungrateful bitch, how dare you*—but she swallowed them. "All right." She got up, moving with the sort of half-pantomime deliberateness that says *See? I'm complying*, and left the room, then turned around. She tried to meet Vanako's eyes, but she was facing away from the doorway, her forehead resting on the fingers of her open hand.

"I had the money on me," Vanako said quietly, "because I was about to go buy the book."

Zaya wanted to reach out for Vanako, in comfort and shared sorrow and pride in her love for her little brother; she wanted to pull back, stone-faced and steel-voiced, and call bullshit, to keep cutting through the layers of lies until she hit the heart of the truth. Her heart was pounding; her chest and head felt like they were pulsing with its beats.

"I want to trust you, Vani," she said, because it was the one thing she was sure of.

"I don't think so," Vanako said.

***

BECAUSE I'M GOING TO *destroy myself, and it won't even save my family:* It wasn't so much that Zaya couldn't say what had brought her back to the Blind Beggar as that she wouldn't, a least not while she was there, in the same shitty booth under the same elephant murals, knocking back the same poor beer served by the same sullen drone of a waitron—but, said or unsaid, she could not help but notice how her thoughts turned to the taste of a mandrill's mind, and its smallness. Dragons of riding size had motor plans distributed across the cephalic brain and several spinal ganglia; their body plans were foreign, a poor fit for human motor abstractions, and the movement of draconic mass through air was a problem so foreign to human neural hardware that she might as easily have learned to speak to the dragon in its own language, if it had one. Wresting fine-grained motor control of a primate was simple by comparison. "Which is why," she found herself explaining to the waitron, "even simpletons like your boy Tjaroon can do it. My people," she said, poking her chest satisfyingly with her thumb for emphasis, "wrote down protocols for safely controlling primates A LITERAL MILLENNIUM AGO and brought them here. If you applied yourself, you too could be a senior thug slash sub-kingpin with a mandrill flunky to do your dirty work. But I understand," she continued, placing a palm on the waitron's forearm, joggling a slop of beer out of the pitcher in their hand. "Your life's path is customer service. It's a noble calling. No. I'm serious. This world demands beer, Sullen Waitron. There are days—so many days—when nothing else will get you through to sunset—"

The waitron mumbled something.

"What?"

A Mrineen woman slid past the waitron to sit across from Zaya—broad-shouldered but slim-waisted, in a tight sleeveless top that showed off biceps the size of papayas. "They said they've won two of the city's top prizes for poetry this year, and if their debut collection keeps selling, they'll probably be able to retire off the royalties."

Zaya looked at the waitron in wonder. "That's amazing. Congratulations."

The waitron shrugged, blushing faintly.

"My drinking companion needs something stronger," said Zaya's new companion. "Bring us two glasses of your—" She stopped and looked Zaya in the eye. "Is tonight a 'finest' night or a 'cheapest' night?"

"This feels like a test."

"It is, but not the kind you pass or fail."

"In that case," said Zaya, "it depends—"

"Sorry," said the stranger, "I apologize, there is in fact a failing answer and it's 'It depends on who's paying.'"

"So what you're testing," Zaya said, "is whether the girl you're flirting with can afford not to care who's paying for expensive drinks." She cocked her head and shrugged theatrically. "Starting to feel like a 'cheapest' night to me."

The waitron squirmed and scribbled something on her pad, then crossed it out.

"Counterpoint," said the stranger. "The top shelf at this establishment, very much begging the pardon of the staff and requesting their discretion—" she raised an eyebrow at the waitron here, whose spine stiffened and whose eyes showed a ring of white around light grey-green irises—"is still priced to move with respect to the clientele—"

"I guess this arguing thing works on most of the straight girls you take home," said Zaya, "but I came here to drink, not prevent the Poet Laureate of Yemareir from collecting tips, so we'll have a bottle of the blackberry peach arrack and two glasses, please. Pitcher of water to go with."

The sullen waitron scribbled down the order and dashed off as if a Cinereal Vore were on her scent.

Zaya leaned forward on her elbows and met the stranger's eyes, which were a beguiling shade of blue, somewhere between sky and sapphire. "Now, Ma'm'selle Colonizer," she said, "was that a 'finest' order, or a 'cheapest' order?"

The stranger smiled with closed lips. "This feels like a test."

"Mostly a test of how often you come here to pull closeted Kayalim girls."

"If that's what you want to know, you could just ask. The answer is once every couple of weeks. But I can make that more often if you're a regular." This smile showed the stranger's teeth, which were gleaming and perfect.

Zaya looked up at the lightless elephant murals on the ceiling, then ran a palm over her still-cropped hair and let a sigh out through her nose. "What's your name, stranger?"

"Kemreen."

"I'm Zaya. The thing, Kemreen, about girls with no experience is that they can confuse a playbook for a personality. You're pretty good at this thing where you trample over boundaries like a mad mother elephant, but I've made it pretty clear I'm onto you, and you're not adapting. Not every Kayalim girl with short hair is trying to pass for straight."

"I've heard rumors that a few of them are actually straight, but I guess that's not you either."

"Correct."

"So what's the deal?"

Zaya laughed softly. "I'd tell you that even gay Kayalim shave their heads when they kill someone, but I don't think you'd believe me."

"Is it true?"

"Yes."

"Then I believe you. Want to talk about it?"

Zaya grinned and opened her mouth to dismiss the idea, but found her throat tight; when she blinked, she felt water on her eyelashes. She cleared her throat and weighed words. All seemed too heavy or too light.

"Sorry," said Kemreen. "I can go back to mad mother elephant seduction tactics if that's safer."

"No. Or, yes, but let's not." She let out a long breath through her nose. "That's just." She rubbed her eyes briefly with her thumb and forefinger. "That's a question I wish I'd been asked sooner by someone I'd known longer."

"So do you want to talk about it?"

As if on cue, the arrack arrived—the bottle already opened and two glasses poured, for maximum speed of delivery. The Poet Laureate of Yemareir sped away from the booth as fast as their legs would take them.

"Later," said Zaya, handing a glass to Kemreen. "You never took the test. Finest, or cheapest?"

"This is a setup, isn't it?"

"Correct," said Zaya. "Cheapest means you think I don't respect your company. No. Finest means you think I'm here to impress you. Also no. I'm here to do a thing, and for what I'm here to do I don't need *cheap* drink, and I don't need *fine* drink. I need *strong* drink. Which is what we have." Zaya took a longer pull than she really wanted; peaches and alcohol stung her behind her eyes, and her shoulders heaved a bit from keeping her cough to herself.

Kemreen took a slower sip, not quite able to hide her distaste for the drink. Then she took a long one, and did hide it. "I don't nurse sad drunk girls back to happiness," she said.

"Sad drunk girls," said Zaya, "make their own happiness, when they're good and ready."

"To making our own happiness," said Kemreen, raising a just-refilled glass. Zaya clinked it against her own and drank.

✳✳✳

*B*ECAUSE *I* DIDN'T KNOW *where else to go:*

Sex with Kemreen was exactly what it needed to be—good enough to feel worth doing, tiring enough that no one wanted to talk, awkward enough to remove any desire to stay the night. Kemreen was fit, rough, and Mrineen, the obverse of Zaya's type in all ways, which was also exactly what it needed to be. But for all that swagger, she couldn't hold her liquor, yet another thing that was exactly what it needed to be. Fit people, in Zaya's experience, were early risers and infrequent drinkers, which conspired with insufficient body mass and general overconfidence to make them crumple against even a middling bottle of arrack.

"So, who'd you kill?" Kemreen had slurred sleepily after they were done, and Zaya had said "Someone who was trying to kill me," and Kemreen had said "That doesn't make it better at all, does it?" and Zaya had been about to say "No, it doesn't," when she was suddenly consumed by the urge to say "Well, yes, it does," and after a moment she realized the problem with either answer, and said it: "I've never killed anyone who *wasn't* trying to kill me." And Kemreen chuckled and snuggled closer, and Zaya felt herself stiffen, but waited until she heard snoring to pull away.

Kemreen didn't wake, or pretended not to—the polite simulation of unconsciousness was a strategy Zaya had used more than once, to make separation easier and, every so often, to observe what her partner might do when they thought they weren't being watched. Her studio was a boring person's idea of austere; she liked suprematist woodcut art but couldn't choose an anchor piece, so there were four haphazardly arranged on the walls, and likewise short swords and throwing knives, of which there were far more than four. Zaya caught herself appraising the artwork and the weapons, and looking out for places where jewelry might hide. But that was a reflex from when her skin and freedom had been worth nothing, or at least that had been how she'd valued them; the scale of what she stood to gain from fencing one none-too-rich woman's none-too-tasteful stuff was so tiny against the gulf of cash she had to cover, she almost laughed out loud. As it was, she laughed silently, and the motion of her ribs and lungs made her unsteady legs reel.

When her body had steadied, she had a plan.

It was a drunken plan; no doubt the blast of the night air would shred it to tatters. But it was enough to get her moving. She dug around on the night table until she found a pot of the same lip paint she could still taste on her own lips, then found the longest, broadest blade in the collection and wrote "same place same time one week if I'm not dead I'll be there" on its shining flat in chunky magenta finger-strokes. Then she collected her clothes and bag and left in all possible silence.

It was easy to find bikes in Cornflower, though not good ones. Zaya made half the trip with an eye out for a five-speed, which would exhaust her less and help muddy her trail. She assumed that the plan would have dissolved and blown away by the time she made the switch, or at least that she would have sobered up enough to back away; but when the handlebars of a five-speed winked back at her in Damask Precinct, she found herself on it and back on her route without hesitation, detail blooming from the bare boughs of her plan unbidden as dandelion. A midnight liquor store was not too hard to find in Vermilion Precinct; and after another quarter-hour, she ditched the five-speed by the Scarlet Precinct broodspire and walked the three blocks to the depot, two fifths of lousy whiskey in her bag and her mind on a diamond-patterned sack of emeralds.

***

Because everything I try to do falls to pieces in my hands:

With her skin uncooled by the bike's slipstream, the night heat closed on Zaya like a fist, dry but heavy. Sweat sprang out, and she let it stay; she didn't want to wipe it off in view of the depot. It felt like a guilty gesture.

The gate guards recognized Zaya and put up their broadspears without her asking. She smiled at them, and they smiled back. She'd come to the depot late before, though usually for early-departing caravans. But the building manager knew she kept some petty cash here for the voyages. That would do to explain her presence if the police came knocking.

There was nothing complicated about the layout of the depot: The north end was storerooms and loading docks, the south end was lockers and offices, and to the east of all that, in the yard outside, were the dragons. Most of them would be sleeping at this hour, snouts tucked into the feathers between their wings, but that wouldn't be a problem; Zaya knew the mindprint she was looking for, she'd slept near it for weeks. She went into the locker room and *reached.*

I know you were sleeping, she said once waking had kindled in the wyrm's brain, *but I have whiskey in my bag.*

The Dawn radiated suspicion at the offer of midnight whiskey.

Whiskey later if you help me now.

What do you need?

What wyrm do you hate most in that pen?

An image bubbled up: A Dusk Stalker, compact and evil-looking in the Dawn's emotion-memory, its grey sickly, the blacks of its crest and wing-feathers utter.

Whiskey if you bite its tail as hard as you can and don't let go. Chew it off it you have to. I'll deliver after things calm down.

Uncertainty shivered in the Dawn's mind. *We don't fly if we fight.*

Everyone will think the other one started it, said Zaya, grasping at straws. *Isn't that right?*

How much whiskey?

Zaya imagined the two bottles in her bag, a bit bigger than life—dragons didn't know whiskey bottles came in standard sizes. Or so she thought, at any rate.

Done.

She felt the Dawn wheel and leap. The wyrm-scream from the pens was instantaneous; fire painted the night. It took almost no time for feet to thump from the barracks at the south of the depot, toward the exit to the pen.

It was into the barracks Zaya ran, eyes wide and face twisted in feigned fear, in case anyone had remained behind—but no one had. Her eyes scanned frantically: The key ring, if it was there, would be large, probably affixed to some deliberately oversized object—and there it was, on the end of a billy club that looked to have seen some use.

She ran again, this time to the storerooms. These were arrayed in two ranks, the space between them open to the air and the north wall open so a wagon might easily back in, and each was secured with a barred gate. Zaya checked the west rank first, her eyes out for a palm velvet sack patterned with diamonds.

She found it almost instantly. It was the other cargo that struck the spark of familiarity: The bags of cumin and coriander, the carved stone statues of eagle- and jackal-headed figures, the gold bracelets inlaid with turquoise. The diamond-patterned bag leaned against a statue's leg, almost invisible in the torchlight. Zaya held up the key ring in triumph. This was storeroom 3; all she had to do was find the key.

There were no labels on the keys.

Zaya fumbled through key after key, swearing silently at herself. The noises of wyrm-scream and shouting seemed to ebb, then crest, then ebb again. Zaya dropped the keys with a vast metallic song that rang out in the night's thick air. *One more key*, she told herself as she picked it up, *and then I run no matter what.*

It took two, but the door opened.

Or it seemed to: The bolt rolled out, but when Zaya pushed the door, it wouldn't budge.

She felt some give in the door, she was sure of it. She put half her weight against it and felt it give a hair. She put her shoulder against it, planted her feet, and shoved with all the strength in her legs.

The door few open as if on greased hinges; Zaya careered in, lost her balance, and fell on top of a crate. It half-buckled under her; the song of shattering glass soared out into an otherwise suddenly, unaccountably silent night. The barred door clattered against the side of the storage room a second later like a thousand tiny gongs.

For a moment, Zaya thought the clangor might have gone un-noticed. Then the shouting resumed, with a new, familiar timbre. Zaya knew a thief-taking shout when she heard one.

She picked her way through the treasures of Nistrium and nearly fell, but she got a finger on the palm velvet sack and it was all she needed: It was under her arm then, and she darted out of the storeroom just in time to hear a guard bellow "They ran inside! Cover the exits!"

She made a few calculations quick as lightning then:

If she dropped the emeralds and the key ring and got back inside the depot, she stood a chance at pretending the thief was never her. She was known, she was trusted... but she was here at a strange time of night, and all the other suspects had been outside pacifying dragons. She might still end up on a work crew for nothing.

She could pull a wyrm from the pens and start setting fire to things. The guards wouldn't stand a chance. But her stomach curdled at the thought of destroying the depot, of killing soldiers who'd never asked for this. And she still might not get free.

If she hid? There was no way to hide in most of these storerooms: Most were empty, the rest would be searched.

While Zaya calculated, the voices of the guards moved—and, she realized, all in one direction. They were looping around the north side of the building, to come in by the entrance where a wagon would back in to load or unload. Because, to a thief who was a stranger to the depot, that would be entrance and exit both: Less well guarded, open to the desert, with a clear path to the eastern foothills. It would be insane to come inside the building; even if they knew it was empty, they'd have to get past the guards at the gate—

So she ducked inside the building, her heart pounding at her ribs like an drunk ex-lover at the door, and sprinted through the north-south corridor in six quick steps before doing what would seal any thief's fate. She exited through the east door, to the pens.

Shouts rang up and down the corridors of the depot; beams of light from torch-charms played through the small windows, making odd tessellated patterns through the glass, which was reinforced with hexagonal wire. From behind the fence of the wyrm-pen, the Dawn met Zaya's eyes and *reached* out with its mind. *Why are you here?*

CHAPTER 7

PREHISTORY OF YEMAREIR AND ENVIRONS. *With an 800-year tenure in Yemareir, the Yemari are newcomers to the region. The Ililuë have been here for at least several millennia, and they don't remember the nomads who founded the season-city... but however ancient those nomads were, it's plain that they were predated by some kind of intelligent life, almost certainly nonhuman.*

These intelligences appear to have been made up entirely of tissues that don't fossilize, or else they were extremely conscientious about cremating their dead. Artifacts are likewise very hard to find. Go down far enough in the geological record, though, and you'll find scars of a war that warped reality, alterations to the rock strata that no natural process could explain. And obviously I don't mean you specifically, O tourist, should pick up a rock hammer and do this...

... but the thing is, if you did, you'd probably find something. Literally every other dig has. This entire region of the continent is built on top of a memorial to a conflict that our species' brain probably isn't wired to visualize.

SEE ALSO: Environment and Climate; Landmarks, Fantastic.

—From "A Visitor's Handbook for Yemareir," by Shenireen Agama

***

"I NEED TO FLY," Zaya said.

Whiskey.

"Ten bottles."

They'll find me. They have before.

"I'll take care of it."

How?

Zaya threw a hastily sketched image into the wyrm's mind. It recoiled. *That won't work.*

The banging and shouting drew closer. "Why would I suggest something as obviously doomed as that if it wasn't going to work?"

I won't be able to fly.

"It's not forever, you baby! I know you don't want to spend the rest of your life behind this fence!"

Zaya knew nothing of the kind, of course; and the realization trickled like ice water down her back as the wyrm stared at her, its iris a thread-fine gold ring around an all-swallowing pupil. She knew Dawn Wyrms better than that: They were homebodies at heart, soarers over fish-filled bays, uncursed by the primate need for new experiences. There was nothing in this dragon's soul that hated fences, any more than there was anything in Zaya's that hated bright fruit or blue water.

But the wyrm sighed, and blue and yellow fire dropped from its mouth, and the fence in front of Zaya melted and fell away.

She ducked through the hole, dimly feeling a new-melted link scratch her shoulder, cauterizing the furrow even as it dug. By the time she was through, the Dawn had knelt in the way well-trained wyrms are taught to do. A memory crossed Zaya's mind as she swung herself up, only a little awkward with the sack of emeralds under her arm. The Dawn's mind rang with some dry, reptilian emotion that might have been a chortle. *Is that how wild ones take riders?*

"Any wyrm who takes a rider isn't wild," said Zaya. "The Mule just liked to make me climb because it was a trash animal with a deformed sense of humor."

The guards finally burst out of the depot into the wyrmyard, yelling words and phrases Zaya didn't so much fail to hear as refuse to listen to. She *reached* into the Dawn's mind and let loose a plume of fire that shut the bluster up—not close enough to damage the guards, but close enough to singe eyebrows and, more importantly, night-blind them for several seconds, each more precious than the last.

She did not have to tell the wyrm to fly; a hideously powerful leap, two wingbeats like typhoons, and they were airborne.

***

THE AIRSPACE OVER YEMAREIR was not, of course, unwatched.

Customs and quarantine for entering wyrms was strict and time-consuming; Zaya and the Dawn knew this firsthand from recent experience. Scrutiny of outbound wyrms was more lax. The Dawn, unladen and without harness, might even be mistaken for a wild wyrm if Zaya hunkered down far enough in its blue shoulder-feathers—if the depot guards were slow in alerting the police.

That seems unlikely, said the Dawn, when Zaya had explained.

"It just depends on whether they're any good at their job," said Zaya. "I like to give people the benefit of the doubt."

Because then you run into a lot fewer unpleasant surprises.

"I *also* like to think the best of people."

Why would you think highly of someone just because you like to?

"My species is the only one on the record with a recipe for whiskey. Don't expect to understand our monkey genius." Zaya turned to check behind them. "Two on our six, paced to overtake. Start descending."

Fire surged in Zaya's mind, blinding her for a moment; she felt its echo in the Dawn's, and it lurched in the air for a terrifying second. When the flame subsided, her head still ached. There was a burning lump like molten silver at the base of her skull.

Owwww.

"First of all, never lash out at me like that again," said Zaya. "You can probably give me a seizure if you really try, but it's going to come back to you through the empathic link and kill us both. Second: I'm not giving up, you dumb death chicken, but we're not going to shake a pair of cops just by flapping your wings as fast as they'll go. You're made to fly ten-hour days in straight lines, not do evasive maneuvers against trained dogfighters. Your shoulders are still sore from what you and I did over Emerald Dunes. They're going to catch up with us, and they've got a lot of things to throw at us." She let the images take the front of her mind: Crossbows, javelins, nets.

They want me back, said the Dawn. *They won't kill me.*

"They'd rather kill both of us than let you get away."

That doesn't make sense. They can find me later.

"At this point it's not about finding you, it's about showing that they're good at their job." She made a directional gesture in the Dawn's mind. "Get as low in that canyon as you can. If we're lucky, they'll see that it's a trap and stay out of it."

Black thoughts on monkeys simmered at the back of the Dawn's brain, but it banked and descended into the canyon, only bridling a bit when Zaya pushed it low enough that its remiges almost scraped the sides. The canyon's walls were smooth as glass, striated with the ancient history of the rock; in the day they would be shades of yellow, red, and white—with one exception, a foot-thick layer that was merely dark under the moonlight but would show up in the day as an oily blue-green.

This is actually a trap, right?

"I'm sure your people have stories about the battles that were fought here, tens, maybe hundreds of thousands of years ago, by a species that commanded magic no longer known to dragon- or humankind?"

No.

"I was kidding, I know 'your people' are feathered lizards with brains smaller than apricots."

I could turn upside down right now.

The *spung* of metal on rock rang in the canyon; Zaya swung her head around to see two dragons behind them. "Short answer, something horrible happened here and covered the ground with some kind of, I don't know, toxic sludge that probably killed all life in an unimaginably large area. Scholars speculate that whatever created it was some kind of blind animal, fighting against sighted enemies, so they created a substance that would react to a certain frequency of sound by—"

The Dawn bellowed and bucked as a quarrel slashed through its crest. Zaya laughed; it was night, the stars were out, and she was riding a dragon bareback away from home and city as fast as its wings would take her. She was half-blind without her goggles, half-frozen without her jacket, and off balance without her saddle-knife, and none of it mattered. The wind brought clarity, certainty, stillness. "All right," Zaya said, "all right. Just scream as high as you can."

High?

A lattice of rope descended over Zaya, and as easily as that, all stillness and clarity evaporated. She clenched her legs around the Dawn's shoulders and dug her fingers into its feathers. "Fuck it," she said, and *reached.* The Dawn's jaws gaped with an ear-piercing keen. Zaya screwed the Dawn's eyes shut, and her own, and the canyon erupted in light.

She pulled the Dawn vertical, hugging its neck as hard as she could with her left arm, hugging the sack of emeralds with her right. The net caught on her head and shoulders, pulling her down like the paw of a massive cat, toward empty air and, beyond it, the canyon walls. She had no illusions about surviving if she should manage to guide her fall to the river that coursed through the canyon like a winding thread; from a height like this, the water might as well be granite.

The Dawn hauled upwards, the net hauled down. Zaya's left shoulder howled against the strain, then yielded; she slid three terrifying feet down the Dawn's back before her hand caught on the Dawn's wing. She clenched her legs as hard as she could and tried not to empty her roiling stomach.

The Dawn's mind pulsed with untranslatable distress, then shot Zaya an image of her own body plan, giving her the very weird sensation of someone staring intensely at her curled right arm. *?!Hang on!?*

"I need those." She sent back images of emeralds, of cash, of Tjaroon's mandrill and his knife. Her left hand was in agony. She tried to thrash her way out of the net, but she couldn't move much without dislodging her hand. The net didn't budge. The Dawn's mind tried to sort through the images she'd thrown at it, with all the success you'd expect. *?!Use the other arm!?*

"No! I can't drop these!"

If you fall, they fall. An image flashed before her with breathstealing clarity: Herself, limbs out, hair long and blue and streaming as she fell from wyrm-flight height over the Emerald Dunes.

Her right arm moved almost without her willing it; she hauled herself up and hugged the Dawn's neck. She moved her leg to catch the bag of emeralds as it fell—and she stopped it, her knee pressed it firmly against the Dawn Wyrm's flank.

Then the net reached the end of its tether. It wrenched her body back all at once; she tightened every muscle she could around Bandit's body and used her free right hand to unsnag it from her shoulder. The net fell away—but it snagged the toe of her right boot for the briefest of moments.

It was enough. Her leg straightened with the force; she shook the net off her boot, and she was free. When she curled her leg back around the Dawn again, the bag of emeralds was gone.

The Dawn shot upward, bursting from the top of the canyon like a firework. Zaya wept like a child into its neck, her whole body heaving with the loss. The slipstream swallowed her sobs so the Dawn didn't hear them, and her tears so they didn't soak its feathers.

You're not hurt, the Dawn said after some time. *Why are you hurting so much?*

Haltingly, over time, Zaya told it.

Soon enough, though, you could hardly call it "telling"; she let the words fall away, replaced by a stream of images and emotions that she guided only by filling in context—more memories—where it was needed. They flew over the rocky landscape in slow strokes and long glides, an endurance gait optimized for desert-crossing, and poured out the weeks into the Dawn's willing mind.

Minutes and wingbeats melted into one another until the night was one smooth streak of shoulder-ache and chill wind, watched over by the constant stars. Zaya said nothing to the Dawn as she would say nothing to herself; there was nothing in need of saying. Desert gave way to veldt, and then to jungle, and then, within the jungle, a clearing with a circle of houses—some small, rude huts, some longhouses that could fit two or three human families, some multi-story buildings that might not have been out of place in some neighborhood of Yemareir.

The Dawn set down in the clearing. Before it could take a breath, it was surrounded on all sides by humans, waving long wooden teeth of wood and metal. It lashed its head from side to side, unsure which was more threatening—they all seemed as terrified as it was realizing it felt, chattering to one another in the yowls and clicks they used—there was one approaching now, it would be easy to cook it—

"Zaya?"

That wasn't the wyrm's name, so why did it sound familiar? It felt a pressure it had forgotten about release, on its shoulder below the wing—no, *Zaya* felt the wyrm feel it, the release of the tension on its feathers as she put a hand to her head, which hurt; to rub her eyes, worn raw by the slipstream. "Zaya!" said the human—not *the human*, the elder, the Ililuë elder, Cerminir's mother, Indiriel, not half as absurd in her sleep-roused nakedness as any human ought to be and, most importantly, not a threat or a meal or anything else in need of meeting the spooked Dawn's flame.

Easy, Zaya said, and then, anxious to explain, "Indiriel," but when she tried to dismount, her legs would not move like a dragon's, and she fell to the packed dirt as limp as a bludgeoned capybara, her mind frantically soothing the Dawn while blood ran from her lip and nose and her limbs taught themselves slowly, ridiculously, how to carry her weight again.

Chapter 8

AMALGAM (ILILUË). *A* SMALL *Ililuë settlement, the only kind that are left within a couple of hundred miles of Yemareir. You can book a guided trip out to one in the green precincts up north (Emerald, Olive, Viridian, and so on). You'll get real hospitality and real worldvine, but most of the rest will be for show. Which isn't to say don't do it! You can learn a lot about a culture from their performance art, and the worldvine experience will be a lifelong memory. Just don't mistake it for real life on the veldt or the jungle fringe.*

Distinguished from the Mlin word "village" for at least one of at least two reasons. On the one hand, most amalgams have a large transient population, as well as a communist ethos and a level of autonomy unlike the villages of old Mlinivoun (which were chartered by, and channeled tribute to, the Great Houses). On the other, it was convenient, back when Yemareir had colonial aspirations much broader than the current city limits, to have a word for inconvenient indigenous settlements that didn't evoke memories of home. (Citation needed. —Ed.) (Please see the bibliography of The Linear Orchards, *by Shenireen Agama, for about four dozen of them. —SA) (Oh, come on. —Ed.) (You cite them, then. —SA)*

SEE ALSO: Conurbation (Ililuë).

—From "A Visitor's Handbook for Yemareir," by Shenireen Agama

***

"You need to make it molt," said Zaya.

Indiriel put a cool green palm on Zaya's forehead and pushed her gently back down on the mat. The smell of weed washed over Zaya; in Indiriel's other hand there glowed a gracefully rolled joint. "You need to take a breath," she said. "Look up, greet the morning, show some gratitude."

Zaya surged back up, then caught herself on a hand as she reeled. "Of *course*, hetman, you can't imagine how grateful I am—"

"Not to me. To the forces all around us who weighed the magnificent improbability of your existence in this moment and, against all the competing permutations of circumstance, allowed this moment to take precedence over all others in the great winnowing of possibilities."

"Hetman, all moments are equally improbable. Can we do this later?"

"No. Morning is best."

"Why?"

"Because morning follows night, and night is the time for eating too much, getting high, and getting laid. If we don't practice gratitude in the morning, we're going to find ourselves practicing regret. What happened to you, anyway?"

This was the sort of argument Indiriel enjoyed, especially with city-dwellers—and even more especially those city-dwellers who might exercise undue influence on her daughter. Zaya stared at the ceiling—really, the underside of a grass-thatched roof, whose shingling of thick rubber-plant leaves still let in dozens of points of light. Indiriel was right; a minute's delay wouldn't make much difference.

But an hour's might, and Zaya was starting to drift off already. She sat up again, making a show of care and slowness, taking a long breath through her nose before she spoke. "It's good to see you, hetman. It's been too long. I wish I could have come with Cerminir to show you Enwë."

"I'd have liked that," said Indiriel, her cheeks webbing with fine wrinkles as she smiled. "I know your voyages keep you away. Have you kept your hair short since Kiriki died? It's fetching, but I always loved the color—"

"Hetman, you need to make the wyrm molt. I know you prefer to move slowly, but its owners will not move slowly. They are surely sending scouts to sweep around Yemareir in widening spirals; once they pick up the location charm on its feathers and scales, they'll send a posse to take it back. Transdesert is one of the great corporations of Yemareir, they'll have the police on their side and maybe hired hunters as well—"

Indiriel's eyes were cool; the light green of their whites made her seem almost treelike, ancient and impassive. She took a long drag on the joint, held the smoke, then let it out in a thick plume. "Why did you bring it here, then?"

Zaya's heart sank. "Hetman, I had nowhere else to go."

"You have your linked domiciles in Lilac and Celadon Precincts, I hope? You have the stable where you once quartered the Mule?"

"They would have found us if we'd stayed."

"The veldt is wide. The jungle is deep."

"I can't force-molt a dragon."

"Has my daughter taught you nothing?" There was less disappointment than pride in Indiriel's smirk.

"She's taught me everything, hetman, but I'm a poor student. All I can learn is pitch, roll, yaw, and the simple minds of dragons."

"That's poetic." Indiriel's voice was as dry as salt.

"Your thoughts on morning gratitude inspired me."

"Force-molting is traumatic," said Indiriel. "We don't inflict it lightly."

"The Dawn wants to be free. That was a condition of its carrying me." Zaya chuckled. "That and ten bottles of whiskey."

"Free?" laughed Indiriel. "To lurch around your streets like our village idiots used to do when they were nothing but cowpaths in the ruins? Have you told your creature what it's losing its feathers for?"

"I'm *not*—"

Indiriel continued as if Zaya hadn't spoken. "You city-dwellers and your 'brimstone slipstream.' It's a colonizer's game, a minor practice of my people warped into a Mrineen fetish, which they became so ashamed of performing in public that they made it a crime—"

"It can have its freedom," said Zaya. "I'm not going back to the 'stream. Even if I were, I'd never force a wyrm to join me. I didn't steal that wyrm to race it."

"Oh?" said Indiriel. "Then why did you?"

"My daughter lost eleven slabs' worth of worldvine tar and now she's in a sea of debt to the dealer she was working for."

That gave Indiriel a moment's pause. In due time, she laughed. "I'd never have thought Taavi had it in her."

"Not Taavi. Vanako."

"Who?"

"She's been with the house for a little over a year. Her mother was a friend of some ex-boyfriend Kirono isn't speaking to any more, she died of kerostasia. We thought it might be useful to have that kind of... understanding in the house."

"You didn't think she might not want to lose a brother the same way she'd lost her mother?"

Zaya sighed and looked at the sky through the smoke-hole in the ceiling of the hut. "We didn't think she wanted to be on the dole as an orphan either. We thought it was kinder to offer her the choice than choose for her."

Indiriel flicked glowing ash from the joint's tip, then ground it under a bare heel. "She doesn't sound like a girl who's good at choosing."

"We've learned that."

"Speaking of which. You're not going to race the wyrm?"

"I told you I'm not going back to the 'stream."

"Aren't you?"

Zaya choked back the urge to shout. "No."

"Why not?"

"I thought it was a colonizer's game? A Mrineen fetish?"

"Don't flatter me with the idea that you give a shit what I think."

Zaya pushed herself up on her elbows. "I do, actually."

"Not that stuff. You think it's easy for me to bitch about coloniz-ers and crap all over the things you need to do to get by when I live out here with my own people. You think I'm an old hag who's so set in my savage tribal ways that I don't understand how complicated it is to be poor and downtrodden in a city that hates you."

"That's weirdly accurate."

"Thank you." Indiriel loosed an elegant plume of weed-smoke.

"And you know I'm right."

"So don't blame me for you being a coward. Also, you're wrong."

"I told you I wasn't going to race the wyrm."

"You didn't tell me how you're going to protect my daughter. And granddaughter."

"Grand*children*. And I'll figure it out."

Indiriel pointed out the hut's door with the burning joint, to where the Dawn slept in the village common. "You stole a bag of gems and a dragon from the people you used to work for. You're not getting any money from them. What else are you going to do? You can't fight, you can't practice law, you can't cook books. Are you going to sell your poetry or are you going to race?"

"You'd be surprised at what people would pay for my poetry." She thought of the Poet Laureate of Yemareir, serving mediocre drinks at one of the worst bars in the city. Indiriel smirked again, probably not actually reading her mind, but who knew? "So you're going to force-molt the wyrm?"

Indiriel twitched the joint back and forth, then took a restless drag. "I was never not going to force-molt the wyrm. I don't want angry city people climbing up my ass any more than you do."

Zaya realized she'd been clenching her arms and chest as tight as guitar strings; she let them rest, lying back flat on the reed mat between her and the earth. "Thank you."

"But you owe me."

"Anything."

Indiriel laughed, a gravelly smoker's laugh that was also rich and round and coffee-bitter. "I'll hold you to that."

"Fine. But how much is a favor from a long-haul wyrm-rider really worth to you?"

"A long-haul wyrm-rider? Not much, unless she's any damn good at stealing from the depot." Indiriel paused; a cloud of smoke passed between Zaya and the hut's thatched ceiling. "A Sky-Eater with a healthy Dawn Wyrm at her command? Don't sell yourself short, my dear."

***

ZAYA HAD NEVER BEEN to Cildinior Amalgam alone. When Cerminir had taken her and Kiriki there for their wedding, there had been feasts, visits, performances; when they had visited after qualifying for the Bisai, they had met with the Amalgam's physiologists, who regarded Cerminir as a terrifying idiot savant whose enthusiasms they were happy to indulge from a distance. They were experts at manipulating the human body through nutrition. Mammalian physiology was an open book. But the foreignness and mutability of dragon bodies was another matter. The only Ililuë who came willingly into contact with dragons were their Sky-Eaters, and it was the rare Sky-Eater who had a head for biology and chemistry; still rarer, the Sky-Eater who could persuade a wyrm to eat any-thing it didn't feel like eating. But if there was one Sky-Eater in Cildinior Amalgam who might have possessed those abilities, it was the one sitting a respectful distance from the Dawn, hands wrapped around his knees, watching it while it slept.

"Hi, Thelendil," Zaya said, dropping to sit beside him.

"Zaya." He was shirtless, sun on sweat outlining the shapes of long muscles under green-black skin; he was lanky like Cerminir, his hair in its customary fade, a new-to-Zaya beard aging him more than the years since they'd seen one another. New, too, were the scars on his upper arm: wyrm-rake, and from a big animal by the spacing of the wounds. He looked appraisingly at her hair. "I killed someone," she said. "I don't want to talk about it."

95

"Is that what the whole head-shaving thing means?" said The-lendil.

"Yes and also no."

"I guess that's unhelpful enough to not count as talking about it."

Zaya reached over and tapped him on the temple. "Good to know the old machete hasn't gone rusty."

"So you're not fucking men these days, then?"

"Starting to revise my thinking on the brain-machete."

Thelendil shrugged. "It seemed like you wanted me to ask."

"I am not fucking men these days, Thelendil."

"Thanks for clarifying," Thelendil said. "I'm so sorry about Kiri-ki, by the way. I'd love to meet her son."

"Also the son of someone else in this conversation."

Thelendil winced. "*Your* son, sorry. What's he now, eight?"

"Seven, and hunted."

"I know. I'm sorry about that as well." Thelendil pointed to the dragon with his chin. "You going to race her? After the feathers grow back?"

"I haven't asked."

"You should. She looks very fit."

Zaya noticed that the Dawn's eye had opened to look at them. When her eyes met its own, it reached out with its mind to touch hers; in a panic, she batted it back. Its eye lingered on her for some time, then closed again. She sighed.

"What was that?" Thelendil asked.

Zaya swallowed, then *reached* tentatively for the wyrm's mind. *I'm sorry,* she said. *I'm worried about doing this after what happened last night. It's not your fault.*

What happened last night?

"Tusk-madness," said Zaya, explaining to the wyrm and Thelendil both. "The wall between our minds fell down after those police chased us. It used to happen with Kayalim construction workers trying to control rhinos and elephants on their own, that's where the name comes from. I hadn't slept, and I'd been afraid for a long time, and my blood was up, and I forgot I was me. That's why I acted so strange last night. I was still locked into the dragon motor schema. It's the risk of being an empath working with large animals—so many motor units to control, and all with instructions that don't work with your own body, you can lose the way back."

Thelendil nodded. "But with a second mind you can share the load. That's why you rode with Kiriki."

"That's right."

Thelendil looked appraisingly at the Dawn. "If you race her, you'll need a second mind."

"No."

He treated her to the full force of his smile, dazzling white teeth against grass-green gums. "You just said you would."

"You're too big."

He looked down at his torso in mock offense. "I can see my ribs!"

"You'll get fat on city food."

"I'll eat only what I can catch and gather. Like a proper savage."

"You made fun of me and Kiriki for using empathy to race," said Zaya. "You said it wasn't real skill."

"The jealous ravings of a feckless youth. I renounce them." Thelendil waved his hand in renunciation.

"You hate Yemareir."

"Ravings. Jealousy."

Zaya looked hard at him. He was too tall to be really light, but he was slim, and the Dawn was strong—stronger than the Mule had ever been, if Zaya was honest, forged by a life of long-hauling over the desert with a rider on its back. He could handle wild wyrms without empathy; he might understand their minds well enough to work inside the Dawn's. And it had been comfortable to settle into their old rhythm, which had flowed around the empty space left by Kiriki without missing a beat. It had summoned memories of the wedding party, where Thelendil had taught them the amalgam's celebratory dances and led its warriors in a malformed, joyous haka; and of quiet nights, him and her and Kiriki leaning against the Mule's flank and sharing palm wine. If she had to share the wyrm with another mind—and, probably, she did—who better?

Well, she could think of one person; but that person had been dead for a long time.

"I don't know, Thelendil," she said. "I don't know how I feel about sharing minds with someone else."

"Kiriki would want you to do what was best for your family."

Zaya glared at Thelendil. "I'm part of my family. Which is something Kiriki knew, and taught me when I forgot."

Thelendil held up spread hands in concession. "Of course. You'll do what's best for everyone. It's what you've always done."

Zaya smiled, not without sadness. "Thank you." She slapped her hands on her thighs, then rocked forward to stand. She walked over to the Dawn and ran a hand over its flank, raking gently with fingers hooked into talons. A rain of pink and blue feathers fell to the earth. She turned to Thelendil. "All right," she said. "What was the last wyrm you rode?"

"A Banshee Liana."

Zaya glowered down at him.

"What?"

"A Liana won't hold two. What gave you that scar?"

"An Irascible Craw. You don't want to get near it."

"I'll tell you what I don't want to get near. You still know its territory?"

"There's a pack of capybaras it uses for a pantry. So do we, that's how we ran into it. Zaya, you do not want to screw around with this wyrm. Your city dragons like humans, they know you. I wooed this bastard for six weeks, had it literally eating out of my hand, but..." He rubbed the scars on his shoulder.

"Perfect," said Zaya. "If you can co-pilot a wild Craw, Cargo Parrot here should be no problem."

Thelendil looked at the Dawn. "That's a magnificent creature. You can't call her Cargo Parrot."

"What would you call it?"

Thelendil thought for a moment. "Diadem."

"Like a tiara? Why?"

"You stole her. Don't you have all these stories about the Diadem of House Iguana getting stolen?"

"Tuatara. And no."

"Sure you do," said Thelendil. "It's like a whole genre with you city folks."

"It's really not."

"What do you know about Mrineen culture anyway? You live in a little Kayalim enclave."

"I live in a city that's two-thirds Mrineen. You live in the literal jungle."

"The last thing I stole was a honey biscuit," said Thelendil. "We're not calling her Honey Biscuit. What was the last thing you stole? Kiriki's Heart would be a nice name."

Zaya shook her head. "I'm not doing that to it, or me. Anyway, I've stolen a lot since then."

"You can't call her Fat Sack of Emeralds, it's a bad omen."

"It's a terrible name, but why's it a bad omen?"

"Fell from the sky." Thelendil eyed the Dawn's plumage. "Also, emerald clashes with her color scheme."

"What else have I stolen?" Zaya rubbed a hand through her hair, barely as long as her thumb was thick. "Bandit's Breath."

"Not bad," said Thelendil. "Speaking of bandits—what do you need to fly a Craw for, anyway?"

"You'll find out tomorrow," said Zaya.

"Why tomorrow?"

"Because they're molting her tonight."

***

ZAYA SPENT THE AFTERNOON and much of the evening reviewing the elements of psionic empathy with Thelendil. It wouldn't be enough for him to do much of anything other than inspect what was going on in a wyrm's brain; but it would be enough for Zaya to shift some of the psionic load over to his mind for execution, which meant enough to protect her against another bout of tusk-madness. When his head wouldn't stop hurting, she let him sleep, and joined Bandit's Breath to sit with it as its feathers loosened.

It was a matter of a few hours after the wyrm gulped down the ritual liquor, which was greasy and bitter and could not, for the sake of Bandit's health, be washed down with alcohol. In the first of those hours, Bandit spread itself as flat as it could across the ground, trying to take in the cool of the earth. Zaya joined it in its mind, letting her own limbs shiver with fever and her own gut churn with nausea, stroking the wyrm's flank as the liquor did its work. Not soon, but soon enough, its body calmed, and hers with it, and feathers began to fall away beneath Zaya's palm. The sun had sunk below the treeline, and Zaya got up for a few minutes to cover the wyrm's back and neck with the stack of blankets the Ililuë of Cildinior had left for them. When the blankets settled, clouds of feathers puffed out from under them to paint the dirt in shades of dawn.

She leaned against Bandit's flank again under a blanket of her own. "You know you're free to leave as soon as your feathers grow back," she said. "But I wonder if you'd like to do something with me."

The question didn't kindle the warmth in Bandit's mind that might have come from a dog, or spark a monkey's fierce passion for attachment. What came from the wyrm was more like the *click* of a lock: A cool, soft sound of alignment, of connection.

Zaya drew breath to speak, but speaking was, of course, beside the point; racing against other dragons through the streets was almost the definition of something that couldn't be described in words. So instead she opened her mind to memory.

For a few stretching seconds, it felt impossible to call more than scraps to mind—and scraps she did not want to share, not yet: The weight of Kiriki's sleep-starved mind, the terrible heat of wyrm-flame in Ashen Precinct, the smell of roasting flesh and feathers as they plunged down to the deserted street. But each scrap summoned more memories like it, and soon there was more than the wyrm could possibly absorb at once. The ache of wings and shoulders, the burning of lungs, the slipstream's liquid rush over face and belly and tail. The merging of the wyrm-mind, whose language was shear and yaw and friction and momentum, with the primate mind whose language was tactics and advantage and the spreading bloom of if-then. Daily feed and celebratory whiskey and a place to sleep where there was no rain. A crew of humans surrounding it with their care: The care of tactics and advantage and if-then, but also the care of food and shelter and touch. The striving for speed, and the rush of attaining it (a rush available only from the primate mind; exultation was not native to reptiles). The ache and awkwardness as bone lengthened and shortened, as chemicals rebalanced in blood and brain, as feathers changed their thickness. The bitterness, too, of failure, which was what brought that sweet ache of change; the cold piercing of tail-spikes, the rake of teeth and talons, the burning pain of wyrm-flame. Zaya could not communicate the emptiness of loss in a form natural to Bandit's mind, because the Mule had never experienced it—it had died first. But she gave it what she could, because that was part of her own life in the 'stream, and for what she was asking she owed that much.

What was all that for? Bandit asked when it was over.

Zaya laughed, the echo seeming to fly a few feet and then fall to the ground in the humid night air. "Don't you want to know what you'd be getting into?"

The calm chill of disinterest and contentment wasn't exactly something that could be cast into words—but if Zaya were to try, she knew exactly what the words would be. *I don't care what I'm getting into. I only care who with.*

She stroked its flank again; the feathers lay in drifts now by its limbs and belly. When it got up, its outline would be painted blue and pink and orange. "Sometimes I think you animals are pretty stupid."

But then you think again and you realize how wise we are?

"No, I think it's pretty clear how stupid you are." Zaya patted its flank; the last few feathers burst off, a soft firework in the dark. "I just forget how useless it is to be smart most of the time."

Chapter 9

BROODSPIRE. *A* HUGE STONE *tower shot through with warrens and chambers that dragons mate and brood in.*

This of course raises many questions: Why do they do this? Why would anyone build something for them to do this in? Why does each species prefer one or a set of broodspires, and how did this preference arise? (BAR FACT: It's not just "wyrms go back to the spire they hatched in"; ethologists have tracked Dawn Wyrms hatched in Cobalt who went on to brood in Lilac and so on; how anyone has the patience to do a thing like that is beyond me.) Do any wyrms breed outside broodspires, and if not, how did they get by before humans came around? DID THEY EVEN EXIST BEFORE HUMANS CAME AROUND? (BAR FACT: This is actually an open question; human-dragon coevolution and even the idea that humans somehow bred and domesticated dragons are real theories held by actual scientists, although their friends are not at all reluctant to describe them to journalists as "froth-dotted cranks.")

The one question we can pretty much answer is "Why are precincts organized around broodspires?" And the answer to that is basically that dragons mate and brood in very regular multi-year cycles, and they get very hungry and testy when they do. So brooding season means everyone around the broodspire needs to move out at once, which in turn means that group of people makes sense as an administrative unit in the city, YAWNNNNN.

The broader question is of course "why would anyone move into a city riddled with dragon nests in the first place," which five seconds with a randomly selected Mrineen should teach you.

SEE ALSO: Dragon; Government; Precinct.

—From "A Visitor's Handbook for Yemareir," by Shenireen Agama

***

IN THE MORNING, ZAYA and Thelendil packed a lunch of dried fish and honeycomb and went Craw-stalking. Zaya had expected that to be a grueling, uncertain affair, but Thelendil had advised her to wait by the capybara pack in plain sight, and sure enough, the Craw came hovering over within half an hour or so to see what the human it had hurt was up to now. That was close enough for Zaya to communicate the notion of two skins of strong palm wine, half payable in advance, with emotions and sense-memories borrowed from the Mule and the new-named Bandit's Breath.

After some skeptical sampling of the first skin, followed by a boilerplate dominance display that left Thelendil terrified and Zaya doing her best not to laugh, the deal was done. Thelendil had to climb up first, to the middle of the wyrm's back with the brace of sacks over his shoulders, using Zaya's hands as a step and the wyrm's rough flank-scales for purchase. Craws were built like brawlers—long, muscular forelegs and massive shoulders—and Thelendil didn't get the wing to hold as he was accustomed to; he nearly fell. Zaya vaulted lightly up, hitched Thelendil's mind to her own and then to the wyrm's, and took off.

She felt the Craw strain to bring them to altitude. These animals were sprinters more than gliders, more used to striking from cover than from the air. Thelendil, too, felt its striving, and a fog of doubt wrapped his mind. She shifted her attention to the Craw, coaching it through the unfamiliar wingbeats, dangling the thought of gliding on thermals as a reward. She could sense its own desire, too, for this new achievement, feel its particular dry triumph at this new altitude, the analytical pleasure of adjusting its visual memory to accommodate the vistas of river, jungle, veldt, and sky it had never seen all at once. She felt a familiar thrill in the base of her throat and the muscles over her shoulder blades, like mustard seeds popping in hot oil. "Feel that?" she said to Thelendil. "Its body's changing. It's turning into a glider."

"What?"

"Come back in two weeks and find it. You'll see it's gotten lighter, flatter. Wider wings, less chest and shoulders."

"Why?"

"Because it loves this, and it can feel how the shape of its body holds it back." She reached forward to scratch the Craw under the soft green down behind its earholes; it did not purr or press against her head, but she felt its buzz of electric pleasure all the same. "All right. Dumping time."

They were out of the jungle now, over an oxbow in the river. A herd of kudu drank on one side, a lanky pair of Ranger Wyrms on the other—these were elephant-eaters, blue-and-tan giants with wingspans that could break windows on either side of any street in Yemareir. They were easily large enough to make a meal of the huffing Craw, whose chest and shoulders were punishingly sore at this point—Zaya reached out to Thelendil with a calming stroke of mind as he made the connection. She regretted it as soon as she'd made contact. It was too intimate. The contours of his mind were subtly wrong: ciliate where Kiriki's had been tight-furled, smooth where hers had always had a sharkskin feel. But she felt him relax and smile. He shrugged a sack from his shoulder and upended it off the side of the Craw.

Zaya banked into a long arc over the river to see what it would look like—she'd imagined a comet-trail of pink, blue, and orange, slowly diffusing into the sky as the wind took Bandit's new-molted scales and feathers where it would. But small objects at that distance lose their features; they quickly became black specks, then disappeared. Maybe enough of them would make it to the river that the Amalgam would notice a slick of Dawn feathers on the water in an hour or two... but more likely not. The world was big enough to absorb these pieces of even a huge beast without showing a trace of them.

Zaya looked west. It had taken less than a night to fly here from Yemareir, but the city could not be seen over the horizon, far off as that was. Even the ocean was no more than a rim of dark blue, a nail-paring. Herds and clutches of grazers roamed the veldt; wyrms loafed in the high sun to warm their blood; a flock of jeweled macaws burst from the canopy, bustling to the shelter of the Supplicant, a statue of a sow-headed woman that towered over the jungle's tallest trees, hands stretched high above her head as though to cup the sun.

"If you like this," said Thelendil, "you must love your job."

Instead of answering, she showed him: Hour after hour of dunes, differing only in shifts of color so gradual that you might travel from green in the morning to blue in the evening without noticing the change. Constant squinting, down for the caravans and up for threats from bandits, wild wyrms, rocs, or simurgs;

crushing sun, rain, storms of shredding dust; the scorn and demeaning liberties of her Mrineen colleagues, the cheeseparings and random debits of expedition-masters, the painful pull of new realms and cities, an arm's length away but, after feeding and watering and grooming and watch-standing and the need of the body to repair muscles not built for day on day of wyrm-clinging, as untouchable as the Supplicant's stone fingernails. Back-watching, knife-stashing, and thinking every day that she might die far away from a family she missed more days than she saw—far from her dying son, and from her daughter who might doom the whole family with her waywardness.

"Forget I said anything," Thelendil said after a moment, and dumped the second sack.

Of its own volition, or so it felt, the Craw banked sharply and tacked downward, plunging like a shark through the cloud of bright feathers. A mist of Dawn colors surrounded Zaya for a moment, a confetti of bayside sunrise over the veldt at noon. She felt Thelendil smile, and this time she did turn around. "Did you do that?"

His only reply was the motor image of the Craw's wings and shoulders, pulling into the maneuver.

On the way back to Cildinior Amalgam, she felt the Craw's mind orient. It was new to the upper air, but after half an hour on the thermals it knew what to expect—and two wyrm-size silhouettes advancing steadily toward them from the west were not among its expectations. They were not quite the size of the elephant-eaters at the oxbow, but they were bigger than any racing wyrm. Big enough to take the Craw, in any case, which was exhausted from a hard flight, and which had never been a dogfighter to begin with. Zaya began guiding the Craw down into the jungle. "You know your way around?" she asked Thelendil. "Even far from home?"

"This isn't far from home. Where are we going?"

"Somewhere they won't find Cildinior Amalgam if they follow us." She felt Thelendil's stomach drop a fraction of an inch. "What's wrong?"

"It's not a city, Zaya."

"It's a giant jungle. Once we let this Craw go, how could they possibly find us?"

"They can't find *us*," said Thelendil. "But they can find Cildinior Amalgam, if that's where they think we're going. And there's nowhere else to go."

"So where would we land if we were going somewhere else?"

The silence hung for a long time as they descended. They were almost below the canopy before Thelendil said, "I might know where."

***

"Thelendil," said Zaya, "what in all the bowers of all the gods is all this shit?" She tried to lean forward from her squat, and squinted for a better look through the brush.

"The most humanity we're going to find near Cildinior Amalgam," Thelendil whispered back.

They were just downstream of a waterfall, if you could call it that, that poured from the cupped hands of the Supplicant; the stream disappeared into mist a hundred or so feet up, but enough of that mist traveled straight down to create a pool, and the pool flowed into a stream. The lush undergrowth was punctuated with man-high boxes, and figures waded through it, covered in bulky white cloth from neck to ankles, with and wire masks over their faces. As Zaya and Thelendil watched, one such figure pulled a slat out from one of the tall boxes and shook it out into a tight-woven basket. They then commenced to slog through the thick jungle toward a tent some distance off.

"What are they doing?"

"Stealing pollen from the bees."

Zaya blinked; the boxes and the bulky outfits made sudden sense. "That's a weird thing to do out here."

"They're probably chasing some craze? You city people always think the jungle is holding out on you."

"So there's nothing at all special about pollen gathered in the shadow of a statue so massive it defies the laws of physics."

"Oh no, taking anything from this area is forbidden on pain of excommunication. Has been for centuries, long before your pale-face overlords ever parked their greedy asses on our coastline. Every settlement within a hundred miles has that taboo. I assume that's why your countrymen there are so keen on it."

"Why is it forbidden?"

"It's the mark of a... ugh."

"What?"

"I forgot your word for the thing."

Zaya stared at him. "Under the circumstances, I'm not going to make fun of you."

"Gûlnír. Bad wizard, the kind that summons things."

"Goetist?"

"That."

"What would a goetist find here?"

"If they told us that, then the kids who wanted to be... go-e -tists... would come here looking for it." Thelendil looked at Zaya in genuine incomprehension. "Don't you city people know how taboos work?"

"Our taboos aren't for actual survival. Mostly they're for making people feel bad for being normal."

Thelendil nodded sagely. "Ah yes, sometimes I forget that your city is run by a worthless junta of rapacious colonizers who fuck with your heads to keep you docile."

"I never forget that."

"Neither do I, but doesn't it make you jealous that I *could*?"

The wire-masked harvester with the pollen basket had almost made it to the tent. "How'd you find out about this operation?"

"They fly wyrms in and out. We noticed the air traffic pretty quickly."

She wiped sweat from her forehead. "If I were flying wyrms in and out of here, I know what I'd be doing." She pointed to the banks of the stream, where there flourished a number of plants with broad, toothed leaves and blunt-shaped buds pointing to the sky. "It's crawling with datura here."

"Ah, the botanical basicness of the urban drug person." Zaya let that one slide. "I saw that too—but you can get datura a lot closer than here. And whatever they're doing with the pollen, it's got nothing to do with the datura. Those only bloom at night. Pollinated by moths, mostly."

"I know datura blooms at night." She hadn't known about the moths, though.

"You didn't know about the moths, though."

Zaya noticed a monkey leaping from tree to tree. It wasn't the first she'd seen, and for a moment she wondered why it had caught her eye. It was moving oddly; it was carrying something. A little satchel on its back. It was moving toward the tent, much faster than the wire-masked worker they'd first seen. "They have empaths," Zaya said.

Thelendil shuddered slightly; Zaya felt an echo of it in her mind. Surprised, she pulled back whatever connection had hung on since the flight with the Craw. "If they have monkeys harvesting, they might have monkey eyes on the perimeter. We should go."

***

As far as they could tell, they were not followed.

About half an hour after they had struck out for Cildinior Amalgam, Thelendil stopped them. The jungle had gone silent. They crouched under a tree with a view of a small hole in the canopy; before long, one hulking sky-blue belly winged across, then another. "Pelagian Coursers," said Zaya. Not elephant-eaters but shark-eaters, with the endurance to fly between far-flung islands and the size to hoist a healthy bull mako out of the water.

"Cop wyrms?"

"Cops wish. War wyrms, if you can get them. I guess Transdesert is pretty serious about collecting."

"They're going the wrong way, at least." Thelendil's silence was the ocean's roar, drowning all else out. "We have to get Bandit out of Cildinior."

Zaya nodded, hoping it wasn't too late.

***

It took most of the evening and the next morning to get back to Cildinior Amalgam. Thelendil guided Zaya along a switchbacking route that kept them under the overgrowth and returned them every few hours to the river; they stopped when the stars came out and slept in the root-crooks of trees old enough that any low branches had been long snapped off and smoothed away, covered with broad rubbery leaves from a plant whose name Zaya was too tired to ask. When she woke in the morning, she found her fingers tangled in his, and snapped them away before he could wake and see it. She wished, for the first time in a long time, that Papa Zinji were around, so she could ask him if it was common to do strange things in your sleep after a bout of tusk-madness; but he wasn't, and Thelendil awoke not much later with nothing to say about hand-holding, and little else either. There wasn't anything to eat, so they set out, but she was pretty sure Thelendil went a little out of the way to take her by a stand of jackfruit he wouldn't have bothered visiting on his own. He didn't say anything about his mystical savage food-finding powers or her hopeless citified ignorance, which was welcome at the time but felt strange later, as they walked. They climbed down a few dozen feet of cataract and veered around the trail of a panther and, eventually, came to Cildinior Amalgam, where Cerminir was waiting in the square as if she'd been standing in the same spot all day.

"You have to get back," she said.

"I know. You must have been worried sick, I'm so sorry, I sent word as soon—"

"We got the message. I'm not talking about any of that. The police came by twice, and someone from Transdesert came by too. Everyone wants to talk to you about the missing death chicken."

"Thirst and famine," Zaya swore. "What have you been telling them?"

"The truth has been pretty good so far," said Cerminir. "You went out to get drunk one night and never came home. If only someone could find you face down in a gutter, drowned in your own vomit, you'd be free and clear."

"Don't tempt me."

"We'd still be on the hook for that dealer's money," Cerminir said. "I don't think it's a good strategy."

"All right," said Zaya. "I'm glad we thought it through."

"Then again, with you gone, we'd have a lot less opposition to cutting Vanako loose."

"... and this just stopped being funny," said Zaya.

"Was she joking?" Thelendil asked.

Cerminir gave him a cool look and shrugged. "Hi, Thelendil. I hear you're Zaya's new co-pilot."

"We'll see how well he takes to city life," Zaya said.

"Let's go," said Cerminir. "I told my pilot he could get fucked up here for a day if he'd wait for a day; he's going to be high as the Supplicant's fingernails for a couple of hours and then take a couple of hours to come down. You need to eat and rest, and then we need to think of a story."

"We need to get Bandit in."

"Bandit is the dragon?" said Cerminir. "Bandit is fine. Your family needs you."

"Transdesert Corporation is looking for it. Eventually they're going to come here. Bandit needs to be gone when they do."

"So it'll get gone. It has wings."

"It doesn't have any feathers, this isn't its biome, it's not used to fending for itself in the wild, and it sticks out of any terrain within fifty miles of here like a jellyfish in a date barrel. Also I owe it my life and ten bottles of whiskey."

"Ten bottles of whiskey?"

"It didn't save my life out of the goodness of its heart."

"You can't give it ten bottles of whiskey."

"I really thought you'd be more concerned about the part where I smuggle a dragon into—"

"I am concerned about that part," said Cerminir, "I'm extremely concerned about that part, you're already a wanted criminal and I left my *baby* in your *house* and now we're going to do *another crime* before I even have the chance to get my *baby* out of your *house* and after *all these crimes* to get this *stupid wyrm* back into the *stupid city* you're going to feed her *ten bottles of whiskey*? How are you going to race her when she's got the burps for two weeks?"

By this point, about half of Cildinior Amalgam was poking their heads out of their domiciles to look with great interest at Cerminir.

"... I see we're somehow already past the part of the conversation where we talk about whether I should race her," Zaya said.

Cerminir turned without a word and walked to her mother's pavilion.

Thelendil started after her; Zaya blocked him with an arm. "Leave her be," she said. "Walking away isn't telling you how serious she is, it's managing how much stuff is in her brain. She needs to be in her own head to figure out what she's feeling. If we try to make her do that while putting a bunch more stuff into her brain, she'll just get more upset and take longer to recover." She looked around, found a face she recognized—Emenduin, a farmer. "Is anything going to market in Yemareir? Like, today?"

He shook his head. "Nothing 'til next week. Ardilë just took a load of cassava in yesterday; we won't have another wagonload for at least three—"

"How much do you have now?"

"A quarter?"

"How much do you usually sell?"

Emenduin shrugged. "A half, two thirds?"

"I'll buy all of it at a 25% discount."

Emenduin looked at Thelendil suspiciously. "Is she good for it?"

"She's never owed me anything before," said Thelendil.

"Would you sell to her on credit?"

"In a heartbeat." He said it instantly but easily, the swiftness of confidence. Only when he turned toward her to smile did she realize she had been staring at his face in something like wonder.

"Done." She clapped a fist to her heart in what she thought she remembered was the Ililuë sign for a done deal; Emenduin smiled and repeated the gesture, though Zaya noticed that he hit his chest with his thumb in, not up. She grinned up at Thelendil; her heart buzzed like a swarm of cicadas. "I can unload a few bales of discount cassava in Damask and Madder in an hour or two."

Emenduin shook his head.

"What? Didn't you just sell me a quarter wagon of cassava?"

"The last wagon was cassava. This is the next wagon."

***

"WHY DID YOU TAKE me?"

Zaya was leaning against Bandit's flank, stippled with tufts of fine new feathers like a poorly plucked chicken. Soon the sun would lean near the horizon, and the trip back to Yemareir could begin. "Did you really want to get free? At this cost?"

Bandit let a jet of superheated air stream from its mouth. *You called me a baby.*

"You didn't care about that."

I've seen babies, they're barely animals. Just loud meat and fat in skin bags. It's very insulting.

Zaya didn't dignify this with a response, but let her mind sing "bullshit" until she got bored.

Some minutes passed. The call went out: It was time to pack the wagon. Zaya got up.

Because you saved my life, said Bandit, *and I didn't want to let you die.*

"Oh, my death chicken," Zaya said. "They wouldn't have killed me. Not for emeralds."

That's not the only way to die.

"What's that supposed to mean?"

Bandit did not answer; maybe it couldn't. It didn't matter. It had been in her mind. She knew what it had seen. A child, a dog, a pool of blood; and then a lifetime, dimly lit and endless.

CHAPTER 10

BRIMSTONE SLIPSTREAM. *(Why not "Slipstream, Brimstone"? —Ed.) (Honestly. —SA) An underground sports league in which scofflaws race dragons through the city streets. Illegal but mostly tolerated; racers, or "'streamers," don't pose much danger to passersby, but it's convenient for the practice to be illegal because it prevents it from growing too much and gives police and lawmakers an easy way to control it if they feel they need to.*

It also makes it difficult to engage in for tourists: You're not likely to find a place at a starting line or finish line unless you already know a guy. If you want to catch the action, your best bet is probably to find one of Yemareir's many charismatic landmarks (see "See also") and just camp out there. The odds aren't in your favor, but at least you're already at a sightseeing spot!

SEE ALSO: Bone Loom; Caldera; Cold Point Preserve; Landmarks, Fantastic; Necropolis; Rosewing Fountain, Stone Forest; White Springs.

—From "A Visitor's Handbook for Yemareir," by Shenireen Agama

***

TWO AND A HALF days later, a Kayalim woman laboring under a heavy sack trudged up to the door of a tenement in Azure Precinct—a shore precinct, south of Cold Point and north of the more comfortable beach neighborhoods of Cadet and Cobalt. Salt wind cut the heavy fug of humidity that hung over the rest of the city, mingling the dock-smell of aging fish guts with the beach-smell of spit-roasted fish over tiny illegal campfires, and with the persistent musk of urine and the yeasty tang of bad beer, and with the horror-scent of sewage and skunk and rotting meat that hung over the woman and her sack like an invisible dome, repelling all comers (except the seagulls and their competitors, the Cormorant Drakelets, who trailed Zaya at a distance, hoping for a morsel to drop). She clapped her hands three times, then rang the doorbell three times, then waited for the third-floor resident to come down to find her.

The stench hit him like a gong; he stumbled backward in the vestibule. He was a Kayalim man, older than he looked, in a new-looking vest over a filthy chest wrap and trousers; his hair was down to his back and beautifully dyed, crimson and deep teal and periwinkle. "Zaya-*ko*," he said, half in annoyance and half in wonder, "what happened to your hair?"

"I killed someone, Papa Zinji."

He looked directly into her eyes: searching, impassive, most likely stoned out of his mind.

"They had it coming."

He nodded. "And why did you bring a sack of durian to my house?"

"Because I couldn't pay anyone to drive a quarter wagonload of it across the city."

"You could have dumped it in the river."

"You should eat," Zaya said. "You never remember to stay fed."

Her living father put a hand to his potbelly like a newly pregnant woman might, curious and questing for new sensations. Then he held his hands out for the durian.

"Papa, I'll carry it up."

"You don't have to, I'll take it."

"May I please, Papa?"

"It's a mess up there, you don't want to see it."

"I do."

"... I have a guest." Zinji looked half protective, half ashamed.

"I'll be nice."

He looked at her for a long moment, then another. Her skin began to crawl. She'd walked across the entire city—who knew how soon Minshoon might give the tip to the police? Could he have told them already? "You need this," he said, almost a question. The intonation was well rehearsed, a mix of resignation and curiosity precision engineered to put a kid on the back foot. *I'm disappointed,* it said, *but maybe if you spill your guts, I'll change my tune.*

"I want it too, Papa. I should have come to see you sooner."

"But you need it?"

"Yes."

He stepped back to let her in. "Anything you need. But I'll carry the durian."

She let him take it, relieved at any tiny diminution of the smell. Neighbors groaned and cursed as they climbed the cramped stair; the sack was dripping juice from several wet spots. When they reached Zinji's apartment, he rapped sharply on the door. "Tevala," he called out, "company. Get decent, please."

The flat was a bit like House Shearwater, if the common room were half the size, the kitchen little more than a stove and a block of counter about the width and depth of Zaya's forearm, and no other rooms. On a narrow bed off to the side, a Kayalim with long grey hair was squirming into trousers under the sheets. "Tevala, this is my daughter Zaya," said Zinji. "She brought durian. Don't ask questions. Zaya, this is my good friend Tevala. They like to come over and get fucked up with me like your Papa Kaalo used to do, which is probably why they have lukewarm old person sex with me every so often like your Papa Kaalo used to do."

Tevala had extricated themselves from the sheets by now and came over to squint at with Zaya. "Zinji never told me he had a beautiful daughter."

"He never told me he'd had lukewarm old person sex with any-one at all," said Zaya, "so I guess we all learned something tonight. But his other daughter is the beautiful one."

Zinji brought the durian over to the tiny block of counter—the only clean space in the apartment, Zaya noticed, free of scraps and grime, gleaming softly in the light of the jaguar mural on the ceiling as though it had been waxed—and began to peel. "So, what brings my beautiful daughter to Azure Precinct this evening?"

"I need to get drunk with you."

He didn't turn, but she saw his shoulders stiffen. "Did some-thing happen?"

"Yes." She'd found most of a bottle of papaya brandy in his liquor cabinet by that point; from the cabinets she found three chipped clay cups, more suitable for mate than spirits, and split the bottle between them. "But not what you're thinking. Everyone in the family is fine." She threw back the cup of brandy; it was sticky and oversweet, the papaya perfume mingling nauseously with the smell of durian. "Correction. Jaliki is still hunted, Yyrreen still thinks we're thieves, and Vani is into some drug gang for more than we can possibly pay back."

"Could be worse?"

"Could be worse."

Zaya handed Zinji his own cup of brandy; he sipped at it. "This is terrible."

"You need to be sober to buy good alcohol."

"A lot of people have told me I need to be sober to do a lot of things," said Zinji, "and so far they've all been wrong." He finished the cup in a long pull, then held it out for more. Zaya bit her tongue and poured. "So what's the problem?"

"There are cops looking for me because they think I stole a dragon." Zaya knocked back another swallow of brandy. "I need an alibi."

Zinji plated three thick slices of durian and handed one to Zaya. She'd quit noticing the stench at this point. "If you need an alibi, that means you stole the dragon."

"Sssh! Not so loud," Zaya stage-whispered. "Your guest might hear."

"If you needed a dragon, you could have come out here."

"I needed it *right then.*"

"Why?"

Zaya sighed, pinched the rim of Zinji's cup between her fingers, and pulled it closer to his face. "We need to have a few more before I get into it."

Zinji nodded and drank, then made a face. "I can't do this any more, it's like you found a bottle of juice that's been outside all summer. Get the cucumber gin, it's a special occasion. Tevala, be a dear and tell Fili a soirée has commenced. Price of admission is one bottle of something, at least half full, or the equivalent in exotic substances. He'll get the word out." Tevala nodded and left; Zaya finished her gin pour. When the door shut, Zinji popped a slice of durian and swallowed it nearly whole. "Fili's a tragic figure—very eager to please, no sense of discernment. He'll get people in here who'll swear they've been here a week and so have you. And they'll really believe it. His friends are idiots. I just hope they're hungry enough to eat down that durian."

"Speaking of which." Zaya raised her glass. "Wanted to wait until your guest was gone, but: To Papa Kaalo."

"To Kaalo," said Zinji. "The sexiest and most horrible idiot I've had the privilege to know."

"To Papa Kaalo," said Zaya. "He made a lot of bad choices, and I needed him to be better than he was. But he's my papa, and I love him, and I wish he were here."

Zinji smiled. "You don't usually add that last bit."

"That's how you know the gin is working."

Zinji held out his cup until it clicked against hers.

***

THE FLAT WAS RANK with packed bodies; Zaya had switched to water, although every time she drank it tasted flat and disappointing and seemed to coat her tongue with some film of tastelessness that she had to resolve to ignore. *"No,"* she corrected whoever had said whatever they had said. *"Not* a wagonload of plucked *chickens,* a plucked *dragon.* In a wagon. Covered in enough durian so the Pelagians couldn't see it from the air."

"Not plucked," said someone. "Molten."

"That's *right*. Molten. Molted. Not plucked. The durian hid the wyrm long enough to get us across the veldt. Without the Pelagians seeing. Then, at the gate, we showed the wyrm carcass."

"Not a real carcass?"

"We *said* it was a carcass. I kept it still and carcass-like," Zaya said with more than a little pride. "Until we passed the gate. Not that uncommon for traders to bring in a wyrm-carcass they've found."

"Didn't they check the pulse?"

"They could not," Zaya intoned, "have given two swings of a dead rat about the pulse. Everybody knows you can't make a wyrm play dead under a pile of durian."

"How'd you explain that it was plucked?"

"We said we figured it was probably sick," said Zaya. "Between that and the durian, no one had any interest in looking for the pulse. Pull that hand back or I'll chew it off." The hand moved off her thigh; Zaya shook her head. "I always forget what creeps Papa Zinji parties with."

"Who?"

Zaya blinked; her would-be groper had left, it seemed, for greener pastures or softer targets, and in his place was a pretty young woman with her hair in thick twists, each dyed separately: midnight blue, bright azure, and dandelion yellow. "I was just going to offer you some worldvine, but if—"

"Not you," Zaya said hastily. "That is, yes you. Yes, you should give me some of that, and not you are one of my father's creepy friends, at least so far."

"Thanks for clarifying," the blue-and-yellow-haired woman said. "My name's Eruen." She held up a length of worldvine, quickly peeled it, and began slicing it expertly into shavings.

"Zaya."

"I know."

A small crowd had formed—or, rather, the density of the crowd had increased around Eruen, whose lap was accumulating a pile of worldvine shavings. She slapped a hand away, not unkindly, then just as not unkindly nicked another with the paring knife. After that, hands kept their distance. She picked up two shavings in one hand, and dangled the first into Zaya's mouth; as Zaya bit down, Eruen's lips closed around the second.

***

ZAYA LAY ON A flat sun-warmed precipice, her head in the lap of a great bear, which sat upright like a human; its fur was shades of red and blue, long as sheep's wool and soft as baby hair and fine as spun sugar. A sapphire ocean pulsed and glowed under pirouetting stars, rainbow-haloed and too bright to look at straight on. The air was sweet and cold and heavy as snowmelt, which she had tasted once high in a mountain range whose name escaped her, and beasts of all kinds and colors danced and chattered and coupled among the gritty, broken trunks of a petrified forest. In her hand was the hand of the goddess of this place, skin silk-fine and coffee-black over copper-dense sinew and slim stone bones from which the indiscriminate heat of magma poured forth.

A tight knot of three radiant comets shot past—or, no, not comets, she realized as one and then the next spread fire-feathered wings to pull ahead. The goddess howled in exultation, a terrible harmony on all frequencies, ear-piercing and bone-shaking; the bear roared. "The Breakers," the goddess said in a voice like molten gold. "You won that once."

"We won more money when we lost it," some person said through Zaya's mouth. Zaya's own attention was on the water and the stars and the hand of the goddess, which pulsed and trembled with the restlessness of the infinite against her palm, inside her fingers.

"You could again."

A swarm of objections buzzed around her head, but she could put words to none of them. She could see them flitting across her field of vision, but all there was was motion; she could see no details, no features, nothing but. Sense of a crowding, choking presence. She waved a hand in front of her face.

"All you need is a wyrm."

This, Zaya thought, was something she could answer, and began the muzzy and uncertain process of building her response, but the bear rumbled "what beautiful black stars," which was so *wrong* that Zaya had to unbuild the response to the goddess so she could correct the bear, and then the goddess said "I've never seen any-thing more beautiful," whose wrongness shattered any attempt at a response she might, partially, have made.

Before she could begin to react to any of it, the bear hauled her up so that she leaned against him, her face pressed into the soft crimson fur of his neck, which smelled of sweat and papaya and cucumber and weed. A chill pierced her palm as the goddess' hand fell from hers. "Time to get you a glass of water and a bit to eat, Zaya-*ko*," rumbled the bear.

The jungle of wondrous beasts and spirits wavered as she moved; this was how worldvine worked, the Zaya far away from her remembered with her mind, it settled in as your senses adapted to a scene, adding filigrees of sight and texture over minutes if only things didn't change too much. Elands and mandrills became

Zinji's scraggly, fucked-up friends; a massive monitor lizard eating a kudu became Tevala, ministering to a young woman who seemed very pleased with them indeed.

The bear—Zinji—was growling softly to a termite mound: "Get the girl with the pretty hair out of here. Blue, blue, yellow. She's a cop."

Zaya's stomach churned—motion sickness was another effect of the worldvine, which had its ways of insisting those who ate it sample its charms. She must have retched a little; Zinji asked, "Are you OK?"

"It's all right," she said. "Nothing worse than a corkscrew barrel roll at top speed, anyway." The Zaya far from her mind had come close again; she remembered a third thing about how worldvine worked, the thing that had practically stopped her brain when Zinji had mentioned black stars: Worldvine visions were shared. People tripping in the same place saw the same things. "You trapped her," said Zaya. "She wasn't high at all."

"Rookie error," Zinji agreed. "She wanted you to admit you had a wyrm."

They were walking down in to the embracing earth through a spiral lava tube whose walls were covered in softly pulsing bioluminescence; every few blinks they resolved into animal murals in the blocky, thick-lined Kayalim style, in this case a vulture going through all positions of a wingbeat along the staircase. Bar the echoes, there was blessed silence; neither the crowd of the roof deck nor the crowd of the party were close enough to fill her ears. "This is what you did for Papa, isn't it," Zaya said. "You kept him safe."

"Like a mother sow keeps her piglet safe," said Zinji. "No dog or hawk or wyrm got near him. But animals can't hunt for shit,

Zaya-*ko*. Pure dumbness and savagery, no thought for the long view. A hawk might go hungry, but the farmer always gets his in the end."

"Who's the farmer in this analogy?"

"For a long time I thought it was datura," said Zinji. "But datura isn't what keeps us all in one place and takes what's ours when it pleases."

A rumbling had been building low in the lava tube, Zaya just realized, without her noticing; now that rumble came with a glow. A tongue of magma lashed out, just missing her; it was scarlet and amethyst and moved very fast and hot indeed. Soon the main flow had pushed up into the tube, jeweled and searing, and Zaya could not help digging her fingers into Zinji's arm, taking no comfort at all in the strong and fine-grained impression of bear-hair beneath her palm and fingertips. "It's OK, baby girl," said Zinji. "Just a dream. No one'll get burned."

He took a step down; she stepped with him; the magma, which some hidden part of Zaya's brain knew was actually a press of people, moved slowly up, making worried noises that were also the rumblings of terrible heat and pressure in the depths of the earth. "I'm scared."

"They're scared." Another step. "'Cause they don't know better." Another. "But you—" Another step down. "You *invited* those cops to find you here." Sweat had sprung out, in the heat of approaching magma, to coat Zaya's skin; she could not tell if the same thing had happened to Zinji. "'Cause what a narrative. Girl who pulled herself up from nothing, to come within a hair's breadth of being the first Kayalim to win the Grand Bisai..." Another step down. "Found on a four-day bender with her junkie dad and a hundred of his worst friends."

"That's not," said Zaya, but she could not finish the sentence—did not know, really, what words would even go there.

"Of course it is," said Zinji. "You use what you have, that's what we always taught you."

"That's what Papa Kaalo told me when I caught him with that bong he made out of a coconut shell."

Zinji laughed.

The crowd was three steps down; the heat was unbearable, the jewel-colored light of their faces blinding. Zaya shrank into Zinji. Even with her eyes closed, her skin burned.

Then the first shoulder jostled her, and it was smooth and cool as water.

She opened her eyes. The lava tube had become a glowing sea-cave; groupers and rays and nurse sharks streamed past, the same color as the magma had been. She moved her hand through the water, feeling its cool resistance to her action, feeling its heaviness in her lungs. She could taste the salt on her tongue, but it didn't taste salty—if anything, it was fresh, almost sweet.

The crowd passed. Below them were two huge mako sharks, one midnight blue and one scab-red. Zaya became immediately conscious of the scene: Two wide-eyed, huge-pupiled Kayalim, waving their hands around and marveling at the lamp-murals of a dingy tenement stairwell.

"That's her, right?" said Red. "Mid-twenties, Kayalim, cropped hair, completely fucked up on substances with the proprietor, who also happens to be her father? Some genius rent-a-cop thought *this* stole a wyrm out of lockdown and shook two Air Guard pilots in a dogfight?"

"Remember how I said I might know this girl?" said the midnight-blue shark, and something about the tone of its voice made

Zaya squint and taken a second look beyond the sharkskin—the uniform, slick and snug to prevent grabs, white to blunt the sun and because no Mrineen ever wore white voluntarily—to the familiar face beneath, whose shape her mouth knew better than her eyes. She opened her mouth to say a name, but something in the set of that shark's body, a certain bracing as though for onslaught, made her stop. "I know this girl."

"The one you stopped in Crimson?"

Blue nodded.

Not Blue. Kemreen.

"Two hours after the report," she said. "Headed west. Probably here, I guess? Didn't seem like she was in any condition to climb up on a wyrm at all, much less break in somewhere and steal one." She shrugged witheringly; Zaya felt shark teeth sink into her chest. "Should we take her in?"

"Fuck," said Red, the words misting from his mouth like whale-blood in water. "The depot staff said she was there."

"So we take her in." The blue mako that was Kemreen glanced at Zaya and—astonishingly, for a shark—winked.

"Sure, let's do that. Then we get pulled into court, you testify that she couldn't possibly have been there, and we both get roasted alive for making an arrest we couldn't deliver. I'm trusting some desk-fucking lookout who couldn't hack it as a bouncer at a children's library to know who was where when? No." Red looked at Zaya with baby-seal-eating eyes. His contempt brought her, for a brief moment, back into Bandit's body; she wanted to skin thin lips back from dagger-teeth, feel the flame-gorge roil through her throat like iron slag. "Where were you about two hours after midnight, three nights ago?"

The air pulsed around Zaya like water. "In bed with a girl I'd just met."

"Did you then go on to take a Dawn Wyrm that didn't belong to you?"

"Sometimes I *summon* them from the thermals above the bay," Zaya said, with what she hoped was an appropriately stoned gesture. "Those are free wyrms, they don't belong to anyone but themselves and the sky."

"I'm going to ask you one more time whether you stole a Dawn Wyrm from the depot, and if the answer I get is anything other than 'yes' or 'no' I will drop you in the Damask Precinct drunk tank by mistake."

If there was a moment Zaya might have blown the whole thing, it was there: *the Damask Precinct drunk tank,* which this lame-brained shark of a cop thought was the ultimate threat—and which it surely was, to whatever soft-livered milk-swillers whose heads he spent most of his nights busting. *The Damask Precinct drunk tank was my vacation home, chum king. The undersides of the cots probably still have my drawings on them. I could pick up a chess game with Head Lice Zeino like I was fifteen again, he never forgets a board.* She felt the words straining against the reins of her better judgment, felt the leather of her will begin to give. But Zinji squeezed her hand—when had he taken her hand?—and she remembered: There was a world of jeweled lava and lush sea-caves and the embers of sweet bedroom memories that was invisible to Red. All he wanted was for her to say "No" so he could leave what he *thought* was a shabby tenement staircase; it seemed cruel not to give it to him. He didn't even know he was a shark—

"You're saying I'm a *what*?"

Zinji quickly shushed to soothe him. "So sorry, Officer, she's just *so* fucked up right now. Absolutely out of her mind."

"No," said Zaya.

Red looked at her. She looked at Red. "No, *what?*" he prompted.

"No sir I did not steal a Dawn Wyrm from the depot sir."

"Seems credible," said Red. "Let's get out of here."

Kemreen nodded, silent and serious.

Red eyed Zaya for a long moment. When he turned to leave, Kemreen allowed herself one flash of a relieved, triumphant grin; and though it should have been shark-toothed and terrifying, the worldvine somehow let it through unaltered, and it poured through Zaya's eyes and into her brain and spine like a lightning strike, leaving her buzzing and wobbly at the knees.

Kemreen turned, then, to join her partner, and their sickle-shaped tails sent them gliding down the lava tube and out toward the open ocean, or however the worldvine might shape the city that night.

***

Zinji had some questions. Zaya heard them no better than she'd have heard the rustle of rose petals in a monsoon. She found her way up the stairs and through the crowds and to the narrow bed in Zinji's common room, and stood at its foot until the occupants grew too uncomfortable with her staring to continue. She tucked herself in, carefully and precisely, and when she closed her eyes the dark was brighter and more vivid than the light. She kept them closed anyway, and the light slowly faded. She heard the scrape of a chair being dragged over to the bedside, felt the settling of a weight into it. A hand rested on her shoulder long enough for her to feel the familiar weight and shape of Zinji's palm. Whether the hand or consciousness left first, she could not say.

CHAPTER 11

SEASONS. SUMMERS ARE HOT *and dry; winters are mild and wet, although we see snow every couple of years. There's a noticeable east-west gradient across the city, where the coastal precincts in the west will have noticeably less extreme temperatures and weather than the precincts near the main gates in the east. If this has any relationship to which dragons brood in which precincts, no one's figured it out.*

We've maintained a few of our spring and autumn festivals from old Mlinivoun, where you actually couldn't grow things or go anywhere in the winter and the ancient Mrineen passed the time by sucking the bones of starved goats and crafting horrible ideologies to justify the conquest of sunnier realms (CITATION NEEDED. —Ed.) (THE WORLD IS MY CITATION —SA). So if you come in the spring and hear people singing about what a relief it is to finish up this bitter winter where they've obviously been strolling outside and gorging on fresh fruit the entire time, that's why. The autumn bonfires are pretty cool, though.

SEE ALSO: Environment and Climate; Religion.

—From "A Visitor's Handbook for Yemareir," by Shenireen Agama

***

IN THE MORNING, ZINJI and Tevala were both gone; Zinji had left a pile of sherds and flinders and a note that said "Buy a big breakfast. Love you." Zaya didn't touch the cash and resolved, nauseous, to skip breakfast as well; but she had not left Azure Precinct before the smell of fried fish in bitter chocolate set her stomach straight, and she spent half an hour sweating out residual blood alcohol with the help of the fish and a cup of hot mate. Then she realized she'd arranged no food for Bandit at the stable, and spent another hour and all her remaining cash finding a fishmonger who'd ship a crate of dried tilapia to Rust Precinct—under the name "Thelendil," which grated, because they had been concerned that Transdesert and/or the police would be looking out for Zaya, which her encounter with Eruen of the beauteous blue and yellow hair had proved they were, although hopefully they were done. With no cash for a rickshaw or a wyrm, she was forced to walk home; her eye was out for a bike, but she didn't find one until she was halfway there, and by then she'd realized she wasn't in any rush for what waited for her.

She wished, trudging past the bike with a pounding head and chafed thighs from the walk, that she'd thought to ask her father what it had been like: To come before a family who expected better of him and confess stupidity and failure and a recklessness with all their lives. Every smug or shitty thing she'd said to Vanako since the night at the Blind Beggar vibrated against the inside of her forehead, grinding drifts of bone-dust out to coat the front of her brain. Maybe they'd grind a hole through and she could avail herself of the mercy of just collapsing dead in the middle of the street. She was pretty sure the front of the brain wasn't that important for basic autonomic functions, but any kind of brain damage would be better than none at this point.

House Shearwater exploded into chaos on her return; the unannounced arrival of Thelendil had already rattled the family, softened only partially by Cerminir's vouching for him, and his story about smuggling Bandit back into Yemareir had enchanted the littler kids and evidently put garlic in everyone else's tea. Enwë and Eäril fought for Zaya's lap, and Gilthiniel peppered her with questions while Taavi looked on in silent concern, and Kirono looked like he was casually trying to get a word in edgewise and Minshoon tried, to no avail, to orchestrate all of it into a state other than chaos, and Cerminir watched it all with genuine but partial attention and no apparent desire to contribute, and Vanako sat so thickly wrapped in sullen silence that it was impossible to tell what she thought or felt, and Jaliki sat as though glued to Zaya's flank, close enough that her body moved with his breathing. In the course of it all, these things were said:

***

GILTHINIEL

WHERE'S THE DRAGON?

ZAYA

At Saavero's stable in Rust Precinct.

***

MINSHOON

YOU'RE SURE THE POLICE are done with you?

ZAYA

I'm sure those two cops said what I said they said. We still need to be careful.

***

EÄRIL

Dɪᴅ ʏᴏᴜ *STEALED* ᴛʜᴇ dragon?

ZAYA *(with a dirty look at Gilthiniel)*

I helped it escape.

***

GILTHINIEL

Wʜᴀᴛ ᴡɪʟʟ ɪᴛ ᴇᴀᴛ?

ZAYA

Dried tilapia, for a couple of days. I have to keep it fed.

***

MINSHOON

Aʀᴇ ᴡᴇ sᴜʀᴇ ɴᴏ one in Cildinior Amalgam will give you away to Transdesert?

THELENDIL

Hey, fuck you, man.

***

JALIKI

You saw Papa Zinji?

ZAYA

Yeah. He helped me out. He misses you like crazy.

JALIKI

He said that?

ZAYA

… yeah.

JALIKI

Is he gonna come visit?

***

GILTHINIEL

Why do they tag the feathers? Why not, like, its eyes?

TAAVI *(rolling her eyes)*

Dead stuff like hair and feathers doesn't resist charms the way live tissue does? And they have to cast the charm at fucka-huge scale to cover an animal that big?

MINSHOON

Language, Taavi—

GILTHINIEL

"Fucka-huge?"

TAAVI

Dipshit?

MINSHOON

Tiamat and AURYN.

TAAVI & GILTHINIEL

Language, Dad.

***

EÄRIL

IT'S TOO COLD? WITH no feathers?

ZAYA

It's fine, sweetheart. Saavero keeps the stable very warm.

EÄRIL

It needs a blanket?

***

MINSHOON

IT'S NOT AN ASPERSION on your people, I just—

THELENDIL

"My people"? Like I'm some kind of jungle tribesman or something?

MINSHOON

No, that's not—I mean, wait, that is literally exactly what you are.

THELENDIL

Sure, but I don't need a colonizer to tell me that.

MINSHOON

I have absolutely no opinion on what you are. I just want to know how sure we are that not a single person in Cildinior Amalgam will snitch on Zaya to Transdesert.

THELENDIL

Mercantilist colonizers like Transdesert are literally why we invented holes with poisoned stakes at the bottom.

***

ZAYA

Maybe, Jali. He's hard to pin down.

JALIKI

Can we go visit him?

ZAYA

I don't—

JALIKI

He said next time we come over we can pick a Dawn out from over the bay. Like you did with the Mule.

ZAYA *(tightly)*

Is that what he said?

***

VANAKO

So let me get this straight. *You*—

ZAYA

Me.

VANAKO

—who put me through ninety-six flavors and five spice levels of Hell for making a questionable decision to earn some money—

ZAYA

Mm-hmm.

VANAKO

—are telling *me*—

ZAYA

Yep.

VANAKO

—that you walked halfway across the city to do a drunken smash-and-grab on a heavily guarded storage facility—

ZAYA

I biked most of it.

VANAKO

—and fucked it up so badly that the only way you could get out of it was stealing a dragon and flying it out to an Ililuë village halfway across the continent?

ZAYA

It's an amalgam, and about two percent of the way across the continent.

VANAKO

How is it still legal for you to be a parent?

THELENDIL

Colonizer laws benefit no one but the colonizers.

ZAYA

Traitor.

VANAKO

If I get pregnant, can I have some bullshit authority over other people's lives too?

ZAYA & MINSHOON & CERMINIR & KIRONO

No.

***

EÄRIL

Papa Zinji was your mommy but now he is your daddy.

ZAYA *(sighing)*

No, sweetheart. He gave birth to me, but he's my daddy.

EÄRIL

And that's why your grandma and grandpa didn't love you?

ZAYA

Who told you that?

EÄRIL

Vani!

VANAKO

... I'm pretty sure there's another Vani at her school.

***

ZAYA

How are you feeling about all this?

KIRONO

It's not the first bad decision one of us has made. It won't be the last.

ZAYA

... you sure?

KIRONO

I mean, it was pretty bad.

ZAYA

I know.

KIRONO

Drastically bad. Don't make big life choices while you're drunk bad.

ZAYA

Yeah.

KIRONO

A brace of sex-crazed mountain goats wouldn't have fucked this far up bad.

ZAYA

... been saving that one?

KIRONO

The students don't appreciate it, I thought I'd try it on a grown-up.

ZAYA

Time for a mercy killing, friendo.

KIRONO

What, all of a sudden you make good life-and-death decisions?

VANAKO

Savage.

KIRONO

Thank you.

***

MINSHOON

I THINK I READ that somewhere, that's literally true, isn't it?

THELENDIL

I literally said literally.

MINSHOON

... I guess you did.

THELENDIL

Do you city people learn anything for yourselves, or do you just read it all? Like have you ever *been* to the jungle?

MINSHOON

I mean, no? Nature is bullshit.

THELENDIL

I won't say you don't have a point there.

VANAKO

Did it get a little hot in here, or is it just me?

***

GILTHINIEL

Explain again why you had to fill the house with durian?

ZAYA

I'm your mother. If I say we're filling the house with durian, we're filling the house with durian.

***

TAAVI

Stop shipping our dad and the jungle tribesman? It's weird?

VANAKO

You see it, though, right?

TAAVI

I don't *not* see it?

MINSHOON

Young lady.

***

CERMINIR

When's your first race?

***

The whole living room went quiet at that one—except for Enwë, who looked around the room of suddenly somber adults and began to laugh.

"You're racing," Minshoon said. Or maybe asked; it was hard to tell.

"I can't work," said Zaya. "It's summer, no one wants to get into the desert in the heat. And even if there's a late caravan leaving for somewhere, Transdesert won't touch me now. And even if they would, I couldn't earn enough in time."

"I can teach," said Minshoon. "So can Cerminir, or she could get work at a pharmacy. Kirono could pick up extra courses, maybe. We don't have to do this."

"If I go to Tjaroon empty-handed and tell him the plan is to make twelve spare slabs appear from teaching and selling ointment to grannies," said Zaya, "he'll just send his people to break all our knees right now. If I race, I at least have a chance at winning big. That can buy us time."

"Vani got us in this situation by committing a crime," said Minshoon. "You made it worse by committing another one. Now you want to pull us out by committing a third? The 'stream is still illegal, Zaya, and you said it yourself—the police are watching you now."

"The 'stream's always been illegal," said Cerminir. "You didn't worry about that before."

"The Mule was Zaya's, free and clear," said Minshoon. "A gift of the sky over the bay. The money went to this." He gestured at the walls around them. "Landlords and taxes. We put that money back in the legal economy. You're talking about using a stolen dragon to win at illegal gambling on an illegal race so we can pay off a criminal we owe because one of ours screwed up while doing crimes for him. If we get caught at any of that, we're on the hook for the whole thing."

"The only thing wrong with that argument," said Zaya, "is that racing the dragon is the only illegal thing we haven't already done. It's the only way to make anything good come of any of it."

"How? The bookies won't take odds from me any more."

"So we don't make fancy bets."

"You say 'don't make fancy bets,' I hear 'don't manage our downside risk.'"

"Minshoon," Kirono said, "I don't even know what downside risk is, but I know we are *so far past* managing it."

Minshoon looked at Kirono for a long time. Kirono looked at the wall.

"Sorry," Minshoon said. "I wasn't trying to... anything."

"It's OK," Kirono said.

"Three to one," Minshoon said. He leaned back on the couch and idly put a hand on Jaliki's scalp, scratching it gently with his fingertips, then looked up at the walrus mural on the ceiling. "All right. If you and Cer and Zaya are for it, all right."

"I'm also for it," said Thelendil.

"You have to be in the house for more than a day to get a vote," said Minshoon.

"Sounds like some colonizer bullshit to me," said Vanako.

Gilthiniel punched her in the shoulder. "Don't rile up the parents."

"They already took the door off my room," said Vanako. "What have I got to lose?"

Zaya looked at all the eyes in the room, pair by pair: Thelendil, Gilthiniel, Vanako, Taavi, Cerminir, Enwë, Eäril, Jaliki, Minshoon. There were so many of them; so many of them were so young. She felt acid rise in her gut; she spoke as much to mask it as anything else. "Before we go through with this, we need to recognize something. We don't have to do this. There's an easy way to get the money." She made the same gesture Minshoon had earlier, encompassing walls, ceilings, kitchen, windows; chairs, tables, couches, the hallway to the bedrooms, even the ker curled up at Jaliki's feet. "We could sell the place. We'd have a bit left over, but probably not enough to buy even in Damask; that's another few years of working and saving and getting lucky. Cer would probably have to go back home if we did that, so there's another option: We could sell the place and leave town. We'd probably have to go farther out than Cildinior to shake them loose, though. Maybe out to Tzadiscari. I don't know how much our sherds and flinders would buy out there, but with our luck we'd probably be poor. Poor in a city where we don't speak the language. But together." Zaya took a deep breath to let the rest of the family speak; no one did. "I'd rather fight for what we made. But it is a fight. Things can happen in a fight. People can get hurt, people can lose what's important. And we don't have to do it. If we do it, we choose to do it. Anyone want to make a different choice?"

Cerminir frowned. "I don't get it. Isn't that exactly what Minshoon said before?"

Minshoon smiled, and in it there was sadness and a little defeat and readiness and a little flint and steel. "Pretty close. But not exactly."

"What's the difference?"

"I said what I said for her. She said what she said for them." And he scratched Jaliki's scalp again, then leaned over to follow it with a kiss. Jaliki leaned his head into Minshoon's chest.

"I still don't get it," said Cerminir. "But I'm over it."

"So," said Vanako. "Since you all had your vote on it—what do we do?"

"Study hard," said Minshoon. "Someone's going to have to bail us out of the work crews when we're done."

CHAPTER 12

HOUSES, GREAT. *In Yemareir, a "house" is a group of people sharing the same surname. In practice, it's almost always Mrineen, and the surname is almost always a reptile.*

(Shenireen. —Ed.)

... the far-seeing editors of this humble volume have divined that you, tourist, are as interested in the spackle of dumb myth-making over the Yemari tradition of shitty oligarchy and power politics as, apparently, they are. How surprising! And unfortunate!

Look: When you think "House," with a capital H, you are surely thinking of the polished political, martial, and sorcerous élites who play the rest of the world like marionettes in whatever literary or dramatic tradition you're burdened with—each with its own colors, its own specialties, its own traditions. And, sure: Tuatara, Amphisbaena, Pogona, Taipan. The names of people you'll never meet, because they're too focused on keeping a stranglehold on this city to mingle with random passersby from away...

... but the rest of us? House Agama, my own, has a sprinkling of peers, a couple of earls and a margravine; we have the estate in Alabaster Precinct, tucked between Taipan and Monitor like a garden shed. If all the Agamas in Yemareir tried to fit in the estate, we'd press ourselves into paté. We have nothing in common and no loyalty to one another. It's just a name.

SEE ALSO: Government.

—From "A Visitor's Handbook for Yemareir," by Shenireen Agama

***

CANDLEGRASS STAND WAS THE kind of attraction that brought folks to Damask Precinct for a night: Wander a few of the sweltering paths cut into the periphery of the stand, where the grass grew slim-stalked and not much higher than your head, then watch a concert or a play in its flickering light, eat some bad Kayalim food with a poorly paired beer, and stagger home. What most of those folks didn't know, and didn't care to know, was what went on in the interior of the Stand, where the towering old stalks grew too thick to cut down easily and the heat of the grass' fiery-globed tips grew close to unbearable. Without paths, you relied on a guide who knew their way around or learned to wayfind by the blazes others had left on the endlessly similar stalks. Police rarely did the first and refused to do the second; so Candlegrass Stand was, among other things, where one went to find a race for a wyrm.

Zaya had dressed lightly for the quest, in a thin linen shift too cool for the brisk spring evening; she'd shivered on the bike ride here, but by the time she entered the labyrinth her thighs were already chafing with sweat. Soon she stuffed the shift into a shoulder bag, leaving only briefs and a halter. That earned her a smattering of laughs and stares from tourists, and one nod of recognition from an Ililuë man as tall and lanky as Thelendil, whose face was ritually scarified in the style of Elduren Convivency and who wore nothing but a pair of filthy hemp rope sandals.

She worked her way to the inner wall of the labyrinth, sweating freely now, then began to look for the entrances—subtly wider spaces between the stalks, pushed permanently apart by centuries of visitors wishing to conduct business in private. They had names, based—or so Zaya had heard—on features of the stalks so subtle as to escape the notice of all but the most careful searchers; she had forgotten the ones for sex, drugs, fights, and politics, but the entrance she had been accustomed to use was called the Trident Gate because, from a certain angle, one could believe that four of the globes formed a row (opinion was divided on whether the fourth globe had grown out in recent years, or whether the ancient namer simply didn't know what a trident was). It took her three passes, but she found it.

The paths within the core of Candlegrass Stand were as much a matter of custom as the entrances, slight expansions of the natural spaces between the stalks marked sparsely by obscure blazes. Picking one's way through was always tricky; the grunts of lovers and the traces of other transactions were never far off, and anything short of iron-walled tunnel vision was asking to get your ass kicked by anyone who didn't care for your attention. Which was tricky if you didn't know exactly what you were looking for. But Zaya did: The clipboard, the feather jewelry, the position two stalks down from a blaze on the left side of the path. She couldn't place him as Mrineen or Kayalim from his features, body shape, or complexion—but he was where a fixer for the 'stream would be, and that was all that mattered. Zaya caught his eye and smiled at him; he looked at her breasts. With an effort, she kept her eyes from rolling. "Tourney?"

"Oh, yes, *cha*." That was the formula; no syllable could be omitted on pain of being found a cop.

"Course?"

"The Broodspire Tour, *cha*."

"Bullshit." This was Zaya's part of the contract; the first course was always bullshit, and anyone who bit was a cop.

"If you must," said the fixer. "The Stone Forest Slalom, then. Who's racing?"

"A new team on Bandit's Breath."

"Who though?"

Zaya paused an examined the fixer; he was obdurate, his jaw out like a bulldog's. "It's a new team," she said. "The wyrm is Bandit's Breath."

"It's not ears I'm in want of, *cha*, it's names."

This was way off script, and it was making Zaya nervous. "Are you new here?" she said. "We don't do names, not in the grass."

"Less new than you, *cha*, or so you've said to me; and, these days, we do."

When the hand clapped down on her shoulder, her stomach sank. A cop, of course, just slightly savvier than average; and this would be his backup. "Have you stinking swine," she sighed, defeated, "*genuinely* no better crime to stop?"

"They do," said a voice from above and behind her, "but the dealers are armed, and they don't want to tangle with the fighters."

Zaya spared a glance up and back; it was a Mrineen man, slim-shouldered but fashionably bulky, in a sleeveless indigo shirt and matching pants that radiated a slight but noticeable cool—though she still smelled sweat on him; it would take more than an off-the-shelf cool charm to be truly comfortable in here. His face was round for a Mrineen—or maybe his size disguised its youth—and something in his wide-set, bright blue eyes looked familiar. She brushed his hand off her shoulder. "Is this a grift, or just some kind of weird cop performance art where you string me along and gain my trust before bringing me in?"

The fixer shot the Mrineen interloper an appraising look, his tongue darting out to moisten his lips. She felt the Mrineen behind and above her shift his weight. The not-a-fixer flared his nostrils, puffed a breath out through his nose, and walked off as though it were his own idea.

Zaya turned to look up at the Mrineen interloper; the bitterness of having to look up at a Mrineen man who'd just-maybe-rescued her foiled her mouth and spread to the back of her throat. She swallowed it down—more was coming. "Thanks for that," she said. "Have we met?"

"I don't think I know you," he said. "But I've just signed up for a race. Let me introduce you to the real fixer."

"You never did answer my question about whether this was cop performance art."

He laughed, but she could feel the annoyance in it. "I'm not a cop," he said. "My name's Shanhoon Krait."

"Kaala," said Zaya, reaching for the first fake name that came to mind. "Nice to meet you."

He motioned her farther into the candlegrass with a jerk of his head. They walked past an entangled pair of shadows on a parallel path, separated from them by maybe a dozen stalks; the sharp staccato of rapid gasps hammered at her forehead. "What do you race?" he asked.

"A Dawn," she said.

"Name?"

"Bandit's Breath."

"Don't know it."

Zaya laughed softly. "Unless you're a Swordwing pilot in the Air Guard, I don't know yours either."

"Monsoon. It's a Melanic Shrike—strong echolocation. Which helps compensate for its size on tight courses; it's not quite a five-course meal, but definitely three and an *amuse-bouche*."

I've eaten meals like that for breakfast, Zaya did not say.

They were in far enough that the bases of the stalks were thigh- rather than arm-thick, the light dulling as the tips stretched higher into the night sky. A lanky Mrineen—lanky for a Mrineen—sat with their back to a stalk of candlegrass as big around as a modestly sized tree, leafing through a thick stack of comics. They looked up as Krait approached. "You can't sign up twice, Krait," they said.

"I'm here on an act of public service," said Krait. "My new friend Kaala would like to join the Brimstone Slipstream."

The fixer eyeballed Zaya as though she were one of a massive herd of small jellyfish washed up on the beach and they were deciding whether the novelty of touching her was worth the risk of getting stung. "Stone Forest Slalom, *cha*," they finally said, after a look to Shanhoon Krait.

"That's what yon doppelgänger of yours tried to fix me up with," said Zaya.

"Their information's not bad," the fixer said diffidently. "Quite a few cops in the 'stream, figure it can't hurt their chances if the new blood get picked off before they hit the start line. Wyrm?"

"And you let them do it?"

"Is that a question?"

"Yes, it was a question. Bandit's Breath, apostrophe between T and S, we're a new team, don't fret if you haven't heard of us. You just let them entrap new 'streamers?"

"In point of fact," said Krait, "I could have let them entrap you, and I didn't."

Zaya turned to stare a dagger or two at him. "Are you with the Standards Board?"

"No. But neither are they, really. No offense, but how are they supposed to chase off a cop?"

"None taken," said the fixer.

"Come on," Zaya said to Krait. "You didn't have to challenge the officer to first blood back there. He knew where he was. You cry 'police' and you've got a crowd of armed folks who came here for privacy to share the load." Krait's face was starting to wobble a bit in the way faces do when they're trying to stay impassive while something's going on beneath the surface. "You didn't think he was afraid of you, did you? You *did*." Through the sweat and the heat and her heart, still racing from the out-of-date fear of being carted off to jail, Zaya laughed. "All right, I'll ask the question. Who's Shanhoon Krait when he's at home?"

Shanhoon was now looking at Zaya as though she were some exceptionally elaborate insect and he was trying to figure out which end was the head. "Shanhoon Krait is the 'streamer who's dominated the scene for almost three years at this point, odds-on favorite to win next year's Grand Bisai. Not to boast—I mean, I'm boasting, but it's facts." Zaya hoped she was better at hiding her feelings than Krait was at hiding his. "You, though. You're someone who knows something about the 'stream, who has *opinions* about it—" His eyes went wide, then his face opened up in a grin. "Kay-alim woman, mid-twenties, riding in a team," said Krait. "I'm so fucking stupid."

"I wasn't asking you."

"I saw your hair and just—but anyone can cut their hair."

"Stone Forest Slalom unlocks seasonal qualifiers for the top three 'streamers," said the fixer. "Entry fee an eighth slab, winnings one slab, half a slab, quarter slab."

"*What?*"

"I can't believe you're back," said Krait. "This is massive. Who's your teammate?"

The fixer droned on as if they hadn't heard Zaya or Krait, although their smirk said plainly that they had. "Psionic dampers will be distributed by the Standards Board immediately before the event; any evidence of tampering with the device is disqualifying. Other disqualifying offenses include—"

"Psionic dampers?" Zaya said. "And an eighth-slab entry fee? Did you paint 'poors need not inquire' on the starting line, just to clear things up for the slow learners?"

"Hold on, Shearwater-*cha*," said Krait. "That's not our colleague's fault. The Standards Board implemented it a few months after you left."

"It might not be their fault. It doesn't change the facts." She turned to the fixer. "If I gave you a wyrm free and clear, could you enter the 'stream with an eighth slab as table stakes?"

The fixer looked up at Krait uncomfortably. "Maybe?"

"Shearwater-*cha*, you of all people can hardly complain about the fee—" Krait began.

"Watch me."

"Most of it goes to the prize. If we'd had those fees when you were in the 'stream, you'd be rich."

"If a nothing course like the Stone Forest Slalom had cost us an eighth slab as table stakes," Zaya said, "I'd still be knocking over liquor stores with my dads. And without psionics, we'd never have placed."

"Give yourselves some credit," Krait said.

"I'm giving us credit for beating all your rare wyrms and your gear with nothing but psionics and hunger. The Standards Board banned both. What else do I need to know?"

Krait took a deep breath through his nose, then let it out. Right or wrong, it felt like he was trying to calm Zaya down rather than himself, which only made her angrier. "I feel like this conversation took a left turn," he said. "I'm so glad you're back. It's going to be great for the 'stream. Maybe it takes you a few races to learn how to be a great racer without psionics. So what? It gives your fans a thing to root for. Sweetens the victory. Where's there to go if you start at the top?"

She imagined the ker speaking Krait's words, its eyes full of the same false doggy comfort. You could waste a life in refutation.

"My team and my eighth slab will be there to accept our psionic dampers and any other bullshit gadgets of oppression the Standards Board may introduce in the meantime. Citizen Krait, Citizen Fixer, thank you for your assistance."

She turned on her heel and left without another word.

It wasn't until halfway home, when a Dawn Wyrm winged overhead while she blazed through the fast lane on the Street of Cracked Hearts, that Zaya realized she didn't know where the race began, or when.

***

"Zaya, my dear, it's so good to see you!"

Zaya pushed up on her tiptoes as far as she could to embrace the graying Mrineen man. He squeezed her with ropy arms whose hardness had always surprised her; the smell of leather, iron, oil, and wyrm-down brought her back six years, to endless nights in bars with Kiriki and this man, when the skies had knelt to them. "Arhoon, my dear, you're still carrying a sword around like some old-timey enemy's about to challenge you to a duel in the street."

"I've fought a couple of duels in my time. Come, sit." Arhoon Pogona gestured toward the red brick patio, lined with trellises of morning glories and half full of breakfasters tucking into spiced pulled pork with parsley-garlic sauce and lime-cooked fish salad. "Tjaliraan's has a kitchen now."

"They served food before," said Zaya.

"A bucket of flour and a pot of boiling oil isn't a kitchen, it's a highly specialized machine shop. Oh, I know, they had a menu and all that, but whether it was 'fried potatoes' or 'crispy fish filets' or 'golden bean curd cubes,' it all came down to edible gin sponges." Arhoon undid a buckle and humped the longsword off his back, then sat on a bench, leaning it by him. It was tall enough that its pommel was at the level of his face, like a third member of the group. Zaya joined him.

Silence hung for a moment—not an awkward one, but not a usual one either. Arhoon and Kiriki had always sparked one another like hammers on hot steel. By now she'd be commenting on some change in his clothes or hair that he hadn't noticed, or he'd be poking fun at... whatever change in Kiriki might have happened if she'd been alive these last six years. Maybe she'd have gotten fat, or they'd have tattoos. He was probably trying not to comment on Zaya's hair. "What's good here now?" she asked.

"Everything. But when they recite the menu, the first and last dishes are yesterday's ingredients. Easier to remember, so you're more likely to order them."

"That's sneaky."

"Pretty standard at these mid-tier places."

The last time Zaya had been to Tjaliraan's, they'd served home-made lemon gin at a price per glass that could have paid a month's rent on a beachfront penthouse in Cobalt Precinct. Arhoon had paid for that as well, by necessity. She hadn't known the tiers went higher than that. "Well, that'll teach me to avoid mid-tier places. How've you been?"

"Doing my best to live out this life of dissipation I've made for myself. Kiriki's death made House Pogona a little skittish about the future of my peerage, so I married briefly. It was nice for a few months, but he was… if I'm honest, he wanted more out of a spouse than I wanted to put in. A house-brother of your brood-sister's, actually. Zeroun Amphisbaena, maybe they know each other?"

"I wouldn't know."

"He's happily married to a viscount of House Ferdelance now, little brood. All very cozy. You still don't talk to Ziyuki?"

"It takes two women not to talk."

Arhoon laughed. "You must have a lot of one-sided conversations."

"I don't have a lot to say to a Grandee of House Amphisbaena."

"She's been Baronet of Ahjanshoun for years, Zaya."

Zaya shrugged. "Proving my point."

A waitron came by, polished and full of energy; Zaya pined briefly for the mumbling poet at the Blind Beggar. She ordered the pulled pork. Arhoon ordered some melange of diced mixed cephalopods, a glass of gin, and a gin fizz. The waitron's eyes sparkled at the thought of gratuities to come. "You don't discourage your customers from drinking gin neat before breakfast?" said Zaya.

"If he doesn't drink it," said the waitron, "you'll have to."

"Fair play," said Zaya, sighing; and when the waitron was headed inside to the kitchen, "Arhoon, I'm back in the 'stream."

Arhoon leaned forward with wide, eager eyes, as though she'd told him how she liked to be licked and who'd last done it. "I'd heard, but never dared to believe. What do you need? Tack, tail spikes, barding? A wyrm, maybe? The market for well-bred rare wyrms is better than it used to be; I know a breeder who just got stuck with a fourth-cohort Saw-Pinioned Dart that's eating him out of house and home, I'm sure we could work out a discount—"

"I don't need you to throw the House Pogona money bin at me. But thanks for offering," she added, not really feeling it. "What I need is—"

"Hold on a second," said Arhoon. "I absolutely respect your right to turn up your stuck-up nose at my hard-earned sherds and flinders." Zaya rolled her eyes at "hard-earned," as was required; Arhoon hadn't earned a flinder for his house in his lifetime, and he knew it. "But you cannot win on a half-drowned Dawn you dragged off the beach and whipped back into the air on cheap fish and whiskey. Psionics is out now. You need to change your game."

"The sweet fuck I do."

"You can't use empathy in the 'stream. Your main advantage is gone."

"No," Zaya said steadily. "I have to wear a 'damper.' My main advantage is..." She shrugged. "Moist."

The drinks had silently arrived; Arhoon tossed half his gin back and pointed a finger at Zaya. "That's denial."

"No disrespect to your noble race, but every Mrineen empath I've met has had the psychic strength of an overboiled noodle," Zaya said. "Not that the potential isn't there, you understand, it's just that the culture encourages laziness." Arhoon clapped a hand over his heart as though he'd been struck by an arrow. "You figure out how to get semi-adequate compliance out of a well-fed primate? Flawless victory! Psionics at that level practically 'damps' itself. Whatever they're passing out to 'streamers is probably just plain tin painted with made-up runes."

"Fine," said Arhoon. "I'm not arguing with you on this one, since my brain's so weak. Just come to me if you need money."

Can you spare twelve slabs? she almost asked. But she knew the shape of that conversation. Arhoon was a peer of House Pogona, but a hereditary one; the house was run by an adoptive sibling, Dvaraan Pogona, who'd been identified as a high-potential individual by one of House Pogona's examinations and brought in when Arhoon was a kid. Just like Ziyuki had been with House Amphisbaena. Arhoon's bloodline was deprecated and his contributions to the House were, from the House's point of view, zero. His stipend wouldn't cover twelve slabs, or even three.

"Can you spare twelve slabs?" she asked.

Arhoon laughed weakly. "I shouldn't make promises I can't keep. Is that why you're back? Wanted to put a down payment on a château in Alabaster Precinct? Or did Minshoon's gambling habits finally get ahead of his brain?"

"More like the second than the first, but not Minshoon. I don't want to get into it. And I'm sorry I asked. I couldn't not."

"If someone's after you for the money, I could maybe look into..." He drew a finger across his throat.

"Ugh, no you couldn't." And, in case he could, "And don't."

"Suit yourself." He finished the gin. "I'll say it one more time, though: The 'stream is a different game now. Rare wyrms left and right—and not wild ones, these are raised to riders. Armor, spikes, blades. Charms. No actual sorcery allowed, but I don't know. It seems to be au courant among the right young people these days."

"And 'the right young people' are in the 'stream." It wasn't a question.

"Gone are the days when noble personages like me and Kanivoon were much admired rarities in a sea of hairy rejects." He said it in a tone of self-mocking, but he let more truth into the words than he meant. "And beautiful strivers like yourself and Kiriki, may Kukulkan remind me to save a drop of gin for her out of the next glass."

"Who do I need to watch?"

"If you're coming in on a scraggly bay wyrm? Everyone."

"The good 'streamers, Arhoon. The winners."

The food arrived, along with a spare glass of gin that Arhoon hadn't asked for but accepted as though he had. It smelled unbelievable. "The winners," Arhoon said. "Let us speak of them."

CHAPTER 13

DRAGONS, COMMON. THESE ARE *the wyrms you're most likely to see in Yemareir and environs:*

Dawn Wyrm. Slim, medium-sized wyrms, usually a mix of magenta, blue, orange, and purple. These live on islands in the bay and on cliffs by it. They're often out at dawn and dusk, circling on the thermals and diving for fish—including small sharks and porpoises. They're the most sociable of the common wyrms, and the most common in the 'stream.

Dusk Stalker. Nocturnal indigo wyrms that stick mostly to the jungle, but occasionally venture out to the veldt and even the bay. As fliers, not as strong as the other common wyrms, but they fly well when visibility's poor, which both 'streamers and law enforcement find useful for different reasons.

Eyrie Shrike. Mountain dwellers, a bit smaller than Dawns. Grey, blue, and white. They like to age their prey by hanging them on inaccessible crags for days or weeks, hence the name. Calm and generally low-energy, but their skill at maneuvering mountain environments has made them prized in the 'stream.

Merlin Wyrm. Cat-sized dragons, as common in the city as dogs or monkeys. Not used in the 'stream for obvious reasons. As dumb and rowdy as any little cousin with something to prove. Cute, but illegal to keep as pets due to fire hazard.

__Ranger Wyrm__. These live mostly on the veldt. Blue and tan, power-fully built, with bushy crests of feathers at the base of their skulls; a few grow big enough to hunt elephants and rhinos on their own. Touchy and wild. You shouldn't approach wyrms in general, but you really shouldn't approach these.

SEE ALSO: Brimstone Slipstream; Dragons, Rare.

—From "A Visitor's Handbook for Yemareir," by Shenireen Agama

***

CARNELIAN PRECINCT: THE STONE FOREST STARTING LINE.

ZAYA AND THELENDIL SAILED in low on dragonback to touch down on the roof of a workhouse in Carnelian Precinct, thick with wyrms and riders and surrounded on all sides by a torchlit audience. The workhouse had once held ranks of seamstresses, each a specialist in some particular hem, seam, or stitch on some specific garment sold however many centuries it had been ago by whatever corporate concern had then been flirting with the mass production of clothing. That corporate concern had leveled a pre-Yemari long-house and installed something similar in its wake—its chief virtue being a wide, flat roof that handily separated racers from onlookers while abetting the act of onlooking, putting the competitors on something rather close to an actual pedestal.

The onlookers were different from the crowds Zaya remembered: Better dressed, better mannered, floating on wine or world-vine rather than beer and arrack.

The wyrms, too, had changed.

Rare wyrms left and right, Arhoon Pogona had said, but the profusion of breeds and plumages wasn't the first thing Zaya noticed. For 'streamers of her vintage, the source of choice for dragons was the bay: Dawns were sociable, plentiful, and biddable, easily motivated by affection and brown spirits. Six years ago, the colors of a race had been magenta, blue, and orange, accented by the common wyrms of the veldt and foothills: the tan-and-blue of Ranger Wyrms, the grey-and-blue of Eyrie Shrikes, the night-blue of Dusk Stalkers. Shanhoon Krait's obsidian-black Melanic Shrike would have stood out like a crow in a flower garden.

Not here.

Thelendil let out a low whistle as he climbed down from Bandit's back. "I never thought I'd see so many different wyrms in the same place."

Zaya unhooked the helmets from Bandit's saddle and handed the larger one to Thelendil. His was simple, a wooden half-shell shape that would cover his scalp; hers was bronze, with a nose-guard and cheek-plates. Reluctantly, Zaya admitted, "Me neither."

There was a Moonturn Moultwyrm in the dregs of its spring plumage, piloted by a Mrineen in matching green accented with deep purple and cadmium yellow; their hair and goggles were the same green. ("Lerikaan Boomslang," Arhoon had said over cocktails and breakfast at Tjaliraan's. "Nice person, straight shooter. Arrow's a little like the Mule used to be, surprisingly good on the corners for such a big wyrm.")

Most of the pilots wore no goggles, though; the faint oil-slick sheen of minor shear fields gleamed and sizzled in the air around their faces. There was a Prismatic Wyvern, unfeathered save for purely ornamental crests and tufts around its face, rainbow scales dull in the half-light ("Shainjoon Monitor. Very serious 'streamer, possibly the only one who actually learned from anything you and Kiriki said about feed and feathers. He'd never credit you, though, because he's a massive asshole."). A Peregrine Gyrdrake, blue and grey and black, dense and compact with a dagger-like snout ("Gyr-drakes are the new Dawns, and Kshalain Honu and Ajiroon Ora are the two major threats on those. The difference is Kshalain is all about fucking you over to win, and Ajiroon is just all about fucking you over."). A Ranger Wyrm nearly the size of the elephant-eaters Zaya and Thelendil had seen from the Craw's back two weeks be-fore ("You might see Carnaug, which is a Ranger Wyrm the size of a mountain. The rider is like seven feet tall and goes by Yaulë and no one knows who they are because they always wear some kind of Ililuë ceremonial mask. They never win, but they always place well, and Carnaug can ruin your life if you get caught behind it.") Common wyrms outnumbered the rare ones, to be sure, but each had some signifier of its owner's investment in the 'stream: a variant coloration, a shaped or decorated crest, a finely detailed piece of barding on its head or neck, a gleaming set of tail-spikes. She caught a glimpse of Monsoon's black head across the rooftop, but Carnaug blocked the view.

All of that Zaya swiftly noticed, but none of it was the first thing she noticed.

"They're so quiet," she said to Thelendil. "They don't move, they don't make a sound."

"Neither does Bandit."

"I know," said Zaya. "That weirds me out about Bandit."

It's not my fault I was well bred.

"No," she said, putting her hand on Bandit's flank. "But these wyrms used to be wild. This didn't use to be a well-bred sport."

Thelendil put an arm around her shoulders and squeezed. "Don't worry, we'll make it barbaric again."

Zaya slid without comment out from the half-embrace. She felt Thelendil's disappointment and confusion (at some remove, echoed through Bandit's mind) and could not quite contain a surge of regret—which he would feel, as well, or might, which only made her feel worse, and so on. This was something she'd never questioned with Kiriki; when they had been with the Mule, their minds had simply fallen in step, and if she had not always wanted to reveal her thoughts and feelings to Kiriki she could at least accept it. She liked Thelendil, but she did not yet trust him enough to accept it.

A young Mrineen with a pen, a sheet of pages, and an armful of amulets caught Zaya's eye and ambled over. She took Zaya and Thelendil's names, then Bandit's, then held two of the amulets out. "Psionic dampers," she said. "Make sure you return them by race's end or you'll have 'stream privileges revoked until the Standards Board's made whole, plus a fine."

"Or you could just keep it and save us all the trouble," Thelendil said, his brilliant grin huge in the half-light.

The girl nodded briskly. "That's very humorous. Good luck." She looked up at Bandit. "Don't see so many of these any more," she said with a world-weariness that, Zaya knew from wearing it when she was younger than this girl, was entirely unearned. She shot Thelendil a glance to say *Do not engage.* He shot her one to say *You never let me have any fun.*

"'Streamers, to wyrmback!'"

Zaya flicked her goggles over her eyes, turning the riotous plumage of her opposition into shades of pine and emerald. She put her arms out, about to create a stirrup for Thelendil, and bumped instead into his head; his arms were outstretched to hug her, his river-long body bent nearly double for a kiss.

She fended his face off with a forearm. "Not when I'm racing." The words were as gentle as she could make them; she didn't need the echo from Bandit to know that it didn't matter. Which was lucky enough, as the echo wasn't there; the damper had muffled it completely. Thelendil looked mock-stricken. "Where'd you go?"

With some effort, she *reached* out to him. *I'm at the finish line already. Didn't you see me race?*

After a second, he laughed, then furrowed his brow in concentration. It took Zaya another second, perhaps two, to feel a sort of scratching on the inside of her scalp; but she could get no meaning from it. "I'm sorry," she said. "Couldn't catch it."

Thelendil raised an eyebrow. "So this only goes one way?"

"Not funny."

"That's all right, I'm into it. Anything for you."

"You should listen when I tell you things aren't funny." She held out her hands as a stirrup for him. "Mount up, or they really will leave us behind."

They quickly tied bandannas over their noses and mouths, then donned the racing goggles and put their helmets over. His swing up to the Mule's back was almost graceful, or at least almost smooth. For herself, she almost lost her balance, swinging up to Bandit's lowered shoulders to hunker between its wings; its feathers were hard and slippery, like lathes of polished wood.

In the groove, the world's variegations sorted themselves out: A few details gleamed razor-bright in the emerald cast of the goggles, the rest fell away. There were about a dozen and a half dragons in this race; the long boulevard ahead would provide some freedom for them to sort themselves out, but after that it would be tight alleys and slim side streets until the Forest itself. To her left—and well above—was Yaulë on Carnaug, the white face of their whole-head mask tapered and schematic and quizzical; to her right was Lerikaan Boomslang, looking sharp in a loose blouse and pantaloons with thin rainbow zigzags on a black background, on Time's Warped Arrow. Both wyrms were armored on their faces and at their shoulders and the base of their necks; both had gleaming spikes on their tails. Zaya tamped down a churn in her guts and forced her eyes forward.

"Wyrms, find your marks!" shouted the announcer. Zaya *reached* harder than she thought she needed to. Bandit crouched, wings poised—but the motion was delayed, imprecise, uncertain. She swore. The lag on her empathic link to Bandit was worse than she'd thought; the delay would be enough to screw up their start, maybe even crash them into another wyrm.

"Steady!"

"What's wrong?" asked Thelendil.

Zaya had no answer. She could build the lag into her *reach*, she realized—just do it early enough to account for the delay—but if Bandit left too soon, it was all over before it would have begun.

Fuck it. Zaya *reached*.

"To the sky!" came just late enough; Bandit was in the air.

***

LILAC PRECINCT: SIX DAYS BEFORE THE RACE.

ZAYA WAS TRYING NOT to get pulled into arguing precinct politics with the usual malcontents when Kirono came out of his room. This, fascinatingly, was the single thing short of a chemically induced stupor that had ever shut the malcontents up entirely; Kirono never came out of his room when there was company—especially not company as loud and full of screeds and edicts as Kiri and Vinaali Petrel. "Zaya," Kirono said, "I've got something."

"By the smell on them, I'd agree," said Kiri, who could not be shut up for long.

"Do they live here?" asked Vinaali.

"Kirono-tē has always lived here," said Zaya. "He smells because he's a scientist. He's working on something for me."

"What does a perfectly nice girl like you need with a scientist in the house?" asked Kiri, stroking his beard flat over his belly. "If he stinks so much."

"Scientists are very intelligent, dear," said Vinaali, placing her fingertips on the swollen-knuckled back of Kiri's hand. "I'm sure Kirono-tē makes himself very useful to Zaya."

Kiri said something skeptical, Vinaali said something tart; Zaya was already up, moving with Kirono toward a bedroom that stank of chalk dust and rotted garlic. "I'm sorry for the smell," Kirono said. "I'm too used to the lab—they've got huge windows and a couple of giant fans, like peacock tail feathers on broomsticks that you can—"

"It's all right," said Zaya, surrendering to the impulse pulling up the corners of her mouth. "Brings back memories."

Kirono's desk was a long granite slab laid across a pair of tree-trunk sections each wider than Zaya's hips, impossible to move with a crew fewer than four, scarred, stained, pocked, and cluttered with beakers, alembics, charm-powered burners, and any number of mixed jars full of pastes, powders, liquids, and granules. There was also an immense beehive and a set of small mismatched plates, each with a Dawn's wing feather on it, ranging from azure to purple-blue. "You remember the last time you flew the Stone Forest Slalom," said Kirono. "Dawn feathers are kind of fluffy; that makes them light, but it also makes them prone to latch onto whatever's in the air. I couldn't figure out something that would protect them without weighing them down." He let himself have a half-unmanaged grin. "I've learned a thing or two in the department, though. Try them out. Control, old recipe, new recipe."

"You were right about the Stone Forest last time," Zaya said, picking up the control feather as a reference point; it was stiff but light and soft. "We came in fifth. The Mule barely stopped to let us off before it went off to the bay for a bath. That stone dust is a bitch." She picked up the second feather; it was stiffer, harder, and felt like an astonishingly lifelike gold sculpture of the first feather. "I don't think this would have done us any favors, though. Not against Vlaana on Bat." Vlaana cha-Zina had been the smallest, most rawboned 'streamer Zaya had ever met, often mistaken for a child by cops and bartenders; Bat o' Fine Tails had been a first-cohort Dusk Stalker practically born to flit through trees, with a feather structure that shed particulates with exceptional efficiency. She hadn't heard from either of them since the Mule and Kiriki died. She picked up the third feather. "Wow. Are you sure this'll grip the air, though? It can't just shed stone dust, it has to keep Bandit off the ground."

"The Mule won with waxes a lot like. this. It feels different on your finger, but it'll work." Kirono licked his lips and the angle of his head and the hesitation on his face made it feel like he was looking up instead. "But it won't help as much as the other thing."

Zaya shook her head—once, sharply. "Thank you, Kirono, but no."

His chest swelled as though he was about to protest, but he swallowed whatever he had been about to say.

"I'm telling you," Kiri was announcing from the common room, "Jina ze-Saibaka is a sellout. A tool of the racist oligarchy just barely Kayalim enough to keep this precinct from opening its eyes and realizing how far short we're falling from what we could be."

Zaya looked at Kirono, but his eyes were down. "Don't say it," she said.

"I would never," he said, but he didn't mean it.

CARNELIAN PRECINCT: THE OPENING STRETCH.

Bandit hit the apex of its leap; its wings snapped out, stopping their fall with a jerk as they gripped the air; it heaved forward with all the fury of a gale in Zaya's face, wind shearing her lips back from her teeth and flattening her shirt against her chest and shoulders; and her mind erupted with two blooms of panic: a hot flume of red fear from Thelendil, who'd lost his grip with one hand and was now flapping like a banner in the slipstream, and a barbed swarm of sparking shadows from Bandit's Breath, who'd never flown in such proximity to so many other worms before and was struggling to cope with the flood of sensation. She *reached* as well as she could, focusing on a lane between the Moultwyrm and the Dusk Stalker in front of it and tweaking Bandit's muscles to slip through. It didn't react—or, no, there it was, along with a trickle of relief at having some kind of direction to sort through the noise; but in the second's delay between her sending and Bandit's action, the lane had closed, and they were sharing the space behind those two lead wyrms with the massive Carnaug.

"Thelendil, head in the game," she said. "Bandit, just tail Arrow and the Dusk as close as you can, we're about to hit a sharp corner and one of them's bound to—" She trailed off; the words felt futile. There was no resonance of acknowledgment in Bandit's mind, and Thelendil's panic wasn't helping; it had lost its overpowering brightness, but its more muted thrum of heat and fear still drowned out whatever subtler signals might be making it through the psionic damper.

Carnaug's massive wingbeats seemed to set the air shivering like an earthquake. Bandit or Thelendil had also caught a nose catching up on their far left, looking for the same kind of opening on the corner that Zaya had been hoping for. She wanted to wipe her goggles; she felt like she was flying blind. She couldn't continue the race like this, couldn't take the risks she needed to. Almost without thinking, she *reached* back into Thelendil's mind, flooding it (as best she could, a river through a pinhole) with calm, reassurance, and love.

***

LILAC PRECINCT: FOUR DAYS BEFORE THE RACE.

"I THOUGHT YOU WEREN'T interested in men," said Thelendil as Zaya swung a leg over him.

She put the heel of her hand on his mouth, less gently than she might have. "It's a tenuous interest. The wrong dumb comment could drive it away entirely."

There weren't any more comments after that.

They'd spent the day in Bistre Precinct on the southern edge of the city, taking Bandit through its paces in an area by the Eyrie Shrike broodspire so long depopulated that a stand of cedars had grown there. Zaya had shown Thelendil the trees blazed with a cruciform shape in bright white paint, one axis much longer than the other and tapered like leaves at the tips. "A shearwater," she'd explained. "At least, close enough to a shearwater for Yyrreen."

"It's a silhouette," he'd said. "Stylized."

"Heavily."

"I wouldn't know. We don't have them by the Amalgam." He'd looked at it for a moment. "Why a shearwater?" Zaya had raised an eyebrow. "I mean, I know it's your name. Why'd you take it?"

"It was Kiriki's idea," Zaya had said. "After Ziyuki joined House Amphisbaena. I was... I don't know how to say it. Not destroyed; we hadn't really liked each other for a long time at that point. But it was one more thing this city had taken from me that I didn't consent to give. Kiriki and I were walking by the cliffs in Ultramarine Precinct, so I could pretend I wasn't in Yemareir, and we saw these petrels with nests on the cliff's edge, diving for fish, and I was feeling however you want to call it, and I just said, 'That bird is us. It makes its home in hard rock over an ocean that'll swallow it the first chance it gets. It sleeps all night soaked in the spray, and it flirts with drowning every time it hunts.' And she told me it was called a shearwater, and that shearwaters are migratory birds, some of them travel over whole oceans to come to these rock nests over the water. And I said fuck it, right? If Ziyuki's new family can name itself after some animal, why can't mine? Birds are closer to dragons than lizards are anyway."

"Naming yourselves after animals," Thelendil had said, shaking his head. "Such a city person thing to do. Out in the real world, you learn that animals are bastards."

Bandit had singed his ear with a lick of flame, and after a string of oaths whose echoes had spooked a flock of starlings into flight, they'd gotten down to flying.

It hadn't been Zaya's first time in Thelendil's head, or even her longest; but if gliding the Craw over the jungle around Cildinior Amalgam was reading a nursery rhyme to a child, drilling Bandit through its paces was teaching an intricate harp solo to a guitarist who only knew three chords. With each quick turn through the course of cedars Yyrreen had built all those years ago, Zaya's mind had bumped up against Thelendil's; and each time, the foreign contours of his consciousness grew more familiar—and more responsive, anticipating the adjustments to the angle of Bandit's tail or the tension in its wings that would go into any given maneuver. Slowly and sweetly, the drills had transformed from a dance frantically choreographed by a Zaya always three beats behind into a partnership, where three minds divided the work fluidly to create flight.

Flying well together wasn't the same as knowing one another; turn of wing wasn't turn of phrase; good timing wasn't a good heart. Zaya knew all that when she invited Thelendil to her room.

But if their minds matched in flight, maybe their bodies would match in bed; and the thirst for her that his mind was too callow to conceal had taken root in hers. She wasn't sure if she shared it, but she wanted to follow where it led.

"I think you should sleep in your own bed tonight," was the first thing she said after. Saying it felt less cruel than not saying it. "You can stay a while if you want, just... don't fall asleep here, all right?"

"Of course," said Thelendil. "Hard warrior-men of the jungle don't snuggle."

"Hard warrior-men of the jungle are more exhausting to talk to than they are to have sex with."

"That's only because I haven't rubbed my special unguent of mandrill sweat and termite-mound dirt on—"

Zaya tweaked a nipple; Thelendil flinched and yipped. "Take a hint, warrior-man." She settled her head back on his shoulder; he kissed her hair, and the queasy feel of regret returned. "Tell me something real."

He dwelt on the question for a long time, enough that she thought she might have to wake him up. "I thought your family would be like one from the Amalgam," he said. "But it's not."

"How's that?"

"Families that start at the same time kind of clump into a bigger family," he said. "Every parent cares for the other kids in the same generation. And childless adults of the parents' generation will join too. Sort of like your family, that's what I was thinking." He drew in a long breath and traced up and down her back with a finger. "But that means that, in the Amalgam, family is about power. You're always thinking about how you're cultivating the people who will hold the future in their hands. Here... family's apart from that."

"Because we don't have any power."

"I know why that's bad," Thelendil said. "It just feels like it might be a relief too. You're Cerminir's refuge from us. Here, family can be that—a refuge from the city. Family can't be a refuge from the Amalgam. I think about that sometimes, how that might make it different to raise a kid. In a good way."

"You got a kid?"

If Thelendil answered, Zaya fell asleep before she heard it. When she woke up, he had gone.

***

CARNELIAN PRECINCT: THE FIRST CORNER.

THE FLOW OF LIGHT and serenity to Thelendil's mind stopped as abruptly as it had begun, ripped away like a loose scarf in the 'stream. It was not the damper that did it; Thelendil's mind, familiar as it was, was the wrong shape, the wrong smell. Those feelings belonged to Kiriki, not Thelendil. But the noisy heat of his fear had ebbed a bit, just in time for her to realize Bandit was about to attempt a corner far too early and far too fast. "Hang on!" Zaya barely had the chance to shout, and they were sideways, staring straight into the huge eyes of a slack-jawed toddler through the window of a shabby twelfth-floor garret as momentum pressed them against Bandit's back in the turn—hurtling straight into the path of the Moultwyrm.

The command to Bandit's muscles would take too long to reach them, so instead of *reaching*, Zaya *shouted* as loudly as she could: "STIFFEN YOUR WINGS!"—along with the image of Bandit colliding with the Moultwyrm. There was a wyrm-scream, a ripple of tension through Bandit's muscles, a rush of air... but there was no impact; only a stomach-turning lurch as Bandit came out of the turn, at about half speed, and the Moultwyrm shot past—and then the elephant-eater Ranger, two Dawns, an Eyrie Shrike, the Gyrdrake...

"Burn!" said Zaya as Bandit struggled to regain speed.

Zaya, Thelendil's voice whispered in her mind, *not yet—*

"Ignore the seasick fool sitting on your spinal ganglion, he's nothing but spoiled meat hallucinating its own sentience, *fucking burn—*"

****

LILAC PRECINCT: THREE DAYS BEFORE THE RACE.

"But why *exactly* eight buckets of Old Cheesefeet's cloudberry moonshine?" Zaya asked.

Enwë popped off Cerminir's breast with a satisfied "ahh," and Cerminir stood, holding the baby's chest against her shoulder and slapping her back while gently bouncing. "It's cheaper than 150-proof spirits," she said. "Especially if you show him your tits."

"No."

Cerminir shrugged. "City men pay money to see them, city women pay money to hide them. I don't understand any of it. Are you afraid he won't ask you to marry him or something?"

"Afraid he *won't* ask?"

"Or whatever?"

"I've never even met Old Cheesefeet."

"He's a confirmed bachelor."

"I don't want to marry him!"

"That's what I'm saying! Who cares if he sees—"

"*Cer.*"

"Have it your way." Enwë let out a glass-rattling belch; Cerminir held her up like a valedictory chalice and made sugary cooing noises, then cast a gimlet glance at her and brought her back to the shoulder. "Didn't get it all."

"The Mule only got booze as a treat. Bandit's good, but it hasn't been that good."

"What Bandit is, is fat," said Cerminir. "Catfish and barley is fine for coasting all day, but it's not racing trim and I can't change it in time. When a wyrm uses its breath weapon, it dumps a load of epinephrine into the blood. A *load* of *epinephrine!*" she said in singsong to Enwë, who had burped again; Cerminir sat, perched the baby on her thigh, let her grab her by the thumbs, and began joggling her up and down. "And *epinephrine* makes it *faster* and *more agile* for a very! Short! Time!" Enwë gurgled and laughed.

Zaya took the kettle off the stove and poured hot water over two cups of mate. "What's the catch?"

"It'll be ridiculously! Exhausted! Afterward!" Cerminir touched her forehead to Enwë's, then drew it back and made a bug-eyed, shocked face; more giggles. "Or at least noticeably sluggish. It'll help get some of that fat off it, though."

"Why didn't we ever do this with the Mule?"

Cerminir made a face; Zaya smelled slightly sour milk in the air. Enwë had spit up all over her front and Cerminir's leg. Zaya brought her a cup of mate and a rag, and Cerminir set to wiping.

"The answer to that is, I hadn't met Old Cheesefeet," she said. "Which is just as well, because we were too broke even for him."

***

DAMASK PRECINCT: RIGHT BEHIND CARNAUG.

A PLUME OF JEWELED flame coruscated in the gathering dusk—Zaya thought she caught a hint of cloudberry in the slipstream—and the wind tore at her face as Bandit surged to overtake.

They had crossed into Damask Precinct, following the glowing blazes on the buildings into a maze of grey tenements with open wounds in the concrete of their exteriors, the balconies decorated in riotous color as if in compensation: murals of wyrms and birds and jungles and veldts and fractals and other eye-catching abstractions, charm-lights twinkling like small varicolored galaxies, bioluminescent plants. Bandit drew up on a knot of wyrms, all darting for position, all failing; the elephant-eater Carnaug was acting like a cork in the twisted bottle of this Damask warren, holding back a half-dozen more maneuverable 'streamers by dint of size alone.

She felt Bandit begin to lunge for the open lane below the pack; without thinking, she grabbed two handfuls of feathers and pulled back to rein it in. To her surprise, it responded quickly and smoothly. *Of course*, she thought, *it's trained to ride with quiet-mind riders; it knows the physical cues. It's not the Mule.* "You can't just grab that lane," she said. She felt a trickle of inquisition coming from Bandit. "Because that's where its claws are," she answered, "and because you don't want to be caught between the cobblestones and a wyrm the size of a bull hippo with a taste for street noodles."

The view of the lane pulsed in Zaya's mind's eye. If this was Bandit's best time—the time its agility and speed were at the highest—the worst thing she could possibly do was waste it cruising behind a knot of wyrms at three-quarters speed. "On three," she said.

Bandit darted down on two.

The elephant-eater Ranger didn't see the drop, or at least Zaya didn't see it cast its eye back, but she saw it get ready; its trajectory grew too steady, as its focus changed from moving unpredictably to occupy the lane, to preparing a drop on Bandit. "It'll have to fold its wings to lose enough altitude fast enough," she said. "Get ready—"

If there was any acknowledgement from Bandit's mind, she didn't hear it. It arrowed on ahead; out of the corner of Thelendil's eye, she vaguely sensed a wyrm dart in to take the same opportunity.

They were under. Zaya looked up because she could not not look up; the sky-blue-bottomed wings folded, the enormous belly swelled in her green-washed field of view; the wyrm behind them—it was the Gyrdrake—surged neck-and-neck with Bandit.

The world spun; a great force wrenched her away from Bandit's back and toward infinity, and she clutched feathers and squeezed knees so it would not take her; images of the Mule and Kiriki leapt up in her mind's eye, bright and sharp as scalpels.

***

LILAC PRECINCT: THREE DAYS BEFORE THE RACE.

"I WISH I COULD help," said Minshoon, his voice not entirely un-slurred by the strong sorghum wine they were sharing from a clay bottle. It was a nice bottle, Zaya observed with what felt like great discernment, pleasingly fat and raked with thin close-together grooves, and reinforced at its fattest point with thick hemp netting.

"You're helping," Zaya said. They were stretched out on the couch, her feet under one of his elbows, legs pressed against one another. "You make the numbers work. You know what the kids need. You're a terrible cook, but I like eating."

"We've never had a cook as good as Kiriki. I still dream about her plantains and rice. My plantains get too soft while the rice is still hard."

"Everything she knew, she learned from Papa Kaalo."

"There's a name I haven't heard in a while." Zaya and Minshoon both took long pulls from their cups; there was a brief silence as they both held in the urge to cough. "He always understood it, you know. The mechanics of it. The mix, like, of the hedging and arbitrage piece with the pure ratfucking trickery of making dumb money dumber."

"He had the killer instinct," Zaya said. "Papa Zinji never had that." Minshoon nodded with the false gravity of a mild buzz. "What he had was a lick of common sense. All the killer instinct in the world couldn't keep Papa Kaalo out of the datura. He was a really smart man, but what he taught me was that self-control beats genius any hour of the day."

"What are your priors on the Stone Forest?" Minshoon asked.

Zaya gave him the half-laugh she usually used for political canvassers and fumbled pickup lines. "Speaking of things I haven't heard in a while. Why do you want to know? I don't even know the competition."

"It's not about you having the right number. It's a sample."

"For a sample to be useful, you need more than one."

Minshoon looked into his cup and shrugged. "It doesn't need to be useful."

"If you start placing bets," Zaya said, "someone's going to hurt you."

"I know."

"Or someone else who sleeps here."

"I *know*. I won't. I'm just curious."

Zaya sighed. "Top half, eight tenths. Top fifth, seven. Place, one. Win... one?"

"Rounding up or down?"

"Up, obviously. What do you think of those chances?"

"You're the 'streamer. My job is to take you at your word."

"Your job? I thought this was just curiosity."

"Old habits." Minshoon's face was inscrutable. "Why so pessimistic on top half?"

"New partner, new wyrm, new competition? Plus the psionic damping. I thought eight tenths was optimistic. Seven tenths on top fifth is really optimistic."

"Fair enough. Why so optimistic?"

"Because I was the best six years ago, and the only thing that could stop me was an ambush from a Vore." She took a drink of wine that wasn't as long as she really wanted it to be. "And because no one who really needs to win can afford to enter."

Minshoon swished some sorghum wine around in his mouth. "Makes sense."

"Satisfied?"

"This is why I like priors. Putting a probability to something can take a conversation to interesting places."

Zaya made a blade out of her toes and poked him in the thigh. "Spoken like a man who wouldn't know a good conversation if it tattooed a double integral on his ass-cheeks."

"We can talk about how Cerminir thinks you're sleeping with Thelendil."

"Bold of you."

"Hmm?"

"To assume that we can talk about it."

"Are you?"

Zaya ran a hand through her hair, almost three inches long. "I've got to get some color in this stuff. People are forgetting who I am."

***

SCARLET PRECINCT: THE BOULEVARD OF DANCERS.

THERE WAS A SMACK of meat on pavement, a bloom of brimstone in the air, wyrm-scream and human-scream commingled—but now Zaya and Thelendil were upright, coursing smoothly, an unbroken wind ripping at their goggles—unbroken and clean, free of the fog of wyrm-breath that Zaya hadn't even noticed until they were shut of it. She added her own whoop of victory to the rush of the slipstream, forced as much of the lightning of her exultation as she could through the damper, felt Bandit's cold, clean triumph as an antiphon—but Thelendil's mind was still throbbing like a wound. She risked a look back at him, fearing to see that he *was* wounded, nicked by a stray claw or bludgeoned by a wing—but any hurts he had sustained could not be seen, at least not with him flattened against Bandit's back like a sloth cub, clinging with both arms and both legs.

Bandit felt Thelendil's fear at the same time, and its wings began to falter before Zaya could whip it back to speed. Frantically she threw the message against the damper: *It's all right, we can't help him by losing this race.*

She could not tell whether Bandit perceived the message, or believed it—but it hauled the air as fiercely as it could.

It wouldn't be enough. There was something growing at the very bottom of Zaya's gut, a seedling of the same vine that had grown inside her during those hell-minutes in Ashen Precinct, when it had become clear that the numbing fog in Kiriki's mind had spread to the Mule's, and the first flare of the Vore had blossomed below. Bandit's surge of speed was ebbing, replaced by a heaviness in its wings, a sluggishness in its mind; its body, trained to coast for hours, was becoming overtaxed by the constant cornering; and it was flagging under Thelendil's fear—and also under his weight. He was slimmer than many of these 'streamers, but also taller, and dense with muscle built by hunt and harvest. They grey tree blazes took them to the Boulevard of Dancers in Scarlet Precinct, a broad, open street flanked by great schematic statues of human figures in stately poses—as crude in outline as one of Eäril's fin-ger-paintings, but bold and true of line enough that, in the periph-ery of one's vision, they did seem to dance. The air glowed with charm-lights and bioluminescent body paint, and thrummed with old Mlin dubstep; there was, as there so often was, a crowd of real dancers here, who gasped and panted as Bandit winged over.

The gasps turned to cheers as the Gyrdrake overtook them.

She knew in an instant that the dam had broken; on this wide street, the elephant-eater Ranger could no longer act as a cork on the course, and swifter wyrms were passing it. She reached out for Kiriki's help—this was her specialty, acting as eyes in the back of Zaya's head so they could fend off would-be overtakers—but Kiriki wasn't there, she'd died six years ago, and Thelendil was flattened against Bandit's back with fear, unreachable as a sobbing child. A Dawn Wyrm shot past, above them; more whoops from the dancers. She *reached* out to Bandit with her ragged mind, but it, too, was roiling too wildly for the damped signal to penetrate; it was exhausted and confused, flying wasn't supposed to be *like* this, this wasn't gliding above a caravan or even one of the mercifully few dogfights it had been in, where you put all your fear and anger into claws and teeth and breath and then you rested, this was just hauling two loud-minded humans at ridiculous and agonizing speeds so they could be in a place they didn't like and wouldn't stay a few seconds before the other humans who also didn't want to be there got there. It was like a game, but without any pleasure, and it felt like *it would never end—*

***

AMETHYST PRECINCT: TWO DAYS BEFORE THE RACE.

"You do it," Jaliki announced with solemn authority, "by rigorous training and practice, so you and the dragon become one." He pronounced the word *rigorous* with careful precision. "So that your mind basically bonds with the dragon and you're like one creature when you're in the air. That's what Kanivain Goanna says."

Thelendil smiled. "Who's Kanivain Goanna?"

"The tied for first best living pilot in Yemareir. She flies an Argent Swordwing in the Air Guard." He shoveled an enormous scoop of lemon cloudberry shaved ice into his mouth. They were, at Jaliki's insistence, in the Sweet Soldier, enjoying the wares and the waste cool from the charms that kept the ice from melting. Zaya had given Jaliki the choice of venue; Thelendil, still jobless and bored, had invited himself, and Jaliki had insisted on Vanako's company, so it was the four of them.

Thelendil's nod clearly said *I don't understand most of these words.* "The Air Guard is a corps of dragon riders the city maintains in case of aerial invasion," said Zaya. "In between, they do exhibitions. The Argent Swordwings have some very beautiful precision formations."

"Ah," said Thelendil. "But, young Jaliki, they're not racers? What I asked was, how do you make a lazy lizard like the average jungle wyrm go *fast*." He shrugged, a bit theatrically. "Maybe the city wyrms are just more industrious? They seem to be zipping around all the time. Jungle wyrms like to find a spot of sunlight and curl up for a while."

Vanako made a disgusted hawking noise over her iced black coffee. "Don't tell him Yemareir's better. Yemareir sucks. The jungle has the right idea."

"I agree with you," said Thelendil, "but I wonder if you'd agree with you after the first time you dug a yam out of the ground with your bare hands. Or the first time you got a fungus on—"

"The answer to your question," said Zaya, "is that you put an image in its mind of how hungry you're both going to be if it loses the race."

"But you're not," said Vanako. "Are you?"

"You tell me," said Zaya. "How much do I owe your boss again?"

As calmly as though she were going to the bathroom, Vanako got up and walked away.

Jaliki exhaled, halfway between a sigh and a shout. "That doesn't help, Mom."

Zaya began composing a defense; but, of course, the child who barely came up to her elbow was right. "I know," said Zaya. "Come on, let's go tell her I'm sorry."

"What?" said Jaliki, muffled through a mouthful of fruit, shaved ice, and grass jelly. "I'm not done eating!"

"I know, my breath, but if I wait she'll get away."

"That's not my fault," said Jaliki, his arms circling protectively around the dish of shaved ice. "I wasn't mean to Vani."

"Just leave him with me," Thelendil said.

Zaya's eyes leapt to the ker, curled up under Jaliki's chair.

"If we're riding together," said Thelendil, "you have to trust me."

Zaya let out a sharp sigh and pulled the pouch out of her shoulder bag. "If it attacks him, you use the fire-charm in there to light the herbs, then you throw the powder at it. Shape an intention in your mind that it falls asleep, then focus on that—don't try to pull it off him, it'll hurt you too if you do." She left him looking, stricken, at Jaliki, who in turn was studiously not acknowledging Thelendil, focused on scraping up every drop of the melting ice.

Outside the shop, she pinged the memories of a few birds and a loitering monkey and followed their memory of a blurry shape with a mess of bright purple hair. Vani was sitting on a stoop in a back alley, curled up tight enough around herself that Zaya almost looked past her. "Vani," she called. "I'm sorry."

Vanako's face was wild with panic and revulsion; unfortunately for her, the alley was a dead end. Zaya walked up to her and sat. Vanako scooted away. "I'm sorry," Zaya repeated. "What I said was cruel. I'm frustrated and scared. I don't want to lose the house, and I don't want to lose you."

"You say all that stuff," Vanako said, "about how House Shearwater doesn't leave anyone behind. So how are you alive when Kiriki is dead?"

How dare you. The speech unfolded effortlessly in Zaya's mind, each cut perfectly placed: *Some street kid I barely know, that I took on as a favor to some ex of Kirono's I didn't even know—how dare you ask me about my wife? How dare you insinuate that I abandoned her when I'm risking it all for your worthless hide? When you had no idea what we were trying to do, trying to build?*

"You're going to have to take my word for the answer," she said instead. "It was a conversation between Kiriki and me. No one else was involved."

"Oh, so I'm the first one who gets to hear the big secret of how you became a widow?"

Zaya looked her levelly in the eye. "No. Everyone who's ever loved Kiriki knows this story, including your seven-year-old brother, plus Taavi and Gilthiniel, a couple of girls in bars, a couple of people I was fucking, a reporter, and a priest." Vanako made a gagging face at *a couple of people I was fucking*, which was satisfying. "It's not a secret, it's just something that hurts too much to tell anyone who might ask me to prove any of it, which I can't. And all it was is this. I made her promise, if something happened in Ashen Precinct and she could get out and I couldn't, that she'd leave me. Because it was a choice between leaving me and leaving everybody else. And she did, but only if I promised the same thing. So I did."

Vanako moistened her lips and stared at the opposite wall, then looked back at Zaya. "What happened?"

"Two of them worked us," said Zaya. "Vores are slow, that's why more people don't die in the Bisai—even the range on their breath weapon isn't great. You just can't let them get close. So one starts coming straight at us down Imshaj Street—it's a big, straight street, we can see it coming, we basically hang the first right we can, because that's going to get us closer to the exit and away from this Vore we can definitely outrun. And before we're done the turn, one comes right up from under us. Hits the Mule right in the guts with its breath weapon, the worst kind of hurt. But it softened the crash as much as it could. I got thrown into the ruin of an old longhouse, Kiriki ended up with a leg stuck under the Mule. She could reach her saddle-knife, but she was stuck under the wyrm, not in the saddle. She couldn't get free."

"Was she at least unconscious?" Vanako asked, when the silence had gotten too long to bear.

"No. She was in incredible pain. I felt it." She didn't try to stop the tears from roughening her voice. "It was hard for me to move, or even see, just from the spillover. But she was conscious. I didn't see her again, actually, or hear her voice." She wiped at the corner of her eye. "It was just the empathic connection. She could feel I wanted to come save her, but she knew she was stuck. She showed me what she was going to do—she was going to distract the Vores, focus their minds on her and the Mule, so I could get out. She showed me a safe route through the street, out of their line of sight. And I said no, and I could feel her smile and say she loved me, and I felt her mind turn away. And I ran, so I could get out of there before they killed her. Because when she died, she wouldn't be able to distract them any more." She let her shoulders down with a juddering sigh. "And that's the story of how I left my wife to die."

"I'm sorry," said Vanako.

"That she died, or that I made it out?"

Vanako made a face as though she'd bitten a moldy lemon. "Come on."

"Be sorry she died," said Zaya. "Kiriki would have been nicer to you than I've been. But don't be sorry for asking. You have the right to know."

Vanako nodded, and it was all Zaya could do not to press the advantage: *Just like I have the right to know why you were selling. When you had everything you needed. We have the right to understand our family. Both of us.* But the ghost of a voice reached forward to say *the family* we *built,* gently chiding, and Zaya leaned forward and rested her head on her forearms and let a few caught sobs dissolve in her throat, Vanako's hand eventually coming to stroke her upper back lightly and awkwardly with her fingertips, like a blind girl learning to read.

***

SCARLET PRECINCT: ENTERING THE STONE FOREST.

THREE MORE WYRMS SHOT by them on the Boulevard of Dancers, the Prismatic Wyvern and two sleek Dawns with hypertrophy in the chest and shoulders that made them look like overbred chickens. Bandit had tried gamely to foul them, but the street was too broad and Zaya's attention too divided; she'd never realized how strongly her style had relied on Kiriki's eyes behind them.

Then it was back to back streets, where Bandit could more easily control the course. They came up behind one of the Dawns, whose rider was even more awkward on the constant cornering than Zaya was with her empathy gone—but what it lacked in agility it made up for in the ferocity of its spiked tail, which lashed until Zaya was tempted to make Bandit bite it. Eventually it pulled ahead, and Zaya told Bandit to save its strength. Thelendil had faded to a buzz of sick anxiety in the bay of her mind; the best use of her mental effort, it seemed, was to keep him out of Bandit's skull.

The smell of the air began to change; Dry, chalky, with a metallic tang at the back of her nostrils. Bandit's Breath cornered once, twice, then wheeled over an avenue and through two marble posts carved in the shapes of tree trunks and into the Stone Forest. Belatedly, Zaya tied a bandanna over her nose and mouth; she shouted for Thelendil to do the same, hoping he would hear or see her and follow suit. She reached to Bandit, tugging at the muscles in its chest to reinforce the tug on its shoulder-feathers it should know as the signal for *ascend*. She dragged a finger over her forearm; fine dust was already beginning to collect there. She ran a palm over a patch of Bandit's feathers, and it came away nearly clean. So far, so good.

The challenges of the Stone Forest Slalom were three. First was the stone dust, which fouled not only lungs and eyes but feathers, weighing them down and allowing them to drift slowly out of alignment, which conspired to make the wyrm work harder for the same speed. Kirono's wax had been designed to repel it—and seemed, at least so far, to be working.

Second was the stone leaves, which grew and fell from the branches of these trees just as they might from the trees of any other forest—but they were still stone for all that, as heavy and hard-edged as any flake of flint. These were more a danger to the 'streamer than the wyrm, and a helmet and a good leather jacket would provide all the protection that could reasonably be had—but a stray leaf could still half-blind an unlucky wyrm, or nick a streamer's throat.

Third—

A flicker of movement caught Bandit's eye from the branches of the first tree they would have to swing around; Zaya, her eyes on the course, only noticed it through the wyrm's eyes. She sent back a flood of alarm, which she knew would penetrate Bandit's mind only in a trickle, and pulled up on its shoulder-feathers to ascend more. It did; even so, she felt the blaze of impact in its flank. She thought it was a glancing blow, but with the fuzziness of the empathy damper blurring Bandit's mind it was hard to be sure.

Some centuries-dead zoologist had dubbed the Stone Forest's inhabitants "litho-orangutans," but they were not apes or even mammals. They were long-armed brachiators, that was true enough, but they were carapaced, ciliated rather than hairy, with at least three different specialized types of eye and internal organs whose operations were paradoxical and occult. They were attracted to the liminal energy of the living stone, and ate the fruits, seeds, and leaves of the stone trees, though not their bark or wood; and they were no fonder of intruders than any other ape. The third hazard of the Stone Forest was the deadly and accurate throwing arms of the lithorangs, and there were two ways to approach it:

1. Keep a safe distance, flying far below the canopy, relying on distance as protection from thrown objects. This was widely acknowledged among 'streamers to be the superior approach to the Stone Forest Slalom—in fact, no one had ever won the course any other way.

2. Charge through the canopy like a spooked boar hog, getting right in the faces of swarm after swarm of furious lithorangs, dodging the graceful boughs of the stone trees for dear life, and setting oneself up for a horrible death by some combination of choking on stone-dust and massive laceration as one's passing dislodged and pulverized enormous quantities of leaves. The main advantage of this approach was creating a wake of falling leaves and pissed-off lithorangs that might have the potential to hurt your immediate followers a quarter to a third as much as it hurt you—which, compounded by the element of surprise, might be enough to retain an any edge you were about to lose to an overtaking wyrm who was better in a slalom than you were.

Every other time Zaya had flown the Stone Forest Slalom, she'd taken the first approach. She knew about how much ground she'd gain with it. It would be a lot.

It wouldn't be enough.

By the time Thelendil had raised his head to say "No no no no no *no NO*—" it was far too late for his thread of white-hot terror to slow Bandit down. He shouted in mingled disgust and pain as a stone turd hit him square in the shoulder—"Get down!" Zaya shrieked, and she felt him shift his weight and hoped he had—and they hit the first tree's canopy like a plate glass window, in an explosion of stone shards, noise, and pain.

✷✷✷

LILAC PRECINCT: SIX DAYS BEFORE THE RACE.

MINSHOON, CERMINIR, KIRONO, AND Thelendil were all waiting when Zaya got back from Candlegrass Stand. They all turned expectant eyes to her, but the smiles and quiet cheers they offered when she gave the thumbs up felt hollow after what she had done and nearly done and learned. So she told them about the near miss with the informant, and the entry fee, and the damper, and that did cast a somber mood over the room—except for Thelendil, who didn't know any better and was clearly a few spliffs farther along than anyone else. "That's amazing," he said when she was done. "They have a whole group of people that this city pays to make sure no one races dragons, and a whole *other* group of people who want to make sure that people like *you* in *particular* don't race dragons, and you're still going out and getting in a dragon-race. It's amazing. You're amazing."

"I can move money around for the entry fee," Minshoon said. "We shouldn't have a problem getting in, this time."

"I can do something about the damper," Kirono said.

"No," said Zaya.

"Zaya," said Minshoon, "you know it's bullshit. Standards has never liked Kayalim teams, it's done things to put you at a disadvantage before. And this is more blatant than any of that."

"I've always gone through appeals and abided by the rulings," said Zaya.

Cerminir chortled. "If by 'abide,' you mean 'show you can win anyway by doing things they didn't have the foresight to call cheating.'"

"That's what the word means," said Zaya.

"This isn't even the questionable courtesy of just letting people buy an advantage by spending money they can't afford," Minshoon said, "it goes directly at Kayalim practice and tradition—"

"Minshoon," said Zaya, "I love you. I know."

"Can you win without it, though?" said Kirono. "Bandit's a new wyrm, it's never raced."

"Bandit's been trained to respond to pressure signals, and it's not used to having empathy as a crutch," she said. "I'm more likely to win on Bandit than I would be on the Mule."

"It's not a *crutch*," said Minshoon. "It's how you race. How can they take that from you? How can you *let*—" He stopped short, there, unprompted, and sat back, flushed with anger and more than a little embarrassment.

"If Standards finds out I've been cheating—" she saw Minshoon's lips whiten and press together at the word 'cheating'—"we're on the hook for all winnings, including gambling winnings, from the point at which the cheating started. And they won't be as understanding as Vani's little dealer. I'd rather run the risk of losing."

"I can make it undetectable," said Kirono. "Smaller than a sunflower seed. You could mount it in a genital piercing." Stares turned on him; he blushed. "So they wouldn't find it."

Zaya stood up. "I'm a 'streamer,'" she said, "again, for good or ill. I've never cheated—by Standards' definition—and I'm not starting now. Anyone can cheat their way to the finish line."

The silence in the common room was neither content nor agreeable.

"Good night," Zaya said. "Keep the ideas coming. I love you."

"We loooooove you too," said Thelendil, letting the cloud of fragrant smoke he'd been holding pour like white water from his mouth.

Zaya got all the way to bed before she began to weep.

***

SCARLET PRECINCT: THE STONE FOREST, STILL.

STONE FLEW BY IN all forms: Lumps and clots that flew dangerously close to Zaya's head, massive lengths that Bandit frantically dodged, shards that seemed to fill every particle of air, raining angry edges down on her leather jacket and pants and occasionally slicing the back of her neck or hands. She'd never heard the high furious keening of the lithorangs up close, nor seen their myriad eyes; it wasn't an experience she could say she'd missed. Thelendil's fear still nagged and itched like a day-old sunburn.

Then they were through to open air. Zaya swung Bandit to the left—they would need to be on the left—and risked a look behind and down. There were wyrms swinging wide of the trunk, wyrms who'd skirled off the course. She couldn't count them, but she saw the plumage of at least one Dawn Wyrm and a gyrdrake, and her heart rose in her chest. Then they hit the foliage again.

A cluster of impacts from all directions hit Bandit all at once, and a clump of something pounded Zaya in the ribs, lodging between her and Bandit. She felt its shoulder blades pull apart and its ribs swell, then contract; the heat and stench of wyrmfire washed over her, though she couldn't see what Bandit had attacked. She idly wondered what it was like to be hit by ragged-edged leaves of superheated stone, and decided she was better off not knowing. She *pushed* herself as best she could into Bandit's visual system, then cast its attention forward. Monsoon and the Moultwyrm were still in the lead; there was another Dawn about two trees ahead.

They were making good time, she realized, better than they had a right to. Bandit wasn't used to sprints or high-agility maneuvers, but it was used to being tired. It didn't coast on thermals of convenience; it didn't stop to nap when it was tired; it kept the same hours as the caravan, whatever they were. It wasn't as *good* as the Mule, and might never be, but it drew from a well of discipline, a tolerance for pain and grinding work, that the Mule, in its free life over the bay, had never had to cultivate.

They broke free of the third tree; Zaya swiftly tipped her goggles open to let a trickle of salt water dissolve into the slipstream. A faint hum of questioning sang through the slim thread of their connection.

"It's no way for a wyrm to be raised," said Zaya. "You deserved better."

Counterfactuals weren't something dragons dwelt on; a sort of mental shrug and the warmth of confused appreciation were the best she could expect. But she got them.

On the fourth tree, or perhaps the fifth, a stray leaf seared edge-on across Zaya's forehead, turning her world into white pain for a handful of seconds so intense that the question of whether she had blacked out was academic. The constant cascades of falling stone seemed to be effective at keeping the rest of the pack back; but, of course, it did nothing to slow Monsoon and the Moultwyrm, who maintained a healthy three-tree lead. She was not hit by too much thrown stone, but enough that she had lost count; her shoulders, thighs, and head were all aching, and a warm weight on her left thigh was definitely, for sure, going to be scat.

Then the lithorang boarded Bandit.

She felt it land, between her and Thelendil; they broke free of the tree, whichever one it was, and the peon on the ground checking that all 'streamers were in technical compliance with the slalom said "Holy shit." Zaya *reached* frantically in the wild hope that the lithorang might somehow be exempt from the damper field; her debilitated mind fetched up against its alien mentality like a wet rag on a stone wall.

They exploded into the foliage of another tree, stone leaves shattering against the lithorang's carapace with a series of staccato reports like fireworks. Zaya wiped blood off her forehead and steered Bandit a little too close to a thick bough to try to shear it off—but Bandit didn't understand the objective, left itself too wide a margin, and it didn't matter much anyway; the thing could see in all directions with its eye-ringed head, and it flattened itself against Bandit's back to dodge the impact.

The saving grace of the situation, for a few seconds, was that the creature seemed to realize the gravity of its peril: It was now aboard a large, dangerous animal moving at extreme speeds at an altitude not conducive to walking away from falls. Which, were Zaya in its place, she thought would have an easy remedy: Simply swing right back off on the next available tree, make peace with the family of lithorangs that lived there long enough to get down from it and back to its own tree, where it could die in peace, perhaps telling its many-eyed children and grandchildren the story of How The Lithorang Rode the Dragon And, Guess What, That Lithorang Was Me around a stony little campfire or the lithorang equivalent.

But they had broken free of the big trees now—all that remained was to pelt to the finish through, or over, a group of sparsely scattered saplings.

The Moultwyrm was less than a length behind Monsoon, harrying it with feints to pull ahead; Monsoon was lashing out half-randomly with its spike-adorned tail, closing lanes out more or less at random. It was slowing them both down—and Zaya could not help, in the split second it took her to apprehend all this, thinking of how easy it would have been to dodge around that sad random flailing on the Mule with psionics undamped; it could dart to the opposite side of a tail-strike as quickly as Zaya could think to do it.

She felt the lithorang's weight settle on Bandit's back, felt (through Bandit) its talons grip feathers. It was getting ready to leap. She battered again at its mind, hoping to stall it, but it was like looking for a door in a boulder.

"Turn around before I fuck your shit up, you bubblebath city slicker of an excuse for an ape!"

The lithorang's weight shifted, its claws gripped and moved and gripped again; Thelendil's ringing threat had landed—and, blessedly, the stone-shitting monster from the dimension next door was not the only creature whose attention he had captured; Shanhoon and the Moultwyrm's rider both whipped their heads around. That divided focus flowed through their bodies to the wyrms, visible in real time; they began, for just a moment, to coast. The gap between Bandit and the two wyrms in the lead began to close. The crowds at the finish line began to whoop and chatter; Zaya's blood sang at hearing it, and Bandit's blood sang just a few notes in response, and the gap closed another length. The bickering between Monsoon and the Moultwyrm grew more desperate, blocks and lunges slowing them yet further.

"One more burn, my heart," said Zaya, "and then—" and she made an image in her mind as bright and fine-lined as she could.

Bandit tilted its neck up to light the night with yellow and cerulean. Monsoon and the Moultwyrm's shadows leapt to the ground, still coursing and squabbling over the lane to the finish.

Four great beats of Bandit's wings took it over the two lead wyrms; Zaya could not see its snout, but imagined it craning gracefully out, nosing just inches ahead of Monsoon and the Moultwyrm.

"Hold tight!" Zaya shouted with voice and mind at one, and she hauled on Bandit as hard as she could, and it followed her hands, turning gracefully through an entire barrel roll.

A voice shouted, a wyrm screamed, Bandit surged; the litho-rang, at least, had fallen away. The roll had jangled Zaya's mind, and blood had smeared her goggles; she wiped frantically; she felt snarling, lashing, a thread of bright pain; the crowd roared; Bandit broke off from the other wyrm, and Zaya heard the crowd gasp, watched them swarm away from the Dawn's path like frightened birds; and the announcer, charm-amplified, intoned:

"Zaya Shearwater, gentlewights, returned after six years to the sport that widowed her, has taken a new co-pilot from Cildinior Amalgam and a new Dawn Wyrm by the name of Bandit's Breath to an astounding second-place finish behind Lerikaan Boomslang and Time's Warped Arrow—"

***

SCARLET PRECINCT: THE FINISH LINE.

Zaya should, perhaps, have known she would be mobbed, but she was not prepared for it. The crowd that had scattered now surged back in, eager hands and concerned words washing over her still-jangled mind and pulling her to her feet. She pushed her goggles up, then winced as the glass dug into the leaf-slash on her forehead. Someone pressed a damp cloth into her hand, which she pressed into the wound, only belatedly wondering where it might have been or what it might be damp with. She realized she had not laid eyes on Thelendil since she'd dismounted, and rose on her tiptoes and craned her neck to look, then reeled and dropped back down before she fell. "My co-pilot," she said to a young Mrineen man with bright magenta hair. "Is he all right?" The young man had to lean down to hear her, then craned his neck to look, then looked back at Zaya and shrugged.

Zaya turned and prepared to push her way through the crowd, but they parted for her. She laid a hand on Bandit's flank, realized it was panting, and removed the damper, whose intricate knot work design now held all the allure of a three-day-old fish head—but the field was still strong even with it in her hand, the incoming signals from Bandit and Thelendil still vague and weak.

Thelendil was sitting in a squat, leaning on Bandit, ashy and panting. When Zaya put a hand on his shoulder, he brushed it off. "Are you all right?" she asked.

"I don't want to talk about it."

"Are you hurt." Her frustration flattened out the question.

Thelendil shook his head. "Not hurt. Just useless."

She knelt and put a hand on his shoulder. He looked into her eyes, his own face softening, and put his hand over hers; she tried not to roll her eyes. "Don't pout in front of the audience. This stuff can get into magazines, papers."

"What do I care?"

"You're not the only person on this team."

Zaya felt a crash from behind; skinny arms cinched her waist and squeezed. She heard barking over the chatter of the crowd. "I saw you come from behind," Jaliki said, loud enough to cut through the noise, "with that thing on Bandit's back, and then you did the barrel roll and it fell right onto that one guy on the black dragon and you were so close, Mom, you were right behind that Moultwyrm, I couldn't even tell if you were first or second, that was *so cool*—"

"It's nice to see you too, my heart," she murmured, twisting around to bury her nose in Jaliki's tight curls and breathe in, searching for the baby-scent that hadn't been there for five years.

"What's wrong with Thelendil?"

Thelendil was scrambling to stand, although his face was still grey and gleaming. "Nothing serious, son. I just bit off a little more than I could chew."

"Who brought you here?" Zaya asked Jaliki.

"Everyone," said Jaliki. "Except Minshoon, he's home with Eäril and Enwë."

"Vani and the twins?"

"Yeah."

"Who's with Vani?"

"You are, *Mom,*" came the surly voice from behind Jaliki. "Thanks for screwing up my bet."

"You were *gambling*?" Zaya asked.

"Minshoon gave everyone two sherds to bet," Jaliki said. "I put all mine on you in first." He trust his chin out at Vanako when he said it, squeezing Zaya around the lower ribs. "Vani put hers all on you in the bottom half."

"The odds were SO GOOD," Vanako said. "I would have won like six plates."

"Good payouts equals terrible odds, genius," Gilthiniel's voice came from behind them. "Which is why I spent mine on a coconut full of some incredibly delicious liquid." He waved a half-coconut above his head. "It was so good I saved half for you."

"Half the coconut?" Taavi clarified. "Zero percent of the liquid? Gil can now embalm things by breathing on them?"

"Taavi's just in a bad mood because she said that before and I breathed down her—"

"Mom?" Taavi said.

Zaya was looking, as best she could, over the crowd, at a teak-brown fade and a pair of cheekbones she knew through hands and mouth: Kemreen, in plainclothes, craning (much more effectively) to see. Their eyes met, then glanced past, like marbles; the *clack* was almost audible. "We should get going," Zaya said.

"Mom!" said Jaliki. "You have to at least stay to get your pin."

"I have a box of second-place pins in a closet somewhere," said Zaya. "But only because the pawnshops wouldn't even take them for free."

Jaliki's embrace relaxed; she could practically feel his face fall. What she could feel was the ker, making circles around their ankles and occasionally leaping up a bit to half-stand against Jaliki, for all the world like a normal dog. She disengaged her son's arms, then knelt to look him in the eye—or try; he turned his head to look at some particular knee within the sea of knees. "Hey, Jali. You're right. I'm sorry. I said that because I'm feeling a way. I didn't want to hurt your feelings, I wasn't thinking."

"It's fine."

"No. Your pride in me is a gift. Let me talk to Vani and maybe we can stay for the pin."

Vanako's head whipped around at the sound of her name. "What?"

Zaya stood and motioned her over. "Did you see any police here?" she said in Vanako's ear, low enough to be swallowed by the crowd.

"Why are you asking me?"

"Because I don't know where Kirono is, Gil's drunker than he thinks, and Taavi is a very smart girl who's spent most of her life reading books in precincts I chose specifically so she wouldn't have to develop a knack for keeping track of cops."

"I mean, so's Gil."

"Gil's a boy, don't be a shit."

Vanako shook her head. "I didn't mean—"

"Great. Sorry I misunderstood. Cops, though."

"No. I mean, I wasn't looking out, but no."

"OK. Next thing. Thelendil needs to get home. I was going to have him take Bandit back to the stable with me, but obviously he can't. Can you?"

Vanako blinked. "Sure."

"Thank you. Now where are the other fucking grown-ups?"

***

SCARLET PRECINCT: THE WINNERS' PODIUM.

THEY FOUND CERMINIR THROWING elbows at journalists and scruffy scions of House Boomslang to pester Lerikaan about quiddities of the Moultwyrm's diet ("She probably lost two minutes on that course to all the *kelp* she feeds it") and passed Kirono on the way to the podium, deep in conversation with a dapper young man about something that might have been a fine point of thaumaturgic control theory or the opening steps of a nerd mating dance, it was hard to tell. Thelendil tried to beg off going to the podium, but Zaya tugged his hand with a look that would not hear no. "Kiriki always went with me," she said, knowing it would be misconstrued, knowing that it would bring him false hope for something between them, because he deserved to have this memory of being recognized for this thing, even if she was not telling the truth entire when she said "You earned it."

She looked for Kemreen in the crowd but did not find her. She was not sure whether to be nervous about it. When she took Thelendil's hand to raise it together with her own when the names were called, he squeezed hers and, not thinking, she squeezed back, because it was what she and Kiriki had always done. Shan-hoon Krait did not look at, still less speak to, either of them on the way to or back from the podium, but when his name was called, he raised both hands in an odd configuration—palms out, thumb and little finger spread, middle three fingers pressed tight together—to a wall of cheers and catcalls.

There were winnings. Zaya hadn't expected that. The 'stream had run on too little, six years ago, to give much more than tokens, and those only to the first-place winner; the money was in gambling. But the twelve plates they gave her was more than she and Kiriki had earned six years before for winning the race outright—more than enough to cover the exorbitant entry fee, Bandit's room and board, and her round in the pub after. It was a life-changing amount, for her old life, and for a moment she wondered why the races weren't flooded with poor Kayalim kids with nothing but a wild Dawn and a dream. She looked at the small sack of cash and shook her head. Thelendil, less bound up in his own misery than he had been, made an inquisitive noise.

"In five years working two jobs and eating nothing but beans and rice, I couldn't have saved up the entry fee for this race," she said.

Thelendil nodded. "I'll just nod sagely as if my tiny savage brain is capable of understanding your big-city finance."

"Money wasn't, like, my idea, you know."

"Too bad, money seems very cool and not at all like a literal promise to bad actors that you society will make it as easy as it possibly can for them to consolidate power and exploit everyone."

"Dammit, Thelendil," she said, and beamed to the crowd as widely as she could.

CHAPTER 14

SEXUALITY. *A* LOT OF *you foreigners are super uptight (Shenireen. —Ed.) that is, hail from societies where sexuality is a delicate topic, so I'll be euphemistic (Shenireen. —Ed.) mindful and brief here.*

One big mistake foreigners make while trying to get laid in Yemareir is getting their hopes up about anatomy based on how a person talks and dresses. I could tell you that all you need to do is be forthright about your preferences and you'll be fine, but that would be a lie; being hung up enough about this to ask is social suicide and will usually earn you the derision of your would-be partner. I'm not saying it's right—and nothing's universal, some people are nice about it! But know the risks.

The other big mistake is observing that Yemari folks are very casual about sex and gender and then inferring that all is permitted. It is not; be respectful, don't take liberties. You might get some "cute" mileage from being a foreigner, but probably not enough to close the deal.

Learning this stuff, which applies mostly but not exclusively to the Mrineen of Yemareir, sometimes leads foreigners to seek out Ililuë or Kayalim partners instead, on the assumption that their sexualities and romantic conventions are "simpler" or "more familiar." This is a mistake.

SEE ALSO: Beaches; Law Enforcement; Substance Use, Recreational. (See? I'm not trying to say you can't have fun.)

—From "A Visitor's Handbook for Yemareir," by Shenireen Agama

***

THELENDIL TOSSED HIS GOGGLES to Vanako, Cerminir and Kirono took him home with the children, and Zaya and Vanako mounted Bandit in near silence for the flight to Saavero's stable.

On the flight itself there was no hope of talking, which was a blessing; the crowds at the finish line had worn Zaya out, and the roar of cool high air and the slow shifts of Bandit's muscles were the perfect antidote. Even its soreness was a benison; she could feel it in detail now, as feelings in a body (though not hers) rather than a distant, muffled signal blaring from somewhere outside her head. She caught a glassy ripple from Bandit's mind, as much like a chuckle as its mentality could create. "What?"

The other one is looking around. It shared an image of a purely mental, only partly comprehensible sensation: An exogenous mind, rummaging haltingly in Bandit's perceptions.

"Huh," said Zaya. "I didn't know she could do that."

They are part of your clutch, said Bandit. *I assumed any child of yours could do it.*

"We're born very stupid," said Zaya. "And stay that way unless we study. She must have studied it."

She studied, but you didn't teach?

"Humans are weird, friendo." Gently, Zaya *reached* out to Vanako. "Want to drive?"

Vanako's mind lurched with shock. Zaya felt her weight shift on Bandit's back, and *reached* out to tighten Vanako's grip on Bandit's feathers, her legs around its flanks.

MOM! Vanako's whine was no less grating in Zaya's mind than it was on her ears; at least the shock was gratifying.

"It's all right," Zaya said, "Thelendil was scared to take control too."

Wounded pride flared; Zaya laughed.

You did that and you thought it would work and you were right and I don't understand why, Bandit said.

"Kind of a social mammal thing, I think," said Zaya. To Vanako, she said, "Just concentrate on some of the natural variation, how it tracks what Bandit does. Then just... push in and tweak it a little."

Almost immediately, Bandit lost tension in its right wing; they keeled and dropped like a stone.

If Zaya hadn't been prepared for something like this, they might have been paste on the streets; but she was, and Bandit almost immediately resumed its glide. Vanako didn't say anything... but she couldn't hide her panic, her embarrassment, or her relief. It was amazing how much that set Zaya at ease. "It's all right," she said. "Thelendil did the same thing. So did I when Papa Zinji taught me. It's different from making a little thread snake dance for you—that's what they tried to teach me to do in Kayalim school. Anything you do wrong with a dragon is going to scare you really badly, because you could fall out of the air and die. That's the hard part. The easy part is, your thread snake doesn't want to dance, but your dragon wants to fly. So you watch more and you do less. And if you're out of your depth, you don't bear down, you let go. Understand?"

Vanako didn't say she understood, but didn't hide it either.

"One of the dumbest tests I ever took," Zaya said, "was in the Pearl Precinct Kayalim school—don't ask how we were ever living there, I don't remember. After I'd been for a couple of weeks, they put a dead snake in front of us, stuck with a bunch of needles. Only it wasn't dead, they'd just anesthetized it. The test was, they'd shout the name of the muscle and some amount of tension, and you had to reach in and tighten *that* muscle *that* amount as fast as you could, and the needles would report how close you got. There were kids in that room who were absolutely unbelievable at it. As fast and precise as you could possibly imagine. It was something their parents would brag about. Papa Zinji didn't get it at all. He'd just say 'Oh, we just taught ours to use wild Dawn Wyrms to knock over liquor stores!' And laugh as if he was kidding."

Cool story, Mom.

"You're the worst daughter," Zaya said. "In the city, I mean."

No, it was cool! It was inspirational, it was relatable, it had a point. Four out of five stars.

"Do mom stories ever get better than four out of five stars?"

I thought the whole point of this story was how we shouldn't get upset about numbers someone pulled out of their ass to measure your performance.

Zaya laughed. "On the one hand, touché, but on the other, no, this is not a story about how you don't have to do well in school."

Mommmmmm.

"What I didn't tell you is how I studied my ass off and beat all of those kids at their dumb, pointless game."

No way.

"Yeah, no," Zaya said. "If I'd done that well at Kayalim school I'd be a priest or a foreman or a newspaper editor or something. I studied my ass off, screwed up the first five calls, then spent the rest of the exam getting my snake to coil up into the shape of a cock and balls. Which it did not do. Never went back. And that's why

I make my living as a long-haul wyrm rider with a side of illegal theft, racing, and gambling."

Vanako's mind was silent for a moment.

Don't talk about it like that.

"That's how it should be talked about," Zaya said. "That's what it is. You don't want this life, my heart. It's not a good one."

No.

Zaya wanted to say more, to grind it in, to force Vanako to understand. But six years raising children had trained her out of that sort of thing. She let Vanako have the last word. When they landed at the stable, Vanako guided Bandit down, and Zaya, mind hovering tautly a hairsbreadth from taking control the entire time, didn't have to help at all.

***

A SECOND BODY AT the stable made things faster—there was fresh and dried fish to haul for feeding, water to pump and oil to pour for grooming, great rough blankets the size of tarps for the rubdown; and it was pleasant, though not necessary, to have a companion for the final ritual before sleep which Zaya and Kiriki had developed with Cerminir for the Mule. "The clearer the wyrm's physical memory of the parts of the race where it did badly," said Zaya, "the better its body will adapt to compensate," and Vanako, for once, just listened.

The ritual itself was a mess. It had never gone well when Zaya had done it on her own—mostly in the run-up to the Bisai, when Kiriki, huge with an almost-born Jaliki, had not had the strength for another few hours of waking after a hard race—and although Vanako's company was welcome, it was in some ways worse than solitude. Vanako wasn't any better at focusing on a boring task than any other kid her age; her mind flitted away from the race to recent memories in the stable, her observations of the other Wyrms, the score-setting and coup-counting of the school and the precinct. And, of course, her presence made the absence of Kiriki ache and gape and echo. Something about that absence made the pain of the ritual harder to endure, as though the meticulous rehearsal of her own fear and disappointment during the race, and the reinstatement of Bandit's pain and exhaustion, would break something open inside her.

All that was surely perceptible to Vanako, who acted largely as a passive amplifier and filter since she hadn't been in the race, and perhaps to Bandit... but Zaya was too wrung out to care. When she ended the ritual, she was sobbing. Bandit, presumably, did not understand the significance of this mammalian social display, and Vanako pretended not to notice, which might have been the best thing she could have done.

They left Saavero's with Zaya mired in fatigue and old sorrow; which is perhaps why it was Vanako who noticed the figure leaning on the hulk of an old factory as they walked toward Lilac Precinct in search of bikes. "Mom, do you know that person?"

"Who?"

But by then Kemreen Gharial had fallen into step beside Zaya.

***

KEMREEN WALKED WITH THE ferocious intensity of a cop pretending to be relaxed; her enthusiasm was unsettling. "Hi, Zaya, what fun to see you all the way out here! Who's your friend?"

"Hi, Kemreen!" Zaya said, with what she hoped was the same plainly fake good cheer. "This is actually my daughter, Vanako, who I've trained from an early age not to lie to cops about things they almost certainly already know! What brings *you* all the way to Rust Precinct? What with your beat being in Azure and all?"

"Oh," said Kemreen, "I'm off duty. But I have a couple of friends from the force that I heard were going to come hang out out here after some big race or something, I think because they thought they might get a chance to talk to the winner or something—and, hey, look, it's them right up there!" She stepped in front of Zaya to wave to two wide Mrineen men who had just materialized from behind a ten-foot pile of trash at the mouth of an alley. As she made the move, her left hand, blocked from their view by her body, reached out to squeeze Zaya's right, light and swift and warm and dry and very, very hard. "Hi there! I know you guys—Yyvvoun, right, and Kanjoon? From the Heliotrope Precinct force? I'm Kemreen Gharial, I work Azure and Cadet out west. What brings two upstanding officers of the law out here on a night like this?"

"Good evening, Officer Gharial," said Yyvvoun, or at any rate the one on the left. "We might ask the same of you."

"Well, then," said Kemreen, "I suppose forthrightness is in short supply all over tonight." She grinned like a panting dog; Zaya thought her tongue might roll out past the end of her chin. "Nice to see you."

She began walking past them—Zaya was still too stunned and scared to move—but Kanjoon, or at any rate the one on the right, showed her his palm in a way that said *stop*. "We were hoping for a word in private with Shearwater-*cha*."

"Finders, keepers." Kemreen reached for Zaya's hand in plain sight this time, then alit on her wrist and grasped it like a shackle. "Whatsername-*cha* will be free another night."

"You don't know who that is?" said Yyvvoun. "There was a raid in your district—everybody says there's a wyrm-stable near here—"

"I don't know about any of that," said Kanjoon. *He doesn't want to arrest me,* Zaya realized, with a heavy chill like a lump of dirty ice in her gut. *If there's a charge, he'll have to bring me in, and he doesn't want that.* "Officer Gharial," Kanjoon continued, "it just happens you've struck up an association with a person with whom Yyvvoun and I very much need to have an informal conversation. I know how hard it is to let go of what's surely shaping up to be a delightful evening... but you can hear the call of duty ringing here, can't you? Help us a little and I can't imagine word of your selfless sacrifice could fail to reach... Sergeant Zalsheen, if I'm not mistaken?"

"I'm more imaginative than you," said Kemreen. "Actually, I'm just drunk enough to imagine I could take the two of you, especially with backup... but it's probably better for all of us if you just say your private 'word' in public and let the grownups go about their business."

If Kemreen shared any of Zaya's terror at the two officers towering over them, none of it showed in the curve of her back, the set of her shoulders. Zaya was pretty sure she was flexing her biceps for effect.

Stop thirsting, Mom, Vanako's voice stage-whispered in Zaya's mind. *This is serious.*

One more word and it's the explosive shits for you, young lady.

You can't do that.

Don't bet your pants on it.

Kanjoon's face had grown red and ugly, but Yyvvoun clapped him on the arm and made a noise of reassurance. "You know what, Officer? I think Shearwater-*cha*'s got the message. I mean, to run into us in Rust Precinct on some future race night? That's a co-incidence, things like that happen all the time. But to run into us *and* Officer Gharial again? That would surpass coincidence. I think Sergeant Zalsheen would agree."

"Sorry," said Zaya. "I think we skipped the part where you actually deliver the message."

"Just rehearsing the legalities of certain actions," said Kanjoon. "Stealing wyrms, racing them in the street. Assaulting respectable members of society in the process."

"Are we talking about the respectable members of society who took third place in that same illegal race?"

"If we protected only perfect people, Shearwater-*cha*, we'd have a much easier job."

"Ggggaaaahhhhhh!" said Vanako, and Zaya whipped her head around to see if she was having a stroke. "Is there a competition on for the worst person in Yemareir, or is it just like a point of pride with you?"

Before she'd fully realized why, Zaya had *reached* for two night-jars and the Bedecked Merlin Wyrm that had been stalking them for dinner—a fine-boned thing no bigger than an underfed tomcat, whose patches of rich red, green, and blue were washed grey by the moonlight. By the time their eyes were trained on Yyvvoun, he was already backing away from a sobbing, spitting Vanako, rolling on the street with her arms wrapped tight around her left leg; the officer had closed the distance between them in a smooth instant, lashing her shin with a steel-toed boot. Kemreen's knife, as long as

Zaya's forearm, was out. It had Yyvvoun's attention, but he didn't seem afraid.

Nor should he have been. Oh, if Zaya had had the mind of a full-sized wyrm to seize, neither of these men would be more than cremains and a few long bones sucked hollow... but a Merlin and two nightjars wouldn't save them. Kemreen knew that as well as Zaya, or she would have made a move already. "She'll recover," Yyvvoun said to Kemreen's knife. "Maybe with a more civil tongue for the law. I don't think you're ready to take it as far as *that*—" he nodded at the knife—"for this."

"You assaulted a child," said Kemreen.

"That's no child, I don't know what you're talking about, and I don't care. I was beat worse than that for singing too loud on Carnival night. That's not assault; that's barely discipline."

Zaya let the Merlin hiss a long, hostile territory-claim call at Yyvvoun, whose disgust seemed to go over and above the initial shock of a Merlin taking a particular interest in him. *Kayalim psionics*, she imagined him saying through the sneer, as if he were saying *piss-drinking* or *mopping up after a bar of puking drunks*—but, if he was thinking it, he kept it to himself. "I don't imagine I need to worry any more about that trash parrot than I do about my colleague's sidearm."

"That depends on whether you think you'll ever get a date again with your nose bitten half off." Zaya kept the Merlin's eyes trained on Yyvvoun while she walked over to kneel by Vanako. "Can you stand?" she whispered.

"I think so."

"Act like it. Don't look like you're leaning on me if you can help it." She grasped Vanako's wrist, then *reached* out to blunt the pain of standing. Vanako's consciousness flooded in—the pain in her shin was overwhelming, and her fear was so much deeper than her anger, which only made Zaya's anger grow. "Cops will give love taps," she said aloud, "but only when words fail them. So it's important to speak slowly and simply. When you use a big word like 'competition,' they worry you might have a couple of friends hidden behind it."

"Mind your tone," said Yyvvoun.

"Don't make it worth our lives to fight you," Zaya said.

Yyvvoun and Kanjoon both snickered at this, as if it was self-evident how little their lives were worth. Kanjoon jerked his head toward Red Sand Street, Yyvvoun nodded, and they both sauntered off without another word.

***

ZAYA RELEASED THE MERLIN and the nightjars. Kemreen got on the other side of Vanako, but she was too tall for the girl to put an arm around her shoulder—still, her waist was better than nothing. They limped along in silence for a while. They passed a brace of bicycles, but there was no point. They would need to catch a wyrm or rickshaw home. Zaya had been sure they'd see a rickshaw first; but in Taupe Precinct they caught the eye of a dashing Kayalim on a sleek, immaculately maintained Dusk Stalker, who couldn't quite hide a yawn as they boarded.

"I suppose I should thank you," Zaya said while Kemreen helped Vanako up. "That could have been much worse without you there. Would have been."

"You suppose you should thank me," said Kemreen, "or you're thanking me?"

The flash of anger in Zaya's chest must have shown on her face; Kemreen shook her head. "That came out wrong," she said. "I wasn't trying to force you to say something you didn't want to say. I just wanted to understand how you were feeling."

"My mom's feeling guilty about being hot for a cop," said Vanako from atop the wyrm. "Which, on the one hand, fair enough, cops are bullshit people who'll apparently break a little girl's shin for mouthing off. But on the other, you did help us out and, I mean, Mom, this cop is a *snack*."

Zaya buried her face in the Dusk Stalker's feathers, which were much itchier and less soft than they looked. After a few long moments, she felt a hard hand on her shoulder. "I'm going now," said Kemreen. "Do you want to maybe look me in the eye before I leave?"

Zaya shook her head, her face firmly pressed against the wyrm's flank. "Can't," she said. "Ever. Please go. Never have children."

The hand lifted, and Zaya felt a cool rush of merciful relief; but, before she could take advantage of that space to flay the skin from her daughter's bones with an enfilade of red-hot barbed invective, it returned—this time accompanied by Kemreen's whole body, pressing lightly against Zaya's back, her hips, the backs of her legs; and by the tumble of hair on her temple, a nose pressed against her jawbone, lips on her ear. "You know where I live," Kemreen said, softly enough for the wyrm's feathers to swallow it.

Then the night air, not even cold, filled the space where Kemreen had been with a knifelike chill; and all that was left of her was the ghost of a squeeze on Zaya's shoulder, a scent in the air that she could neither name nor mistake for anything she could name.

She swung up without a word.

"Your drawers are so wet right now," Vanako said.

"I'll toss you off this wyrm to die broken in the street."

"Hey!" said the driver. "Liability here."

"Fine," said Zaya. "I'll wait and strangle her in her sleep."

"Works for me," said the driver, and they were airborne, and the slipstream devoured all hope of speaking.

CHAPTER 15

CURRENCY. FOUR DENOMINATIONS, EACH worth 24 of the previous ones: Flinders, sherds, plates, and slabs. I won't subject myself to arithmetic just to give you the value of a slab in flinders (331,776. —Ed.), but basically a handful of flinders is small change, you're probably buying a meal in sherds, a well-made sword in plates, and a house or a dragon in slabs. It also means you'll never lay eyes on a slab coin in the wild. There are a few in circulation, but they are the size of saucers and have a hole punched into them so you can tie them to something as thick as your thumb. The mint and the treasury in Ivory Precinct have them under glass, chained to their pedestals.

The denominations are named after the various sizes of pottery pieces that were unearthed here as the early settlers started digging up the streets to build. This is also, in a way, why our cash is made of ceramic. I mean, I'm sure it was intentionally evocative or whatever, but it also happens that we can easily mint coins for the same reason proto-Yemari made a lot of pottery: The delta is full of clay, and it's cheap. (People who understand this stuff will also talk about the counter-inflationary effects of having cash that breaks easily. Sure, fine.)

SEE ALSO: Bright Thread River; Prehistory.

—From "A Visitor's Handbook for Yemareir," by Shenireen Agama

***

WHEN ZAYA STUMBLED INTO her room, there was a note on the bed.

Papa Minshoon showed me a couple of good arbitrages in the odds. I had to bet against you a couple times, though. I hope you're not mad. —Taavi

There was a twist of butcher paper under the note. When Zaya opened it, coins fell out—a mix, well leavened with black flinders and copper-plated sherds, as well as several silvered plates. All together it added up to almost half a slab.

Zaya sank to her knees with her fists squeezed tight around the coins, anointing them with a huge, shuddering breath. Then she threw them on her bed, slammed her door open with a window-rattling crash, and tore out like a Dawn Wyrm to a whiskey-cask.

***

SHE WAS LOOMING IN the door to Minshoon's room like an avenging revenant before he'd even rolled over; Vanako's door clicked open, as did Kirono's, Taavi and Gilthiniel's, Jaliki's. She closed Minshoon's door and locked it. That cut off the light from the main common area, which meant she could see him sit up but, backlit by the dim light of the city outside, could not see his face. She threw Taavi's crumpled note at his chest, where it bounced away somewhere. "What is this?"

"I have no idea," said Minshoon. "I don't even know where it went. What's going on?"

"You. Taught. Taavi. To gamble. On the 'stream."

"This is a lot coming from someone who dropped a dangerous extradimensional creature on a scion of a noble house for the privilege of *second place.*"

"Involving our children was never supposed to be part of this."

"You stood up in front of everyone and asked us to affirm that we were all in on the crime-doing or else we could sell the house."

"That means they do what needs to be done, it doesn't mean them going out and finding ways to dig us in deeper. What if she'd had to pay up?"

"She didn't, by the way, and that's not just luck. Her instincts are good, she can spot arbs without coaching, she has an eye for opportunities. But if she had to pay, so what? She'd have lost her nut. It's a lesson."

"How leveraged was she, Minshoon? How much did you borrow?"

"Nothing."

"Horseshit."

"Don't call me a liar."

Zaya could hear the ice creeping into his voice. When she couldn't control her anger, she went hot, but Minshoon would go cold. As long as one of them was in control, they'd be all right in the morning. She made herself walk back from the flame. "If you didn't borrow, and she wasn't leveraged, how is there half a slab on my pillow?"

"Half a slab?" The ice was ebbing now. "She told me half a plate."

"Well, the amount of currency sitting on my pillow right now is nineteen flinders shy of half a slab."

"Zaya," said Minshoon, "I pledge on the souls of everyone we've lost that I didn't say a word about borrowing to any of our children, and I would have chased them away from it with fire if they'd asked."

The molten rage that had brought Zaya crashing through her best and oldest friend's door had cooled to a massive casting of slag—heavy, smooth-edged, fused to her flesh. "You didn't have to," she said dully. "Taavi's smart enough to think of it herself. So's Gil, so's Vani." She could see his eyes gleaming from the dim streetlamp-light through his window. "Taavi has a future. Now every time she picks up a book, she has to ask herself: Why study this stuff when I could be gambling to support my family? That's not what should be on her mind." She shook her head. "You're right, though. I'm not any better. Shanhoon sent some cop friends after us at the stable."

"Tiamat," breathed Minshoon. "Are you, is Vani—"

"Fine. She'll have a bad bruise on her shin for a while, but that's the worst of it. We talked our way out." She sighed and shook her head. "That's a lie. Right before I fucked up at the depot, I slept with a cop. I didn't know she was a cop. She got wind of what was going to happen, got in front of it, and saved my ass."

Minshoon chuckled. "She sounds nice."

"I don't even know. She's a giraffe Mrineen and also a cop. She likes knives and bad arrack and girls who are mostly straight. Vani teases me because she thinks it's funny her mom is horny for a cop, which would be easier to deal with if I *weren't* horny or it *weren't* funny, or if I knew who some of her stupid crushes were so I could tell her how stupid they are. But I like this stupid cop, and if I stay with her she's going to fuck me over because she's a cop."

Minshoon patted the bed beside him. Zaya sat, and he put his arm around her waist; she leaned into his shoulder. "Let the thing with the cop be what it is. I'll talk to Taavi about leverage. The thing with Vani... it sounds like you shouldn't be alone out in the city for a while. At least at night."

"I wasn't. I was with Vani and Kemreen and someone still got hurt."

"Then we stay away from empty streets, big crowds, and anything shy of full daylight. We'll get through it. We've been there before."

"'There' is the definition of the place I never want to be again." Zaya swallowed a lump forming in her throat. "The worst place I've ever been is 'there.' I ran so hard from 'there' I lost my wife and my wyrm and almost everything else. I did everything I could to become the kind of person who can't survive 'there' because the things you have to do to survive 'there' are things that no one should ever do. How did Taavi put up enough cash to win half a slab?"

"I swear I gave her two sherds, just like the other kids. I was surprised she could win half a plate. Half a slab is... something else."

"Gil spent his money on drinks," said Zaya. "But Vani said she lost hers betting on me to place in the bottom half. She acted like she didn't know how odds worked." She looked up at Minshoon. "I'm so stupid. How did I not know that was an act?"

"If Vani can pretend, so can Gilthiniel."

"But between the two of them, one already has a history of going behind our backs to get money. I can't do this, Minshoon."

"You're the strongest person in this house. You can."

"I don't mean I can't take it. I mean I have no credibility. How can I tell her to stay safe and keep it legal when I've already told everyone the only way out is through?"

"Maybe there's another explanation," said Minshoon. "We can't assume it's Vani. She's barely had a second alone since you found her at the Blind Beggar. She doesn't even have a door."

The weight of the day seemed to fall on Zaya all at once. She pushed through heavy air to get up. "Maybe. Good night, Minshoon. I'm sorry I woke you. And, you know, reamed you out like a grapefruit."

"Don't ever do that again, please." He reached out and squeezed her hand. "At least we learned one good thing today."

"What's that?"

"Six years out of practice, and you're still the fastest 'streamer in Yemareir."

"Second fastest."

"Bullshit."

Zaya squeezed his hand back, then went to bed.

Chapter 16

PUBLIC ART. WE LIKE to say we have a rich tradition of public art, although I can't say many of us have ever been anywhere else we could compare. At any rate, most precincts take up regular collections for sculpture, public gardens, environmental enchantments, and the like. The Boulevard of Dancers in Damask Precinct, the Sea-King's Wrath off the shore in Cerulean, the Kitchen-Garden in Heliotrope, and the Ministers of the Open Hand by the Souk of All Worlds in Citrine Precinct are worth taking the time to see.

We also like to paint on other people's walls a lot—especially in poorer precincts, honestly, where tax takings are lower and more desperately needed. (Funny how that works— (REDACTED. —Ed.) (Fine. —SA)) Anyway, the best murals are mostly not in the best neighborhoods (exceptions: Lilac, Crimson), but Rust, Damask, Madder, Rose, Azure, and Cadet are packed with fantastic wall art. Where and what is always changing with the concerns of the hour, but ask around for the latest from Kaana te-Tekko, Slider (yes, just Slider), or Shaizo ze-Gaaka. People will know.

SEE ALSO: Landmarks, Fantastic; Landmarks, Historic.

—From "A Visitor's Handbook for Yemareir," by Shenireen Agama

* * *

SOMEONE HAD BROUGHT TWO huge, greasy bags of pão de queijo the next morning. They were still warm when Zaya woke up, and she munched in silence while Minshoon finished the mate. Then they fell to counting sherds and flinders.

Zaya was good at arithmetic and estimation where currency was concerned, and Minshoon was better; but they had both learned better to guess at sums they had not counted. So Zaya did sigh in relief when the winnings from the race and Taavi's gambling takings added up to thirty-seven plates and change—eleven shy of the two slabs they needed for Tjaroon, but they had eleven saved.

But they didn't have another eleven. Tjaroon's next collection would be in two weeks.

The three older children had already left for school when the counting was finished. Kirono was teaching, Cerminir was asleep with Enwë, and Minshoon had bills to pay and dinner to cook; so Zaya and Jaliki took Eäril to school.

Not more than a minute passed outside before Zaya felt the weight of staring eyes on her. She ignored it at first—residual guilt, she was sure, over her return to a life of illegal dragon-racing—until she turned the corner and saw the mural.

There was no mistaking that it was her, nine feet tall from the base of her neck to the crown of her scalp, rendered in the colors of a Dawn Wyrm's plumage—rich magenta and pale turquoise, with accents of purple and orange. Her goggles were finely detailed with rivets and decorative bevels, catching the light on perfect, unscratched lenses; her hair, painted at its usual rather than its actual length, streamed in an unseen wind. The face of a schematic Dawn

Wyrm who looked nothing like Bandit peeked out from behind her. A wide scroll above her face bore a few characters of Kayalim script, rendered in ornate block print: "VERAAMAKA NAVO!" It stopped Jaliki in his tracks with a low "whoa"; Eäril goggled for a moment, then began to jump with arms flung out, spinning in a circle as she shouted "Mama! Mama! Mama!"

Her squeals brought stares; Zaya could see eyes widen in recognition, heads turn to companions and receive nods of confirmation. She put a hand on Eäril's shoulder and hustled her away, leaving Jaliki and the ker to follow; a pair of young Kayalim with bright, flowing hair cheered "veraamaka navo!" as she passed.

"What did they say?" Jaliki asked, panting, when he caught up.

The ker was capering around the little group, yipping and pawing; Zaya found she did not have to fight as hard as she might against the urge to kick it. "It means 'our dragonrider,'" she said, tousling his night-black curls.

***

Swallowing a bitter fear in the back of her throat, Zaya brought Jaliki to Rust Precinct to feed Bandit.

He was a strong biker, at least for his age. They went slowly but did not rest too often, and easily outpaced the ker, which simply appeared mid-stride alongside Jaliki's bike when he was too far ahead. She couldn't shake the image of the dog sinking its teeth into his ankle, pulling him down into the street, planting a blood-soaked muzzle into his throat... but it was a normal dog today, as it had been since Zaya had returned—save, of course, for the ways in which it was not: its blinking in and out of existence to stay close to Jaliki, its unsociability to other dogs, its disinterest in food.

The ride was long, though; Jaliki had to stop a few times to catch his breath. About two thirds of the way through, they stopped at Slorm Pond and joined the other shoreside picnickers to eat sticky rice and pork out of banana leaves and watch the octopus change color as they dreamed. "Why do they all change at once?" asked Jaliki, watching a wave of orange spread out from a point far in the middle of the pond, supplanting the azure and coral patches of the octopus on the pond's periphery. "Are they dreaming the same thing?"

Zaya nodded. "All octopus brains are wired the exact same way, down to each individual nerve cell. They're all always thinking the same thing, even when they're awake."

Jaliki looked at her suspiciously. "No they're not."

"Sure they are."

"They can learn."

"Whatever one of them learns, they all know."

"No, scientists do experiments and stuff. Each one has to learn on its own. Otherwise they'd know how to do all the experiments."

"Good thinking." Zaya pointed her banana leaf at a small island in the middle of the pond. "The real reason is, that island has a ton of worldvine growing on it. Do you know what that is?"

"If you eat it, you see things that aren't real, but it's the same thing as other people who ate it."

"That's right. Where'd you learn that?"

"Kids talk about it in school."

"I learned it from Grandpapa Kaalo."

"Because he used it a lot?"

"Yeah."

"Did he make you use it?"

The question was so unexpected that Zaya laughed much louder than she meant; a few picnickers turned to look, and the nearby octopus briefly seemed to disappear, taking on the blotchy brown of the lake floor mud before returning to the emerald of their dreams. "My breath, your grandfathers would have—" She stopped before she could say *beaten me senseless*. "They would have laid a clutch of ostrich eggs before they let me near any of that." *At least when I was little*, she appended in her mind. "It's why I'm so hard on your sister, a bit. I can't think of worldvine without thinking of all the people I knew who spent so much time in *that* world they were no use in this one."

"Vani's not selling worldvine," Jaliki said through pork and sticky rice.

Zaya felt as though she'd hit her funny bone, except that instead of her elbow, the electric numbness was coursing up and down her spine. *She told* me *she was selling worldvine tar*, she did not say, followed swiftly and in equal silence by, *and according to her she isn't selling anything any more.* "No?" she said instead, with what felt like the world's least convincing shrug. She wanted to go after this like a badger, worrying away at it until it gave; everything inside her screamed that he was six, that he was gentle and guileless as any boy she'd known, that she should be able to crack him like a rotten coconut.

Maybe—but six years of mothering gave her doubts. Defying his mother, that was second nature. Betraying a conspiracy with his favorite sister, his indisputably *coolest* sister, the sister who had won his heart with an always-open door and an endless stream of lemon cloudberry shaved ice when Taavi and Gilthiniel had retreated into apprenticeship and study and, perhaps, fear of the ker that Vanako had always, from the first moment of their acquaintance, treated as a mild nuisance, a thing not quite beneath contempt.... that, maybe, was another matter.

Jaliki seemed to be aware that he had let something slip. "She called it something else," he said. "I forget what."

They ate in silence for a bit, watching the octopus change; scarlet, indigo, brown with green stripes, ivory, celadon, stark white with tessellated blue hexagons, a strange pattern of overlaid squares in shades of pink and purple. "She just wants to help," said Jaliki. "She doesn't like to say that's what she wants, but it's true."

"I know," Zaya said, not sure whether she believed it.

Jaliki breathed deep in through his nose and then back out; the ker, dozing, did the same. "She *can* help," said Jaliki.

"I know."

He did not contradict her, but everything in his body spoke disbelief: The set of his shoulders, the tension in his lips, the arch of his eyebrows. He picked up a pebble, threw it into the pond; there was a brief ripple of cadmium yellow in the octopus where it landed.

A man's voice came from behind them: "Have mercy, son. Let them sleep."

Jaliki's face brightened and his jaw dropped; he sprang to his feet. "Grandpa!"

The ker kept pace with him, barking, as he charged the old man—he was taller than Zinji's shoulder now, and staggered him into a stutter-step as he crashed into his arms. Zinji cackled an old-junkie cackle and kissed him on the temple. "Little bird told me I might find you here."

"By a 'little bird' your grandfather means your mother," Zaya said, dry as dust.

Zinji took Jaliki's shoulders and pushed him out a foot or so to look at him. "Your mother's right, I should give her the credit she deserves," he said, looking over Jaliki to meet Zaya's eyes. She did not smile, but nodded. He looked at Jaliki again. "Now finish your lunch so you can go show me your dragon."

***

THE MEETING WITH ZINJI had been a pain to arrange, but it paid dividends at the stable: Zaya could sail through the things that needed doing, while Zinji could take all the time he wanted teaching a rapt pupil how to check wyrmdown for parasites, or how to communicate with Bandit's mind. For its own part, Bandit kept Zaya supplied with a stream of Jaliki's more unexpected or alarming observations, and peppered her with questions about the relationship between herself, Zinji, and Jaliki, which was a great source of confusion—it had begun to understand the idea of training outside one's brood, but the idea of a close relationship between family members separated by more than a generation was difficult to grasp.

This old one would be a better rider than the tall one, Bandit said, while Zaya was cleaning its teeth. *Its mind is nimbler and it's not so large.*

"You just like the fact that he has a lot of memories of giving whiskey to Dawn Wyrms."

I would like to have a friend like this, yes.

"You already do. It's been a long time since Zinji's rolled over a liquor store—I don't think he remembered how much he missed getting into a dragon's head. But he's too old to be a racer."

You said one thing but you meant something else. Tell me what you meant.

Zaya paused in her work, idly scratching along Bandit's jawbone. She was not too surprised it could tell "too old" was not the whole truth; that had been a white lie to herself as much as anything. But, from Bandit, *Tell me what you meant* was new. The Mule, always more raw and wild than Bandit, would simply have said *Lying* and, depending on mood and circumstance, its mind might observe with detached amusement or erupt in flames of rage and betrayal. From Bandit she would have expected the question, *What did you mean?*, but not an order. "He's not reliable," she said.

Bandit's mind pulsed briefly in understanding. *The young one is also small and has a good mind,* it said. *But it is hunted.*

Reflexively Zaya looked over at Zinji and Jaliki and realized the ker was not there. She didn't remember it leaving, but she was used to it ceasing and resuming existence at its own cadence, and in any case she hated it so much that she ignored it whenever she possibly could. She could not remember noticing it in the stable at all.

She'd heard stories about dragons fighting kers, even eating them—those were the stories you heard as the parent of a hunted child, and in any group of patients larger than a double handful there was at least one believer. But the streets of Yemareir were full of dragons and, shittily, of kers as well. Zaya had seen a young Dawn Wyrm eat a colobus monkey; she'd seen more than one Merlin eat a skink or sparrow or cockroach, she'd seen a Dusk Stalker pluck a bat out of the air and swallow it whole on the fly, she'd seen a Ranger run down a kudu on the veldt. If any of those animals had been a ker, there would surely have been an uproar, if only from the gleeful quarry, who'd just been handed back a life.

"We call the thing that's hunting him a ker," said Zaya. "Are you afraid of kers?"

Nothing from Bandit's mind but noncommittal static.

"Are you afraid to have Jaliki ride you because the ker is hunting him?"

Jaliki can ride me when he likes. But he spends enough time running for his own life. He shouldn't have to run for yours.

Zaya closed her eyes and focused on the feelings in her body: The soft down of Bandit's jaw, the cool toughness of its skin under her palm, the scent of guano and ripe fish in the close air of the stable. In time, her throat loosened, and when she opened her eyes and looked at her face through Bandit's eyes, they were not red at all.

***

THEN IT WAS BACK to Azure and Tevala for Zinji, up to Amethyst and shaved ice with Thelendil and Vanako for Jaliki, and for Zaya, back to Chartreuse and the Blind Beggar and Tjaroon, cash in hand. She spent the twenty minutes before the meeting cozening a spider monkey to accompany her. It was too small to do much damage to Tjaroon or his mandrill, but it would be enough to buy her a few seconds' head start if she needed it.

Tjaroon had arrived first. He had not brought the mandrill, which spoke well of his tactical thinking—unless, like Zaya and the spider monkey, he'd taken advantage of his early arrival to hide it somewhere. He greeted her with what seemed to be genuine warmth. "Shearwater-*cha*, it's pleasant to see you, and that goes double if you have cash. I'm afraid I must ask you a few questions before we part company."

"How much do I take off the bill for you wasting my time?"

"Not how it works. It's just a set of names, I'd like to know if they sound familiar."

"Fine."

"Tvanshaan Anaconda."

"No."

"Fanjoon Tegu."

"No."

"Fsanreen Gharial."

Zaya blinked. "No."

"Something familiar?"

"I know another Gharial. She drinks here. Common enough name, I think?"

"Ah, thanks. Jalhoon Slider?"

"No."

"Javashi te-Zaako."

It took a moment for the name to come to her. "Yes. Her daughter's hunted. We were in a parents' group together for a bit."

"All right. Talarindor Monitor."

"No."

"Thank you."

Zaya blinked again. "You don't want anything else?"

"Something to get off your chest, Shearwater-*cha*?"

"No." It took a moment for her mind to put it together. "You were selling to these people." Tjaroon's blank face did not deny it. "You want to know if I was involved in Vanako's business."

"That's astute."

"Is Javashi going to disappear because I know her?"

"No."

"Has she disappeared already?"

"No. Neither has your Gharial. Or the one that isn't yours."

"You wanted to know if I'd *notice* if they disappeared."

"If you wouldn't before, you definitely will now."

Zaya narrowed her eyes and thought about telling the spider monkey to bite off Tjaroon's frenulum.

"Fuck not around with the criminal," said Tjaroon, "lest ye find out."

"Don't sell yourself short," said Zaya.

"Come again?"

"You're not a criminal, you're a middle manager."

"Hey, I move some product. I'm like a Senior Controlled Substance Displacement Engineer."

Zaya thumped the pouch of cash on the table. "That's two slabs even, spare me your dad jokes. If Javashi disappears, I'm telling the cops."

"You won't be the first, I hope. Look, take a quarter slab off. I made some good money on you and that dumb giraffe you had puking off the back of that fine Dawn Wyrm."

"His name's Thelendil, he's worth ten of you, and no. If you give me discounts when you win, you're putting me right on the hook for when you lose. No fucking way."

"For you, upside only. Promise."

"Fuck your upside. Vanako is a child. Zayeni is a child. I'm not taking gifts from a middle manager who exploits children for a living, no matter how subtle or quick to anger he thinks he is."

Tjaroon raised an eyebrow, a gesture Zaya could easily imagine him making while a goon of some kind was beating the shit out of a dealer who'd come up short. "Vanako is a very capable young person who worked for me on a completely voluntary basis until a staggering amount of product went missing. Since you're on the hook to make me whole, and a quarter-slab is a pretty big chunk of your next payment, if I were you, I'd swallow your pride and take the cash."

She could hear Minshoon, lecturing in his most infuriating tone: *Making this idiot richer won't help us keep the house. This is no different than hedging our bets with some money on a different wyrm. It's about survival, not pride.* She counted out four plates and forty-eight sherds, forcing herself to take her time. She thought about counting out an extra plate in front of him, just to force him to stop her. But he might not stop her, and the smirk she imagined on his face as he sent her off with that stolen-in-plain-sight seventh plate was too much to bear.

"Thank you for the race," said Tjaroon. "It was a pleasure to watch." Zaya grunted in acknowledgement. "Hey, win a few more and maybe we can discuss throwing one."

The spider monkey jumped into the booth table and screamed straight into Tjaroon's face. He yelped, staggered, and flailed. The monkey ran. Chatter and snickering bubbled all around the bar.

"Talk to me about throwing a race again," said Zaya, "and you *will* lose your frenulum."

"With an attitude like that," said Tjaroon, "you could throw one race and never have to work again."

"With an attitude like *that*, I'd never win enough for anyone to bet against me losing."

"Don't sell yourself short, veraamaka navo." Tjaroon's Kayalim accent was horrible. "I've seen longer grifts pay off at longer odds."

"You probably didn't spill the trick in front of a bar full of people before the grift had even started."

"In theory, the grift's already well under way. This is just how we make it stick." But Tjaroon did look around the bar and, clearly, saw more eyes on him than he preferred. "But I take your point. At any rate, I have a date with a dictionary." Zaya did not ask why, but Tjaroon proceeded as if she had. "To look up 'frenulum'? I assume it's a part of my penis? But I look forward to figuring out which!"

Zaya let him go without another word. When she sat back down, there was a pint glass full of peach arrack in front of her. She looked around and saw the back of the silent waitron shuffling toward the bar. She tucked a small pile of sherds behind the glass and left before she could start drinking.

***

WHEN ZAYA OPENED THE door to House Shearwater, it hit something soft but solid.

Images of blood and torn flesh filled her mind. "Jaliki, baby," she said through the fine dust of her calm, "is that you?" and she put her weight against the door, planning to push him gently, just far enough to let her through, but the resistance vanished mid-lean, and she stumbled in.

Minshoon was halfway to the door, smelling of durian, his hands covered in flour. "What's going on? Did the drop go all right?"

"I felt a body in front of the door," Zaya said, aware that her eyes were the size of mandarin oranges, unable to make them smaller. "There was a body in front of the door."

"There's no body."

"I can see there's no body. I'm saying I *felt* one and then it moved." Absurdly, she looked around; it was not as though Minshoon could have failed to notice Jaliki's body on the floor of the living room. There was no body.

But there was a furry shape in the shadows of the far corner—dappled blue and white by the softly glowing ceiling-mural of an orca, nose tucked under its tail.

"That thing never sleeps out here," said Zaya.

"Doesn't it?"

"Is Jaliki all right?"

"I didn't hear anything—" Minshoon began, but Zaya was already on her way to his room.

Sheets and books in disarray, the smell of blood and shit from torn guts like a breaker in her face, lanky arms and legs curled in on themselves in a corner—these were what she expected, what she even saw, for a moment, etched on the versatile dark of Jaliki's room in the middle of the night; but, an even slightly dark-adapted eye could see, not what was there. Belatedly, she heard the shush of his breath cut through the night's thick silence, heard the sheets rustle in time. "He's all right," she said, half-whispering. She realized she was trying not to wake the ker. Not quite believing it, she rifled through the sheets to feel Jaliki's hands, head, and stomach. They were all present, dry and whole, his belly rising and falling with his breathing. He moaned and turned, but did not wake. "He's not hurt," she said.

Minshoon was leaning in the doorframe, a broad silhouette against the soft light of the common room. "I'm always listening for it," he said. "I would have heard."

There was a trace of hurt in his voice, but Zaya's tattered heart was in no shape to manage it. "Why is it out there?"

"Mmmph," said Jaliki, batting at something, and Minshoon said "Let him sleep." Zaya left the room, then gently closed the door, then immediately regretted it; she wanted to wrap her arms around him and squeeze until her fingertips touched her shoulders, to put her nose in the fine hairs at his temple and breathe her scent in as though he were a baby. Instead she took a deep breath full of flour and durian. "I've decided to stop talking like a person who's losing her mind," said Zaya. "But it would be a mistake to think I'm feeling calm right now. Split a beer?"

Minshoon nodded and went to pour. Zaya walked over to the couch, kicked her shoes off, and curled her legs under her. Minshoon handed her a cup, then clinked his against hers. Instead of a long pull, she took a sip.

"You really haven't noticed that it always sleeps in his room?" Zaya said, trying not to sound as judgmental as she felt.

"Now that you're asking, I can't remember it ever sleeping out here, but that's not the same thing." Her eyes must have widened or her face fallen; he reached out to touch her knuckles with floury fingers. "If you say it's unusual, I believe you. I just don't know what to make of it. Isn't it better if it's far away from him?"

"I don't know, that's why I had to check."

"I know. That was the right thing."

Zaya turned her body to look at the ker. It had opened its eyes and was looking in their direction, as though it was listening.

"Fuck you," she said to it. "Die in that corner."

The ker buried its nose under its tail and closed its eyes. Zaya stared at it in silence; it neither moved nor turned. Her neck and back began to ache from being held in the twist; she turned back to face Minshoon. "It's got something up its sleeve," she said.

"Maybe," said Minshoon. "I don't think so."

Zaya took another sip. It felt like a raindrop in the Emerald Dunes.

"How'd the drop go?"

She put her fingertips to her not-quite-empty pouch of cash, and sighed, and told him.

***

SHE WOKE UP ON the couch to Eäril bolting into the common room, leaping into her lap and screeching for breakfast. Her cup of beer, undrained, still rested on the coffee table. The ker still slept in its far corner, motionless except for the rise and fall of its ribs.

CHAPTER 17

THAUMOBIOME. I WAS ALWAYS *told the definition of a thaumobiome was "An area whose environment has been sorcerously altered." People like to cite Cold Point in Indigo Precinct and the Tundra Mile out in the Emerald Dunes because they have charismatic animals and weird weather, but there are of course debates over whether, say, the Rosewing Fountain or even the more strenuously managed gardens of the House estates might count.*

It doesn't take like a semiotician to tell that "sorcerously altered" implies a sorcerer *making an* alteration—*but no magician I've talked to has given me the faintest shred of evidence that this ever happened... except for the House gardens, and it's telling that those are viewed as edge cases. It makes magicians nervous when I point this out. Magic in Yemareir is tightly managed by guilds; no one is setting up a rain forest in Argent Precinct without permits granted and fees paid. But if there's something about Yemareir that just burps up major geomancy without so much as consulting human opinion, then...*

... I mean, everyone knows the original city was built as a seasonal settlement by nomads. Everyone knows the nomads are gone. No one knows why. If we can't prove that, say, all the air in Yemareir didn't just *spontaneously disappear* one day, *then how do we know what happened to them won't happen to us?*

SEE ALSO: Landmarks, Fantastic; Houses, Noble; Magic; Proto-Yemari.

—From "A Visitor's Handbook for Yemareir," by Shenireen Agama

***

OVER THE NEXT TWO days, life was as calm as it could be in a family of eleven on the brink of financial free fall. Taavi and Gilthiniel studied and squabbled; Vanako sullenly attended school and dutifully ground out her apprenticeship; Jaliki and Eäril did chores and read and learned their sums from Cerminir and, to a lesser extent, Zaya; and Enwë bounced from Cerminir's breast to Minshoon's arms or, when he was cooking, to a swaddle on his chest, where she tugged on his beard and sank slobbery fists into any dough or fruit that happened to be inside her reach.

On the morning of the third day, Zaya woke with the sweat of Candlegrass Stand still dried on her skin, dressed, and walked out into the common area, where she greeted her family with three words:

"Cold Point Chasse."

***

MINSHOON

NEXT RACE?

ZAYA

(nods)

CERMINIR

Good. We know how to win the Cold Point Chasse.

ZAYA

(*shakes head*)

VANAKO

What's a chasse?

GILTHINIEL

It's just an old word for chase, right?

ZAYA

(*shakes head*)

CERMINIR

Wait, why isn't it good? We have a huge natural advantage in the Chasse.

VANAKO

What's. A. Chasse.

TAAVI

Maybe it's like chess?

ZAYA

(*shakes head*)

KIRONO

Had a natural advantage. Three of them. All of which we're short of now.

GILTHINIEL

Oh no, I remember. It is like an old word for chase! But it means *hunt.*

MINSHOON

Cold Point has a sorcerous microclimate. The cliffs are shot through with fissures that lead into caves, and in the caves are—

CERMINIR

Do not come *near* me with your remedial colonizer zoology.

MINSHOON

I wouldn't dream of it, Cer... but unlike you, our children are not genetically endowed with intimate knowledge of all the secrets and subtleties of the Cold Point thaumobiome.

CERMINIR

Fine. Permission to continue lecturing.

VANAKO

Let the record show I asked about a "chasse" and no one except my dirtbag brother has come within ten miles of explaining it to me.

CERMINIR

If you were genetically endowed with intimate knowledge of all the secrets and subtleties of the Cold Point thaumobiome, this would all go much faster.

VANAKO

Thanks, I'll file a complaint with my birth parents.

JALIKI

Walrus bats!

ZAYA

(*nods*)

VANAKO

Your birth parents are walrus bats. (*to Zaya*) No offense, Mom.

TAAVI

Walrus bats aren't a thing? That's like something out of a kids' book?

JALIKI & EÄRIL

Wing Windtwister!

KIRONO

Those were stoat bats.

TAAVI

Whatever? You can't just mash animals together? Especially flying animals with animals that are nothing but tusks and lard?

MINSHOON

They're called walrus bats because, in their native habitats, they hunt walruses.

CERMINIR

The ones who live here don't grow so big, they eat mostly tuna. And small sharks.

KIRONO

And a chasse means a hunt, like Gilthiniel said.

MINSHOON

Cross the finish line without a walrus bat in tow, you're disqualified.

KIRONO

Which we would be sure to crush, six years ago. Zaya and Kiriki were the only 'streamers in the history of the 'stream ever to bring a live bat back from Cold Point.

TAAVI, GILTHINIEL, VANAKO, JALIKI

Whoa.

EÄRIL

Mama!

KIRONO

But we don't have—I'm sorry, Thelendil—we don't have a second competent empath.

THELENDIL

You're fine.

KIRONO

And, even if we did, Zaya put the strength of her psionics at about ten percent within the damping field. So we don't really have the advantage of empathy at all.

ZAYA

(*nods*)

MINSHOON

What we do have is a week. Zaya and Bandit can drill the hell out of it.

KIRONO

But not at Cold Point. Those bats are a protected species. The Standards Board has a lifetime ban out for anyone caught poaching—which is why we didn't practice there last time.

MINSHOON (*rubbing his temples*)

Fuck. You're right.

EÄRIL

Papa!

TAAVI, GILTHINIEL, & VANAKO

Laaaaaanguage, Daaaaaad.

KIRONO

And we don't have Yyrreen.

ZAYA

(*nods*)

***

ZAYA HAD BEEN WATERING the irises when a Merlin Wyrm scratched at her window with a note attached to its foreleg. *Zaya, Rosewing Fountain, an hour before sunset. AP.* Before she let it go, she looked into its mind to confirm its memory of Arhoon—and no memory of Shanhoon Krait.

The Rosewing Fountain was thick with butterflies getting their last sips of nectar before the dangers of dusk set in, and visitors who'd come to watch them. Arhoon sat by a kiosk a few feet from the central geyser, holding his sword out and gazing at the tip; an enormous butterfly sat on it, lazily opening and closing wings that were mostly black with a symmetric lacework of aquamarine. "If you put a little honey on the tip, sometimes you get lucky," he said.

"Not getting anywhere near that one," Zaya said, sitting. "What's going on?"

"You missed the afterparty," Arhoon said. "How dare you, honestly? The talk of the 'stream. You could have sent someone else to take your sleek new wyrm back to Saavero's."

"No, I couldn't. Thelendil was—"

"Exactly." Arhoon swung the sword to point accusingly at Zaya; the butterfly flew off. "What's wrong with your co-pilot? Don't tell me you picked someone with a fear of heights."

"No, he's a Sky-Eater with Cildinior Amalgam. He's on dragonback all the time. But not like this. Being in close with half a dozen other wyrms, doing precision maneuvers at high speed... he wasn't going to know about this until it happened."

"He was the difference between you and first place."

"Maybe."

"Zaya."

"You don't know. I wouldn't have picked up the lithorang I'd dumped on Krait if I hadn't been desperate and gone through the canopy. No desperation? Maybe I run a normal race, Monsoon and Arrow both edge me out, and I'm third."

"Horseshit. Your wyrm—what's its name?"

"Bandit's Breath. You can call it Bandit."

"Bandit. It's stronger and hardier than the Mule ever was, and that's before its body starts adapting to the 'stream. Sure, it's bigger and not so nimble, but endurance is agility late in the game. And you can fall back on physical signals when psionics don't work, which, correct me if I'm wrong, is one hundred percent of the time now. It's a real asset, Zaya. Work with it. Don't go ignoring it so you can mumble superstitious shit about how, really, getting blasted in the face with a thousand stone shards was all for the best."

"Fine." A butterfly had landed on the back of her hand, shades of topaz and amethyst. "What, then? Do you have another co-pilot for me?"

"Do you need one? Psionics isn't working."

"It is, a little. I'm at about ten percent efficiency with a pretty bad lag. With just me on the wyrm, it'd be worse."

"At ten percent efficiency, is the weight of a co-pilot actually worth it?"

"Yes."

Arhoon almost said something, then shut his mouth and leaned back. "OK. So the after party."

"I'm sure the cream of the 'stream had a perfectly splendid party without me."

"No such thing."

"As the cream of the 'stream?"

"As a perfectly splendid party without you." Arhoon grinned. "Nonetheless, I met a guy. I caught his beer when he dropped it. He had to pick it up between his palms; seems his fingers weren't working right for a bit. Get me?"

Zaya nodded. "Working off the tusk-madness. OK. Is he any good?"

"As a 'streamer, he's trash. Finished somewhere in the bottom half. I'm not saying no potential, but... it's the Stone Forest Slalom, not the Gathering of the Elite, you know?"

Be kind, the mother in Zaya's head whispered, *you don't know what folks have overcome to get where they are.* Zaya shushed the mother in her head and assimilated Arhoon's judgment with a brisk nod. "Here we are, though," she said, "talking about him."

"He found a couple mice in the walls, got them up on the table in front of me, and had them doing a little mouse paso doble in about ten seconds. Obviously a bit he'd practiced, but—"

"Directing two minds through a new precision routine isn't easy," said Zaya. "What's his name?"

"Zeino te-Zeino."

"Background?"

Arhoon gave her a perplexed look. "Kayalim?"

"I know that, I'm asking whether he's ever used psionics for a living. Construction, transportation?"

"He said he was an investigator with the Russet Precinct gendarmerie for a bit, but he didn't like using animals to hunt down people mostly stealing to feed their families."

"What kind of animals?"

"I don't know, what do cops usually use? Dogs, birds, monkeys? They don't use Dawn Wyrms for it, if that's what you want to know."

"Any big animal was what I was looking for," Zaya said. "It's all right. I guess I'll ask him about it."

"Good. We can meet at Tjaliraan's. Fine gin is the great tearer-down of walls and builder of bridges."

"Or the other way around." Zaya moved the hand with the butterfly up closer to her face to look at the patterns on its wings; it folded and unfolded them obligingly. "Anything else good at the after-party? Did Shanhoon Krait brag about the cops he sent to break my kneecaps?"

Arhoon leaned over to look at Zaya's knees, then straightened back up. "Did Bandit eat them?"

"The cops? No, they decided that a verbal warning about dropping things on Krait was enough for the night." She didn't want to tell Arhoon about Kemreen yet; she didn't trust him to keep his mouth shut. "Seriously, though, did he say anything?"

"Not about you in particular. The usual excuse-making and swagger. Don't worry about him."

"He sent attack dogs after me. I'm worried."

"I'll talk to him."

Zaya laughed. "That's gallant, but is he really going to listen to someone who's probably my most famous known associate?"

"We know people in common. I think he'll back off." Arhoon patted the pommel of his sword. "Anyway, if he doesn't want to listen to me, he can listen to my little friend here."

Zaya rolled her eyes. "Thanks, Arhoon. I'm sure your little friend will talk him right down out of my business." But she did feel something unhitch in her chest—as if a steel band wrapped around her ribs had suddenly been loosened.

***

THEY WERE OUT SWIMMING in Azure Precinct when Zaya first saw the mark on Jaliki's wrist. She could almost have mistaken it for a fleck of dirt, or freckles; his skin was dark enough that, an inch of two farther away, she'd have missed it. She grabbed him by the wrist as he was about to go play in the water and knelt for a closer look. It was a deep inky purple-black, a pattern of dots and lines that seemed to have been drawn over an implicit five-dot grid. "What's this?" she asked.

He squirmed; she tightened her grip reflexively, as she had done when he was younger and would run away to avoid an apology or a confession. She let go and put the hand on his hard, skinny shoulder instead; he shied a bit but did not pull away. She bobbled in her squat, then put a knee down on the wet sand to steady herself. "I just drew it," he said. "I got bored."

She wet a thumb and smudged at it.

"Ow!"

"What?"

"You rubbed sand on it!"

"Is it tender?"

"No."

"I wasn't rubbing that hard."

"It doesn't feel hard to you, you're rubbing it."

"All right." Zaya looked him in the eye; she felt the effort that it took for him not to turn away. She looked around. Zinji was smoking on a filthy scrap of rug; the ker was lolling by him, still sunk in its new state of sickly lethargy, eyeing a seagull as a cat might from behind a window; Cerminir, Eäril, and Enwë were already out in the waves. "What made you think of the pattern?"

"Mom, I want to swim."

She lifted her hand from his shoulder; he was off into the surf like a hare sprinting from a hound.

Normally she would have thrown off her own clothes and followed him in—but Cerminir was there, and Jaliki was a strong swimmer, and the whole thing nagged like a hangnail. She walked over to Zinji, not missing the opportunity to kick sand in the ker's face; it weakly spat and rubbed its eye with a paw, too deep in its malaise to so much as give her a wounded look. She sat on her father's other side; he thumped the ker's flank companionably. "No need for that," he said.

"That thing has torn away, swallowed, and digested the living flesh of your only grandson, you feckless dotard," she said. "You're damn right there's a need for it."

"All the sand in the world won't stop it eating," said Zinji. "If it would, I'd be right beside you, kicking for our boy until this beach was bare rock. But all you do is hurt it and hurt you."

"Hurt me? How do you figure?"

"By being a person who causes pain when there's no earthly use to it."

"There's a use to it."

"What's that, then?"

"Teaching myself that I'm the kind of person who doesn't give up on my people. You wouldn't understand."

"Might not at that." He moved a hand to pet the ker again, then thought better of it. "You think I see your father in it. Thing out of control, bottomless appetite, no thought for hurt."

"You said it, not me."

"Well, you wouldn't be wrong if you did. We all have our weaknesses."

Zaya made a disgusted noise, then picked up a tiny shell from the sand and threw it at the ker. "You ever see someone with a tattoo of dots and lines?" said Zaya. "A little square of them?" She drew an example in the sand with her finger, as best she could remember. Zinji leaned over to look. "Not exactly that, but like that."

"Looks familiar," said Zinji. "Can't place it. Want me to ask around?"

"Probably," said Zaya. "I saw it on Jaliki's arm. He's being weird about it."

"Tiamat," said Zinji. "And you think I was a shit dad. If I'd seen a tattoo I didn't know on you, I'd beat the story out of you."

"What kind of information do you think you'd have gotten if you did that?"

He laughed, then coughed, then finished laughing. "You wouldn't understand."

"I'll figure it out. I'll learn more faster if he thinks I've forgotten."

The sun was too hot on her skin, the sand too dry on her feet; she longed to be in the water. She watched a trio of Dawn Wyrms soaring on thermals; they drifted slowly north, parallel to the coast, perhaps tracking a school of fish or a pod of dolphins. Jaliki was acting strange, the ker was acting strange, Vanako was acting strange. There must be a connection. No, that wasn't right—coincidences happened all the time. And Vanako hadn't really even done anything out of character. Assuming Zaya understood anything about Vanako's character, which more and more it seemed she didn't. And Taavi gambling with AURYN knew who on Zaya's race? Was that in character? She would have expected it from Gilthiniel, who ran with rough boys and didn't like studying anything that wasn't numbers. Did she know anything about any of her children? What secrets was Enwë hiding inside her perfectly round little head? "You ever sell worldvine tar?" Zaya asked.

"You buying?"

"Sizing the market," said Zaya. "Pure curiosity. How much could you buy for a slab?"

Zinji held out his palm and used his other finger to draw a circle around it. "A cake about that big around and half as thick. But I haven't been paying much attention to the market."

That tracked, anyway. "Hell of a product, if you can pick up a plate for an amount you could hide in your shoe."

Zinji chuckled. "Don't hide it in your shoe. The contact high would knock you flat in about five minutes. That's a rough high too, something about taking it through the skin brings out the vicious side of it. Bats and goddamn manta rays dive-bombing you when you least expect it for eight hours or so."

"This is starting to sound like first-hand experience."

"I can't think of a thing I've learned any other way. Kaalo was the book-smart one." Zinji cleared his throat. "Also, though, you stick a plug of it in your shoe and bike across town for an hour, and whoever you're selling to might as well be buying used chewing tobacco. You need a charm-sealed box just to keep it out of contact with the air."

"Pain in the ass," Zaya said.

"Right."

"Thanks, Papa."

Zinji stretched out on his back and closed his eyes. "Didn't crush a dream of yours, I hope?"

"Like I said. Pure curiosity."

Zinji's chest was already rising and falling slowly with the deep breaths of sleep. Zaya dug her toes into the sand and squeezed, thinking about dozens of tiny charm-sealed boxes.

***

She told Minshoon the story late at night, in his own darkened room, while he bounced Enwë on his shoulder—the day's beach outing had taken too much out of Cerminir, so Minshoon was stepping in for nighttime wakings. Enwë would snore happily on his shoulder, but he hadn't figured out how to put her down. Talk didn't seem to bother her, though. "I don't know if I know what it means," Minshoon said.

"Eleven slabs of product," said Zaya. "That requires a charm-sealed box per customer to maintain potency. If they're going to do that, they might as well track the deliveries, in case something happens that is *just like what supposedly actually happened* to this *incredibly valuable product.*"

"Maybe they're cheap—"

"But imagine, for a moment, that our friend Tjaroon, who represents that he is massively cheesed off about and in serious trouble for this *shrinkage*, was too cheap to shell out for this minor augmentation—"

"How do you know it's minor?"

"I asked Kirono. He said it is *miiiiiiiiiinorrrrrrrr.*"

Minshoon shrugged. He clearly didn't like where this was going, but he wasn't going to contradict Kirono on charms and enchantments.

"Even if Tjaroon was too cheap for a tracking charm, he would have had to keep everything in tiny boxes. You have to figure Vani wasn't selling more than a plate or two per customer—"

"Why?"

"Because worldvine tar isn't habit-forming, because it doesn't go bad, because she was selling to a bunch of Mrineen from common houses and Javashi te-Zaako. Look, it doesn't matter. If she was selling a slab of it per customer, that's eleven separate boxes that have to hold something the size of your palm. Think about carrying that under your arm. That's the first thing she said about it—that it was a stash you could fit under your arm. Minshoon, none of this tracks."

"I remember her saying that," said Minshoon. Enwë stirred and let out a tiny wail; he stroked her head and shushed her, and she settled. "What do you figure? If she's lying, why?"

"She was obviously selling something incredibly expensive. She needed a cover story with something she could easily carry around the city on a bike. She's a stupid kid, so she figured the best idea was to pick something expensive that no one here has even heard of, because why would a grown-up check up on her story?" She grimaced. "Maybe she was banking on me still wanting to keep Papa Zinji at arm's length."

"So she wanted us to think it was one expensive drug and not another. Why?"

"Because she knows me," said Zaya. "She already saw how much trouble she was in for selling anything for this idiot Tjaroon. If I found out that she was ruining people's lives dealing something like datura or amethyst..."

"What would you do?"

Zaya sighed and sat on his bed. She sank her hands into her hair and pulled. "I don't know. She lost her mother to a fox ker. We're going to lose Jaliki. I want to be kind... but she knows what it's like. How can she be dealing to Javashi?"

"You didn't answer the question."

"I don't know the answer. I told her no one's guaranteed a place here, that there are some things that can't be lived with. I don't know if this is one of them. Javashi's got nothing, Minshoon. Vani can't do this."

"I don't know if this is related," said Minshoon. "But guess who Zayeni saw Vani eating shaved ice with at the Sweet Soldier?"

"Tiamat, don't do this to me." She blew air out through her nose. "Jevain Tuatara."

"Close. Ziyuki."

The water in Zaya's spine went cold. "And she was in the Sweet Soldier? Talking to Vani? What about?"

"Zayeni didn't hear. Said the two of them were keeping it pretty quiet."

Zaya made herself say it. "Ziyuki wants her."

"For House Amphisbaena?" Zaya couldn't see Minshoon's face in the dark, but she could imagine it: the line deepening in his forehead, the face like he'd just tasted spoiled milk. "No disrespect to our daughter, but why?"

"I don't know. Why'd they take Ziyuki?"

"She's a prodigy who eats other politicians for breakfast?" Enwë stirred and sighed, as if in agreement.

"Prodigies see things the rest of us don't. Look, Vani wouldn't be my pick either, except... out of our kids, she would be. Right?" She seized a fistful of her hair, just long enough to give a satisfying yank. "We have to let her fly."

"What? No. Why?"

"It's what she wants. She thinks because I won't fly with her, I don't..." She wasn't even sure what. Respect her? Believe she cared about the family? Love her?

"Zaya..." Minshoon sighed and ran a hand through his hair. "I love what we've built here, it's everything to me. You know that. But House Amphisbaena is a Great House of Mlinivoun. Not just a branch, the house itself. The heir came to settle here."

"That life's not for everyone."

"I'm not saying it is. But if it is for Vani, a ride on Bandit won't change that. And if it isn't, it's not because of Bandit."

"If she leaves," said Zaya, "and I haven't done *everything*—"

"Everything?" said Minshoon, with a strange wildness at the back of his throat. "What if she wants to go back to dealing world-vine tar? Or datura, or dragon eggs, or stolen babies? What if she wants to try on contract killing?"

"Limper's ankle, Minshoon—"

"You think I'm stretching when I make those comparisons," said Minshoon. "But on a pro rata basis, they are all provably safer careers than riding a wyrm with you."

Chapter 18

SOCIAL SERVICES. NOT DIRECTLY *relevant to you, O tourist—I hope—but maybe a useful orienting concept is "the dole." This is a system of free dormitories, kitchens, schools, and clinics that supports the large fraction of Yemari citizens who do not get paid enough to afford these things at market prices. It's also a source of well-paid sinecures for the bureaucrats who administer (we're confident that Dr. Agama will be able to find an appropriate scholarly venue for the long essay that follows, which we are regrettably unable to reproduce in this brief and friendly visitors' guide. —Ed.)*

... to summarize, I guess: The dole is complicated. It's good to keep people housed and fed, and more Yemari than not will find themselves on the dole at some point in their lives. But, intentionally or not, it also helps the city separate its poorer citizens from power. It atomizes them by separating them into small, scattered sites, easily surveilled by the government and controlled by a manageable mobilization of law enforcement; it segregates them from their more fortunate neighbors by providing a completely separate stream of services...

I use the word "them" with reservations. I've been on the dole as well, longer even than I've been off it—which is pretty good, honestly, for a journalist not born to money. But I've been out of that world long enough that I don't know if I can claim solidarity. There's a phrase for this, I think, but I've forgotten what it is.

SEE ALSO: Currency; Economy; Law Enforcement.

—From "A Visitor's Handbook for Yemareir," by Shenireen Agama

***

"I WOKE THE BABY," said Zaya. "I woke the five-year-old, and the seven-year-old, and the fourteen-year-old, and the twins. They're seventeen. Minshoon never goes above this sort of stern dad-voice where it suddenly goes really deep and, like, *dense*, without being *loud*. I can do that too, but fuck it. I'm sorry my voice didn't flatten him against a wall. The Chiefs know I was trying." She wiped a tear away and reached for her glass—it was water, which fell so insolently short of what she needed that she wanted to throw the glass to shatter in the street. But the hard hand that alit to rub circles on her shoulder blades helped her think of other things. "It's all true, by the way. I killed my wife, I could easily have killed Thelendil, and I'll kill Vani if she rides with me. But at least then Jaliki won't have to watch her walk away."

"I'd really like to say you won't kill her," said Kemreen. "And I'm pretty sure it's true. But I feel like that's me blessing you risking the life of a child, and I'm not comfortable with that."

They sat side by side on the stoop of a tenement cattycorner to the Blind Beggar, drinking from borrowed glasses. Zaya had come hoping to find her, assuming she wouldn't; she had had trouble hiding her shock when Kemreen was there, in a corner of the bar where she could see the door, smiling as though for a lover who'd been unknowably, unavoidably detained.

"This is where I drink now," Kemreen had said by way of explanation. "I come and I wait for you. And now you're here."

Zaya had refused Kemreen's offer to buy her a drink, and the bartender's offer of a free one, thinking she'd need her wits about her. It didn't matter much. Vani's debt, her own return to the 'stream, her bad blood with Yyrreen—it all fell out. The only thing she kept to herself was how she'd come by Bandit. They'd moved out to the stoop when the live music had begun, making the Beggar too crowded as well as unbearably loud.

Zaya laughed. "But you're fine with me flying a two-ton fire-breathing lizard through the streets, breaking two or three dozen different laws in the process."

Kemreen took a pull from her drink, and the beer on her breath made the back of Zaya's throat feel sand-dry and scratchy. "There's two kinds of police, by and large," she said. "The ones who join to stop the true bad things from happening, or at least help when they do; and the kind who join to push people around."

"And everyone thinks they're the first kind."

"No." Kemreen looked up at the moon-painted clouds. "Men like Kanjoon and Yyvvoun know what they are. But some of us do lie to ourselves."

"Including you?"

"No." She flashed Zaya a quick, broad grin. "I'll admit that I sometimes find myself pushing people around and realize I'm enjoying it. On the job, I mean. Not in bed."

"I understood what you meant."

Kemreen sighed, "You're having complicated feelings about sleeping with a cop, aren't you?"

"I'm having one set of complicated feelings about sleeping with anyone at all, and a largely unrelated set of feelings about having one time, unknowingly, slept with a cop."

"I got into this to stop rapists and killers, not people joy-flying around on dragons."

"I bet that distinction got a lot clearer in your mind when you discovered a dragon-joy-flyer-around-er you didn't feel like arresting."

"Not only do I not want to arrest you, I don't want anyone else to arrest you."

"I'm sure that sounded really sweet in your head," said Zaya.

Kemreen sighed and looked at her glass, turning it in her hand to change the refraction from the streetlight. "You stole that dragon."

"That's a vile slander."

"You did, though."

Zaya turned to stare straight at Kemreen. "You looked your colleague in the eye and gave your professional opinion that I was far too fucked up on drugs to have committed the horrible, tragic crime of which I was—in your *professional opinion*—unjustly accused."

"About that," Kemreen said carefully. "Transdesert Corporation has issued an... objection? To that particular call. They'd like us to look more deeply into it."

Zaya laughed; the sound rattled like seeds in a dried gourd. "For a middleweight common wyrm? They've already scoured the veldt for the bastard and come up empty. How far are they going to go for this? Does it have gold bones or something?"

"No," said Kemreen. "But it's got thousands of miles of endurance flying under its belt, and it's been blooded in a dogfight. It's not just any old third-cohort Dawn you'd pick up on a beach in Azure Precinct. And it's a dangerous precedent to let it go. There are a lot of empaths in this city."

"It sounds," Zaya said, "like they plan to make an example out of whatever idiot stole their wyrm, to make absolutely sure it doesn't happen again."

Kemreen gave Zaya a long look, her face grave, her eyes wide.

Zaya laughed a third time, this time with tears in it. She put her hand on Kemreen's, squeezed, tried to choke back tears to say something. When they wouldn't clear her throat, she solved the issue by leaning forward and kissing Kemreen on the lips.

It wasn't their first kiss—it wasn't their tenth—but it almost had the feel of one: Not a fluttering, uncertain thing, not a greedy draught of lust. A brick-and-mortar kiss, the sun-heat long baked in. Kemreen's hard hand came up to cradle Zaya's head, its heel under the hinge of Zaya's jaw, her fingertips strong and separate against the back of her skull. When they drew back, it had the feel of a parting.

"Thank you," Zaya said, no longer caring for the tear-roughness of her voice.

"Don't be afraid," said Kemreen, in a voice that was obviously afraid. "It'll be OK."

"It's not even about fear," said Zaya. "I'm just trying to get my family through another day. But some company that's rich enough to buy and sell sacks of emeralds the size of my head thinks I'm the enemy."

"You did steal an entire dragon," Kemreen said.

"If you want to sleep with me again, you're going to have to teach yourself to stop thinking like a cop."

"I was trying to think like a captain of industry."

"If you think that's not thinking like a cop, you're still thinking like a cop."

Kemreen moved her face closer to Zaya's, mouth parted slightly as if to meet an incoming kiss. Zaya did not oblige her, and she pulled back. "Do I get to appeal this decision?"

"Sorry, when it comes to the Court of Who Gets To Sleep With Zaya Shearwater, I'm the Chief Justice."

"You realize being a cop is my job."

Zaya closed her eyes, sighed, squeezed Kemreen's shoulder, and stood. Kemreen followed suit, her eyes faintly panicked. "All right, Justice Shearwater" she said. "I accept your ruling." Her voice was flippant, cool, self-confident. She was very convincing. If Zaya hadn't just kissed her, she might have believed the act.

"I didn't kiss you because you did a good job arguing with me," said Zaya. "I did it because you helped me and I needed it and you didn't have to." She kissed Kemreen on the cheek. "Good night."

"That's it?"

"For tonight. If I'm alive in a week, I'll see you then."

"I'll be at the Chasse."

"In uniform?"

"Absolutely not."

Zaya smiled. "All right, then maybe sooner."

"Come home with me."

***

ZAYA DIDN'T, BUT SHE spent more time than she'd have liked to admit alone in bed, her own restless hands poor substitutes for Kemreen's absent mouth and fingers, imagining she had.

CHAPTER 19

LAW ENFORCEMENT. IF YOU'RE reading this, you're probably already in trouble. Am I right? If not, why are you here?

Anyway, most enforcement actions are taken by the precinct departments, which makes some visitors (not you, wise reader!) think that they can avoid consequences by just getting out of the precinct in which they did crimes. Unfortunately for these idiots, jurisdiction doesn't work like that. Criminal law is citywide, and precincts report up to sheriffs and then the Constable General, so there's coordination. Whether all these agencies work well together in practice is another issue, but you'd be wise to assume they will.

Another thing that can come as a rude surprise to would-be scofflaws is that Yemareir police are enhanciles, and yes, that includes the precinct ones. Strength, reflexes, night vision, the works. They're not demigods, but they'd have about an even chance against a tiger if they played their cards right.

Also, they ride dragons. What can I say? Even the death chickens can't resist the lure of a government paycheck.

SEE ALSO: Defense; Government; Precinct; Substance Abuse, Recreational.

—From "A Visitor's Handbook for Yemareir," by Shenireen Agama

***

THE COLD POINT CHASSE started and ended in Cyan Precinct, but not in the same place. It was tradition to roast the walrus-bats obtained on the Chasse over driftwood fires on Galaxy Beach, named for the tiny blue-and-yellow starfish that seemed to outnumber the grains of sand. But the presence of any number of wyrms on the beaches of Cyan Precinct would raise the alarm at the Cold Point Preserve; so the wyrms and their riders gathered in the shelter of Yymroun's Cove, unlikely to be spotted by a casual flyover.

Kirono and Cerminir were applying the last coat of this race's wax to Bandit's feathers—a light, water-shedding layer that wouldn't last long in racing conditions. Zaya, Zeino, and Bandit were reviewing tactics. "Your major advantage is that Bandit can do the work at Cold Point itself," said Zaya. "Flame a bat, catch it, get out. *Don't eat it,*" she said to Bandit. Turning back to Zeino: "So your spear and net are for... ?"

"Emergencies," said Zeino, grinning as though he would like to see an emergency.

"Emergencies meaning a bat is coming right at you or me. It doesn't happen often; usually they're busy running for cover. But every so often you get one brave enough to go after the human running the show. Unless that happens, our entire job at the Point is to be Bandit's eyes in the back of its head. We let it know where important things are. And I'm going to lean harder on you for that because... ?"

"You've got the mental map of the Point."

"I know you've got it all, Zeino-*cha*. I just can't afford to screw this up."

Zeino shrugged. "That's OK, I can."

Zaya laughed politely, because now was not the time to skin her partner and wear his face as a mask; but some of her flash of anger must have bled through Bandit's mind to Zeino, because he held out a conciliatory hand. "Sorry, *veraamaka navo*. You know I'm here to win."

Can I not eat any *of the bat?* Bandit asked.

Zaya was about to answer when the static of a damper field fell over her mind like pins and needles. She turned, a snarky greeting on her lips, then shot up like a rat with a mashed tail. "Adjudicator," she said.

Zeino rose behind her, more leisurely. "Adjudicator… ?"

"Jenirain Gila," said Zaya. "An Adjudicator of the Standards Board—the governing body of the 'stream."

"Chief Adjudicator," said Gila, "and a stickler for detail. I'm surprised you weren't aware—but I hear you've been scarce in the 'stream since you came back. If this is Zeino te-Zeino, please hand him his damper along with yours, there's a girl." Jenirain Gila fixed Zaya with a hawk's eye. She both loomed and hulked, her shoulders broad enough and thighs thick enough that they made a none-too-trim waist seem narrow, her blunt-featured face impassive on a head that rose easily six and a third feet. If she had aged in the last six years, it did not show. "I never did offer my condolences in person," she said. "Kiriki's death created quite a lot of extra work for us, it was a busy time—but that's not much of an excuse for six years' silence. I'm sorry, for your loss and my own neglect."

Zaya handed Zeino's damper to him. "Is that why you volunteered to deliver this?" she asked. "To offer six-year-late condolences on my widowhood?"

"A little," said Gila. "Also, you should know that the Board has summarily dismissed an ethics complaint from Shanhoon Krait about you violating the rules against attacking other racers with projectiles."

"What?"

"You dumped a lithorang on him. He's going to pursue an amendment to the bylaws. The third reason I'm here is I figured you'd like to share some of your usual bullshit concerning the psionic damper, and I wanted a preview of it while your wyrm's in the damping field, so you can't send it after me."

"What could I possibly say that would surprise you?"

"Probably nothing, you were always unbelievably predictable. Except in the 'stream, of course. So bore me."

"Dampers are a tactic to exclude Kayalim on their face. What else do you need?"

"That's interesting though, because when you and Kiriki argued that *allowing* psionics wasn't granting special privileges to Kayalim racers, your counterargument was that anyone can learn it."

"Anyone can. For some reason, only Kayalim do."

Gila smiled thinly. "That argument cuts both ways."

"No it doesn't."

"We're restoring the sport to its roots. Neither the Sky-Eaters nor the early 'streamers used psionic empathy."

"The Sky-Eaters didn't race at all," said Zaya, "especially not in Ashen Precinct during hatching season. Ashen Precinct in hatching season is why they had a whole taboo on visiting the season-city at all. And the early 'streamers didn't use tail-spikes."

"Still bitter about that one after all these years?"

Zaya realized she'd drawn a minor crowd—or, at least, it felt like a crowd; it was mostly far-away eyes, 'streamers and their ground crews gawking over to see who was shouting at the Chief Adjudicator. She looked back at Gila, whose fine-lined face seemed to vibrate with the barest hum of smugness. "Get what you wanted?"

"Yes, thanks."

Zaya turned back to Bandit. "Reminded everyone what a joyless little complainer Zaya Shearwater is."

"That's not what I wanted. Anyway, you should appreciate those dampers. They stimulate your people's economy."

"My *people's* economy?" Zaya said, not sure whether she should be angry or confused.

"'Streamers, to wyrmback!" came the call.

Gila tilted her head toward Bandit. "Go on, then," she said. "Your quarry awaits. I really am sorry about Kiriki."

Keep that precious name off your tongue, Zaya did not say. Zeino was already in the rear seat; she could practically feel his empathy butting up against the damper, like trying to fit his head through his shirt's armhole. She wondered if he felt the same from her—but it was too late to ask; wyrms were fanning out on the beach, necks lunging impatiently north, toward the out-of-place clouds that always glowered over the Cold Point thaumobiome.

"She really hates you, doesn't she?" said Zeino.

"I don't think so."

Zeino snorted. "Could have fooled me."

Zaya felt herself starting to dislike this man, who took liberties of manners he hadn't earned. Definitely the kind of person who congratulated himself in private for being a straight shooter. "That might be part of the point," she said. "We have history, but it's not like that. It seems like she wanted me to say all that in front of a crowd. I'm not sure why."

"I've got a simpler explanation. But you'd know better, I guess."

"Wyrms, find your marks!"

Bandit's mark was between Monsoon and Time's Warped Arrow, the latter now through its spring molt and in fresh summer plumage of desert red-brown with royal purple bands on the wings. Lerikaan had dyed their own hair to match, down to the band. "Is that true?" they called to Zaya. "They didn't use to allow tail-spikes?"

"Not until six years ago," Zaya called back.

"When this one and her wife used Kayalim magic to beat a slew of better riders," Shanhoon put in, "and the Standards Board had to do something about it."

"Remember when I beat that one guy at Stone Forest with a damper on?" Zaya shouted to Lerikaan.

"Leaving us all wondering," called Shanhoon. "How did a woman who only ever learned to control a dragon with her mind do so well in a race where she wasn't allowed to use it?"

She snatched a glimpse of him through Bandit's eyes, and wished she hadn't—his smug face made her want to throw her saddle-knife at it. More than that, though, it struck a spark of familiarity brighter than his features ever could. He hadn't been a 'streamer when she and Kiriki had been coming up; he was too young, for one, and she'd have recognized the name. How did she know that smirk?

"There's more to my mind than empathy, though I don't know if his lordship can say the same," said Zaya, talking to him while looking at Lerikaan. "How much did that barding set you back?"

Lerikaan licked their lips, rapped the wyrm's neck-plate with her knuckles, and stared ahead at the clouds above Cold Point.

"To the sky!"

***

ZAYA KEPT BANDIT REINED in on the flight up the coast, following charm-lights placed along the high-tide line. They started out in perhaps fifth place, but wyrms gradually overtook them; she intercepted those attempts where she could, but did not put much effort into it. "The game on the way up is to save energy," she had said to Zeino during their practice run. "A few more seconds hunting walrus-bats won't make the difference between winning and losing. The real race will be among the teams that are first to catch a bat. As long as we don't lag too far behind the pack, we'll be one of them."

Zeino had shrugged. "If you say so. I'm just an empath. I'm not cool enough to hunt giant bats from the back of a dragon."

"Me neither. Bandit will take care of it."

"... how's that special, though? Can't everyone else train their wyrm to hunt?"

"Sure. They do, and they have, and some of those other wyrms will make a quick catch, and those will be our competitors. But—look, you've worked with tracker dogs. And it's not their job to chase cats, so you train them not to chase cats. But then there's that one time that the thief puts the diamond necklace on his cat..."

"Sure, happens all the time."

"The point is, in this irregular situation, do you want your dog to fall back on its training, which is wrong? Or do you reach into its head and tell it what to do, just this once?"

Zeino had nodded along. "All right. But you said we're not actually going to be able to use psionics?"

"Not in the race," Zaya had said. "But we can do it in advance."

They were pulling up on the border of the Cold Point thaumo-biome; Zaya *reached* with the trickle of empathy that she was able to summon to remind Bandit what was next. Slowly she felt herself fill with the faint memory of copper and raw meat.

"Oh, shit," Zeino said. "On our right."

Two lightly armored riders on Dusk Stalker worms were winging toward the pack from Cold Point. One called out in a sorcerously amplified voice: "THIS IS A PROTECTED NATURAL PRESERVE! WYRM-RIDING AND HUNTING ARE PROHIBITED! TRESPASSERS WILL BE EXPELLED BY ANY MEANS NECESSARY!"

Zaya shook her head. "It's like I said before. These guys have to be seen doing this, or they'll lose their jobs, but they're not going to start a dogfight when they're outnumbered eleven to one. They know what they're in for if they take one of us down, and it's not a nice dinner with the spouse and spawn."

The slipstream swallowed whatever Zeino had to say in answer. Zaya could see a flurry of activity in the channels between the onrushing cliffs—bats, most likely, that had detected what was coming and wanted no part of it, headed for the sanctuary of caves. Three strong wingbeats and the pack of wyrms dissolved like a rotten orange thrown against a wall, scattered in all directions to hunt their prey in the suddenly frigid air of Cold Point.

A thread of dismay and uncertainty from Bandit came through Zaya's empathic link.

"Go to the closest place where you saw the most," Zaya said, guessing at the details. She sent along as strong an angle and position as she could.

Bandit veered in that direction, but its mind was perceptibly dissatisfied. Zaya soon saw why—there were three wyrms in that channel already, each already getting in the others' way. They were clustered around a cave, it appeared, but the bats' concentration—or maybe just the presence of young—had emboldened them; a few of the brilliant white bats were harrying the wyrms, throwing themselves directly at the faces of dragon and rider alike. She felt a filament of sick worry from Zeino. "It's OK," she said. "You're in the rear."

It was hard to tell whether he felt consoled. She didn't exactly dig for it.

A big Dawn broke out of the group—to find greener pastures, Zaya thought, but it looped back around and headed for the cave, chest swelling. "This'll be good," she said, shifting Bandit's angle slightly with the reins, "but not for them. Thanks for the favor, Dawnie, we appreciate you—"

A plume of blue-and-yellow fire burst from the Dawn's gaping mouth and into the cave; and, as if they'd been waiting for just such an insult, a chittering swarm of bats belched forth, filling the channel with a carpet of white.

Riding the Mule, without a damper, she would have used his wings as an extension of her own body, roaring through the air to seize one of these purblind things before it adapted to the light. Any resistance it might have harbored to the prospect of charging a flume of hundreds of screeching bats, each the size of a bulldog with wings longer than Zaya was tall, would have surrendered to the Mule's trust in Zaya and Kiriki; her control would have been perfect, seamless, and she would have felt the fur and skin part under her talons as the Mule seized its prey and peeled off to gain the finish—

—all these commands, these images, she flung at Bandit as hard as she could, though the damper made her feel like a child throwing a handful of pebbles at a stone wall.

And Bandit did not charge.

It *dove.*

"No no no no no," shouted Zaya, "don't be scared, go back, those bats are terrified and confused, it's fine, *please*—" and then the blurry, faint image at the back of her mind came into focus—a pair of arms and a head, flailing in the water, their movement steadily slowing.

"You rubber-headed buzzard's bastard," she shouted, "you dry strip of chicken breast, you understuffed feather bed, you dull boot-scraper—" But it was no use. Bandit was resolved to make this rescue.

Then a black bolt of *something* shot through Zaya's brain, and Bandit pulled up short in its dive.

Another black wave; Bandit's wings hauled gracelessly upward.

Zaya turned back, furious, and screamed at Zeino: "What are you doing?"

Winning this race for you, his mind-voice replied, clearer through the damper's fog than she ever expected it to be.

The initial lift from the sudden snap-out of Bandit's wings had worn off. The Dawn took a halfhearted lurch upward... then, even though the veil of the Damper, Zaya felt the wyrm's resolve harden, and there was no further motion of its wing. They hung in the air a moment, then began to plunge.

Come on, you stubborn slug, Zaya felt Zeino think. In this moment, she realized several truths:

- Zeino, not a 'streamer, had no idea how far Bandit could fall before it became incapable of stopping the descent before they hit the water.

- Zeino, an empath far stronger than she had given him

credit for, could possibly bind up Bandit's motor programs long enough to make a crash inevitable.

- Zeino, used to swift compliance from animals with little experience with racing or dogfighting, had no idea what he might be up against.

- Bandit, a reptile incapable of regulating its own internal temperature, might, in the near-freezing water of the Cold Point thaumobiome, die *surprisingly quickly.*

The slipstream of their fall began to tear at her face; Bandit flailed against Zeino's hold on its mind, but could not break it. Desperate, she threw her mind in with Bandit's, hoping to tip the balance.

It's not going to work, she realized. *It takes less to screw up Bandit's brain than it takes to create a coherent motor pattern. Zeino thinks he's winning, but with the damper, the best he can do is fight Bandit to a draw.*

And a draw means we're in the water.

By the time she had finished thinking it, Bandit's wings had snapped open, heaving them up toward the diffusing cloud of flame-spooked bats.

It took a moment for her to understand why. "You heard my thoughts," she said. "You knew you had to give in."

The damper made the worm's thoughts too blurry and dull to recognize as words; but there was no mistaking the cool, sharp crackle of reptilian fury.

"We'll never fly with this dogshit wingman again, that I promise you," said Zaya.

I can hear you, Zeino's voice echoed in her mind, damper-faint but distinct.

"As if I care."

A bat winged past her head; then a barbed arrow did likewise. Around her were nets, harpoons, even lassos, lashing out at bats and, occasionally, other wyrms and other riders; the Cold Point Chasse was well known as a venue for score-settling. All around, too, was fire; Monsoon and Time's Warped Arrow, Lerikaan Boom-slang's Moultwyrm, were tagging the huge bats with some regularity. Even as she watched, Arrow hit a bat head-on with a jet of flame—only to have it snatched by an Eyrie Shrike, who swiftly wheeled off, a screaming Moultwyrm in hot pursuit.

"Remember what we said," Zaya said to Bandit. "Find one and chase it until it gets away. Don't be like these idiots lashing out at everything. We need one bat, in your claws, and then we leave."

Bandit's first lunge was straight up; Zaya felt Zeino's weight lurch as he scrambled to stay on, and the cold tang of wyrm-smugness seeped into her consciousness. It was soon replaced by the tunnel vision of the hunt: She could not see the bat over Bandit's head, or through its eyes, but the hunt was shot all through its snakelike darts and jackknifes through the frigid air, the short, sharp wingbeats that fueled them. Her skin felt as though it might peel off in clammy sheets. It would not be too long now before Bandit would start to slow in the cold, not much longer after that before the bats' hot blood secured them an insuperable advantage; too much persistence could kill wyrms in the Cold Point Chasse, and the icy water below would not long spare 'streamers either—

—the girdle of Bandit's ribs contracted; the smell of sulphur filled Zaya's nostrils—sulphur and, blessedly, burning hair and meat; and Bandit lurched downward at a crashing pitch, so Zaya was, for just a moment, staring in the face of a foam-laced sea, painted white and black with moonlight; and there was impact, jerking Bandit down toward that white-traced sea for the finest filament of time before it peeled off, up and out of the bat-spangled pillars of the Point, the coast to its left wing, its south south, toward Galaxy Beach and the finish line.

They plunged out of the Cold Point thaumobiome and into the blessed fug of sea air on a warm spring night.

It had always been Kiriki who threw her arms out in exaltation, who keened and hooted their moments of triumph. It was the gesture she'd been famous for in the stream, which made it, curiously, an object of private joy for Zaya—to be the only one, or one of few, who understood how rare and strange such abandon was for her. Kiriki had been a small woman, smaller than Zaya, but the triumphal throwing-out of her arms would always catch the wind, slowing the Mule down for just a moment with the increased drag...

... which was why it took her a moment to realize that the jolt she felt behind her was unusual and out of place. Because Zeino was not Kiriki; because he was not secure enough on dragonback to release his grip on Bandit's feathers; because the force of the jolt was in the wrong direction for a rejoicing body snapping out to catch the wind, but in the right direction for taking an impact from behind.

The damper delayed the pain, but only by a second; it blunted it, but Zaya still chirped out the beginnings of a scream.

She pressed herself into Bandit and shinnied back, reaching back with one toe to find Zeino; he was still there. "Can you hang on?" she asked.

"For now."

"Who is it?"

As if in answer, an arrow sliced the air above her. If she'd been sitting up, it would have pierced a lung.

"The guards from Cold Point. Two men on Dusk Stalkers. Why are they following us?"

"Zaya Shearwater!" one voice called. "This is the Aquamarine Precinct police! Bring your wyrm over and land on the beach immediately!"

Zaya closed her eyes for a moment, bracing for pain. "Get rid of your damper."

"What? Fuck no. I need that money."

Zaya pulled hers off and threw it back at Zeino; it bounced off him, into the sea. "There. We're disqualified. You're not getting paid. Now help me save your worthless hide."

An arrow sank into Bandit's haunch. It screamed; Zaya felt the charred carcass fall from its jaws, and the spasm of its pain nearly bucked Zeino off. She felt him scrabble; his weight shifted, and the stifling field of the damper fell away like a cloak of pelts, bringing lightness and cool and clarity.

She *reached* out to Bandit, shunting through Zeino almost as fluidly as she had done so long ago with Kiriki, and its mind and muscles came alive inside her.

She did a hairpin turn, down and back, putting more torque on Bandit's muscles than she would ever do voluntarily on her own, trusting Zeino to absorb enough stress and pain to let her carry the maneuver through. Pain shot through its right wing—but she blunted it, then surged through it, coming up under one Stalker while it was still turning to face her. Zeino, mind-shredded and screaming, clung for his life; the Dusk Stalker, for its part, recoiled from Bandit's attack. But Bandit did not use its flame, and its claws scratched and harried but did not dig deep. It was looking for something thin, soft, and all-important—and found it.

The harness of the dragonrider's saddle parted under Bandit's talon; and, *reaching* out to the Dusk, Zaya felt the reins slacken, felt the rider's weight slip and then fall away.

Before Bandit peeled off, Zaya reached swiftly into the Stalker's mind to fill it with one final thing: A great yearning, a crushing thirst, a deep and overpowering horniness.

What the fucking fuck, said Zeino in her mind, to the sound of wyrm-scream as the Stalker wheeled and charged its comrade.

"Dusk Stalker males are show-offs," Zaya replied, "and the females will just fucking kill a competitor. One way or another, our friend is going to keep its friend busy."

They surged toward the city, seeking cover in the shoreline of Cobalt Precinct: A richer seaside jurisdiction, with villas fronting the beach and a phalanx of gaudy tenements directly behind. It would be a popular destination on a pretty night; they would lose themselves easily among taxi- and courier-worms.

"You're an abomination," Zeino said. "You don't do that to an animal. I'm ashamed to know you."

"Not so ashamed you wouldn't take my money, you scumbag hypocrite," said Zaya, who was sick of this shit.

"No," said Zeino, exhausted and scared and in pain. "No, not as ashamed as that."

Chapter 20

ECONOMY. *YOU ARE A tourist and I'm a dummy, so I'll make this quick. The basic question of "how do all those people eat?" is answered by the bay, food imports from nearby Ililuë settlements, and the outlying farms to the east and south. Most of the farms are state-run at this point, and a large fraction of the labor is done by work crews, which is to say convicts. Most of the food produced that way goes back to feed folks on the dole, but it can be a minor revenue stream for the city depending on commodity prices.*

In terms of balance of trade and whatnot, we take in mostly raw materials and export mostly manufactured items, art, and culture. We're one of not that many economies that can produce charms and ensorcelled weapons at scale, and there are apparently a lot of people who will buy any dumb thing as long as it came from "the City of Dragons." I mean, hey, you're reading this, right? (Shenireen. —Ed.) Kidding of course; my readers are discerning, tasteful, and almost supernaturally attractive. (Co-signed. We appreciate you! —Ed.)

SEE ALSO: Currency; Law Enforcement; Social Services.

—From "A Visitor's Handbook for Yemareir," by Shenireen Agama

***

THE AZURE PRECINCT FREE Clinic was full up that night, but Zaya didn't need to wait: Zeino limped away as fast as he could, the arrow still in his thigh. She and Bandit coasted down the seaside boulevards of the shore precincts, stopping briefly to pay a courier to take a note to Minshoon at the finish line. Then they veered inland, back toward Rust Precinct and Saavero's stable.

She more than half expected Kemreen, or her cop friends, or Shanhoon, or Yyrreen—even Tjaroon or a police officer, anyone to break the solitude—but no one was there. Even the stalls were half empty; a number of these wyrms had gone to compete in the Chasse.

This was the first arrow she'd had to pull from the haunch of a dragon—but not the first arrow Bandit had had to have pulled out. The rider who'd done it, whenever it was, had been skilled and sure-handed, and Bandit's memory together with Zaya's pain-blunting empathy made the extraction and wound-binding easier than it had any right to be. When she was done, she went to Bandit's locker and produced a fifth of whiskey, a bucket, and a stoneware mug. She filled the mug, then poured the rest of the bottle into the bucket and brought it to Bandit, pausing to hug and kiss its snout. It nuzzled her in acknowledgment of the gesture. She sat on the log that Bandit used as a chew toy and took a deliberately dainty sip. It took a long slurp from the bucket.

"I'm sorry," she said.

She felt a mental shrug from Bandit. *You didn't shoot me.*

"You understand why I'm apologizing, though."

No.

"Do you care at all about why I think I should apologize?"

I don't understand the question.

"I know someone might be after me. Was after me. I didn't think it'd happen during a race. But I should have."

Bandit took a long slurp from the bucket.

"They want to make an example out of me. Of course they'd do it during a race. Killing me on top of my dragon would have been perfect."

Bandit's mind made a mild noise of interrogation; it was focused on the whiskey.

"They're trying to kill me because I stole you."

Bandit's mind made another noise, this time of disdain.

The stable's great bay door opened at the other end; Bandit perked up as another wyrm entered. "Who's that?"

Aubade. It awkwardly reproduced the sound in its mind, stripped of meaning. Zaya heard footsteps approaching Bandit's enclosure; a young Kayalim man appeared in the door. "Holy shit, you're alive!"

Zaya sighed. "And what's your name, son?"

"Tuuro te-Kaneva. Were you really attacked by plainclothes cops?"

Zaya auditioned any number of biting responses, then dissolved them all in a mouthful of whiskey. "Yes. Who told you, and how'd they know?"

"Cymoraan Mamba saw the body."

Zaya drank again instead of saying *shit*. "One of them drowned, I guess? Washed ashore?"

"Drowned?" Tuuro laughed a laugh with too much volume, too much echo—a laugh like a rap on a coffin-lid. "No, Cairn—that's Cymoraan's wyrm—Cairn flamed him while the other Stalker was trying to fuck it in midair. Then Cairn pulled him out of the saddle and dropped him on the beach."

"Bow-backed Chief of Thirst and Famine," said Zaya.

"That's not even the best part. Some other 'streamer pulled the other one out of the water, brought him to the beach, and a whole crew beat him to within an inch of his life."

Zaya put her head in her hands.

"That way it wasn't just Cymoraan," said Tuuro. "Standards Board can't disavow a dozen and a half 'streamers, and the cops can't kill that many without raising suspicions. No one fucks with *veraamaka navo*."

There were so many things Zaya could say to that. They could plant a bomb at the starting line; they could target only 'stream-ers like Tuuro, whom most of this city wouldn't miss; they could simply carry on with their original plan, to make an example out of Zaya Shearwater, to prove to every would-be wyrmjacker in every precinct that stealing a dragon wasn't worth the consequences. But this kid's heart was fuller than her whiskey mug tonight, and emptying it wouldn't help her in any way that mattered. "This race, they did," she said, "but I can't not drink to that." She did. "Who won, anyway?"

"Krait."

"Ah, fuckpig."

"Go on, then," a voice put in from outside the enclosure. "Tell her who took second." It was an older Kayalim man, hair cropped and grey-black, whose family resemblance to Tuuro was unmissable. "Zetaala te-Kaana," he said by way of introduction.

One look in Tuuro's eyes was all it took. Zaya dropped her mug, heedless of Bandit's hiss at wasted whiskey, and bolted up, hooting and crowing, to enfold Tuuro in a tear-stained embrace.

***

Wyrm-taxis were out in force on the warm night, but Zaya couldn't stomach the thought of taking one. At first she told herself it was because she couldn't stand the thought of touching another dragon tonight, which admittedly wasn't wrong; then she observed that it was perhaps because she was in no rush to see her family, which she absolutely wasn't. But as the dozenth coach-liveried Dawn Wyrm of the night coasted over her while her quadriceps sang madrigals of agony pushing a rusty-spoked bike up through the red glinting gravel of Garnet Hill, the reason became clear: She didn't feel right doing it because taking a wing to cover ground her feet would walk for free was what rich people did. It wasn't for criminals who lived in dole-flats. That wasn't her now, of course, but it had been, and at some point her mind had settled that it would be again—or at least it was the modal future, possibly not inevitable but the default, the gravitation from which her family would have to tear free.

Unknowingly, she had braced for a barrage of relieved hugs and outraged questions; the silence that greeted her instead hit her like a wave, so strong she nearly missed the still, tense bodies gathered around the coffee table. After a few long moments, Minshoon whispered, "Tiamat, thank you," but it only served to make the quiet deeper.

"Good news!" she said. "I'm not dead!"

The adults were up, the kids were not: Minshoon, Kirono, and Cerminir were joined by Kiri, Vinaali, Zayeni's mother Kaala, and Kemreen.

As soon as she saw her, Kemreen leapt out from the tableau so strongly Zaya couldn't imagine how she'd failed to notice her: She was too big for the couch and too pale for the lighting, the ceiling mural's colors lurid on her skin. "She's a cop," Zaya said, and immediately regretted it—then retracted her regret; Kemreen seemed entirely unstung.

"Among other things," Kemreen said in mock annoyance, patting the seat beside her.

Zaya went and took the seat, sitting stiffly straight to keep from touching her. What was she thinking, coming here? What did *they* think? "I told them you were alive," said Kemreen. "Yyvvoun saw you fly off. Word got around."

"Among the cops, you mean."

"Yeah," Kemreen said, annoyed, "among the cops."

"I sent a courier," said Zaya.

"We got it," said Kirono. "But... it was kind of Kemreen to share what she knew. We thought, if she cares about you, she shouldn't wait up alone."

"Plus, Vanako wouldn't let her go," said Cerminir.

"If a cop tried to kill one of you," said Zaya, "I wouldn't have a cop over to my house just because they said they were sleeping with you."

"Oh, I don't think anyone said anything about that," said Vinaali. "Congratulations, Zaya, she seems just lovely."

"Vani said she helped you in Rust Precinct," Kirono said hastily. "We took her word, not Kemreen's."

"Vani, the kid who was dealing behind our backs and probably lying to us about what it was?" said Zaya. "Is that the person whose word you're taking?"

"For someone who's so concerned about a *cop* in your house," Kemreen said bitterly, "you sure aren't taking a whole lot of care when you're talking about crime."

That silenced the room. All eyes drifted to Kemreen.

She looked around, confused and maybe a little bit panicked, sensing the change. "That wasn't a threat," she said. "I didn't mean it like that." She waited for someone to acknowledge her correction, but the silence didn't crack. "You have to believe," she said. "I'd never actually—"

"It's not the best look, in a group like this," said Zaya, "throwing your weight around like that."

Minshoon shot her a look. "We believe you," he said to Kemreen. "But about this, she's right."

"All right," said Kemreen, standing. "I guess I've overstayed my welcome."

No one contradicted her. She shrugged and walked over to the door.

"Thank you for what you did tonight," Kirono called as she put her hand on the knob.

"But don't stop leaving," said Kiri.

"I'm sorry the whole sex situation is probably over now," said Cerminir, "I hope it was f—"

If Kemreen didn't slam the door hard enough to rattle the cups in the kitchen, she at least closed it hard enough to make Zaya's heart skip. She sighed heavily into the silence.

"I thought that was a nice clarification Kirono made just then," said Vinaali.

"I have to get some sleep," said Zaya.

"No," said Minshoon.

Six pairs of eyes drifted to rest on him.

"When we talked about this," Minshoon said, "you said the only crime we hadn't committed yet was racing the dragon."

"It's not technically a crime to fraternize with cops," said Zaya.

"I think it was a crime how you treated that girl, if I'm being candid," said Vinaali.

"Eh, die mad about it," said Kiri.

"You attacked an officer," said Minshoon. "In self-defense," he hastily added, showing a conciliatory palm, "but that's not a distinction your lovely friend's co-workers will appreciate. And we lost our entry fee and everything we put up to bet."

"Sorry for saving my own life instead of finishing," said Zaya.

"Don't be shitty," snapped Minshoon. "You know everyone cares more about your life than the money. But you almost got killed tonight and we're out an eighth-slab on this race. We had to at least double that money and now it's gone. We are so far behind, Zaya. What are we going to do?"

Every single word he said stoked an unfair, unreasoning fury—but she could not help but hear the catch in his voice when he said the money was gone. That was university money for Taavi, Gilthiniel, and maybe Vanako, treatment money for Jaliki, tax money for House Shearwater, off-season money to buy food for everyone when the summer made the Emerald Dunes impassable and Zaya could no longer earn from long-haul caravaning. It was the life of the family, as much as air or water, and they had staked it on her and Bandit and that fuckstick Zeino, and it was gone.

Because, although Minshoon would never say it, she—*veraa-maka navo*—couldn't outfly a couple of cops long enough to get one blessed bat carcass to the finish line.

"What do you think we should do?" she asked.

It felt as though a cylinder of air-clear glass around Minshoon had cracked, then fallen to flinders; a softness in his face materialized to match the softness of her voice. "It feels like you've barely been back, and I hate to cut your summers short, but... if you could find a security job, one that'd take you out of town for a few weeks..."

"... it'd bring in some money," said Zaya, "and take me out of the police's reach for a bit." Zaya nodded. "But it doesn't protect you. From the police or from Tjaroon. And I might not find something. Summer is really bad for security gigs." She had to work to keep the boredom from her voice.

Her own objections, obvious, had been preordained; so were Minshoon's rejoinders. "We can borrow against your pay to keep Tjaroon happy if we have to," he said. "The neighborhood will help us with the cops if we keep our heads down—Kemreen, too, maybe, if you haven't soured her on us for good."

"They won't pay Zaya enough to pay Tjaroon back," said Cerminir. "She's never made ten slabs at one job. Why would they pay her that much?"

"We can borrow more than the money coming in, as long as there's money coming in."

"What good does that do?" said Cerminir. "Now, instead of owing money to a criminal, we'll owe someone who can put us in jail if we don't pay."

"It buys us time," said Minshoon.

"What the fuck good has *time* done us so far?" said Cerminir.

Kirono stepped so he was side by side with Cerminir; she looked down at him, and he looked back up at her. "Squeeze?" he asked.

She nodded, too upset to speak. He put an arm around her waist, then pressed her close.

"We always knew we could lose this," he said in a low soft voice, as though comforting a hurt child. "We always knew the thing we made could break. It's amazing it lasted as long as it did."

"That doesn't make it all right," said Cerminir.

"Don't give up already," said Minshoon. "We don't know that's going to happen."

"Describe to me how anything else happens," said Cerminir. "No miracles."

I can tell you how, said Zaya, but she couldn't say it. And no one else had any ideas; so silence fell.

"Fuck Vani," said Cerminir at last. "And fuck all of you for choosing to save her instead of the rest of us. And fuck me for not loving her enough to see it your way, and for being too broken to fix any of it." She loosed herself from Kirono's arm and stalked back toward her room.

"We love you," Kirono said; but she did not turn.

Zaya realized it was her cue to speak. "I'll go knock on some doors in the morning," she said. "With any luck, I'll be on dragonback by night."

"Don't go," said Kirono. "Don't waste the time we have here with each other."

"I'll waste it if I think I could have spent it fighting," said Zaya. The predictability of the whole thing made her want to cry—whether from boredom or from real self-hate, she wasn't sure. The numb despair was so strong, it took her a moment to realize that this, at least, was not a lie. She saw Vinaali nod out of the corner of her eye: *Brave girl.*

She was, she knew, brave. But brave felt less like *brave* than *old.*

"I don't see what all the fuss is about," said Kiri. "You've all lived on the dole before—thousands of people do, hundreds of thousands. You're lucky you have something you can sell off to pay."

"We haven't," said Kirono. The words sounded, for a moment, like macaw-scream or the hoot of a monkey—they weren't part of the dance, the arc of concession and promises hat had stretched, grey and determinate, before Zaya when she had asked Minshoon what she should do. "Not all of us."

"Still," said Kiri. "Even in Lilac, there are thousands on it. And you'll have more cash than most of them."

"Not Cer," said Kirono. "She can't live with strangers—not so close. She never could. We found her in the streets."

Kiri drew a breath, and Zaya wondered for a brief breathless moment if he was going to say she could go back. Instead, he nodded. "But she has Enwë now. What'll she do?"

"She'll go back to Cildinior Amalgam," said Zaya, with every needed not of heavy sadness in her voice, no indication—that she could perceive, in any case—of the globe of cold rock that her heart had become. "To her mother. The reason she left."

***

THE FEELING OF ROTE motion and foreordainment was still with Zaya when she woke. She packed, ate, explained, kissed, hugged, wiped tears, and reassured as though watching herself in a play whose lines she had memorized. The cold comfort of predictability seemed to widen her field of view: She could see Cerminir struggling with fear and rage, Minshoon with doubt, Jaliki and the twins with the growing certainty that this was all worse than it seemed.

Vanako, slightly more tactless and grating than usual, was gutted.

It's OK, Zaya wanted to tell her. *I have a plan.* It wasn't a deep want, like a sand-throat thirst or a deep skin itch or the desire for a woman near enough to touch knees with; it was more like finishing breakfast and realizing you'd have liked another half an apple. She would have given Vanako an extra-tight squeeze when she left, but Vanako wouldn't even acknowledge that a hug was incoming, so she didn't. "Take care of the irises," she said instead. "Please?"

Vanako made a hawking noise and grumbled something that was possibly "Why?"

"They were Kiriki's favorites," Zaya said. "They just need a little water every day. Please."

Vanako shrugged. "I've always wanted to snoop around your room, I guess."

Zaya leaned in close to Vanako's ear and whispered *Just don't let the baby play with the sex toys,* and Vanako shouted "Ugh!" and batted her away, and for a moment it felt like real life Zaya was walking through, fluid and responsive and opinionated, not the rigid chained machinery of an assembly line—

—and then she was out, in the open air with nothing but a bag of clothes and cash, and now instead of feeling separated from herself by the proscenium of a stage it was more like spying on herself from behind the curtain. But she did not let herself come out yet. There were a few more steps to dance.

They didn't do hiring at the depot. You were supposed to find one of the hangouts in Damask or Madder or Tan or Taupe, in front of a Kayalim restaurant or bodega or boarding-house, where everyone knew to look for day labor and contract work. But if you were a professional, you'd been at some point to the routing office in Ivory, where they took down some information if you let them and after, sometimes, if you let them know where you could be found, someone would tell you to go to Kanireen and ask about a job that would always pay more than the usual run. Kanireen liked owls, and some kind of statue or sculpture or little print of one always found its way to her desk after Zaya finished one of those high-paying runs, because if there was one thing she'd learned in a quarter-century of colonized living it was that paper-pushing was more powerful than sorcery and you wanted to get in good with its practitioners. Zaya was more comfortable at the hangouts, but she was also short on time, so she biked to Ivory and walked into the routing office with sweat still gleaming on her skin.

Kanireen was at the desk, her owls arrayed around her in a neat arc. She raised an eyebrow at Zaya. The ivory parent and child owls were all the way to Kanireen's left, nearly out of her sight. "Turning yourself in?" Kanireen said.

"Not today. Who's got work for me?"

"Zaya." Kanireen's look was almost pitying.

"I know. I haven't taken leave of my senses; we're just going through a trial separation. It's not that I don't understand what you feel like you shouldn't have to say to me, it's just that I need you to actually say it, so I can say you said it. Not that anyone will ask. Just to myself."

"I'm not signing anything," Kanireen said, not looking up.

"Fine."

Kanireen looked Zaya straight in the eye. "Then fine. No one will hire you to fly a wyrm ever again. Everyone knows you stole that Dawn, everyone knows you were trying to steal that bag of emeralds, everyone knows you're back to trying to be some hot-shit racer on the back of a stolen wyrm because you can't afford a trained one and you can't use your Kayalim brain magic or whatever to cheat any more. You're a shitty little thief, and that's what you'll be for the rest of your life, and the only good thing about me wasting breaths I'll never get back on a shitty little thief like you is that I at least get the chance to curse you out for ever making me like you at all, you shitty little thief!"

Zaya closed her eyes and drew in an enormous draught of air. She held it for what felt like an hour—it was two seconds, maybe three—and when she let it out, the shreds of the dulling caul around her mind came with it.

"When you said nobody will hire me again, that's not, like, hyperbole?"

"No!"

Zaya nodded slowly. It felt like trying to understand a complicated long division problem five seconds after being awakened from the middle of a very deep sleep. "Thank you. That's very clear."

"THIEF!" Kanireen shrieked as loudly as she could plainly hoping that the police would hear.

Zaya stepped outside and looked around There were no police in sight, but that didn't mean none in earshot. There was a pair of colobus monkeys in a tree, and a small Ranger Wyrm, about the size of a greyhound—the first cohort had hatched a few months ago, and there was a broodspire in Eggshell Precinct, not far to the east. The wyrm had spotted the monkeys. The monkeys, secure in their high perch, chattered and hooted at the wyrm. She found the wyrm's hunger and grew it, deepened it. A rope of drool dropped from its jaws; it danced from foot to foot in frustration. Zaya cultivated, in her own mind, the sight and smell of a fruit-laden papaya tree, with just-fallen fruit scattered split on the ground beneath it.

She turned it over and around before her mind's eye, adjusted the green of its leaves, the fine texture of its bark, the smell of the fruit.

Then she put it in the monkeys' minds, sudden and resplendent, along with a strong directional cue: *Inside the routing office.*

Animals that lived for any length of time around Kayalim learned quickly to distrust any mental images of unknown provenance—but not many Kayalim came around to Ivory Precinct. The monkeys made for the routing office as fast as they could; the Ranger Wyrm, insane with implanted hunger, followed, leading with a plume of blue-and-yellow flame.

Zaya was around the corner before Kanireen could scream.

***

SHE FOUND A COURIER with his own pen and paper to deliver a message to the house: *Found a job. En route to Tzadiscari. Wish me thick clouds and cool air. All my love.*

Then she hopped a bike and pedaled to Rust Precinct as fast as the road would take her.

CHAPTER 21

LANDMARKS, FANTASTIC. Surely part of the reason you've come to this place is the weird magic that perfuses the environment. Like all things in Yemareir, it is unequally distributed; most of our streets are supremely mundane (except for the fire-breathing lizards everywhere), but then you run into a place like the Frogs' Theater, an amphitheater where gravity loosens as you get lower down. (If the Four Elements Children's Repertory is doing a Wing Windtwister play there, you get tickets. I don't care how old you are.)

There's a map with a standard list, locations, and descriptions in the back. But, tourist, these are more than random experiences scattered around for your amusement. The proto-Yemari nomads who built this city's first incarnation achieved magical feats that are still beyond us. Did they cultivate that virtuosity by studying these eruptions of weird energy, or are they human creations? Either way, why did they build a city around them?

No one has figured it out yet, and we've been here a while. You've got as good a shot as anyone.

SEE ALSO: Ashen Precinct; Environment, Local; Landmarks, Historic; Thaumobiome.

—From "A Visitor's Handbook for Yemareir," by Shenireen Agama

***

ZAYA ENTERS THE FIRST RACE.

Zaya came to Candlegrass Stand in fresh-sweat-baptized linen against the unseasonable cold. She stepped through the incantations impatiently, her voice a steel piston, hard and pushing ever forward.

"The Course Fabricant," said the fixer, appraising.

***

ZAYA ENTERS THE SECOND RACE.

Zaya came to Candlegrass Stand in her usual ensemble, easily removed in the glowing stalks' heat. She gritted through the incantations grimly, her voice a pitted machete, hewing doggedly forward.

"The White Steeplechase," said the fixer, pitying.

***

ZAYA ENTERS THE THIRD RACE.

ZAYA CAME TO CANDLEGRASS Stand naked to the waist against the coming summer's heat. She stumbled through the incantations uncertainly, her voice a dull needle, sinking only with reluctance into the fabric of the call-and-response.

"The Angels' Tribute," said the fixer, shaking their head.

***

THREE DAYS BEFORE THE COURSE FABRICANT.

BANDIT DIDN'T QUESTION THE long rubdown, the careful brushing of its teeth, or the personal feeding, complete with a fifth of rather decent whiskey, on that first night. It was only when Zaya was nearly dead with fatigue, curled up on the hay, that it touched her mind with an inquiring filament of concern.

"Yeah, buddy," she said. "I'm staying here for a while."

Its thoughts were still not in a shape Zaya could interpret as words, but the filament of contact grew brighter with inquisition.

"Everyone's fine. Cer and Kirono and Vani and Thelendil are all fine," she said, noticing their images flitting through Bandit's mind. "They don't know I'm doing this. They think it's not a good idea any more.

"That's a good question," she said, in response to a still-vague pulse of inquiry. "I didn't have the strength for the fight. Not physical strength, strength in my mind. I wanted to save my strength for this."

Bandit's mind pulsed with cool satisfaction. *You need a strong mind to ride me well. To reach out and make me race well.*

"That's not what I meant. But maybe you're right." She breathed in the scent of hay, then regretted it; the funk of guano also hung heavy this close to the floor. "If I'm being honest, though, it wasn't about preserving my mind. I was afraid I'd destroy my family. I still am. But at least I haven't done it yet."

The thread from Bandit's mind cooled into an accepting incomprehension. Zaya curled up into the mound of hay she'd pulled around herself, trying to convince herself it was as warm as a blanket, as soft as a mattress. She put her arm over a packed pile of it as though it were Jaliki or Eäril, or a much younger Taavi or Gilthiniel—or the thin, hot chest of Papa Kaalo, who had always caved to her requests to snuggle when Zinji had refused, begging off because he couldn't sleep.

Bandit's feathered bulk dropped gently around her, one wing stretched over her like a crude tent. It did not give off much body heat—Zaya resisted asking it to do a small burn just to warm her—but her own soon concentrated in the little hollow Bandit had made of its body, and she felt it curl closer around the gathering warmth.

"No better dragon than one that can take a hint," she said.

***

JUST BEFORE THE COURSE FABRICANT.

"Jenirain Gila," Zaya said to Jenirain Gila, who was approaching her with dampers draped over her forearm.

"Only one damper today?" said Gila.

"Flying with a co-pilot is deadweight if my empathy's no good," said Zaya.

"Good," said Gila. "You're stopping to think. Paying attention. You're starting to understand that things have changed."

"I'm not blind."

"Seeing isn't believing, not for humans. You've only understood when you've begun to adapt."

"You're an oversized old bat who's grown philosophical in her dotage, Jenirain."

"You said you're not blind." Gila's lip curled. "Prove it."

She shoved the damper into Zaya's hands, then turned on her heel. The damper's plain, flat back, free of the tracery and runic etchings that decorated the front, was faceing up. A single tiny mark drew Zaya's eye. It was an S-shape, tapered at the ends, wide in the middle; from one end protruded a fine extension in the shape of the letter Y, attached to the S by its stem:

"A snake?" she muttered as she donned the amulet.

"'Streamers," came the call, "to wyrmback!"

Zaya mounted up, the mark already forgotten.

***

JUST BEFORE THE WHITE STEEPLECHASE.

BANDIT'S BREATH WAS NOWHERE near Monsoon as they prepared, but she trusted the wyrm to behave itself—though not enough so that she didn't say *behave* as she walked over to Shanhoon Krait. She saw him see her, saw his weight shift, his spine straighten, his eyes go anywhere but toward her. "Hi," he said, a shade too loudly for how close she was. "Can I help you?"

"Empathy isn't cheating," she said.

"Rules say it is," Krait said shortly.

"It wasn't before Kiriki died, and it isn't now. All this shit is to exclude Kayalim racers and you know it."

"Kayalim empaths—any empaths—have an unfair advantage," said Krait. "How are the rest of us supposed to compete with a direct mind-to-mind connection?"

"How are *we* supposed to compete with *that*?" she said, pointing at Monsoon. "Not everyone can sell the spare silver to buy a rare wyrm and barding and tail-spikes."

"I earned every flinder I spend in the 'stream."

"Ha. Right. 'Earned' by being born a Krait."

"I wasn't born a Krait." Krait seemed sincerely hurt by this error. "Your brood-sibling's an Amphisbaena."

"Tell me something I don't know. She didn't earn that any more than you did."

"House Krait isn't rich like House Amphisbaena."

"I'm sure you built up that beautiful Alabaster Precinct estate one shovelful of goatshit at a time."

"I'm sure I don't have to justify my family's trade to you."

"But you want to." She looked him in the eye and imagined clutching his mind, drawing what she wanted out of it. Then she made herself not do it. "Go ahead, Shanhoon Krait." She leaned on the family name, twisted it a bit. "Tell a poor shiftless Kayalim how to get rich doing honest work."

"You wouldn't believe how many Kayalim take home a day's wages for their work on one of our products," Krait said. "A single one. Sourcing, production, quality control. No one calls me 'veraamaka navo,' but House Taipan stands between more Kayalim and the dole than you or your wife ever did."

"One of your products?" said Zaya, pitching her voice to cut over the ambient noise of 'streamers preparing their dragons for the race. "And what does House Krait produce?"

Shanhoon stiffened. "High-quality talismans. We mostly contract with the army and private industry on confidential projects."

"Talismans?" said Zaya. "So is it House Krait I have to thank for this thing?" She held up the damper like a dead rat. She saw a couple of gazes flicker over, then turn back to their business.

"No." He wouldn't look at her when he said it.

"I don't believe you," Zaya said. "Why would you lie about that?"

His eyes flickered left and right; he could see there were eyes on him. "If I were lying," he said, his voice now pitched to be heard, "it would probably be to protect some kind of trade secret."

"Maybe it's a secret the rest of us deserve to know. You seem pretty proud that psionics are out of the 'stream. If that was such a good deed, why won't you own up to it?"

The other 'streamers stared openly now. Zaya imagined Minshoon making a book of bets: Would a fight start, who'd start it, would the first blow land? No one would bet on a wyrm with him these days, but maybe they'd bet on a fight.

"Why won't I spill trade secrets to the estimable competition here?" He spread out his hands to encompass the onlookers.

"These people aren't House Krait's competition."

"Of course not," said Krait. "They're just a group of very fine racers with an understandable interest in making sure the rules of the 'stream promote fair play."

"That's right, that's what we want," a voice called out. It was Tuuro te-Kaneva, standing next to his grandfather, who was staring at him in naked surprise. "But fair play to you means you get to buy weapons for your wyrm that can kill these other 'very fine racers,' and if they can't or won't armor up, fuck 'em. You think the poors should be your sacrifices, and you don't like psionics because it lets us protect ourselves for free. Did you know," he said to the crowd, "that as little as ten years ago, armor, weapons, and even dampers were against—"

"'Streamers," the call came, "to wyrmback!" And the rest of Tuuro's words were lost in the scramble. Zaya tried to look in eyes, to see if the message had penetrated anywhere; but whatever thoughts were in the heads of the 'streamers, their eyes were not disclosing.

***

JUST BEFORE THE ANGELS' TRIBUTE.

"You look like shit," said Jenirain Gila.

Zaya felt like shit. "Rough race."

"I heard what happened after." She sat with Zaya on the bench where she was sitting, elbows on her knees, head in her hands. "Are you sure you should be getting back in so soon?"

"Is it exhausting to pretend to care about people, or is it more like a fun way to escape your real personality for a minute? Because I can see the appeal. For you specifically, I mean."

"I received some interesting correspondence a couple of days ago," said Gila. "I'm afraid the Board is going to have to look into it."

"That's good," said Zaya. "It's nice to keep busy."

Gila shrugged and looked back at Bandit. "I thought co-pilots were deadweight when you couldn't use empathy."

Zaya finally made the effort to lift her head and turn it, so she could look Gila in the eye. "I thought so too," she said. "And what I discovered was that I'd fallen into the trap of thinking like one of you. You fucking colonizers have turned this sport into a resource allocation problem, because as a species or whatever your entire thing is finding resources and allocating them to yourselves. But nothing can take away the fact that this whole dumb thing boils down to animals working together, and the way Kayalim work with big, intelligent animals has always been *as equals* and, not unrelated, *in threes*, which is nothing more than the recognition that an animal's soul is powerful and wild and a lone human mind can't dominate it without losing its own humanity, and what made it all click for me was that none of this is any less true just because we're being forced to wear one of your cursed amulets."

"You're so full of shit," said Gila. "I sincerely wish you the absolute best of luck."

Zaya could tell she meant all of it.

She looked back at Bandit and vertigo gripped her, pulling at the bottom of her throat like a living thing inside her scrabbling to get out. She made herself fixate on it, feel the ghost-memories of wings weighing down her upper back and deforming her shoulders, of a tail splitting her butt and splaying her legs, of a mind that observed the world minutely and divided it remorselessly. The more she thought about it, the more convinced she became that the Bandit she "knew" was a fiction, a personality overlaid on a set of foreign mental impulses that her own mind could not interpret except by organizing them, however absurdly, along human lines. People see faces everywhere; why not here?

She turned her eye to her co-pilot, long hair a rich plum-purple, rubbing the worm's long muzzle and spouting some nonsense at it. She liked to talk to it as though it were a baby, or a puppy—or, rather, as someone else would talk to a baby or a puppy; Zaya had never seen her react that way to either. Kiriki had talked to Jaliki like that, even though he had been too young to smile.

Kiriki had hated purple, though.

With effort, Zaya stood; her shoulders and hamstrings ached like an old man's. It was about time—

"'Streamers, to wyrmback!"

***

THE COURSE FABRICANT.

WHEN ZAYA AND KIRIKI had flown the Course Fabricant, the field had been the most mixed she'd seen: Kayalim with good jobs as empath-foremen or security or anything else above board would try their luck, out in the decrepit southern precincts where the old manufactories had sprung up three centuries or so ago—at the height of Yemareir's population, before the wars. Police didn't have much interest in what went on out here, where the only things to protect were squatters, crumbling properties held by trusts that didn't see the upside in maintaining them, and some of the less sociable wyrms. There was a sort of Mrineen 'streamer—thrill-seeking, prestige-minded, their star on the rise—for whom that disinterest from the police made the race more boring, and a sort of Kayalim (and the occasional Ililuë) for whom it made the race possible at all.

Zaya and Kiriki, desperate enough at that point to be eating exclusively from dole-kitchens and feeding Bandit by taking it to the bay to fish, were not that sort of Kayalim. They would have raced a dozen laps around the Secretariat of the Gendarmerie in Ivory Precinct dropping manure and cherry bombs if they thought they could win money on it. But the Course Fabricant had been their first race anyway, and they had talked in bed afterwards about what it had been like to see all those stolid, respectable Kayalim 'streamers, with their cropped hair and care-lined faces, applying a last-minute coat of bespoke wax to an undersized wyrm, or measuring out a last-minute snack, side by side and to all appearances coequal with the Mrineen doing the same—and giving them, two bright-haired girls holding hands and overwhelmed by it all, the same nods of respect they had just given some Mrineen dandy with a sword strapped to his back, striding toward his Argent Swordwing as if he owned the world.

They would find out, later, how little faith to put in those appearances. But, for Zaya at least, the memories remained, coming forth to balm her mind on the oddest occasions, like jockeying for position with a Saw-Pinioned Dart in the hulk of the Yldren Meat Packing Company.

The Dart was a stubby, emerald-green wyrm with no tail to speak of, and wings that rattled in a blur, like a hummingbird's. Its rider was some minor Tuatara scion whose name Zaya had forgotten, and there was no question they had opted to try to replace competence with money. It was clear the Dart was trained about well enough to point itself where the reins led it and go as fast as it could... and the fact that it was beating Bandit for seventh place rather than walking away with the trophy already was testament to its rider's shortage of technique. Unfortunately, the thing was still nimble as a housefly and could lacerate Bandit with a touch of its wings, and they were plunging toward the Forest of Chains.

The Course Fabricant was a tour through four manufactories in Madder, Taupe, and Sandalwood Precincts, of which the Yldren Meat Packing Company was second. The floors were open and high-ceilinged for the most part—the smells of death and butchery had needed dispersing—but most of the vast Meat Locker #96 was festooned with long hook-tipped chains.

The sign on the door said "Megafauna," and 'streamers were grateful for it—the chains were spaced for huge carcasses, wyrms and elephants and ground sloths and apatosaurs, the "New Eating" that had made Yldren briefly famous for bringing the flavors of the veldt to Yemareir's home cooks. In the end, Yemareir's home cooks decided by a considerable margin that they preferred pork and seafood to the flavors of the veldt, and Yldren closed its doors, leaving a number of carcasses still on the chains. More than one glistening rib cage still hung from its hook, big enough to be a giant's coffin or the frame of a small boat.

The generally accepted way to take the lead in the Forest of Chains was to have it going in, then use your wyrm's tail to lash the chains behind you into swinging, making it perilous to follow closely. The generally accepted countermeasure, if you were behind, was to fly higher, where the chains couldn't swing so widely, and try to overtake from above, optionally heating the chains ahead with a belch of flame to make life riskier for your opponent. This countermeasure was difficult to pull off, since the hole in the wall that brought 'streamers to the meat locker floor and out was rather low down. But rapid altitude changes and nimble dodges between closely spaced obstacles were precisely what a Saw-Pinioned Dart was built for, and the damned thing had just cut Zaya off from above.

The situation's only saving grace was the Dart's lack of a tail: It couldn't leave much of a wake of swinging chains. But it was nimble, and it knew its goal. Again and again it blocked Zaya's attempts to cut in front.

In open air none of that would have mattered. The Dart was fast but predictable; Zaya could have drawn it out with a feint, then surged past it in the opened lane. But in a meat locker full of dangling chains, lateral movements required high precision, and with her mind separated from Bandit's, that precision was impossible to achieve.

Or maybe it only felt impossible.

"Come on, veraamaka navo," she said to herself. "All or nothing."

She counted chains as they swept by, one-two-three-four-five, until she had the rhythm in her head. At the next gap, she would feint; the one after, accounting for Bandit's reaction time, she would streak around the Dart.

She feinted. Her head came not inches from the finger-thick links of a massive chain. The Dart moved to block. She lunged around.

Even as Bandit began to move, Zaya felt the timing fall apart. Bandit's shoulders plowed into a chain, which caught at the base of its wing. It heaved in the opposite direction, shying instinctively from anything that might stop its flight and send it crashing, and ran into two chains on the opposite side of its body. Bandit's panicked wingbeat had been strong, its recoil from the first chain frighteningly fast; its impact with the second sent their hooked tips whipping up, light from a hole in the roof glinting from their rust-splotched steel.

All Zaya could do was hug Bandit's back like a tick and hope they missed her.

Bandit heaved again, this time vertically, taking them up past the height of the hooks before they could begin their arc down and wrap or impale them both. Zaya felt a surge of pride—it was a fast learner, faster than the Mule had been. Then it went in the only safe direction: Down, below the chains.

By the time they left the meat locker, a Dusk Stalker had passed them from behind, coming above, through the chains, to the exit. The Dart was long gone.

***

THE WHITE STEEPLECHASE.

THIS RACE COULD NEVER start where it ought to. There was nowhere in Eggshell, Ivory, Cream, Alabaster, or Argent where a handful of dozen illegal racing wyrms could congregate long enough to kick off a race without being noticed by police; and a police response to a huge mass of wyrms in the city core, the seat of the noble houses and the Courts of Moon and Stars, would guarantee a massacre. So instead the wyrms gathered in Olive Precinct, north of Yemareir's White Heart, and made an almost ceremonial procession down the Boulevard of Watchmakers until it intersected the fairy-lit cobbles of Monitor Street, which would take them west into Cream. Not long before that turn was the Washerwomen's Shrine, a temple that took up collections to help the numerous Ililuë domestics who lived in the northeast of the city. Zaya didn't know any Ililuë domestics and had never visited the temple, but the last time they'd run this race, Kiriki had brought a small bag of loose shards and flinders.

"For luck," she'd explained. "Those wicker hampers in front of the Shrine are collection baskets. In this race it's traditional to toss something in as you fly by. If you make it into a basket, you'll do better in the race."

"Has a single person who's taken the trouble to do this ever actually won the race?" Zaya had asked.

Kiriki had shrugged. "No one knows whose stuff actually makes it in the baskets," she'd said. "The abbot collects it all pretty fast."

"If the washerwomen get it regardless of whether it goes in the basket, why does it matter whether it goes in the basket?"

"That's the spirit," Kiriki had said, and kissed her temple.

And maybe it had been? They'd won a commanding victory, their first in a truly competitive field. Khefthoon Gecko and Willful Child, his storied Argent Swordwing, had come out of retirement for this race; Santoun Agama and the vast Eyrie Shrike he called Peace would soon retire as well. Their rivalry had been the chatter of the 'stream before the race was flown: Which legend would bring home victory for their final run at the White Steeplechase?

When it was over, though, the conversation had changed. Now the two Kayalim girls on their oversized Dawn had become the story on every 'streamer's lips, the two great racers' losses to such unknowns so shameful they never raced again—at least while she and Kiriki were in the 'stream.

That had been more satisfying then than it was now.

In that first White Steeplechase, Zaya and Kiriki had striven to be in the lead from the starting line, breathing down the neck of Gecko and Agama, as if falling behind was death. Time and the 'stream had cured her of that. As Shanhoon Krait, Lerikaan Boomslang, Arhoon Pogona, and the rest of the front pack wheeled onto Monitor Street, a rain of parcels and pouches pelted the flagstone patio in front of the Washerwomen's Shrine.

Not a single one made it into a basket.

Zaya and Bandit were behind, but not far behind; she drew a bead on her parcel and let fly. She tried to track it; but the glorious everything of Bandit's senses rushed into her mind like a crashing breaker of scent and sound and color and roaring air under reaching wings, and she couldn't tell if she'd missed the ring of steel on stone because her mind was otherwise occupied, or because she'd made the shot.

***

ONE DAY BEFORE THE WHITE STEEPLECHASE.

"There'll be three things," Zaya said. "Two pouches of money and an ugly amulet. The amulet will screw with your empathy, so careful flying. One pouch is for the Washerwomen, and one's for you."

Zayeni grinned. "OK, veraamaka navo," she said, "but how do you know I don't take both? Are you gonna check with the washerwomen?"

"I won't know," Zaya said. "But I only get the luck if the wash-erwomen get their cut; and if you want more jobs like this, I need all the luck I can get.

"What you should be asking is, 'What do I do with the amulet?'"

***

THE ANGELS' TRIBUTE.

THE RUINED SEASON-CITY ON which Captain Yymroun Amphisbaena stumbled when he made landfall on this continent had no single place or method for burying the dead: The migrants had availed themselves of sea, sky, and river along with earth and fire, and un-stirred bone-holes and pots of cremains could be found alongside elaborate tombs housing what looked to be generations of deco-rated skeletons. Some of the tombs were badly cursed, or booby trapped; some of the bone-holes carried spells that tripped when a human drew near, prompting an illusion of a song or a prayer or simply a tear-choked oration, all in the language called ur-Yemari by scholars who had not managed to translate a word of it.

The Mrineen colonizers had arrived searching for a new way of life, but also for a balm to the dislocations of that search. There was an appeal to prebuilt customs, new to them but fully formed, with the weight of tradition already attached. And so, when burying time came, they looked to the strip on the south shore of the Bright Thread River called, unimaginatively, the Necropolis.

The Necropolis was not demarcated—someone unacquainted with the architecture of the season-city might easily stumble into it not knowing what the buildings surrounding them were used for, at least until they noticed the lack of windows. That misapprehension would be short-lived, though, because within a minute or two of idling in the Necropolis, that notional someone would be visited by the spirit of someone they had lost—aiming, more likely than not, to dissect the dallier's self-image through a brutal and incisive exhumation of their life's wrong turns.

The Mrineen colonizers, at ease with self-evisceration, took no time at all to designate this land as their lost ones' final resting place.

Fences were thrown up, plots cleared for reuse, customs developed. As the centuries passed, various Departments of Thanatology reconfirmed and re-reconfirmed the fundamental principle of the Necropolis: Everything that happened there was inside the head. No external, objectively measurable spiritual influence was present, only a persistent low-energy thaumaturgic field indecipherable to the sorcerous élites. But these results came far too late to intercept the ceremony around Yemari funerals, which hold that the dead are summoned by their gathered loved ones to welcome a new soul into that long river-shore of graveyard.

The reason for the choice of the *south* shore was discovered at around a similar period of time, 200 years after the city's founding, and long after the riverbed was clad in stone: The river was, or had been, moving gradually south. This had been known since the cladding of the riverbed began, and psionically guided hippos and crocodiles had begun to pull gravestones and tomb doors and ceremonially decorated corpses from the muck, but the reason for it had been found inside a tomb long regarded as impassable, guarded as it was by one of the world's few genuine undead—an invulnerable wight who readily butchered several dozen heavily armed research teams. The issue was solved, as so few ever are, by a pair of Kayalim empaths and the largest dragon that would submit to them, a Dawn large enough not only to hunt full-grown orcas but to lift them out of the water and drop them on a rock to age a few days before digging in. It applied more or less the same strategy to the wight—which did not die, and in fact immediately set about carving a path back to its post... but that would take days of slogging along the sea floor, by which time the research team had already reproduced or extracted its key findings, evacuated its route, and vacated its station so it could return in peace.

The text remains untranslatable, but a diagram makes it plain: the Necropolis' placement was intended to solve the problem of all graveyards, namely that they fill up with memorials that, in a few generations, are valuable to no one. The movement of the river would naturally recycle the oldest monuments and remains; the need for and tradition of south-shore burial would lead to the gradual abandonment or repurposing of any permanent structures on the graveyard's southern edge, leading to a natural and harmonious evolution of the site along with the city and its nourishing river.

None of which particularly played into its choice as a race-course for the 'stream, which was down to (1) its elongated shape and (2) the ghosts, of whom Kiriki's in particular was proving a major distraction at a bad time, sitting on the base of Bandit's neck to block Zaya's field of view while she was trying to come up from behind Monsoon and Time's Warped Arrow.

"Move aside, K," Zaya said. "You're not even buried here."

"I don't have to be. I don't even have to be dead. You just have to think I'm dead."

Zaya craned her neck to look around Kiriki's ghost, who leaned to block her vision. Zaya fought the urge to reach an arm out in case she fell. "So if you're really just in my head, can you, like, do what I ask and just get behind me so I can see? Or maybe come back when I'm in bed."

Kiriki shook her head. "This is just how you do these things, my breath. Shanhoon Krait gloats over his ghosts, Vani just endures hers, but that's not your style. You do vision quests and big reveals. Remember Zinji's mom, last time?"

"You live in my brain," said Zaya. "I know you know her name."

"I'm making an effort to stay in character here."

Who are you talking to? said Bandit.

"We talked about this, remember?" Zaya said.

Oh, that, said Bandit.

"Just," said Kiriki, "like old dead Grandma Whatsername—"

"Shazaya-*taki*—"

"—right, who wouldn't stop fucking with you until you hauled her up and bitched her out about how her disowning Papa Zinji forced you to grow up dirt-poor with a couple of strung-out whiskey-thieves and that had like stunted your experience of childhood—"

"—and I had the epiphany that I couldn't be at peace with my horrible extended family until I made a real effort to understand my dads."

"Right. Did that all go as badly as I said it was going to go?"

"Bitch, you're in my brain, you figure it out."

Mom, Vanako's voice interjected into Zaya's mind. *Fast Dawn on our six. Another team, looks like.*

"Ugh," said Zaya. "Tuuro and his dad. They're great people. Look, just drift on the lane a bit—the longer we can string them along thinking we don't realize they're there, the better."

Vanako and Bandit's minds pulsed affirmation.

"Papa Kaalo dying put kind of a kink in that particular vision quest," Zaya said to Kiriki. "It's been easier for us not to see too much of each other. A couple months ago I filled Zinji's entire house with durian and got massively wrecked on bad booze and worldvine with a thousand of his closest friends. But you knew that."

"Imagine pretending I didn't. I'm very disappointed in you, young lady."

"It was sort of a bonding experience. We're seeing more of him now. Jaliki's so happy when we visit."

Kiriki's face softened in the way it always used to when she'd look at Jaliki. "I miss him."

"There'd better be something good at the end of this vision quest," Zaya said, her voice rough. "Like you're going to dissolve into a mountain of cash. Non-hallucinatory cash."

"Then it would be a cash quest. Vision quests are strictly revelatory, it's in the name."

No, Vanako said in Zaya's mind, *not that way*—and Aubade darted into the lane freed by Bandit's feint, streaking over its left shoulder, tail nearly lashing Zaya's face.

Instinctively, Zaya darted back into Vanako's mind to guide Bandit's response; Vanako picked up what she was doing, more or less, handled her half, and Bandit shot up to wrangle Aubade for position. From above, it wasn't hard to push the other Dawn a little, and too late the other team realized they were about to crash into one of the Necropolis' many beautiful shade trees. They peeled off to dodge it; Bandit surged back into third.

It was only in the moments after that Zaya remembered the other woman who'd drifted into the corner of her mind's eye. She was older than Zaya, maybe by five years, not thin but still drawn and wasted-looking, overshadowed in every way by the brilliant red fox that hung around her neck like a yoke. It had six legs, three tails, and an extra eye blazing in the middle of its forehead; its fur was shot through with silver quills that shone like polished steel. Every so often it lapped blood from a fang-torn hole in the woman's neck; its muzzle and nose were wet with it.

She looked back at Kiriki. Kiriki returned the look, faintly ill. "You'll lose this race if you don't concentrate on what you're doing."

"You're the one who said this is a vision quest."

"It's also a thing where two-ton lizards throw themselves through the air trying to be the first to get to a place, and you're not first."

"You're not even real! Why are you being evasive? You can't tell me anything I don't already know!"

"I don't know, Zaya, why would anyone's mind ever resist admitting something to itself?"

"You know what, fuck it. You're right. I'll just focus on the race if you'll just get out of my way."

Kiriki reached out and put a hand over Zaya's goggles.

The world blacked out but for three slivers of light. Zaya flailed, but Kiriki's ghost-arm wasn't there, it wasn't something her body could dislodge. Which seemed unfair and, honestly, inconsistent, since Zaya could feel the warmth of her palm, the hardness of her knuckles. "Ask the question," Kiriki said.

"The last time we ran this race," Zaya said. "When I saw Shaza-ya-*taki*."

"Say the whole thing," Kiriki said.

"I saw what was in your mind. I saw that you saw yourself. You were your own ghost."

Zaya felt Kiriki nod through the pressure of her nonexistent palm.

"And afterward, when I asked about it, you told me it was fine. You said there was another person in the scene, that I'd missed some key piece of context but you didn't want to talk about it right then."

"I did."

"And I thought you were lying, but I let it—"

"It was a lie," said Kiriki, "and you knew it."

"My heart, please—"

"No, my breath," said Kiriki. "It's a vision quest, not a redemption quest. I'm not here to forgive you. I'm not even here."

Mom, said Vanako, *we're coming up on the spire—*

How dare you call her mother, the woman with the fox on her neck burbled dimly, the echo from Vanako's mind distant in Zaya's. *I raised you. When you were a helpless little thing, I protected you. And you let me die.*

*Vani—*Zaya began, her heart breaking.

Your ghost wife is cooler than my ghost mom, don't make it a thing. We need *you—*

"Why did you think you were going to die?" Zaya said to Kiriki.

"There's a reason Shanhoon looks familiar," Kiriki said, and, smiling, tipped herself back off the wyrm.

Zaya almost lurched to grab her. Then she looked up and saw the column of obsidian and basalt rushing up to meet them.

"Shiiiiiiiiit!" she screamed, but the motor program for Bandit was locked in her mind, brighter and more precise than it had ever been when she'd run the Angels' Tribute with Kiriki and the Mule, and she effortlessly shipped Vanako her half and together they eased it into Bandit's nerves and muscles and the Dawn swung up and around to start a spiral up the height of the Deathspire, whose apex was the finish line.

***

THE COURSE FABRICANT: THE FINISH LINE.

IF THERE EVER HAD to be an indoor finish line, the massive production floor of Zharquaat Textiles was indisputably the perfect place to do it. The old hand-looms and sewing-stations had been looted long ago, save a few smashed ones tossed to the side, the only reason anyone knew what had been there in the first place. It was high-ceilinged as well, and open to the air—not by design, but the far wall had been in poor enough condition that the race's designers had found it easy to tear out completely, some two or three lifetimes ago.

To reach that production floor, though, involved a mess of near misses and hairpin turns through a massive once-half-automated spinning machine (powered by elephants partnered with Kayalim empaths, as testified by the yokes attached to its great axle), the brightly stained dyeing vats (and the brilliant ultramarine skeleton at the bottom of the blue vat), and finally the massive floor-to-ceiling bobbins, still fat with huge masses of fused, faded thread. When Zaya and Kiriki had last come through here, the Mule had snagged a thread from each color it could, so they came to the finish line trailing a wake of color—and they had been the only wyrm who finished; the subsequent pileup of wyrms in the thread warehouse, tangled in the Mule's wake, had made it impassable.

The results of that race had been invalidated, and Zaya and Kiriki had been stripped of their prize money (though not Minshoon's gambling winnings) and hauled before the Standards Board. The complaint had been brought by one Kanivoon Taipan, a highly-ranked 'streamer who'd claimed he could have won from behind had there not been Unsporting Interference, or however that category of malfeasance was written in the rules.

Kiriki's counter had been straightforward: "Use of environmental factors to obtain an advantage is specifically protected in the Standards. Its stated rationale is to reward ingenuity, finesse, and knowledge of the course."

"No one else's wyrm," the Adjudicator had countered, "could execute a maneuver like that. It's not rewarding ingenuity or finesse, it's rewarding one team's adherence to a particular cultural custom."

"I can't afford to feed my wyrm up on specially raised sardines to double its burn capacity," Kiriki had said, "which is how M. Taipan achieved his, let's be frank, distant second-place ranking. In contrast, he could have learned everything my partner and I know about Kayalim empathy at the same cost we paid, which was nothing."

"M. Taipan's time is worth something," the judge had countered.

"If he decides his time is worth more than winning," Kiriki had said, "I don't see why this board should contradict him."

Jenirain Gila had smiled liplessly at that. "You know, Tjeloun," she'd said to the other Adjudicator, "I went back to have a look at the crime scene after the race. After all that old thread got pulled off, those bobbins are brighter than they've been in my lifetime. All that color, just waiting for the old faded stuff to get pulled off. We're not going to give a prize to the man who brought a dragon to fight a few strands of thread and lost. Are we?"

The discussion had continued, but for practical purposes that was the end of it. Jenirain Gila had found them later. "Never appeal to their sense of fair play when you can appeal to their fear of weakness," she'd said, and glided off like a smug bat.

Zaya had thought that the bobbin maneuver might enter the 'stream's lexicon of customs, like throwing tribute to the Washerwomen's Shrine. But, without empathy, it was too hard to train a wyrm to do; and when she passed them in eighth place, her empathic connection to Bandit squeezed down to a trickle by the damper, the old thread stayed wrapped tightly around itself.

***

THE WHITE STEEPLECHASE: THE FINISH LINE.

ZAYA HAD FLOWN BANDIT with unfettered empathy before, but only, she realized, when she'd been fighting for her life: The dogfight over the Emerald Desert, the flight to Cildinior Amalgam, shaking the police loose in the Cold Point Chasse. She'd never really *raced* it without the damper; and when the cursed thing fell away at the Washerwomen's Shrine, it was sunrise on a warm morning over the bay. Right out of that hard corner into Monitor Street, she'd been able to jump five places, from trailing the leading pack straight into the middle of it; lanes that came and went inside the window of Bandit's reaction time to her physical direction now yawned and lingered, and with her eye for opportunities wired directly into Bandit's mind and muscles, it was easy.

It was sharing a bottle of arrack at night on the beach, it was dancing to the sound of taiko drums and the smell of grilled boar at a Madder Precinct summer block party, it was lying on a new-bought bed with a newborn baby fast asleep. It was the scent, the shadow, the echo of Kiriki, and if Zaya's heart was pouring out its blood to feel her so close and not have her, at least the 'stream was scouring it away, dissolving it into the ready air. Bandit, she was dimly aware, watched all this unfold in her mind with a combination of awe, bewilderment, and disgust; but its hard, angular love never wavered, as the Mule's never had, and that too was a heart-cut, to which it bore witness as patiently as it did the rest.

Zaya swept into Cream Precinct in the center of a nine-wyrm pack. Cream was wide blossom-edged streets, gentle curves and rises engineered to serve up new visual delights at a carefully controlled frequency, stately museums, noble monuments; there was not much opportunity for fine maneuvering, but two wyrms behind Zaya and one ahead began to flag and fall behind, tapped out by the effort of surging to an early lead.

From Cream, the major artery to Ivory Precinct was the Street of Poets, whose real name honored some then-much-revered functionary who'd been dead for centuries. Its generally recognized name had come in recognition of the encrustation of boutiques that sold pens, nibs, ink, paper, blank books, blotter, and sundry other tools of the writer's trade. The name was more ironic than not, though—the main customers of those boutiques were the administrators of Ivory Precinct, whose uses of the written word were some of the least poetic known to humanity.

Ivory itself was far older than Cream, built for function and at need, and the course through it was full of narrow alleys and hairpin turns that fouled some of the bigger wyrms who'd held their leads on stamina and strong wings. By the time they reached the Office of the Court of Stars— a complex of seven half-fused marble buildings full of skyways and dead ends—Carnaug and a muscular Dawn in the colors of House Tegu had dropped back, and Zaya had fought past the Tuatara Dart and Time's Warped Arrow, and almost contemptuously dodged a lash from Monsoon's spiked tail to take the lead.

When she screamed with the exultation, Bandit screamed too, and government staffers all across the Court of Stars spilled spiced drinks and dodged behind corners in fear.

Eggshell and Alabaster Precincts were residentials—Eggshell adjacent to and built much like Ivory, dense with tenements and built to house and feed the staff of the administrative state. A few of the Houses of the Moon—the newer, the smaller, Ferdelance and Loggerhead and Honu—made their homes in Eggshell, but most were headquartered in Alabaster, which was as spacious and ornamental as Cream Precinct but less well planned.

It was in Eggshell, as it usually was, that the first White Guest entered the race.

It was a commonplace among 'streamers that no one knew when the tradition of White Guests had entered the White Steeplechase, but after Zaya and Kiriki had drunkenly described it over gin at Tjaliraan's, Arhoon Pogona had insisted that the Standards Board could not possibly have failed to document it, and he had been right. In 3011 by the Mlinivoun reckoning, or 562 years after Captain Yymroun had first made landfall in the bay, a retired Director of the Office of Air Superiority named Kinithoon Ora had been dining on the deck of his Alabaster Precinct villa when he saw the wyrms wheel in from what would become Eggshell Precinct. Ora, a marquis of the House with the airs of a duke and the personality of a goat, had always viewed the 'stream as an abomination and, seeing the opportunity to ruin it, made the attempt: He rushed down to his stable, mounted his retired Argent Swordwing, and joined the race in the middle of the pack.

This is all known because, as Arhoon had intuited, the Standards Board had belatedly registered him and his wyrm, with an asterisk saying "Guest racer, Alabaster entrance." His victory is also recorded. The prize and his consequent celebrity warmed him to the 'stream; he became an ardent advocate and regular competitor, although he never won again. But his example inspired imitators from the White precincts, and his fame constrained the Board to accept the legitimacy of their bids.

In nearly three subsequent centuries, no subsequent White Guest has ever won the White Steeplechase—but the well-dressed young pilot on the Peregrine Gyrdrake surging up behind Zaya seemed confident enough in breaking that streak.

The streets of Eggshell Precinct were not as cramped or unpredictable as those of Ivory, but the tenements were still tall and close together, and it was not too much effort to keep the lead. When the close-packed buildings of Eggshell Precinct gave way to the more spacious boulevards of Alabaster, the game became more difficult. The Gyrdrake harried Zaya, surging toward an open lane at every opportunity; without the empathic connection to Bandit, she'd never have kept up. She'd just fended off another attempt to break her lead when a bolt of lightning crackled by her face. She felt its heat on her temple, felt another bolt burn Bandit's flank. It wouldn't be any worse than a burn from a hot pan, especially with its feathers for protection, but it hurt like hell, and their flight path wavered as its wings twitched with the pain.

"Fuck off with your sorcery!" Zaya shouted, turning to face the rider on the Gyrdrake. He shouted something back at her that was lost in the 'stream, and then the shitty grin on his face gave way to an intense focus on some invisible thing in the middle distance, and Zaya dropped Bandit a gut-churning ten feet to dodge the forthcoming bolt, and Shanhoon Krait shot into the open lane, taking the lead by several lengths with a series of wingbeats that sent a wake of wind into Zaya's face.

Bandit lurched upward, trying to take the lane back; but the White Guest on the Gyrdrake darted forward, joined by Lerikaan Boomslang on the Moultwyrm and Tuuro te-Kaneva on Aubade. The rest of the pack didn't try to surge by, but they were still keeping up, the smell of brimstone and the warmth of fiery breath hanging even in the slipstream. A pit of fire, a searing gravity, was swelling in Zaya's heart.

The pack skimmed down the Hall of Crowds, a wide street lined with ancient mirrors that were rumored to have cooked souls at certain intersections of the reflected light when the sun was bright enough. Bandit shrank from the welter of reflected wings, but only for a moment. Some gadfly in its brain reminded it that the wyrms in front of it were meant to be behind it, and it forced itself to spread its wings and surge forward in defiance of the testament of its eyes, putting the green-and-yellow Moultwyrm behind it and pulling nose-to-tail with the other Dawn.

Then the Hall of Crowds ended and they were in Argent Precinct, the gleaming white broodspire of the Argent Swordwings bisecting the sky like light streaming through a cracked door to another world, and the searing pit moved from Bandit's heart into its throat. Yellow-and-blue flame streamed from its mouth; the other Dawn, thinking it was under attack, wheeled off course, both wyrm and rider screaming in outrage; and Bandit, hungry to pass (but why?) the Gyrdrake and the Melanic Shrike, almost forgot to swing by the statue of Jevain Tuatara, from whose outstretched Hand a gleaming bauble dangled. *Why* was it important to veer near the statue, when there were wyrms to be beaten, was difficult to understand—

—and then the damper field tore Zaya's mind away from Bandit's and thrust it back into her own head with an electric black impact that left her brain upside down inside her skull, and *shit shit shit I need to grab it*, but her arm barely remembered what to do—but her body *lurched* and her chin strained and there was a horrible second of a deathly, choking pressure on her neck and then it was gone, and the relief at having the damper dangling between her breasts again was almost too foul to bear.

Then she fell forward against Bandit's back.

Somewhere in her arms and legs she found the will to tense up, which kept her from falling off immediately—but Bandit banked hard, then eased off when it felt her slip. A thread of concern trickled through the damper field.

"Fuck it," Zaya tried to say, but it came out a slurring snarl. *Just get over the line.*

Her vision was all pink and purple feathers, save a slice of sky and city small and blurry to her left. She could see enough to see a wyrm pass through it.

The Limper eat your fucking heart, you skidmark of a wyrm, of all the times to lose your spine—

She stopped, she had to. She could feel Bandit shaking with the effort of maintaining its tightening bank on the in-spiraling home stretch while keeping up its pace and stopping her from slipping off its back. She got a palm under her, then another, pushed hard enough to lift her head a few inches, then collapsed back. There were at least two wyrms ahead of her—Monsoon and the Gyrdrake—and there was one coming up on the inside. She hauled on Bandit to tighten the turn. There was a wyrmish snarl and a human curse in a familiar voice.

Zaya recognized it was Tuuro te-Kaneva's just as she felt a plume of flame nearly sear her leg.

She cast an unbelieving eye at Tuuro, but his eyes faced obdurately forward. Aubade had a look in its eyes that was more than familiar—it wasn't truly its eyes, but the set of its shoulders, the tension of its neck. It was about to lunge for Bandit.

She hauled again, in and back, bringing Bandit in range of Aubade while howling as loudly as she could through that thread of connection. Bandit lashed out with its tail, suddenly far closer to Aubade than it or Tuuro had expected. She felt a familiar impact—resistance, then nothing.

When she looked behind her, she saw Aubade skirling off the course, pulled off the spiral by the weight of Tuuro, hanging from his saddle by a single strap. She passed a hand through her hair in relief.

On her outside was Yaulë on Carnaug. Zaya pressed her body into Bandit, trying to imitate the force of the forward lean it knew to mean "go faster"... but she was practically flat against its back in any case, and it could go no faster without dumping her.

A cheer went up from the Argent Broodspire. The White Heart of Yemareir tolerated the Steeplechase, but barely; once the finish line was crossed, finishers would repair back to Olive Precinct for festivities. As Bandit rounded on the Argent Broodspire, Zaya flopped her whole body into a half-twist to point an eye up at the sky.

As if in answer, Monsoon's black bulk shot over her, wings spread in exultation, yellow and blue flames streaming from its mouth.

$$***$$

THE ANGELS' TRIBUTE: THE FINISH LINE.

NOT MANY WYRMS ARE well adapted for the upward surge. The Merlin Wyrm is, of course, a known master of swift takeoffs from a standstill, but a Merlin is about the size of a sickly hawk or an unusually hale pigeon. The Arboreal Blindwyrm—named not for poor eyesight but for the blinds it builds for ground-to-air ambushes—sometimes grows large enough to ride; but Blindwyrms rely on surprise and speed exclusively, they have no endurance for a race. Of the four wyrms now coursing vertically up the Deathspire, none had any particular physiological advantage in this upward portion of the race. But Bandit's experience as a caravan wyrm meant it knew how to gain altitude quickly—unlike these lifelong racing wyrms, which had trained their whole lives to stay low.

And that was true enough; but Aubade, a wild Dawn that had spent its whole life soaring on thermals above the bay, knew something about rapid height changes as well.

The Deathspire, like a true broodspire, was more or less a cone in shape, wide as a large house at the bottom and tapering to something that was very nearly a point at its summit. Inside the warrens with which it was riddled were not bowers and egg-chambers, but crematoria and, occasionally, tombs, the latter of which contained full mummified corpses or heaps of gilded bones. Because it was the only object of its height in an otherwise lightless strip of city, there was a lantern at the top that was lit every day at dusk to save any more dragons from colliding with it on nighttime flights. If you returned to the finish line with the lantern in hand, you won, no matter who was ahead of you; otherwise, you lost. There was no second place in the Angels' Tribute.

Get ready, Zaya said to Vanako. *This is all going to happen very fast.*

Bandit flew up the side in its own lane for a few wingbeats, then pulsed ahead of Time's Warped Arrow with a smooth lateral shift, blowing a gust from a powerful wingbeat into the Moultwyrm's face. Zaya didn't dare look back, but there was a flare of triumph from Vanako's mind, an image of the wyrm falling away as though off a cliff.

There were wyrmish snarls and screams, there was an impact; a human scream joined the chorus as well. Zaya could not suppress a guilty wave of relief that it all seemed to be happening behind her—from below. She concentrated her mind behind Bandit's eyes, inside its jaws, letting Vanako take the flying completely.

This was where empathy could gain her a half-wyrm-length's advantage. Without the mental connection, there was no way to train a wyrm to retrieve an object of no intrinsic interest—not while racing, not in the time required. But, guided by her mind, Bandit would take the lantern in its jaws as obligingly as any dog. At this point, though, she might not even need it—Monsoon, her closest pursuer, was more than a length behind—

A shout rang out, two syllables—or three, or five?—that Zaya recognized but could not recall. The smell of sage and burnt bone threaded through her nostrils; the lamp took wing, streaking down off the tower like a falcon in the stoop.

Bandit's pitiless, precise eyes showed it to her: the lantern slowing, like a hunting hawk, to alight inside Shanhoon's gloved hand. Monsoon peeling off like a turned page, tail-spikes streaked and dripping red.

"Oh, shit," said Zaya, and turned Bandit around.

There would be time and time for tears, for rage, for motions with the Standards Board. But what would not wait—

"Oh, shit," said Vanako, not a second later.

—what would not wait was Tuuro te-Kaneva, pulling frantically to extract his grandfather from under the flank of Aubade, who scrabbled weakly at the flagstones of the necropolis, blood pouring and pooling from three smooth-edged holes in its neck.

***

AFTER THE COURSE FABRICANT.

TAN PRECINCT, THE FINISH line, would be where the main celebrations were: The winners would drink there, as would their fans and hangers-on, and anyone who wanted to be seen in the aura of victory. The victory parties changed locations from race to race, but the losers always drank their pain off in the same places: The cheap dives near the stables, the Asp & Adder in Rust Precinct and Brimming in Heather Precinct and Saltfeather's in Lapis. Zaya and

Kiriki had been a fixture at all of them; with nothing else to do in the evening, it felt like time to return to her roots.

She ended up at a circular table with Tuuro te-Kaneva and a number of other Kayalim, whose cropped black hair kept her on edge no matter how friendly they were. And they were: A boulder-shaped man named Shozo toasted *"veraamaka navo!"* on the first round, which was embarrassing and also deeply, deeply heartwarming. When she proposed "fuck the Standards Board!" as a second, there was widespread confusion.

"The Standards Board," said Zaya to the doe-eyed woman with distracting cheekbones next to her, "is supposed to be in charge of maintaining the integrity of the 'stream, but ever since Kiriki and I started winning, the only thing they've been good for is making wins easier to buy than earn. Like, there didn't use to be entry fees, and armor and weapons on wyrms were outlawed for at least a century before we won the Mariposa Annulus—"

"Wait, *what*?" said Tuuro.

"Right? And I don't know when they started using dampers, but it wasn't until after Kiriki died. It would have been against the rules before, same as those little shear-fields half the 'streamers use instead of goggles now—'no enchantment and no sorcery' meant none. They turned the 'stream into a way for rich kids to show off their toys. Which it always was, but not like it is today." She remembered Jenirain Gila pushing the damper at her, awkwardly angling it to make sure she showed the snake mark on the back. "Who makes those, anyway? Some company named after a snake—the mark goes kind of like this..." She traced an S in the air.

Shrugs and glances traveled around the table. Zaya's neighbor with the interesting cheekbones spent more than a glance looking at Zetaala, who was staring down into his beer, and that made

Zaya notice that Tuuro was looking away from his father with an intensity that felt very much on purpose; and maybe it was Zaya examining him that made him look up and meet her eyes. Zetaala's shoulders rose and fell, just a fraction of an inch, and he said "Taipan Invotechnic."

It was difficult to read the gaze that Tuuro shot at him, but impossible to miss.

"That's your firm, Zetaala!" said a man across the table—construction worker, at Zaya's guess, from the thick chest and shoulders and the mass of tiny dents and scars on his hands. "Come on, man, how's veraamaka navo supposed to win races when you're out there fucking with her biggest advantage?"

Zetaala smiled thinly. "She's got years of experience, a well-trained wyrm, and a fine head on her shoulders. There's nothing an old man like me could possibly do to stop her."

"Except be the better racer," Tuuro put in.

The construction worker snorted. "I guess you always were a dreamer, Tuuro."

"I took second in the Cold Point Chasse," Tuuro said, full of a cold fury.

"The cops knocked out veraamaka navo," said the construction worker, as though no more needed to be said.

"My name's Zaya," Zaya said. "What's yours?"

The construction worker looked at her in confusion for a moment before he answered. "Haanen."

"How do you know Tuuro and Zetaala?"

"Used to work with Zetaala. He used to be one of the best foreman-empaths you'd ever seen—he and Siila could get an elephant to do jobs in fifteen minutes that other foremen would still be trying to get them to understand. Except when we were getting paid by the hour, then the same job'd take thirty—thanks for that, by the way." Haanen raised his glass; Zetaala raised his own. "Then he went and got a desk job, the traitor."

Zaya laughed. "A desk job? As an empath? What do you do, Zetaala?"

"QC," said Tuuro. "R&D. Probably some other letters."

Zaya wanted to laugh that off and press the point, but as the stranger at the table, she gave it a moment, and nothing about that moment gave her any courage—it was all uncomfortable looks: at her, at Tuuro, at empty points off in the middle distance. She drained her glass, shrugged, and prepared her exit lines.

***

AFTER THE WHITE STEEPLECHASE.

THE LANDING IN OLIVE Precinct wasn't as bad as the landing at Cildinior Amalgam had been, but it was bad. The damper had thrown her back into her own mind, at least, sparing her the experience of trying to breathe fire at strangers; but her body was rubber-limbed and disobedient. When she dismounted, she hit the cobblestones of the plaza with her full weight on her knees, and her arms could not quite save her head from following with a sight-blackening impact.

It was hard to tell how much time had passed, but when she was able to lift her head she could tell a crowd had formed—or, at least, that was what she inferred from the detached patches of color that swam through air full of blurry murmurs around her. She tried to fold her legs under her and sit up, but she couldn't quite lift her trunk off the ground and settled for rolling over. There was something sticky stinging one eye. She felt a pair of strong hands on her upper back hinge her up to sitting, then an arm around her shoulder, a presence sitting beside her. A male voice made some pronouncement, but the voice in her mind was clear: *Don't try to talk.* With the voice came a self-image: It was Zetaala, much younger, taller, and clearer-skinned than he was in life. *OK?*

OK, she said.

Good, you understand my thoughts. Here, sit with me. He opened up his mind, showing her clearly what he meant by "with me."

You'll fall.

I'll do most of the work. You just help me out.

She felt the loss of tone when she *reached* to help pilot his body—felt it internally, but also felt his body slump slightly against her, his arm drag at her shoulders. It was a moment's lapse, though; the memory of a human motor schema snapped back as if it had never been gone, and the defiant meat-logs that had betrayed her to the wiles of gravity became her arms and legs again. He ceded more control and she filled in, the motor pattern burning brighter. She felt her body beginning to support itself. *The Dancer, Zetaala, thank you,* she spoke in her mind, flooded with relief. He replied with words and mind:

"You learn a few things in construction, and one of them's what to do when someone's hit her head."

You learn a few things in construction, and one of them's how to fix an overstretched mind.

In the crowd gathered around her, she saw Shanhoon Krait. She ripped the damper from her neck—how had Zetaala done all that through the damper?—and tossed it at Shanhoon; it fell short, but the intention was clear enough. "There's that back, Dr. Krait," she said, in a voice clear enough to cut through the chatter of the crowd, which, bisected, fell away. "Many riches may it bring you." She felt Zetaala stiffen beside her and quailed a little; but she could not stop halfway. "What's next, make us wear two each? I mean, what a business plan."

Krait was smart enough to stop himself from talking—to know that nothing in his mind at this moment, sandbagged and full of a patrician's anger, could possibly help him against a wounded widow lobbing accusations from the cobblestones. He was not fast enough to stop his eyes from narrowing, his lip from curling.

She twisted the knife: "Scared to admit it, scared to deny it. Fine. At least we can all feel good for the prize money. It'll go to a nice home where it can socialize with others of its kind."

"You should take your complaints to the Standards Board," said Krait.

"If the Standards Board had known you worked for the company selling them the dampers," Zaya said, "they might have made a different call."

The crowd parted; Jenirain Gila stalked through, with two middle-aged Mrineen men Zaya faintly recognized—mediocrities, she realized, former eighth- and twelfth-placers trying to redeem their lack of skill by declaring themselves to have outgrown the race itself and moving into administration. "Pronouncements are being made," Jenirain intoned, "about what the Standards Board would or would not have done had the world been other than it has. The Board has always acted in the interests of the 'stream. If you believe our standards to be at variance with those interests, I invite you to summon the courage of your convictions and file. A. Complaint." She looked down her nose at Zaya. "Rather than borrowing trouble from a would-be folk hero who's plainly suffering from some kind of brain injury."

That sneer, so natural on Jenirain's sharp face, flooded Zaya's mind with doubt. Jenirain had pointed her at the Taipan logo on purpose—hadn't she? If this wasn't what she wanted, why make such a show of it?

Maybe it was just a way to goad Zaya into alienating the other 'streamers with ravings and conspiracy theories. Or maybe this sneer was the show, so any action Jenirain took against Krait later wouldn't be corrupted with favoritism.

I hope you know what you're doing, Zetaala said in the corner of her mind.

Zaya did not reply *Me too*.

***

AFTER THE ANGELS' TRIBUTE.

WITH THE HELP OF Bandit's Breath, Zaya and Vanako had moved Aubade off the still-breathing Zetaala; but his body was twisted, his skull red and soft where it had hit the stones, and his breathing had softly ended long before Lerikaan Boomslang had arrived with the Yemareir Guild of Hospitalers. Tuuro held his hand the whole time and did not speak.

The Hospitalers were trailed shortly by the police. Zaya tried in vain to get Tuuro and Vanako to leave, but neither would. Of course, one of the officers to show up was Kemreen. She took Zaya aside while her partner inspected the scene—for what, Zaya could not imagine.

"I told Kanzhoon I'd handle the interviews," Kemreen said. "I don't think he knows you by sight, but it's not safe for you to be here."

"Tuuro's grieving. He's just lost someone he cares about—and his wyrm to boot. He needs someone who knows what that's like."

"What am I gonna hear from him?"

"If he's in the mood for talking to a cop? The truth. His wyrm got hit in the throat with a tail-spike trying to overtake a 'streamer name of Shanhoon Krait. You get a couple of these each year, it's a standard risk 'streamers assume when they mount up. He'll bury all that in a few opinions—again, if he says anything at all—but that's where you'll end up."

"How are you?"

"I'm good, I'm good, I'm so not having this conversation with you in uniform and your partner in spitting distance of my daughter."

Kemreen's face darkened, but when she spoke, her voice was even. "That makes sense. I didn't think. We can talk later. If you want."

"Why did they send you on this one?"

"I have a reputation. They know I like the 'stream, they know I know some people. I didn't hear anything about you being involved. Were you even involved? Why are you here?"

"I told you. Tuuro."

"But how did you—"

"I was about to win this race when the fucker who killed Zetaala cheated."

"Why is Vani here?"

"She's the only co-pilot in this city worth her weight in raw sewage."

"You mean the only one who'll fly with you."

"I said what I said. My wife—we've talked about my wife?"

"Your family filled me in."

"I'm sorry," Zaya said, forcing her eyes to hold Kemreen's with a steadiness she did not feel. "I should have done that."

"Thank you."

Zaya took a breath. "I met her at the beach, getting proposed to by a Mrineen boy who at least in my mind has always been a lot like Shanhoon Krait. I was seventeen, and I'd just snared a dragon, and I scared the absolute shit out of this besotted kid with my new wyrm, and then I offered Kiriki a ride. And she looked at me, and—Kemreen, it was love at first sight, it does happen, I felt it then and I was right. And she said, 'Not like this.' It took six months to get her on the Mule's back—and not six months of, like, *wooing* her, just six months of being decent. Six months of not doing impulsive shit, of not stealing any more, of learning. To hear her when she said I'd hurt her instead of defending myself. It wasn't until a couple of years later that I realized not everyone would have gotten six months. That Mrineen boy, even though I was the asshole in that situation, he wouldn't have gotten six months—not because she wasn't into men, or not *just*, but because he wouldn't hear it when she said she didn't want him. Don't try to banter with me when you're in uniform, Kemreen, it's not as cute as you think it is."

"Tiamat," Kemreen said softly. "Are you always like this?"

"The girl you met at the Blind Beggar was me, too," said Zaya. "But that girl doesn't stick around. That girl isn't in a good place."

Kemreen cast an eye to the bodies of Aubade and Zetaala behind her. "And this girl is?"

"This girl has a dragon. And someone to fly it with."

"And *that* girl." Kemreen pointed at Zaya. "She got six months from Kiriki."

Zaya nodded. "And that is my dead wife's gift to you."

Kemreen's face sort of wobbled, and Zaya sighed and said, "It's OK, you can smile," and then she did, and Zaya's ribs cracked open and a fine thread of light came in.

***

ONE DAY AFTER THE COURSE FABRICANT.

"Go away," said Yrreen.

"No."

"I heard how you flamed out last night."

"So you're checking up on me now?" Zaya said it lightly, with a smile.

"You're lucky I don't snitch on you to Minshoon. I'm not helping you."

"That's not what I'm here for."

"What, then?"

"Two things. First, if we have to go back on the dole—Taavi and Gilthiniel will be fine, we'll figure out the younger kids, but Vani is a gifted artist. She's been apprenticing with a draughtsman in Viridian Precinct... or at least she was until she started selling drugs. Again. But she's *good*. She could help you. If we do go on the dole... find her some work. Please."

"AURYN and Ouroboros," Yyrreen muttered. "They just keep coming, don't they?" She looked at Zaya with her jaw thrust out. "If she can draw worth a damn and she'll do the work, that puts her ahead of anyone I've seen so far. I'll take a look. What's your second thing, just so I can laugh with cruel joy as I refuse it?"

"You're the only person I know who knows anything about business. There's a company I heard about recently, Taipan Invotechnic. I assume it's owned by House Taipan."

"If it hasn't been sued out of existence for using House Taipan's name, it's owned by House Taipan."

"Would they pull in people from other houses?"

"Sure? I mean, it depends? They're too aristocratic to do much real work, they're going to be pulling in Sliders and Goannas and so on for lab techs and janitors and what have you. But they're one of the great houses, they're not going to let, like, Ziyuki work there, or Arhoon—those people aren't going to want to mix reagents and test out summoning circles or whatever—you said 'Invotechnic'?" Zaya nodded. "They're going to want to boss people around and maybe do high theory if they know how."

"OK, let me ask you this. What do you know about House Krait?"

"Oh, interesting." Yyrreen had clearly forgotten who she was talking to; she was wholly on her bullshit, reading out signals from the pulse-beat of high society in Yemareir. "I worked with them a while back to scope out some lab space in Scarlet and Incarnadine, didn't work out. But they're mostly specialists concentrated in that invotechnic space—systematizing and scaling talismans for mass production. Very much a corporate house rather than an aristocratic one... although in practice they're mostly adopting their top people from fancy houses, I doubt you're going to find a real decision-maker at Krait who was born a Loggerhead or like a Skink. A joint venture with Taipan in invotechnics, with Taipan's name on the door and Krait doing the heavy lifting? That tracks."

"Especially if they adopted somebody from Taipan to work on it, right?"

"I mean, sure, that would smooth things out." Yyrreen blinked; Zaya could practically hear the impact as her feet hit the ground. "Why do you care about all this stuff?"

"Do you really want to know?"

Yyrreen fixed Zaya's eyes for a moment, then steepled her fingers and looked at them. "That's fair enough. I'm saying, out loud, to you, that's a fair enough question." She met Zaya's eyes again. "I do, actually."

"And you helped me, so I'll tell you. But can I ask why?"

Yyrreen looked as though she was about to swallow something bitter. "I've been thinking about what you said. I still think you owe me my portion of the house, and I still think your new daughter has something shady going on—"

"You're right about that."

"Yeah?" A flash of concern, then one of sadness, crossed her face. "I'm sorry. That has to be hard. I mean, I don't know anything about what it's like to raise kids. I barely knew Taavi and Gilthiniel before I left; Jaliki was just, like, a skin bag wrapped around a pair of lungs…" She looked around. "I don't need to be a parent to your kids. But I'd like to know them." She took a breath, then let it out. "And I don't want to be another version of the thug you're dealing with now, always waving his monkey at you and bitching about what he's owed."

"Thank you," said Zaya. "I feel like I should come back and say we'll find a way for you to get your piece of the house. But I don't know. We can't do anything with money right now. I don't know if we'll ever be able to. If we're all still alive and have the house in six months..."

Her throat closed and her eyes stung, and Yyrreen didn't reach across the table to comfort her, which was the right call. "Not exactly speaking from the high ground," Yyrreen said, "but I don't think sneaking into races behind your family's back is good for anyone. Like, emotionally."

"I'm gambling that keeping all our kneecaps in one piece will offset the emotional dimension."

"Bold of you."

"Thank you." Zaya sighed and set her shoulders. "I hate to ask, but if there's anything else you can hunt up about this maybe Krait-Taipan joint venture..."

"I'll send it to you care of Saver."

"Thank you."

"Anything for House Shearwater," Yyrreen said, looking back down at her work. Zaya left her to it.

***

ONE DAY AFTER THE WHITE STEEPLECHASE.

When Zaya left Bandit's enclosure to find a place to pee, Zetaala was there. He locked her eyes kindly but firmly, raised his eyebrows in a fatherly way, and opened his mouth to speak; she, groggy and still moving awkwardly, as though her body was not quite her own, pointed between her legs and did the universal dance and mumbled "I gotta," and he stopped and waved her away.

When she emerged from the public relief on Betel Street, he was waiting at a distance. "Can I buy you breakfast?" he asked. "There's a cart a couple of blocks down that'll sell you a proper bowl of grits with spicy pork."

She stopped in her tracks. "This had better be real, Grandpa. I'm one disappointment away from taking Bandit up in the air and bathing Argent Precinct in cleansing fire until the Air Guard shoots me down."

"It's real. But maybe keep the mass murder stuff to yourself until we have the food in hand."

It was a hot morning—too hot for grits, really—but Zaya was all in after one whiff of the pork, and she sweated happily as they ate at a too-small folding table by the cart. "This is just like a place my d... my parents would take me after..." She realized she did not yet trust Zetaala to know her fathers were queer, or former liquor-store robbers for that matter. "After they came into a little money."

"It was my mother's specialty," said Zetaala. "Working men got served first, everyone else got leftovers. Except on holidays, that was the only time a kid could get a chance at some of the meat."

"Neither of my parents was much of a cook."

The proprietor slid a couple glasses of mate in front of them, with a pat on the shoulder for Zaya. "On the house, veraamaka navo."

Zetaala chuckled and said what Zaya was thinking: "My son would have hated that."

"Is that why we're here?"

"No, actually." Zaya picked up a glass and sipped while Zetaala spoke. "He thinks we're better 'streamers than you, we're doing everything right, you left the 'stream, you need to make way for new blood. Never mind I'm half again your age and you're starting on a new wyrm with a new co-pilot. Tuuro's in the scene more nights than not, trying to make a name for himself. For us. He thought, that night he met you, that you were… handing over the mantle. I said you could be happy about your victory today and still work like hell to beat us tomorrow. He didn't think so."

Zaya shrugged uncomfortably. "Maybe he's right."

"I don't know. But it's not why we're here. We're here so you can promise me you'll never pull a stunt like that again."

Zaya sighed. "What, cutting you off on the approach?" She *clinked* her spoon on the table with more force than she intended. "Even if I did make that promise—"

"No, Shearwater-*cha*." He put his palms out in conciliation. "I mean racing a wyrm one-minded." He dug into the small satchel he carried slung over his shoulder and produced a damper.

Zaya looked at it as you might at half a slug, freshly split and writhing. "I see enough of those when I can't avoid them, thanks."

"I can teach you how to get your mind around it," said Zetaala. "Not perfectly, but better than you'll do on your own. No more ditching and retrieving. But I won't teach it to you unless you promise to race with a partner."

"Why would you teach it to me at all? I'll be honest, Zetaala, if it was me in your chair, I'm not sure I'd do you the favor."

"The noble answer would be what my son said last night: because I don't want to beat you with an unfair advantage."

Zaya laughed. "I like it. Why not go with that?"

"Because fuck the Standards Board."

Zaya laughed again, more deeply this time. "Sold."

***

ONE DAY AFTER THE ANGELS' TRIBUTE.

ZAYA WOKE UP EMBRACED: by a feathered flank against her back, a warm weight on her shoulder, soft hair on her cheek. For a few half-conscious seconds, the weight and texture against her body made her feel like she was floating, supported by and cradled by a perfect warmth, a perfect softness. Then she swallowed, felt hair on her tongue, jerked her head away to free her mouth of the hair; her cheek began to itch, the feathers began to poke, the ache in her shoulder from supporting Vanako's head began to make itself known. Vanako stirred, grunted, pulled away.

"You drank a lot last night," Vanako said.

"So did you."

"Tuuro made me."

"Same."

"No," said Vanako. "He was with me the whole time."

Zaya smiled. "He was. Poor kid."

"What's your excuse?"

"I have to go home today."

Now you know how I feel, Zaya could imagine her saying; or *That's hurtful*, or simply *Rude*; but she just looked at Zaya and nodded with eyes full of knowledge. She'd have to go home, empty-handed, broke, caught out in her own lie by the note she'd had to send the night before: *Vani's safe, she's with me.* "It's all right," Vanako said, fingering the green glass of the goggles still hanging by a strap around her neck. "We'll do it together."

***

A DAY AND A HALF AFTER THE WHITE STEEPLE-CHASE.

ZAYA AND BANDIT GLIDED through the night on silent wings. She felt exposed in the open air, like Minshoon or Eäril might peek out from a cloud and catch her out. But, of course, she might have been any of a thousand Kayalim women on a thousand Dawn Wyrms looking to trade passage for a spare sherd or two; and if anyone noticed them, they kept it to themselves.

The first delivery was to a small letterbox in Incarnadine Precinct, by a faintly shabby block of offices that, Zaya knew, looked much nicer on the inside. In small, neat letters, the box was marked "Office of Standards and Adjustments, Slipstream Industries," and below the name, "Please file notices and complaints here." She dropped the envelope marked *ATTN: Jenirain Gila* before the soul at the one lit window could notice she was there.

The trip from Incarnadine to Lilac Precinct seemed to last only a few wingbeats. Before long, the tenement that housed House Shearwater hove into view. Third floor, north side, third window: A small packet arced through the air to land on the window box, bending the stem of one of the irises. A paper wrapped around the leather strap held instructions: A places, a time, an alibi. Green lenses glittered in the lamplight.

CHAPTER 22

SUBSTANCE USE, RECREATIONAL. WE'RE *near the end of the letter "S," tourist, and at this point we should be able to be candid with one another. In that spirit, let me say I recognize that this topic is likely to be an organizing impulse behind your visit, and that's OK. What I'm here to do is to try to help you stay safe. Consciousness alteration in Yemareir has roughly three tiers, in roughly ascending order of potency:*

***Everyday/social.** Alcohol, cannabis, betel nut, and worldvine are available at licensed establishments. For foreigners, being high in public is fine if it's after sunset, you're in a respectable precinct, and you're not showing the entirety of your ass. You might be able to get away with two out of three; don't try for one.*

***Tolerated.** Most of the more interesting things you'll have heard of are in this category: blue, salvia, mescaline, alagos, opium. You won't see them on shelves, but a lot of barkeeps and street markets have a secret menu, and of course there are individual entrepreneurs. These folks mostly won't screw locals, but foreigners are a different story; get references before buying. Your main risks are bad product and misdemeanor disorderly conduct.*

***Banned.** Amethyst, datura, a couple others. You don't have to worry about stumbling on them accidentally, because by default no one will want to sell them to you. These are viciously addictive substances that will make you dangerously mean or deeply paranoid very quickly. The* *business model leans on repeat customers in desperate situations, which means you're a low-value prospect. Be happy about it.*

SEE ALSO: Amalgam (Ililuë); Law enforcement.

—From "A Visitor's Handbook for Yemareir," by Shenireen Agama

***

Zaya and Vanako entered House Shearwater to the clearing-up of breakfast: Minshoon scraping dishes off into a bin, Cerminir and Kirono bringing them to the counter, Taavi and Gilthiniel keeping the younger kids entertained. They turned to face her and a sickening déjà vu coursed through her stomach: The sitting around the table, the hurt looks, the *talking*. Jaliki ran to her, the ker right behind him, and with her arm over his shoulders she felt the urge, the need, to turn around: she could close the door, hustle him down the stairs, be out of the building before they could catch her.

But their eyes weren't on her. They were on Vanako.

"What did you do?" Minshoon said.

"What did *she* do?" asked Zaya.

"Whoever. What was done. What transpired. What eventuated."

"I told you," Zaya said. "In the note. I was racing, Vani joined me. That's where we were. Did you not get the note?"

"The note didn't say anything about the debt," said Minshoon.

"What about the debt?"

"Exactly!" said Minshoon, his eyes dangerously bright. "What about it, Zaya?"

"It's gone," said Kirono, his eyes on Zaya's, probing. "Tjaroon sent a message. We got it a little before yours. Vani's been made whole by an anonymous benefactor. Did you know that?"

"I had no idea," said Zaya. "It wasn't me."

All eyes went to Vanako.

"It wasn't me either," Vanako said. "I don't know where it's from."

The hesitation, the awkwardness of the phrasing, the tiny shift in Vanako's posture. These were all things, Zaya realized, she would have read much differently before spending so much time in Vanako's mind. Maybe she didn't know where the money was from, but she knew something.

"This is bullshit," said Cerminir.

The children froze like startled animals at her pronouncement. Cerminir was always the distant one, the silly one, the one who receded when things got loud or rough or intense. She was not the one staking claims with iron in her spine and saltpeter in her voice.

"Cer," said Zaya, "I know I shouldn't—"

"You're *damn* right," Cerminir said. "You should have known better. You are better. What scares me most about this whole thing—more than the dole, more than raising my girl at the Amalgam—is seeing you, the woman who built this house, reduced to lying and sneaking and stealing because some snot-nosed teenager won't come clean about what we've all always known is a lie."

Vanako's lip curled. "If you don't want me here, I'll go."

"I don't want you here," said Cerminir, "but I bet you won't."

"Cerminir," said Zaya with all the steel she could muster, "there are children here—"

"I wouldn't miss you if you left," said Cerminir as though Zaya hadn't spoken. "What I want, as opposed to you, is a safe place to raise my baby. First you were in debt to some thug drug dealer, and that scared the shit out of me, but Zaya and Minshoon said it was all right, they were handling it. But they weren't handling it, because we can't handle a debt that size unless we sell the house, so even through that wishful bullshitting it got pretty clear where we were headed. That wasn't all right, but it made sense. I had a plan. I could go back to the Amalgam. If I couldn't convince Zaya and Minshoon to call you on your stupid, obvious lie and throw you out to save the house then at least I had a plan. But *now*," Cerminir said with a deep breath in through her nose, "now the house is saved, I guess, and *I have no idea why.* I don't have a plan. I don't know what shitty deal you made to cancel the debt, what you're going to have to do or when. So I'm going to say it now, while I'm still mad enough to be brave, so I can never take it back. Come clean or I'm through. I'm not going to live in a house of people who let this shit go. Come clean so I can make a plan, or I will never see any person in this room again."

"Same." The voice cracked a little; it was, shockingly, Gilthiniel. "I love you, Vani, but same. You should never have put us in danger like that. Zaya and Minshoon should never have let you. You owe us."

"I can't," Vanako whispered.

"Vani," said Taavi. "Come on? What good is whatever you did if it rips the house apart anyway?"

"I didn't do it for your stupid fucking house!"

"Ziyuki-*kana.*"

All eyes in the room came to rest on Jaliki.

Vanako covered her face with her hands. "Dammit."

"Ever since you talked to her, things were supposed to get better, but they didn't." Jaliki's eyes were wide, and there were tears behind his voice waiting to burst through. "They're gonna figure it out. You have to talk about it now."

Zaya knelt beside Jaliki. His eyes were wide, brimming; she let her hand rest on his shoulder, as lightly as she could. "My breath," she said, "when was the last time you saw your aunt?"

"I never did," said Jaliki. "Vani said she wanted to bring me, but Ziyuki-*kana* was worried I would tell."

"You promised you wouldn't," Vanako said tightly, through tears. "You shouldn't. You're worth more than this stupid fucking house your family's so obsessed with."

"Vani's right," said Cerminir. "You shouldn't tell. She should."

"It's not going to save your stupid—"

"—fucking house, we know." Cerminir was walking over to Vanako. Zaya could see how she controlled her body's motion through space, gliding rather than bustling, reining in any haphazard motions of her arms that might read threatening. Vanako would not see, most likely, the effort that went into that unremarkable motion, but despite the harshness of her words, Cerminir was trying to set Vanako at ease. Her deep green eyes in light green sclerae gently took hold of Vanako's—that was a trick straight out of Indiriel's playbook, and Zaya had never understood how she did it either. "Lying and hiding things hasn't worked," she said. "If we know the truth, we can face it. We won't be living in the dark any more. I'm so tired of living in the dark, Vani."

Zaya caught herself mouthing *I think you are too*, but that wasn't Cerminir's style. She didn't trust her thoughts about other people enough to say them out loud.

Silent, Vanako moved to the couch. Cerminir moved as well, sitting next to Vanako, where the girl would not look too often. The rest of the house took their own places around the coffee table.

"Ziyuki-*cha* invited me for shaved ice at the Sweet Soldier," she said, using the honorific for general respect rather than respected family. "I thought it was to offer me a place in House Amphisbaena. Like she'd been offered. But she wanted to talk about my stash."

***

VANAKO SPOKE:

I guess I should start from the beginning. I really did get hit. I didn't arrange it or anything. I had to tell Javashi te-Zaako that she was short, that I couldn't give her the month's dose for Shaavo. I thought there'd be... like I'd had those conversations before, there's this way they tend to go, denial then hope then pleading then promising, and you usually don't get to violence for a minute or so if it's going to happen. But Javashi had gone through all of that in her own head, I think, before I ever showed up, and knew where it ended. So she just decked me.

And so I'm on the ground, trying to get up, thinking What if she takes everything and runs? *But she doesn't. She just stands there, arms crossed, and waits for me to pull myself up off the ground, and while I'm still getting my legs under me, she starts talking.*

I don't remember the whole thing, but you can guess. The usual stuff about how I'm leaving Shaavo to die...

... or, no, you can't guess it, can you? Anyway, the part that I remember is:

"How dare you come to me with a box of medicine and tell me I can't have any, when your own little stepbrother is getting that shit for free?"

And I just give her this dumb look and say, "No one gets any of this shit for free."

And she looks at me like I'm a slug smeared on the sole of her shoe and turns to go.

And I almost let her, but instead I pick out a dose of yliaster and just, foomp, wing it at her, right between the shoulder blades.

And then we do the thing where she turns around to almost curse me out, then realizes what I've done, we have like a wordless moment with, like, eye contact, tears, all that. All the drama.

So now she's gone, and I'm short a dose, and my head hurts. And I'm feeling like the worst idiot. Because who would hit the streets for months, selling the very thing their brother needs to live, and not insist on taking some? How was that ever not part of the deal?

***

"What did you say it was called?" asked Zaya. "Illi..."

"Yliaster," said Thelendil. "The substance that unifies body and soul."

"Well, that's what the old natural philosophers said it did," said Kirono.

"Were they wrong?" Thelendil said coolly.

"There were some uses they didn't anticipate," said Kirono. "The really old texts talk a lot about turning lead into gold or whatever. That was all theory, in practice you can't use it for physical transmutation—or, you can, but the energy cost is massive, like 'line up an army of dragons and see if you can suck up the heat from all their flames at once' level massive. Once Etrimain Monitor worked those numbers out, everyone got sad and no one thought about it for a couple of centuries, and then the Yellow School started taking the 'unifies body and soul' thing seriously and investigated telepathic uses. So you have some wild old monographs about goety, dream-sending, mind control—and *that* stuff is provably feasible... but now you have the opposite problem as physical transmutation, because organic brains really aren't adapted for telepathy, which is why psionic traditions from the old country are crusted in all these rituals and exercises and you only do complicated stuff in pairs and all that. But our alchemists in Kerkakan and Mlinivoun don't have a folk tradition of telepathy to put the risks in context. So they all die of strokes and dementia a few years after their breakthrough results, except the ones who get eaten by demons."

Cerminir had a thoughtful look on her face. "It sounds like this is all leading up to Jaliki secretly being a goetist and Vani secretly helping him summon demons," she said. "But I feel like if you could summon a demon to eat your ker, I'd have heard about it?" The ker, lying on top of Jaliki's feet, seemed to twitch its ears. Zaya stopped herself from kicking it... then realized how long it had been since she'd seen it close enough to kick. Weeks? It had been avoiding Jaliki not that long ago.

Kirono raised an eyebrow at Vanako. "You want to take it from here?"

"I had no clue about any of that shit," said Vanako. "All I know is that I talked about yliaster being able to manage kerostasia and you went down a whole rabbit hole about a bunch of dead old demon summoners going batshit."

"Being able to manage what?" Zaya said, half choking.

Vanako sighed. "I was getting to that."

"You were dealing *medicine*?"

"Isn't it all medicine?" Vanako said, spreading her hands philosophically. "If you think about it?"

Four pairs of eyes stared like eight poisoned spearpoints at Vanako.

Vanako looked to Kirono. Kirono sat up a little straighter and smoothed out his vest. "No one's been able to make telepathic uses of yliaster safe... but a few labs have shown *anti*-telepathic uses that seem to be safe. Amplifying your brain to summon a really big demon will drive most people crazy, but you can fuzz the connection to a demon you've summoned so it doesn't eat you, and that's probably fine. A ker isn't what we think of as a demon because no one summons one on purpose and we don't know how to control them. But reality doesn't care what we call things; the telepathic connection is the same, and you can cut it the same way."

"There." Vanako gestured to Kirono. "That's what I was going to say."

There was a beat of silence in the room. Into it, Enwë whined and reached for Cerminir, who took her from Gilthiniel's lap and freed a breast to nurse; Minshoon made space for her to sit. "So," he said, leaning on the back of the same armchair he'd just vacated. "There you stood. Nursing a bruise on your face, alone, and short a dose. Where'd the rest of it go?"

Vanako nodded. "All right. I'll actually start at the beginning this time."

✳✳✳

Look, Zayeni had been *trying to get me to deal for Tjaroon since we met—she knew where I'd come up, she thought it'd be a big deal if she recruited me. But I wasn't interested in moving blue or datura, I got out of that for a reason.*

But then she told me about a cure for kerostasia.

She knew. She didn't know about my mom, but she knew about Jaliki.

The apprenticeship in Viridian was a perfect cover. I could skip whenever I felt like it, it wasn't anything worse than Ora-shan already expected of a Kayalim student. I could bike out to Eggshell and Incarnadine, make a couple of sales, bring the money back to Tjaroon in Chartreuse, be back for dinner.

I was happy for a little bit. I was helping. I was saving. But I was always asking for new work, and I never got it. I would have done anything—skipped school, left all of you, moved back to Celadon, any fucking thing just to move more of it. So I could set something aside for Jaliki.

But no matter how much I earned, the price went up faster.

I dealt and I dealt, to all these Mrineen folks. The price went up, and sometimes my client list would change—some charity case getting a discount would drop off, some society matron would come on, and my cut would get a little bigger... but everything I'd saved for was even farther away. And my brother was still dying.

It didn't feel like I was helping any more.

So yeah. I took the opportunity. Eleven six-dose packs of yliaster. Eleven years for Jaliki.

***

"Vani," said Minshoon, his eyes bright. "You didn't have to do this. We could have found the money—we could have *bought* him a dose already—"

"But he's had one already, hasn't he?" said Zaya.

Vanako looked at Zaya the way she might at a lioness a quarter mile off on the veldt. Then she nodded.

Zaya looked at Jaliki. "I opened the door on the ker that one night," Zaya said. "I thought it was you for a minute, that you'd had an attack while I was gone and no one had known. I saw that thing sleeping in the common room and I thought maybe, somehow, you were getting better. But everyone knows you don't get better from this." She looked down at the ker, curled up on Jaliki's feet. "It wouldn't get near him for a while. But that was a few weeks ago, and now it's wearing off. Is that right?"

Minshoon looked at Vanako in growing alarm. "Why is it wearing off?"

"Each one is good for a month or two at most," Vanako said. "You have to keep..." She looked over to Jaliki. "It's OK. You can show."

Jaliki held out his arm, palm up. The dot-and-line design Zaya had noticed at the beach was there, the crisp dark purple of the marks mostly faded to dull grey.

"Vani," said Minshoon, "why didn't you get him another dose?"

"I told you," Vanako said. "Ziyuki-*cha*."

****

I HID THE STASH in his room, so you wouldn't find it if you searched mine. And I took him to a tattooist in Viridian Precinct for the first rune. And it worked!

But then... you were all so scared. I was in so much trouble, and you were getting deeper and deeper in just to help me, and Minshoon was staying up later and later trying to move money around, Kirono was doing his consulting thing and hating it, Cer wasn't looking for work because someone needed to be there for Enwë but she can feel everyone's pain and fear worse than anybody else...

... quit looking at me like that. You think I'm the kind of person who keeps her head up her own ass because she's in love with the view. But I knew we were headed for the dole if nothing changed. And what was

panicking me about the dole was, no offense to this stupid fucking house, not the idea of leaving this stupid fucking house. It was the thought of carrying around eleven slabs' worth of yliaster with nowhere safe to put it. And it was the thought of Tjaroon and his people finally getting pissed off enough to take what they felt like they were owed out of Zaya's hide, or mine, or Jali's.

So I'm not asking questions when Ziyuki-cha offers to take me out for shaved ice.

Like I said, I thought she was recruiting me. And if she was recruiting me, I thought maybe I could ask for a loan—pay Tjaroon back, keep us off the dole, make it all right again. I was so eager I went straight for it, didn't stop to ask if I was right.

What an idiot.

House Amphisbaena doesn't want me. What Ziyuki-cha wanted was the stash. She said she'd pay Tjaroon back—well, now we know she did it. She said she'd guarantee Jaliki's rune—once every six weeks, or more if he somehow needs it, for life.

That made no sense to me. And I said that to Ziyuki-cha. House Amphisbaena is already going to take a loss on the payback—the debt he set was for more than the whole stash cost, and he's getting less than the whole stash. Setting that aside, Jaliki's going to live more than eleven years if the ker doesn't get him. He could cost them eight, nine, ten times the amount that stash is worth in a lifetime. And what she tells me is this:

✳✳✳

VANAKO'S EYES WERE RED and gleaming now, and when she spoke she tore the words from the air like a coyote worrying meat from a bone.

"'The offer comes with one, and only one, condition. If I ever learn that my sister knows about this, the deal's off.'

"And I said, 'OK.'

"And we took a wing here and I gave her the stash. And she gave me a date four days from now for his next treatment. And now you know. And the deal's off."

***

A SILENCE HUNG OVER the House Shearwater common room.

"I don't see what's hard about this," Cerminir said. "I won't tell Ziyuki Zaya knows if no one else does."

"She's an alderwight," said Vanako, voice thick, eyes bright. "She has spies, she has charms. She's probably already heard me spill it."

Minshoon shook his head, his smile sad and somehow proud. "No, Vani. Nothing that elaborate, or that simple."

"Who died and made you the Wise Old Wilderness Guide?"

"Ziyuki-*kana* chooses her words carefully," said Kirono. "She doesn't care if Zaya knows. She's worried about what Zaya will do. She wasn't threatening you, she was threatening Zaya."

Vanako looked to Zaya. Her child's eyes brought her, somehow, back into her body, which felt light, the brow she had not known she had been creasing with concentration now fallen loose, unclouded. "Vani, my breath. My sweet girl. You didn't have to carry all of this. It must have been so hard."

"It really was," Vanako whispered, and the latch of her throat unlocked and the tears began to pour, and Zaya gathered her daughter in her arms, Kiriki's goggles—still hanging around Vanako's neck—digging into her collarbone.

At last they pulled apart, and Zaya pushed back a damp hank of brilliant purple hair from Vanako's cheek. "I screwed up so much," said Vanako. "I told so many lies."

"So did I," said Zaya. "I stole something valuable from someone powerful who wants it back, and I lied to the family. I've been holding your sins over you like I'm any better, but I'm not."

"You did it because of me."

"And you did it for your brother. We both did stupid things for good reasons. We both have debts to pay."

"If you mean that," said Minshoon, "you can start by getting out of the 'stream."

Vanako nodded, but Zaya shook her head. "Maybe I should say yes. But no."

The effort to stay calm didn't register in Minshoon's voice, but Zaya saw it in his hands. "Why?"

"Because we still need money to eat. I can't work for Transdesert or any of the long-haul companies any more."

"Get into construction."

"There are literally murals about me on the walls of the city. How many construction companies are going to hire me?"

"You don't know."

"You're right." Zaya ran a hand through her hair, made a fist to feel the pull on her scalp. It was long enough now; she should put some color in. "Maybe, if I tromp around the city for months, I can find a construction job where a month's wages would give me a fraction of what I can make in a single race. Or I could be a wing-for-hire and whisk people who can pay from one end of the city to another. It'd probably only take me a year to work off the permit. Or I could join a circus."

"You're not being serious—"

"I *am.*" Zaya discovered the slightest ember of anger, heating up in the bottom of her throat. "You haven't said 'honest work' yet because you're better than that, but it's right on the tip of your tongue, I can smell it. The honest jobs for poor Kayalim with psionics but no education are chutes to the dole, Minshoon. Long-hauling was different because bandits don't care who's on the wyrm—and even then, there were Mrineen ex-'streamers with no wins who were making more than me on their first flights. In the 'stream, I can support us—and I'm out in front of our people."

"There we go," said Minshoon. "That's what we're actually talking about."

Vanako's face went dark with fury. "What if it is?"

"Vani," said Zaya.

Minshoon looked at Vanako, his face half-calm, half-stricken, clear, open. "I'm sorry, Vani," he said. "I didn't mean it like that. All I meant was... what I said. That that's what we're really talking about. And so that's what we should talk about. Zaya's become someone who's important to the Kayalim of Yemareir, and that's bound up with the 'stream. All right. So you're going to be an inspiration to the people. What do you do with that?"

"What do I need to *do* with that?" said Zaya. "The point is to win all day and not apologize."

"Sure. Only I'm looking at the woman who stole a dragon to save her daughter."

"What's that supposed to mean?"

"Bluntly? It means it's only a matter of time until you find something you think the admiration of a big group of people is going to be useful for, whether or not it's dangerous. You've probably already thought of five things, Tiamat knows there's no shortage of horrors in this city. There's a reason Ziyuki didn't want you to know about her trade with Vani. You don't want to be a celebrity, you want to be a hero."

Jaliki squirmed a little and squeezed her arm; Eäril whispered "Mama!" *That's not what he means,* she wanted to say to them—but the want vanished like smoke into open air. She squeezed Jaliki back and, since she couldn't reach Eäril, took Vanako's hand. "I never thought of it that way," she said to Minshoon. "But, yes, that's what I want."

Minshoon blinked; he'd expected her to deny it. "That's going to put our family at risk. People in this room could get hurt or killed."

"What do you think I'm going to do?"

"I think you're going to try to get more yliaster to people who need it. And I think you're going to end up trying to fight House Amphisbaena to do it."

"You've thought farther ahead than me. I figured I'd just end up fighting Tjaroon and his mandrill. But I wasn't going to throw the first punch."

"For a man like that," said Cerminir, "threatening his business counts as a punch."

Zaya looked up at her, trying to get a read from her face and posture. As usual, it was useless. "What do you think, Cer?" she said softly. "Is this better?"

"I'm still afraid," she said. "But I know what I'm afraid of now, and what it's for."

Zaya realized her shoulders were up, bracing for impact; she let them drop. "I'm glad." She shook her head with a rueful grin. "Of course, how I'm actually going to get my hands on any of it is academic at this point. Maybe I'll just be Tjaroon's best customer."

"Oh," said Thelendil, "that part's easy."

CHAPTER 23

BEACHES. *A* POPULAR ATTRACTION *in late spring through early fall. Stick to Azure, Cadet, or Cobalt Precincts. Cerulean is mostly the Port of Yemareir; the other coastal precincts are cut up by private beaches, and some of the owners (especially in Ultramarine) absolutely will not scruple to kill "trespassers." Attractions of the Yemari shore include bonfires, drinking, cheap alcohol, fabulous street food, and public nudity; hazards include buried kindling, mean drunks, litter, jellyfish, dogfish, riptides, and public nudity.*

Here is how to approach the beach. Travel in the morning: Wake up late, eat a good meal beforehand, arrive an hour or so before noon. Plan one to two hours of each of the following: Reading, sleeping, swimming, walking (optionally: conversation). Separate each activity with some fruit or juice bought on the boardwalk. You'll be tempted to get a kebab or some divine-smelling fried thing from a cart; discipline yourself! You'll thank me. Half an hour before sunset, pick up a huge, too-sweet, too-strong drink from the boardwalk and settle into a spot to watch the sunset and the Dawn Wyrms' evening hunt. Sip your libation and allow yourself to be gobsmacked by the soul-fracturing beauty of half-starved monster lizards dive-bombing for grouper and porpoises. As soon as the sun edges below the sea, get your starving, wobbling carcass to the boardwalk and crush your buzz under a mountain of fried mussels, hot pepper shrimp, or honestly whatever's closest, you can't go wrong. Then back to the beach for a bonfire, into the streets for a more usual nightlife type scene, or home to sleep it all off.

(Co-signed. —Ed.)

SEE ALSO: Dragons, Common; Landmarks, Natural; Substance Use, Recreational.

—From "A Visitor's Handbook for Yemareir," by Shenireen Agama

***

THE NEXT DAY WAS clear and hot, so they went to the beach. Not just Zaya and Jaliki, but all of them; even Cerminir, who hated both sand and salt water, and Minshoon, whose relationship with the sun was complex at best, and Enwë, who would have to be watched constantly so she didn't put her mouth on a beached jellyfish, or crawl into the surf.

The actual getting there was, of course, a massive annoyance. Kirono would not leave until he'd found his swimming garment; the finding of bikes, scarce on a day of perfect weather, took two and a half precincts, at which point Eäril got cold feet and had to be coaxed to sit on the handlebars, and then only with Cerminir, who already had a sleeping Enwë strapped to her back; so Enwë had to be awakened, screaming, and transferred to Kirono, who was happy to carry a baby and not at all happy to be screamed at. By the time ten minutes had passed on the bikes, Vanako and Gilthiniel began insisting that a bite to eat or at least a cold drink was necessary to forestall the swift and lethal onset of dehydration and overheating; which complaining would have subsided on its own had Minshoon not made the perfectly benign observation that none of the charming cafes and food carts had seating that would accommodate a family of ten on eight bikes, therefore implicitly approving any stop that *would* accommodate a family of ten on eight bikes, and opening up a running series of arguments about whether a given provisioner would accommodate a family of ten on eight bikes. These were still going when they rolled up to the border of Cinnabar Precinct, which was closed for the brooding of the Painted Mockingwyrms, and Minshoon and Cerminir had just gotten into the second minute of an argument about whether to go north or south to route around it when Zaya rolled forward, waving the rest along.

"They're ambush hunters," she said as protests erupted. "And they're nocturnal. We'll be fine."

It was strange, to see city streets so quiet on a perfect day—though quiet was not silent: monkeys, fennecs, even jackals, and birds of all kinds had gravitated to the empty blocks, hungry for a reprieve from the constant pressure of humanity. A pair of mockingwyrms tracked them for a few minutes, their blue-black-yellow plumage brilliant against the sky, imitating the noises of their breathing, the clank of chains in the gears of their bikes.

Zaya's mind gave way to memories of Ashen Precinct, as it sometimes did in precincts emptied for a brooding season—especially on bright, hot days like this, like the summer day when Kiriki had died. But her mind quickly moved on from Ashen Precinct, from the lash of flame, the sickly throat-filling plunge, the smell of burning feathers; to the memory of Kiriki's mind that day. She had been so tired—then and weeks before, even before Jaliki was born, though Kiriki blamed her fatigue on his then-ceaseless-seeming demands to nurse and to be held. Of course, she'd never really seen a colicky baby until Enwë... and Cerminir had never been half as tired as Kiriki; why was that? Then again, Cerminir hadn't been racing wyrms while she was pregnant, and Zaya had never reached into her mind and felt her feelings the way she had with Kiriki... but Zaya herself had been more tired when she was helping Cerminir with Enwë than she had ever been helping with Jaliki. She was older now, of course, and long-hauling took a toll of its own. But twenty-four was not all that old, however it felt at times.

The night terrors, though. Kiriki had blamed them on the pregnancy, on lack of sleep... but Cerminir had never had them. Zinji had never talked about them. How many mothers did she know? Not as many as she should. Something was feeling wronger and wronger about this. How had she not seen it before?

Had she been let into her extended family, she would have seen it. How many of her cousins had she barely met, who would have had children at the time? Kaalo's family was huge. How many pregnancies would she have heard about over dinner, through gossip?

Set that aside—thinking wouldn't close those wounds. This had always been in her mind, she'd known it at some level. Kiriki's ghost had slapped her in the face with it during the Angels' Tribute: To herself, a few days before the Bisai, Kiriki had already been dead.

But she hadn't wanted to die. Zaya had been in her mind. She would have known that. Wouldn't she? How could Kiriki hide a thing like that?

Anyway, that wasn't where the ghost had taken the conversation. She'd spent all that time talking about revelations and vision quests; if that was where she'd been going, she'd have answered that very clear objection. But instead she'd said *There's a reason Shanhoon looks familiar* before taking her swan dive off the wyrm.

She thought back to the starting line of the Bisai. Arhoon Pogona and Ice on her right, and on her left...

Kanivoon Taipan.

He and Shanhoon looked less alike than Zaya and Ziyuki, but they looked alike. Kanivoon Taipan had been the favorite to win the Bisai before Kiriki and Zaya began roaring up the rankings. Yyrreen had practically traced it out: House Krait recruited mostly from prestigious houses. The Krait-Taipan collaboration on the psionic dampers made even more sense if there was already a relationship with a ranking scion of House Taipan. Maybe that was even the reason Shanhoon had been brought in, to seal a partnership. Kanivoon Taipan and Shanhoon Krait were brood-brothers. Cousins, maybe. Related by blood, anyway.

Shanhoon might be twenty now; what would he have looked like at fourteen? Now that she looked for him in her memory, he wasn't hard to find—a hanger-on in Kanivoon's entourage, an occasional substitute in the ground crew, sometimes with his eye on the starting line, sometimes with his nose in a grimoire. He was an applied sorcerer, then. But of course, with the way he'd stolen her victory in the Angels' Tribute, she knew that already.

So they were brood-brothers, brood-cousins, whatever it was. Why did any of that matter?

The sight of a person walking nearly jarred her off her bike. They had emerged in Cobalt Precinct, and the ocean waited.

***

THEY SWUNG NORTH TO Azure Precinct and met Kemreen and Zinji on the boardwalk, where no time was wasted in getting spiced nuts, pork rinds, and shaved ice into bellies hungry from the bike trek.

At the shore itself, the group split, as it was accustomed to do: The three older children looked for friends or interesting prospects, Zinji did the same, and Jaliki and Eäril ran for the water, the ker close behind. Normally Zaya would have followed them, but Kemreen's presence stopped her; she did not want to leave her alone with the family. "They good swimmers?" Kemreen asked.

"He is. She's careful, and he'll watch her."

"Good. I hear some Ililuë don't teach their kids to swim, they're afraid of the poison water or something?"

"That's an overgeneralization of the Doom of Feä-Finnë Conurbation," said Cerminir, "whereby anyone with the blood of Finnë or Feä will be physically torn apart by sea-spirits if they come into contact with so much as a drop of seawater, which is what you get when you have a threesome with the Sea-King's son and heir. Which is why those people don't get out much, because no one wants them starting families who can't go to the beach."

"Holy shit," said Kemreen. "Was it worth it?"

"Well, they gave their names to a whole city of people who can't go to the beach. Even if the sex was great, it would have been kind of gross to rub it in. Did you know there are rivers and lakes inland?"

"Huh?"

"Rivers and lakes. Inland."

"Sure."

"Did you know you can swim in fresh water?"

"Of course I... oh."

"I'm not mad," Cerminir said, pulling Enwë around to suckle.

Kemreen looked to Zaya, questioning.

"She actually isn't," said Zaya. "She just feels very sorry for people who are wrong about things. Cer, OK if we take a walk?"

"I'll keep an eye on the swimmers," said Minshoon. Zaya nodded and gestured down the beach with her head, then grabbed Kemreen's hand and pulled her along.

After a few steps, Zaya looked up at her. "You don't hold hands much, do you?"

"Not when I'm sober, no."

"It shows."

"The problem is that you're so short. It kind of hurts my back."

"I hold hands with small children all the time," said Zaya. "Suck it up. This is what happens when you don't practice being with girls who aren't in the closet. Your skills wither."

"I have skills. I know you know I have skills."

"Let's not talk about them out on the beach, where nice people might hear." Zaya sighed. "Kemreen, what do you know about yliaster?"

Kemreen stiffened. "Not much. Context might help?"

"Why is it illegal?"

"Do you know what it does?"

"You can use it to amplify or dampen telepathic connections. So you can use it to manage kerostasia."

Kemreen sighed. "Yeah. Or you can use it to manage a demon that's too big for your brain to handle. Same idea. What keeps people from summoning demons is the fact that, unless you're really good, the demon will eat you first—"

"That's not the only thing that keeps people from summoning demons."

"I don't know what makes people do terrible things. I just know you saw a lot more of these crime scenes when it was legal."

"Which crime scenes?"

"The ones where the demon ate a dozen random passersby and whoever summoned it walked away from a clean summoning circle."

"When was this all happening?"

"Four, five years ago?" Kemreen's face grew troubled, uncertain. "I don't quite know the right way to say this."

Zaya kept herself from sighing. "It's OK."

"The news didn't exactly get out much—it mostly happened in Ililuë and Kayalim neighborhoods. Rust, Emerald, Madder, Viridian. I'm not saying it's right you don't see that reporting—"

Zaya slid an arm around Kemreen's waist and squeezed. "It's all right. I understand."

They walked along the edge of a tide pool for a few moments, Zaya's arm around Kemreen's waist, Kemreen's arm around Zaya's shoulders. Sweat sprang from their skin under the sun; Kemreen pulled up the hood of her thin linen blouse.

"When we first saw that ker curled up next to Jaliki," said Zaya, "it was such a strange experience—on the one hand, we knew what it meant, but on the other, here was this tiny little thing, that looked like a new life. That was a new life, although not the kind it looked like. It's a developmental stage of some otherworldly entity that just happens to need to feed on this-worldly entities to move on to the next developmental stage, or at least that's what they tell you at the support groups, because supposedly it helps you cope if you understand it. And for weeks, we all treated it like a cute little puppy even though we *knew* because that's what it looked like. What else were we going to do?

"And then it bit him. And even that we treated like a puppy bite, it wasn't that bad, we'd all had worse from a random dog or monkey somewhere. Only Jaliki was sick in bed for two days, and that thing doubled in size overnight. He's lost strength in his left hand because it took a bite out of his arm while we all watched. Any minute of the day could be the one where it attacks him. Unless we can stop it, one day I'm going to find my child in a pool of blood on the floor, with his guts torn out. If he's lucky and I'm not, I'll be there when it happens; if I am and he's not, he'll die alone. That's what I think about when I think about yliaster."

"I mentioned crime scenes before," said Kemreen.

"I know. I could show you numbers."

"I know. And same. This is violence that harms your people. The anti-kerostatic uses help mostly rich Mrineen scions. I admit I kind of thought you'd be all right with that."

"It only helps rich people because it costs. If it were legal, the price would go down."

"And we'd have demons in the streets again. Zaya, I don't write the laws."

"So if I gave you the name of a dealer, you'd go after him?"

Kemreen sighed and ran a hand through her hair, then flicked off the spray that had built up there. "We probably already know about the operation. There are a few we've been directed to back off from until we can build a stronger case. We know the goods are going to people using them for..." She looked back up the beach until she caught sight of the kids playing in the surf, the ker scampering and biting at waves like any normal dog—except when a breaker threatened to soak it, and it would blink out of existence and reappear in shallower surf. "People like Jaliki. Not a threat to public safety."

"Not people like Jaliki," Zaya said. "People who can pay."

"I know."

"So it's fine," Zaya said, "as long as you're sneaking around and giving all your savings to criminals to save your kid's life. It's only a problem if there's enough of it for everybody." She felt like she was outside her own skull, watching a woman with her face say those words without snarling or shouting. If it hadn't been her, she'd have marveled at that woman's restraint. But there was nothing to restrain, was there? It was numbness; or maybe a callus on her heart, an armor of hard, dead skin to turn the world's spearpoints and dagger-blades.

"Right now there isn't much of it," Kemreen said, "and we know who has it. That's safe, and a couple thousand people can manage their condition who couldn't otherwise. The more there is, the cheaper it gets, the less we know. And the more likely we get another massacre outside a school in Viridian Precinct. A school, Zaya."

"Last question," said Zaya. "Last question and then I stop ruining the nice day at the beach."

"If it's been like the ones so far, you won't like the answer."

"Knowing is better. Forget a dealer." She was thinking about Shanhoon Krait and Kanivoon Taipan now, about psionic dampers with the sigil of House Taipan on the back. "If I told you I knew about an industrial use case, where a couple of houses were involved in a joint venture selling, I don't know, *derivative products* to an illegal enterprise, would that be of interest to anyone in your organization?"

Kemreen closed her eyes. Her chest rose and fell, and she squeezed Zaya's hand as if she was afraid it would fly off like a sparrow. "I'm sorry."

"You know what I'm talking about."

"I know a couple of things that sound like what you're talking about. If we haven't already shut them down, we've got reasons."

Zaya let Kemreen's hand go.

"I don't like it either. Zaya, if every officer had to agree with every law on the books, we wouldn't have police."

"I know."

"You'd be fine with that."

"I'm not here to insult your livelihood," said Zaya. "Or to tell you I think you're doing bad things."

"You've been clear enough on all that before."

"Which is why I'm not doing it now." Zaya drew in a deep salt breath and watched the ker for a moment, writhing on its back to scratch an itch out on the hard-packed sand on the tide line. "But after everything you've just told me... this is why I and mine don't feel protected by you and yours. You're telling me this yliaster stuff is a threat to public safety, but the only thing you actually want to enforce is making sure the public isn't able to use it to make themselves safe. Houses, corporations, and people with money are all good. Because you don't trust us, but you trust them."

"That's not fair."

"How?"

"I trust your family." Kemreen took a deep breath. "Look, we've seized a little bit here and there, I can probably get—"

"No."

"There's a lot I can't do, but I can do something."

"It's not about my family. We're good. And I mean actually good, not just that I don't want your help. But you risking your job to help my son doesn't make these bigger things go away."

"It's not doing any good in lockup." Kemreen stopped walking; Zaya stopped too, and they turned toward each other. Kemreen was closer to the water, putting her eye level a little closer to Zaya's—though not so close that Zaya didn't have to crane her neck to meet her gaze.

"Maybe," Kemreen said, "I'm not brave enough to go at the really big things yet. Or I'm not sure I should—and I know it hurts you that I'm not sure, and I'm sorry. But maybe I could do a little thing. Something you can't do, that would help a little. And it might be a start."

Zaya's eyes widened for a moment. This would be so much easier than the path she and Cerminir and Thelendil had mapped out the night before. There'd be no midnight flight, no skulking through the jungle. No risk, for once, to anyone in her family at all. Kemreen could walk into a room and come out with what they needed. And if she screwed it up, it would all be on her.

Actually, I could use a few doses after all. That was all she needed to say. She could imagine the words, the exact pitch and volume she'd need to use to get them across over the roar of the wind and waves. She could imagine taking Kemreen's hand and pulling her down for a kiss; she could imagine the relief softening Kemreen's mouth, then pulling it into a smile over hers.

It was an image she'd cut herself with, later, if everything went to shit.

"There's a group that meets in the Square of the New Philosophers," Zaya said, "in Lilac Precinct, on odd days at four and a half past noon. If it's raining, they'll have a tent. You'll know who they are when you see the kers." She barely remembered the faces in the group, but she remembered the kers: Jaano's tiny boar piglet, Zejaki's eagle, the three-eyed orangutan with blue streaks on its face that followed Vaasho. "There's a boy there with an orangutan ker, if he's still..." She swallowed and blinked hard. "If not him, then find the family whose ker is farthest along. Probably Shozeki te-Shaazo, with the cheetah. If they don't know what to do with it, tell them to take it to Keivai ze-Rezemi in Damask Precinct. Tell them Zaya Shearwater will cover the fee."

Kemreen's face was shouting that she was regretting this already, that she had thought about the concrete details of walking into a locked room and out with an unbelievably valuable substance that was going to go missing and unaccounted for. But she didn't say anything. How could you say anything? She was going to buy a few weeks of life for a child.

And she was going to expect, when she was done, to feel better about it. But she was going to walk away from the New Philosophers group thinking about all the other kers there, and all the other children who would be getting no new lease on life that day, and maybe, if she was who Zaya thought she was, it would, in fact, be a start.

So Zaya tugged back and down on her fingers and turned up her mouth and gave her the kiss she'd been imagining. If she was going to cut herself with it later, she might as well have the real thing.

✳✳✳

THE SUN HUNG AND soaked the beach with light. Eäril and Jaliki brought back shells and sea glass and surf-sculpted driftwood, ate and drank, complained of boredom, went back out again; the older children brought back snacks and drinks, then rejoined their crowd, now in sight, in the water; Zinji returned and played with Enwë while Cerminir slept. Gilthiniel returned, then left to walk with Kirono. Taavi and Vanako joined Jaliki; Eäril joined Zinji, awakening a territorial instinct in Enwë, who didn't know this adult very well but knew that he was hers. Accusations flew, then sand, then tears; Cerminir woke up enough to offer Enwë a breast as comfort; Zinji brought Eäril to the water; Kemreen fell asleep; and, as the sun sauntered down the sky to paint the sea, it was just Zaya and Minshoon, the latter pale and sprawling in a thin linen caftan, a wide white hat, and dark glasses the same bottle-green as Kiriki's goggles; and, after a stretch of silence watching the Dawn Wyrms come out for their evening fish hunt, Minshoon asked, "So what's the plan after tonight?"

"I've been thinking about that."

"I know you have. But what are you going to do?"

"I'll give you a hint. Umber Precinct."

"OK." She could feel the gears mesh behind his eyes. "The Shadowrun?"

"Warm. Very warm."

"I don't know, Zaya. It'll play to Monsoon's strengths—isn't that thing an echolocator?" Zaya shrugged. "And Umber hates anything to do with the city, especially the 'stream."

"Of course. And that'll be reflected in the odds against me."

"You're thinking Krait and Monsoon come out of Omari first and get the brunt of the punishment," said Minshoon. "But that'll be priced into the odds too, and he'll be ready for it, and there'll be enough for you."

Umber Precinct was on the northwest edge of the city, and for centuries it had been controlled by separatists. They grudgingly maintained more or less open borders, paid something like their share into city taxes, and sent an alderwight to the House of the Stars, whose principal responsibility was to hold forth on the floor of the chamber when permitted, throw sand in the procedural gears when possible, and vote with the opposition on everything.

They did not acknowledge the legitimacy of the Reeve and the Chambers of the Sky, and Zaya had no idea how they were governed or policed except that it was nothing like the rest of the precincts of Yemareir.

That was most of what Zaya knew about Umber Precinct—except that the underground portion of the Omari Shadowrun ended in the foothills above it, and that the residents of Umber Precinct made a game of pelting the 'streamers, invariably floundering through the air as their wyrms' dark-adapted eyes adjusted to the brightness of the day, with anything to hand.

"Yes," said Zaya. "Your bookie friends will do all the smart things. The odds will give Shanhoon a haircut for being first out of Omari and having garbage thrown at him by the fine citizens of Umber Precinct, but they're also going to price in the fact that Monsoon is an echolocator and I'm a washed-up has-been and probably they're going to give him a boost for cheating in the Angels' Tribute, which is the kind of bullshit that won't help him here. But they won't price in my secret weapon."

"What's that?"

"Veraamaka navo."

Minshoon sighed. "Always so reassuring to hear someone trying to cash in on their tiny measure of highly localized minor fame."

"Please," said Zaya. "That's the problem with you numbers people, you think small things don't matter. There is literally nothing more powerful than highly localized minor fame."

***

By the time the sun had sunk below the sea, the fires had sprung up: Little campfires, massive bonfires, the occasional road of man-tall torches leading seekers to wherever they might find whatever they might be seeking. The older children were sent out with cash to bring back dinner and returned with company, a moon-eyed Ililuë girl who insisted on sitting shoulder to shoulder with Taavi and a small gaggle of Kayalim boys and girls who seemed to know Zinji a bit, who accepted their share of food easily and offered no contribution of their own. They ate tough, greasy pepper steak with chopsticks and drank oversweet fruit ices from waxed banana leaves, the adults spiking the latter with a flask of mezcal produced by Zinji. Gilthiniel flirted with a chisel-jawed Kayalim boy who refused to say a word, and Taavi let the moon-eyed girl down easily when no one was listening, and Vanako punched a boy in the mouth when he got too familiar. Kirono played Zinji's guitar while Cerminir sang, and Zaya and Kemreen swam out until the water came up to Kemreen's chin and kissed for a long time in the water, Zaya's toes inches that might as well have been fathoms above the sand, floating in the summer-warm water and the firelight and the hands of her lover, which held her head above the water as surely as any coracle, then roamed as light as fish to all the places Zaya wanted them to be.

When they finally resolved to go, hours later than they'd intended, Zinji invited them to stay, and they accepted—all but Kemreen, who said something about work the next day, which was surely true and entirely beside the point. She invited Zaya with a raised eyebrow, and Zaya declined with a tiny shake of the head and a smile, knowing the wanting that she would feel waking in her father's house would be sweeter than the having.

And she did wake up, and the wanting was sweet, and she whispered something to Zinji before they bedded down all over the floor to sleep, and that night, when even the baby was so exhausted from the day's efforts as to be unwakeable, she and Thelendil tiptoed out to the beach to catch a Dawn.

CHAPTER 24

ENVIRONMENT AND CLIMATE. *READER, this volume aims to elucidate what is unique about the city you've chosen (one assumes) to visit—the peculiar anguishes, rare pleasures, and general quiddities of the Yemari condition as they present themselves to foreign eyes. It is with a heavy heart, then, that I approach the subject, about which I can say nothing original or interesting, of the configurations of dirt and patterns of more and less hot air that (Shenireen, for fuck's sake. —Ed.) (Are we a dirty travel guide now? I'll need to do some revising. —SA) (Just do the entry. No entry, no money. —Ed.) (SEE ALSO: Sex Work, Consumer Protections In. —SA) (SHENIREEN. —Ed.)*

... AS I WAS VERY MUCH SAYING, Yemareir lies just south of the Omari Mountains—a few northern precincts, like Umber and Viridian, are arguably in the foothills. Immediately around the city and stretching west is the veldt, which you might have learned as "steppe" or "pampas" depending on which Mlin dictionary you were studying. Veldt shades into desert if you veer north or jungle if you veer south. Summers are hot but not blistering; winters are wet and mild. yEmArEiR hAs A fAbUlOuS dIvErSiTy Of ClImAtE aNd GeOgRaPhY wItH sOmEtHiNg FoR vIsItOrS oF aLl kInDs AnD pReFeReNcEs. (How long did it take you to write that sentence that way? —Ed.) (Hopefully less time than it'll take you to typeset it, you monster. —SA)

SEE ALSO: Amalgam (Ililuë); Conurbation (Ililuë); Faranmithir Forest; Jeweled Desert; Landmarks, Fantastic; Thaumobiome; Veldt.

—From "A Visitor's Handbook for Yemareir," by Shenireen Agama

***

"WE HAVE A DRAGON in a stable," Thelendil said, shaking himself against chill from the breeze off the bay. "We know it likes me. Why do we need a new dragon?"

"The dragon in the stable is stolen property," Zaya said. "We don't want to get caught leaving the city on it." The sand had become cool, hard and damp under their feet; they had crossed the high tide line. "Will you light that torch?"

Thelendil lit the torch, and they stepped into the surf and then began walking out. The Cobalt Precinct beach had always been the best for this—its slope was gentle, you could walk out a long way before the water came above your knees, which helped separate your little summoning-flame from the beachside bonfires and torches the bay wyrms had learned to ignore. "I forgot you used to do this a lot," he said. "How does it feel now that the student has become the teacher?"

"That's not what it feels like," Zaya said. "For one thing, I'm not bringing my child along."

"You've got a whole family staying back with them," said Thelendil. "Kaalo and Zinji didn't have that. They just had the two minds they needed to guide the wyrm, and you."

"What if I'd gotten hurt?"

"What if they'd left you, and they hadn't come back?"

Zaya let it go. Now that Thelendil had brought it up, she did feel a certain thrill of recognition, as though she was carrying the torch as she had used to do and if she looked up to either side she might see Kaalo or Zinji, wild-eyed but finely focused, the set of their shoulders and the curve of their spines seeming to cast a net of gravity over the night sky. It had felt unimaginable that a wyrm would spurn those men; and if one ever had, Zaya couldn't remember it. But in the present moment, Zaya knew keenly that it was not, in fact, possible to cast a net of gravity over the night sky, certainly not with psionics, and she felt herself trying to imitate her fathers' bearing, to communicate with her body (which, in the moment, felt as small and imprecise as a little girl's) that this was a proposition no dragon could refuse.

She heard Thelendil's sharp intake of breath before she saw it; then there was a great splash and she was soaked and blinded—again, after so long, at last—by the cold salt spray.

The Dawn stared down at the pair of them. It was perhaps a fifth- or sixth-cohort wyrm, much larger than Bandit or the Mule, with a claw-rake on the left side of its snout and forelegs nearly as thick as her own waist—perfect for a long flight with two passengers. Zaya felt the same awe, the same terror as she had done when she was half the size she was now and thin as a wet rat... but in a corner of her mind, away from the part that had come here to do a thing. She *reached* out with her mind and said, "My colleague and I would like to retain your services for a night. We brought drinks."

***

THE NEGOTIATION WAS SWIFT enough; there were, of course, the two other fifths of whiskey they had left on the beach as a way to establish trust, as well as the portion available only on completion. The wyrm seemed to understand the negotiations better than Zaya remembered from the empathic eavesdropping she had been able to do when she was young, and she wondered if it was one whose services Kaalo and Zinji had used in the past. It wasn't long before they were agreed, the whiskey was swallowed, and they were airborne.

Unpursued, there was no real need to join with the wyrm's mind, but Zaya did by reflex and Thelendil fell in without resistance. Zaya kept half a mind's eye on him, taking in the feeling of a first flight into the upper air, the view of the city from the heights: A frantic constellation, a cluster of stars in the black sky that was the ocean and the veldt.

"This is how you got Kiriki to fall in love with you," Thelendil said. It wasn't a question; it had been scudding along the surface of Zaya's mind, her first memory with Kiriki on the Mule above the bay.

"I don't know," said Zaya. "I think so. She wouldn't have come if she didn't trust me. But I don't think it was love until we were airborne."

"And when did you fall in love with her?" asked Thelendil.

"Same, I think."

"Makes sense," he said. "You were inside her mind. You knew exactly what you were getting."

But she could ride with you, she heard him think and then not say.

"Kemreen can't," she said. "I taught you to join Bandit's mind. I don't think I could teach her."

She could not hear him sigh through the slipstream, but she could feel his chest rise and fall—and she could feel him remember her own memory of locking her arms around that chest, squeezing hard enough to bruise his ribs, feeling his breath come faster and faster until it all rushed out at once.

"It feels like I said the wrong thing," she said. "I thought it would help."

She felt the tears sting his eyes beneath the goggles. "As long as it was because I was a shit 'streamer, it made sense. Now you're telling me you like a cop without an ounce of empathy better than me."

"Exactly. How could a decision that bad possibly have anything to do with you?"

She felt him sink into Bandit's back—a mix of resignation and relief. "I'm glad I was in your mind to hear you say that. Just speaking it, I don't think I'd believe you."

"You can ride with me, you know." She hadn't really meant to say it—maybe she hadn't said it; she remembered, with Kiriki, how easy it had been for stray thoughts to become statements. "Low altitude, high torque, that's not for you. But you were with me up here, out here. I didn't just bring you out for the smash and grab. I trust you up here. We may not be alone when we make the trip back."

Thelendil didn't respond with mouth or mind, but she could feel something hulking, a heavy shadow in his mind just beyond the space where thoughts turned into words. "I can feel it," she said. "What's going on?"

"History," he said after a few moments. "I love the house. But it's... you all know each other so well. I don't know where I fit in."

"You don't, necessarily."

She felt his heartbeat pick up, his breath grow a little shallower, and hoped she'd done the right thing. "Then why am I still here?"

"I'm not saying we don't want you. If that were true, you wouldn't still be around. But you're right, everyone in the house is pretty tight, and we've all gone through some things together you weren't around for, and maybe there's a reason only kids have joined since Kiriki died. Shit, even pulling in an older kid has been agonizing. I love Vani and I'll do anything for her, but it might have been a better idea to let her go on the dole. I don't know."

At *I'll do anything for her*, a spike of pain and sadness had pierced his mind like a hot needle. She didn't know if he'd failed to hide it or just wasn't trying; but he didn't say anything, so she continued. "I don't have answers for you, Thelendil. You joined at a hell of a time, and you're here because you wanted to help and we like you and we have space and *you didn't leave*. But—look, Vani is our responsibility. She's a child, and we've set ourselves above her, as parents, and so there are things she owes us and things we owe her. We've accepted you too, and so maybe it seems like—"

"I get it," Thelendil said. "No need to spell it out."

He was angry, he was feeling rejected. He wasn't trying to hide that. But that wasn't the dark presence that seemed to be pulling on his thoughts like a magnet. "There's something else," Zaya said.

"There's not," he said, and the landscape of his mind glitched and blurred.

If there weren't, you wouldn't be hiding it, she almost said; but after weeks of back-and-forths like this with Vanako, she thought she'd maybe developed a sense for how not to make a bad conversation worse. "I'm not saying you don't belong," she said. "I don't think anybody thinks that except you. Which is why, and I'm saying this with all the love I've got, I think it's on you to figure out where that's coming from."

"Please," Thelendil said, "don't talk to me about love. Unless…"

An old memory drew itself in Zaya's mind: A boy on a beach, facing Kiriki at the edge of the surf, pledging himself to her in mangled verses on an exquisite summer day. *My breath,* she said to herself where Thelendil couldn't hear, *where were you when I needed the rock-bottom common sense to not fuck a guy out of nothing but curiosity?*

To Thelendil, she said, "Of course. I'm sorry."

The dark shape in his mind was fogged, now, but she could still sense it: Its contours, its location, its gravity. The pain of her rejection gleamed in its shadow, separate.

***

THEY LANDED IN A sparse patch of jungle northwest of the Supplicant, reasoning that any encampment was likely to be closer to Yemareir rather than farther away. They left the Dawn with another fifth of whiskey and an admonition to be still and quiet. It bolted the whiskey, put its chin on its paws, and closed its eyes.

"Do we want it to sleep?" said Thelendil.

"We asked it to be still and quiet," said Zaya. "If it doesn't sleep, it's going to find something else to do."

"What if we need to leave in a hurry?"

Zaya tapped her temple. "As soon as I'm in reach, I'll make sure it's ready."

Thelendil nodded, not entirely easy with the plan, and led the way to the camp.

Zaya, for her part, was keeping a wide open mind for monkeys, parrots, wyrms, or anything else they might find useful. The best way to do this was always going to be a monkey. Thelendil had assured her that there were night monkeys in this patch of jungle—he called them galagos—but it was difficult to latch on to any animal here. The range of their senses was better than the range of her empathy, she guessed, and they weren't city animals whose fear of humans had worn off from constant contact. They were probably running away before she could detect them.

Also, the ones who didn't run away, she couldn't see, and from their minds it wasn't always so easy for a city girl to tell what they were.

"Four legs," she whispered to Thelendil. "Bad eyesight, good smell, close to the ground. Probably a mammal."

"Bushpig."

"Reptile, no legs, I assume it's a snake. Up in a tree somewhere. Weird rough skin."

"Porcupine viper."

"Not the time to fuck with the city girl, Thelendil."

"I swear it's a thing. They're not really porcupine quills, it's more like durian spines."

"I'll bury you at the foot of this obscenely large tree my dumb hood ass doesn't know the name of."

"It is real, and extremely venomous."

"Is there anything out here that can see for shit?"

"It's night. These animals didn't start coming out at night because they were hot shit at seeing stuff."

"Nature is the worst."

"Give the bushpig a chance, they come out during the day sometimes."

"How is a bushpig going to hold a vial of yliaster?"

Thelendil was too good a hunter to sigh, but she could feel his mind vibrate with exasperation. "We could have done this right, you know. Taken our time to find a suitable animal, spy during the day when we can see, come back at night for the actual execution. We still could."

"The race is in three days. Anyway, that Dawn won't wait."

"Then maybe quit bitching about nature and take the bushpig."

Zaya *reached* out to the bushpig. It was skittish, but curious enough not to run out of range immediately; Zaya found its images of their scents and sounds, hers and Thelendil's, and replayed them, adding good visual images to ease its mind, pairing all of it with her best emanations of calm and serenity. She did the same with the porcupine viper, modified for what she knew of reptilian minds—snakes and lizards typically didn't respond to caring or social energy the way mammals did; they preferred feelings of physical warmth and extreme quiet. Eventually the bushpig came to them.

It wasn't alone—four piglets and a mate followed.

"Six-course meal," Zaya muttered. "This had better be helpful." To the pig's inquiring mind, she imaged the scent of roasting potatoes over a fire. This immediately seized its interest.

The pig family tagged along patiently; she thought the young, especially, might be a liability, but they slipped through the brush more silently than she and Thelendil did, and seemed to have no trouble keeping up. They picked their way southwest until Thelendil said *stop*.

What's going on? He directed her mindsense; she caught it immediately. *Oh hell yes, a monkey!*

Don't fuck with it.

???

If it hasn't run away, it could be a perimeter guard. Someone else could already be in its mind.

Fuuuuuuck. Good spot.

Thank yourself. You warned me about this the last time we were here. I wouldn't have thought of it on my own.

A spark of cold interest flickered in the trees above.

Oh, shit, Thelendil, said Zaya. *I've still got the durian snake.*

Porcupine viper. You want to send it after the monkey?

I could.

She could practically feel the sick feeling in her stomach bleed into his mind. *You don't want to,* he said.

It's not the monkey's fault. It doesn't deserve this. She thought hard for a moment. *It's OK. We can use this.*

I don't like the sound of this.

Why?

Because the only thing we can "use" the monkey for is a distraction.

Yeah.

Which means one or both of us is going to get chased by whatever guards they've got on at this time of night.

Yeah.

And if it's not me getting chased, it's probably going to be me going in for the smash and grab. Since we don't have a monkey of our own to do it for us.

Well, I've got some good news for you, Zaya said.

What's that?

I'm not going to have to do too much explaining. You've pretty much got the idea already.

✶✶✶

FOR A DAUGHTER OF Yemareir, born and raised in the barrios and projects of Madder and Azure and Russet Precincts, there was nothing natural about crouching, sweating and cramped, in the jungle with six bushpigs, a porcupine viper, and a spy monkey; but there was an awful excitement to it, as though she were in a mine with an arm-thick vein of gold separated from her by a bare half-inch of rock.

Zaya counted fifty heartbeats, then a hundred, two hundred. She tried to keep her mind as far as she could from the bored, restless bushpigs without losing her grip on them completely. The porcupine viper's mentality was the one she needed, watchful and patient. Four hundred. Unfortunately, there wasn't anything here the viper was particularly watching for; it would rather be in some other tree, richer in opportunities. Six hundred. She clenched her back teeth, did her best to wipe the sweat off her forehead without rustling the underbrush overmuch, and ignored her aching thighs. The viper hearkened to some interesting odor; the piglets began butting each other in frustration. Eight hundred. The spy monkey sat, stiller than any monkey had a right to be.

One thousand.

With near-orgasmic relief at being able to do something, any-thing, Zaya *reached* out and looked through the monkey's eyes.

It wasn't focused on her and the pigs; it didn't know they were there. That was good. It did know she was in its mind, and through its mind she felt its own alarm echo in another. She withdrew her own mind as fast as she could, which wasn't as clear a message as making the monkey scream *COME GET ME FUCKPIGS* would have been, but verisimilitude was key here.

Now she was in the bushpigs' minds, looking out for whatever might be coming. It would, or at least should, be human guards; vanity empaths like Tjaroon might not consider the dangers of having a companion animal when you were up against another empath, but these people were professionals, or so she assumed—

The bushpigs heard the crack of branches before she did; their hearing went high enough to catch the alarm calls of far-off animals she couldn't hear. Their hackles went up. They smelled something they'd smelled before, that wasn't human.

The plan had been for them to rush through the night-blind guards, bowling them over with a charge and then making, squealing, for the scrap heap. That was gone now. Zaya said *Run* in all six little minds, which were happy to oblige, and began scanning the night just as the stink of sulfur began to waft toward her through the still, stifling night air.

She found a mind—a wyrm's mind, that much she could tell by feel, seeking and curious and not a little hungry—and then she was thrust out of it, evicted by a force so overpowering it had to be an incredibly strong empath.

One incredibly strong one, or two adequate ones.

No time to tell herself *of course* and tear her hair; she needed to know how big, how far, how fast. Unfortunately, there was no sane animal that had stayed close enough to tell her—

Desperately, she seized the monkey's mind.

Whoever had thought to put two empaths on the wyrm had neglected their sentry monkey; its memories were an open book to her. She caught a sense-memory of a long creature, stub-legged but wide-winged, covered in green feathers; and now the monkey was running, swinging away as far and fast as it could, because it knew the creature had the most agonizing—

Zaya threw herself to the side with her arms wrapped tight over her ears just as the wyrm screamed.

It felt like hot nails through her skull; it felt like her ears had been turned inside out and whatever was inside them had been poured on a bed of burning coal; her gorge rose, her limbs twitched, lightning ran up her spine and back down. A tongue of bright cerulean flame licked out where she'd been.

She didn't try to get her hands and feet under her. She didn't know what would happen if she did. All she could do was send the viper plunging, coils ready, fangs out.

It landed on the wyrm's face. That was good and bad. She felt her fangs sink deep as they were meant to, felt the venom course into the wyrm's flesh as it was good and right to do—and then a crushing, a ripping pain around her midsection, and she pulled out of the viper's mind as the other empaths must have been doing from the wyrm's, and she scrambled to her feet and lurched back in the jungle before she could think otherwise. By the time the next scream came it was a mere brand of pain in her temples, which already pulsed and throbbed so horribly with the residuals of the first scream that the new pain was merely an interesting variation on an agonizing theme.

She did not know when her path converged with Thelendil's; she did not even care to ask him if he had found what they had been looking for. But he pushed into her mind, and she was not capable of caring enough about the intrusion to bother fighting him off, and as they both scrambled, lungs full of fire and legs as limp and heavy as unfired bricks, onto the waiting Dawn, he sent the exultant image: Eleven finger-thick pouches, bulging, in the bottom of his satchel.

***

"Oh," Thelendil had said, "that part's easy," and all eyes in House Shearwater had turned to him; and, a night in the jungle and a day at the beach earlier, Thelendil had expanded: "It's the Supplicant taboo. Kirono said it. Your friend Tjamoon or whatever has figured out how to make everyone in the city a gûlnír."

"Goetist," said Cerminir.

"Romalango," said Thelendil.

"That means 'show-off,'" said Cerminir. "Actually it literally means 'horn-throat'—not 'horn' like on a kudu, but like you blow—"

"You're doing it again," said Thelendil.

Cerminir smiled with an awful lot of teeth.

"How is the Supplicant involved in all this?" said Kirono.

"There's some kind of pollen-collecting operation at the foot of it," said Zaya. "Thelendil and I ran into it when... it's a long story."

Minshoon looked at her like Death looks at a cat on its eighth life.

"You'll get the recap eventually," Zaya said. "But Thelendil's right. I mean, I think Thelendil's right. I mean, I don't know what pollen has to do with... yliaster?"

"What kind of pollen?" asked Kirono.

"It's a jungle," said Zaya. "There's a million plants there, and we didn't have time to follow the bees. There was a lot of datura there, though."

"Zaya was very keen on the datura," said Thelendil.

"Good," said Kirono. "That narrows it down. I guess there probably wouldn't be any hermit's pearl in an area that warm?" Thelendil shrugged. "What about brightwick?"

Thelendil frowned, then looked to Cerminir. "Galícuma?"

"Yeah."

"I saw some lianas that could have been... that. I wouldn't have seen the blossoms, obviously."

"You can get brightwick in the foothills," said Zaya. "Why would you go all the way out to the Supplicant?"

"Brightwick only grows on top of huge trees," said Kirono. "Datura only grows out where it's dry and sunny. Except out at the Supplicant. Because, as far as anyone can tell, anything can grow in the water that comes from the Supplicant. Which means you can get the same pollinators coming after both. So at this point you've got a bunch of dueling principles, sun-moon, earth-sky, high-low... now, most modern alchemical theories will tell you that if you get a few of these two-in-one principles in close proximity, you can use them to manipulate other dualities—move them farther apart or closer together. This is the unifying principle of alchemy and sorcery, that the mind-body duality can be not only the patient of something like sun-moon or earth-sky, like what we're seeing here, but also an agent impinging on, like, matter-energy..."

"The dragon people who failed out of Basic Mixing Things Together are just nodding along at this point," said Zaya.

"Look, it's just some alchemist getting smart about a natural experiment," Kirono said. "Botanical alchemy is hard because plants in the same biome almost always have similar characteristics. The Supplicant has this miracle water that allows its biome to support plants that play into multiple dualities at once. The common telos of the pollinators binds those dualities and amplifies the intrinsic tensions. Plants are similar enough that the yield of actual yliaster must be tiny—but with bugs doing all the work for you, it's *cheap*, and you don't have to move mind-body all that far to see effects. Separate them a little, you can close off empathic or telepathic channels; move them a little closer, and..." Kirono shrugged. "Strokes, dementia, eaten by demons."

"Which is why the getting of more yliaster is easy," said Thelendil. "You just have to get out to the Supplicant and collect the materials."

"Children," said Zaya. "Away."

Vanako and Enwë whined; but Taavi dealt with Vanako, Gilthiniel scooped up Enwë, and soon only the five adults remained in the common room. "Thelendil," Zaya said, "one does not simply walk into the controlled substance operation and set up shop."

"Why? You're not going to take anything from them. The Supplicant makes plenty of water, they're set up within, what, a few hundred feet of it? The water doesn't lose its potency that quickly—"

"Remember that whole money thing that's so cool and normal about Yemareir?" Zaya asked.

"Ohhhh," Thelendil said. "I forgot about the supply and greed thing."

"Demand. Supply and demand."

"We translate it as 'greed,'" said Cerminir. "'Milmë armaryë.' It's catchier."

"So yes," said Zaya, "we're taking something from them."

Thelendil sighed. "I mean, this doesn't sound like such a good idea any more."

"No," said Zaya, keeping her voice low against the sharp ears of spying children. "I don't mean we *would be* taking something from them *if* we set up our own shop. I mean we're going to go out and take their stuff."

"This is very much a thing that hasn't worked out well in the recent past," said Minshoon, visibly trying not to shiver apart into his component molecules.

"I don't care," said Zaya. "Jaliki's set for life now, no thanks to me—"

"You don't actually have to be the individual person to cure an incurable curse," said Minshoon. "That's not in your job description. You can set that guilt down and never pick it back up."

"Says you, but that's not the point—"

"It is absolutely the point."

"No," said Cerminir.

Minshoon looked to her, his face softening. "I thought you'd have my back on this one," he said.

"I know you did. That's why I spoke." She flared her nostrils, blew a breath out through her nose. "We have all the information now. Not many others do. We could tell someone else, hope they do the right thing, but how is that fair? We decide what's right and let someone else take the risk? We know this is right. We have to get it. Even if we get one dose, that's a life."

"For today."

"Life is always for today."

"Someone could die. Zaya's taken so many horrible risks already—"

"Someone could die. So instead of lying and pretending everything is OK and everyone is safe, Zaya's bringing us in. The point of *us* isn't to be safe all the time. We can't. The point is to bring each other in. Zaya is right. We need to get some of the goods, so we can show people what this is on our own terms. Everyone else agrees. So let's make a plan."

Minshoon brought his hand up to his face, pinched his temples between his thumb and forefinger. "It's just." His voice was ragged. "I built this. So did everyone; but I, in particular, built this. I cooked the food and did the wash and rocked the children to sleep and walked them to school and paid the bills and moved the money around and managed the risks, and I made the bets that everything else came from. And now you're all telling me it's OK if we just knock it all down. Which isn't what you're telling me. But..."

They let the silence hang until it was clear Minshoon wasn't going to finish. Then Zaya said, "That's the feeling of knowing that, no matter what you do, you can't make anything this city can't take away from you."

"I've known that for a long time."

"You didn't grow up with it. It hits different."

"Fine." He looked to Cerminir. "I won't let the kids come to harm, not if I can help it." *No one is going to let anyone get hurt if they can help it*, Zaya thought; but all Cerminir did was nod, and she let her leave it there. "Let's make a plan."

***

ZAYA AND THELENDIL FLEW low for a while, to the north-northeast, the wrong direction; and when the sun began to tint the sky and they could see wyrm-free air from horizon to horizon, they wheeled around toward the city.

When they reached the veldt near Yemareir, where the river swelled with tributaries and began to teem with early-rising wyrms and antelope and kudu and crocodiles, they landed by a Ranger Wyrm that was big enough for the both of them and negotiated a transfer—Thelendil projecting drool-worthy mental images of arrack and whiskey while Zaya reviewed the Dawn's instructions for its final leg of the mission. The Dawn took flight first; when it was out of sight, Thelendil and Zaya took flight on the Ranger, one satchel lighter.

They landed at one of the bays outside the city gates reserved for inspections of in-flying travelers and submitted graciously to the searching hands of Yemareir's protectors. They made Thelendil dump a few twists of cheap weed on the sand, then looked for something they could force Zaya to part with—or so it seemed to her; their words, their names, had already sluiced like water from the folds of her brain. When the whole demeaning thing was done, they sent the Ranger off into the sky with a slap on its flank and walked past the suddenly slack-jawed guards back into their city.

They were too saddle-sore to bike home, but they hadn't brought enough cash to flag down a wyrm, so they walked. The way to Lilac was the high street, along the north side of the river—which was not as wide as contemporary levels of usage would have preferred it, but it was fronted by more than the usual number of old structures from the season-city, shrines and longhouses and mausoleums, the odd slab table or gateway, the stairstep-sided auditorium that still saw use for plays and concerts, though they were obliged to work around the altar in the middle of the stage. It ended at the Grove of Colors.

"I'm glad you brought me here during the day," Thelendil said—the first words of substance they had exchanged since the Ranger had touched ground.

"It's a must-see," said Zaya. "Also the most direct way home. But you should see it."

The Grove was a massive stand of argan trees, each of which had leaves of a different color—though all were brightly saturated, almost blinding in their purity. There was no rhyme or reason to the dispersion of the colors as far as she knew. The vibrancy of the colors stood in strange but welcome contrast to the cool offered by the broad leaves. The grove was full of wanderers, Mrineen and

Ililuë and Kayalim and foreigners, resting in the shade or wandering from tree to tree or simply taking the road through the grove a little slower.

"I've seen these in the desert," said Thelendil. "Goats climb in them to eat the nuts. And they only come in green."

"My dads told me they were part of the land," said Zaya. "Like Candlegrass Stand or the Rosewing Fountain, some weird feature of the land here that you'd never see anywhere else. They're where the names of the precincts came from, but they're also why we dye our hair—to say we have as much of a right to be here as any Mrineen colonizer. The Grove of Colors is older than all of us." She laughed a little. "Then Taavi and Gilthiniel went to actual school and learned that the old nomads enchanted the trees. That was how they kept telling the story of the place they would come back to—the place with the colorful argan grove. By comparison to some of the man-made magic around here, it's simple. No one knows how Cold Point was created, or how Ashen Precinct keeps the Vores in, but they know how this one works. A lot of kids learn to cast it before university. The Grove's even been disenchanted by vandals a few times since the city was founded." Zaya sighed. "That made me start wondering other things. Like why straight Kayalim don't dye their hair. Of course, that question answered itself. Kaalo and Zinji weren't lying about why we do it. But it's not just Mrineen that we're talking to."

"Straight?"

"You know. Heterosexual."

Thelendil squinted at her.

"Boys who like girls and girls who like boys. Not, you know, any other arrangement of genders."

"Oh." Thelendil nodded. "You teach jungle savage new word! Jungle savage no thank you enough."

Zaya punched him in the shoulder. "You asked, jerk."

Thelendil looked up and around at the sun winking through the varicolored leaves. "It's not like we don't have words for those things. I just never really had to learn them in Mlin. It's a big deal for you?"

"It's why I don't know my grandparents, or my uncles and aunts. Ziyuki does, a little—she was old enough when Papa Zinji came out that she has some memories. I was a baby when it happened; I don't remember him passing as a woman at all. And I don't re-member them."

"Shame."

"Not really."

"I mean for them. I just feel for anyone who doesn't get to look at Zinji's hair, you know? You city folks can't do much, but you can get a really nice, even tone out of a hair dye."

"Papa Kaalo was amazing at that," said Zaya. "He taught all of us—Papa Zinji and Kiriki and me."

They left the Grove, continuing along the high street toward the edge of Heliotrope Precinct and then to Lilac. The sun seemed to hang a bit heavier in the sky; sweat misted Zaya's skin as they walked.

"You really believe that wyrm's going to get the stuff to Zinji?" Thelendil asked after a bit.

Zaya laughed. "You haven't done this long enough. Stick with it and you'll learn that animals are more reliable than people. Which is why it's so hard to get them to agree to things."

"How's that?"

"When you really mean the promises you make, you don't give your word lightly."

Thelendil breathed a deep sigh at that. "I guess not. What about the people piece of it? You think they're going to be reliable?"

"Sure. I'm not going to ask them to promise anything. I'm going to give them something, and tell them something. They'll know how it fits together."

CHAPTER 25

ARGENT PRECINCT. H*OME OF the only Argent Swordwing broodspire. Secondarily, home to the Reeve's Palace, the Courts of the Moon and Stars, and the estates of a few truly old and powerful houses: Tuatara, Taipan, Amphisbaena. I'm supposed to tell you how it's full of beautiful architecture, public art, and history; and it is, it's all true. But why is it in Argent Precinct and not elsewhere? Why should we be proud that our caretakers have cloaked their own place in memory and beauty, when they won't extend that care to the rest of Yemareir?*

(This is a lot to put on the reader before they're even through the letter A. —Ed.) (I trust my readership. —SA)

SEE ALSO: Government; Law Enforcement; Umber Precinct.

—From "A Visitor's Handbook for Yemareir," by Shenireen Agama

***

T*HERE WASN'T QUITE A* wall around the border of Umber Precinct, but there might as well have been: Watchful eyes hit you as soon as you even breathed in the direction of Wiremakers' Street, and if you crossed it, the broad-shouldered men and women who owned those eyes had no qualms about following you openly, waiting for you to make a false move. Zaya didn't cross yet, but she gave the border guards a cheerful smile and a wave, and leaned against a pine tree to wait.

It didn't take long for her companions to arrive: A Kayalim woman, with close-cropped hair and eyes aged early into haggardness in a face that could not yet be thirty; a boy, younger than Jaliki, only just growing out of baby-softness into the long, lean lines of childhood, holding his mother's hand with the only arm he had; and a hyena, six-legged and taller than the boy at the shoulder, its fur and mane streaked with iridescent blue and its mouth trailing wisps of dark blue vapor that hung in the air. Even the Umber border guards were unsettled by it. "Javashi," Zaya said. "It's been a minute."

"Hey, Zaya," Javashi said. "Shaavo, do you remember Shearwater-*cha*? Jaliki's mom?"

"Jaliki had the puppy," Shaavo said. He looked back at the hyena; the hyena gave Zaya an appraising look.

Zaya squatted down to get to Shaavo's eye level, pulling out the best smile she could manage with an eldritch monster in an increasingly implausible hyena suit breathing spooky vapors into her air. "I hate to say it, Shaavo-*jiji*, but it's a big dog now. Not as big as your guy here, but bigger than it was. But we're here to change that for you. Did your mother explain what we're doing today?"

Shaavo nodded. The hyena made a small chattering noise in the back of its throat.

"OK then," she said. "I have one little secret for you, though, something that can help if the needle hurts a little bit. You want to hear it?"

"Yeah."

"Keep your eye on the sky. If you do, you might be the first one to see something really cool."

"See what?"

Zaya shook her head, smiling. "I'm keeping it a surprise. But I promise it'll be worth it."

They left the shade of the pine and crossed Wiremakers' Street, and the granite-eyed border guards stared openly as they entered Umber Precinct. She could see Shaavo turn his head to look back. "Don't bother," Zaya said, touching his shoulder. "You're not going to see anything that's going to help you. They do this to everyone."

"Why?"

"Because they don't want us here."

"Why?"

"They don't want anyone here. They consider themselves a sovereign precinct. That means they think they're their own city and they can say who does and doesn't belong," she said, sensing him about to fill his lungs for the question. "Of course, if that were true, they could just kick us out instead of trying to scare us away." She knew it wasn't a good idea to raise her voice so they knew she knew they could hear, but she did it anyway. One of them trailed off to saunter along behind them. Javashi gave Zaya a look that was one hundred percent deserved.

The hyena ker looked back at the man following them and growled, too loud for Zaya's comfort. "It won't attack," she said to Javashi. "Right? I'm just realizing that I haven't spent much time with one of these that imitates a, uh, large predator."

"I've never seen it attack a stranger for no reason," said Javashi. "And I'll tell you, there are times when it would have been helpful. Large predator my ass, I don't see how you get to call yourself a predator when there's some cop getting in my face about a sack of dates some fruit stand fascist accused me of stealing when I wouldn't let him gouge me for them. I can't eat a sack of dates in five seconds! I'd be surrounded by pits. But this good-for-nothing just stares like it wishes it were a police dog. Go be a police dog, you bastard, leave my family alone." Javashi's face did with a laugh what Zaya's nose sometimes did with a sneeze that died halfway through. She stared far off for a moment. "I always think it'll help me feel better if I give it shit," she said. "It doesn't care, but at least I can be funny. But I can't be funny. How can anyone laugh at a joke about a thing that…" She squeezed Shaavo's hand. "That does what that thing does."

"I don't feel better either, but I don't let that stop me," Zaya said. "Sometimes you just have to do what's right, even if it doesn't do a damn bit of good."

"I guess," said Javashi. She thought for a moment, as if rolling the idea around her mouth to see how it tasted. "That doesn't make me feel any better."

"Sure doesn't," Zaya said.

They walked in tense silence, trailed by the Umber border guard, until they reached Loggerhead Square and the broodspire. The tattooist was easy enough to find; she'd already set up a table with her inks and needles, and sparked a small fire-charm as Zaya watched. There was a sign with her name on the table—"Terikko te-Vala: Charms and Sorceries for the Strengthening of the Body and the Clarification of the Mind." She was taller and broader than the man following them. Terikko glanced quickly at their approach, but her eye lingered on the ker. "You must be veraamaka navo. And spouse and son?"

"No," Javashi said the same time Zaya did, and Zaya let her speak. "I'm Javashi te-Zaako and this is my son, Shaavo. We know Zaya from a families' group for hunted kids."

Terikko fixed a gimlet eye on Shaavo. "That ker's dogging your heels, Shaavo te-Zaako. I'll be straight with you: You look smaller than you ought to be by an arm, give or take. That must have been a hell of a time for you, little son. Was it bad?"

Javashi's face grew dark, but she didn't speak. Shaavo nodded, bright-eyed.

"You're a strong one, to come out the other side of a thing like that. And with a straight back and a grin on your face, no less. Stronger than me, Shaavo te-Zaako. Don't think I can't tell what you're thinking behind that look." He was, in fact, looking at her with a polite but vast skepticism, as if she were a beloved great-aunt pitching him on a multilevel marketing endeavor. "You're thinking I'm buttering you up so you'll be brave for the needle. And I am, little son, I am. Because the needle won't help you if I draw the sigil wrong, and I'll draw the sigil wrong if you can't be still, and it takes a brave little son to be still when it hurts. But, Shaavo, here's my secret: I'm buttering you up, but what I'm telling you is still true. You survived an attack by an unkillable demon from Hell. More than one, by the looks of the thing. Compared to that, I couldn't hurt you with this little needle if I wanted to—and I don't; I'll be as gentle as I can. Do you think you can be still for that?"

Shaavo nodded again, his skepticism not gone but much receded. Terikko patted the cushioned chair beside her, and he looked up at Javashi. At her nod, he hopped in. The ker curled up at his feet, and Terikko put some needles into the fire. Shaavo looked up at the sky, but there was nothing there but clouds and a bird or two.

A few interested onlookers were pausing on their way through the square to see what was happening. Loggerhead Square was run down in a way that was both nobler and sadder than your average block in a poor precinct like Rust or Damask; the people were straighter-backed if shabbier-dressed, but the buildings were much worse, many missing walls and one or two slumped in on themselves in crumbled heaps. Zaya looked up at the sky again, but there was nothing there. Terikko lit another fire-charm, which she used to light a thick stick of incense that spat a bit before sending a thick plume of violet-blue smoke into the air. "Help our visibility," she said.

"You thought of everything," said Zaya. "You do this a lot?"

"Maybe in your precinct there are more fun things to do than watch an occult tattooist at work," said Terikko. "Welcome to Umber. You want to get started?"

Zaya looked at the crowd again. "Give it a minute."

"You've got their interest. That won't keep."

"It's a ten-minute job?" said Zaya.

"Less."

"Give it a minute."

"I'm just saying, that gentleman cleaning his ear out with that butcher knife isn't going to stand there forever." Zaya looked around and found him easily; the knife wasn't an actual butcher knife, but it was a single-edged dagger near the size of one, with thick saw-teeth at the base. "Man like that has places to be, wonders to gaze upon."

"I thought you said Umber Precinct was boring."

"Sure, but he's about to pull a really interesting-looking chunk of brain out through that ear."

Shaavo laughed; Terikko held her fist out, and he bumped it with his. He looked up at Javashi, grinning like Terikko had said he was when he hadn't been, and Zaya decided maybe she and Terikko should date.

Terikko picked up a pot of ink, then turned the underside of Jaliki's forearm up to look at the prior designs. The ker looked up at her, interested, maybe a bit tense. "Go back to sleep, you abscess," said Javashi. "I hope you choke on a million pounds of rotten fish guts. I hope your mother disowns you in a letter and your father rips the middles out of all your favorite books."

"You didn't pay for the special ink," said Terikko.

"How much for the special ink?" said Javashi.

"When I figure out the one that can make it choke on a million pounds of fish guts, I'll let you know."

"Ewwwww," said Shaavo.

"Veraamaka navo," said Terikko, "I know you've got some, like, effect you're trying to achieve here. But as a specialist in the area of tattooing children—which is not something a lot of people can say!—I want to point out that letting the subject get bored and squirmy isn't what we in the profession would call a recipe for success."

Shaavo looked up at the sky again. "All right," Zaya said, "I think you can start."

Javashi sucked a breath in through her teeth when the needle hit Shaavo's skin. He flinched and whispered, and Terikko put a hand on his back and whispered something in his ear, and he pressed his lips and eyes together and sat very straight and still. A few onlookers winced in sympathy, then pressed in for a closer look.

"Hey," Zaya said to the man who'd been cleaning his ear—he was big and potbellied, maybe twice Zaya's age with grey hair dyed lavender, and his knife was no longer in evidence. "You know this kid is hunted, right?"

"The six-legged hyena was kind of a clue." Still, he edged back a tick from Zaya. "I'm sorry, though, that's a bitch. You his mom?"

"Friend of. Now, Terikko over there—that tattoo she's giving him is to help him. It'll keep the ker away from him for a few weeks. Special magic ink, magic design. Watch."

As the tattoo's grid took shape, the ker scooted back from the chair, then stood up and backed away, head down, whimpering. The crowd made way for it.

"My mom died of that," said the man with the big knife. "Warthog ker."

"I'm so sorry," said Zaya.

"I was there when it killed her. It sprouted bat wings while I watched, and this like... ridge of spines on its back." He ran a hand over his upper spine to indicate. "I almost came for it, but I was too chickenshit."

"No," said Zaya. "You can't kill those things, but they can kill you." She held up her left forearm with the bite scar. "That's not my son, but my son's hunted as well. I got off easy. It wasn't much bigger than a puppy when it did this."

"So what's your angle?" he said, shifting his hips in a way that thrust the big knife on his belt right toward her. "Because what I see is a southerner coming into our town and showing off... for what? Help your friend's business? You know, I've seen one or two of you southerners going to visit Terikko, thinking no one here'll notice how nice you dress even when you're trying not to. Terikko, now, she's one of us, she spends what she earns in the neighborhood and we all eat off it. What I can't figure out is why someone like you would come to a town like this and do a whole stunt in front of everyone to tell them how rich you are."

Zaya nodded and tried not to swallow too audibly. "I'm not rich. I'm not poor, not the way some of you folks know what poor is, though I know it too because I've been it. I'm not rich. But you might have seen me on a wall somewhere."

He gave her an appraising eye, then laughed. "Veraamaka navo. All right, that's interesting. I still don't get it. Swinging your golden balls around might get you somewhere in Argent Precinct. Not here."

"I told you, I don't have golden balls. And what I do have, I'm giving to you."

"Pull the other one."

She *reached* up, and made contact, and the crowd parted, screaming, as Bandit's Breath landed, its blue and orange and magenta plumage fairly flaming before her eyes in the sun-soaked morning.

When the roil and din had subsided, Vanako stood on Bandit's wing joints and shouted, loud enough to echo off the ruin and rubble that bordered Loggerhead Square:

"Whoever wants their kid to be next for a tattoo, bring your ker and get in line! First ten served free, and keep order or the wyrm will do it for you!"

That got Loggerhead Square's attention. The crowd began to roil again; one parent worked their way to the front, dragging a fat, solemn eight-year-old behind them, trailed by a massive monitor lizard whose scales shone an iridescent blue. A mother towered over by a gangling teenager pushed through close behind, confusing Zaya with their lack of a ker until she saw the griffon vulture watching from an argan tree on the edge of the square.

The knife-man looked at the short queue forming. "Pretty good, veraamaka navo," he said. "What happens when the eleventh kid gets in line?"

"There's always an eleventh kid," said Zaya.

"And that's what everyone will do everything they can not to be." The knife came back out to clean a fingernail that didn't seem to need it. "So what's the plan? You'll just roast everyone with that Dawn of yours?"

"The Dawn will do what it has to. I didn't bring Javashi and Shaavo here to get eaten by Umber folks just because we reminded you to be mad at the world." A third group joined the queue: A father with a little child on his shoulders, still not through their baby fat, trailed by a dog not yet grown into its own feet. Before the first attack, Zaya found herself praying; before that precious skin ever felt the touch of teeth. "You're not wrong to ask, but you didn't let me finish. There's always an eleventh child, that's a fact."

"I never said it wasn't."

"Five minutes ago, there wasn't a Dawn Wyrm in Loggerhead Square. Also a fact."

The knife-man twirled his dagger between his fingers like a bored child might do with a pencil. "Well, all right."

"You don't have to believe me."

"Sure don't. But it's a thing to hear."

"What's your name?" Zaya asked.

"Chashu."

"That's not a name, that's lunch."

"So eat it."

Zaya chuckled. "All right, Chashu, a question for you from ver-aamaka navo."

"I'm honored?"

"How's your throwing arm?"

***

Zaya hadn't realized how rarely she saw Arhoon Pogona outside of Tjaliraan's or the 'stream until she saw him lying on the rim of the Pilgrim's Square fountain, trying to balance his dumb greatsword point-up on his chest. She, Vanako, and Jaliki were on the way to the fish market; the ker, debilitated from Jaliki's most recent treatment, trailed far enough behind them that she'd almost forgotten about it. As they watched, the greatsword pointed at the clouds for a full three seconds before wobbling and falling. Arhoon caught it neatly, not quite before the blade could dip into the fountain; he dried it on his shirt. Then he saw who he'd clearly been looking for. "*Veraamaka navo!*" he called out in the most atrocious Kayalim accent Zaya had ever heard. "A word?"

"Anything for a fan," Zaya said. "You maybe met Jaliki when he was a baby? The other one is Vanako, my co-pilot."

"Arhoon Pogona," said Arhoon Pogona. "Disgraced and sidelined scion of House Pogona, condemned to waltz around the city dropping swords into fountains and otherwise wallowing in self-parody. Sort of like a cross between your mother and her sister, if your mother were an amusing failure instead of a widely adored celebrity whose star is justly rising."

"Walk with us to the market?" said Zaya. "I'm enjoying the compliments, but not so much I want to miss the last sardines at Kaizeki's." Arhoon sheathed the sword in the baldric on his back with a smooth no-look motion that she had to admit, in the privacy of her mind, was pretty badass, and fell in with them.

"I see the unwanted guest is trailing rather far behind," he said, jerking his head back to indicate the ker. "I'm glad to see it. Far behind, I mean."

"We're very lucky."

"Sounds like there are some similarly, uh, afflicted individuals in Umber Precinct who think they should share the privilege. Who knows where they'd get that idea?"

"It's almost like they're mad that poor people are dying in agony when rich people can get treatment on the black market," said Vanako.

"Yes, when you put it that way the whole situation sounds very bad."

"How else would you put it?" Vanako asked

"Your mother clearly hasn't introduced you to enough individuals of my lofty social stature," said Arhoon. "When the air you breathe is thin enough, a lot of... novel ideas start sounding reasonable."

"When the air you breathe is thin enough, you get brain damage," said Vanako.

"What the young woman lacks in the finer elements of the social graces, she makes up in true facts about human neurology," said Arhoon. "And since the sardines at Kaizeki's aren't getting any younger, I should let her directness inspire me."

"Eughhhhhhh," said Vanako, but quietly.

Arhoon forged forward: "Not long ago, Zaya, you came to me asking for money to offset a debt to a questionable individual. You've now secured the resources not only to help your own child but to run a philanthropic program in Umber Precinct. I'm not well acquainted with what the bean counters would call your 'income streams,' but based on what I know and what your wondrous daughter has just articulated, I have to believe you've cracked the code for inexpensive yliaster."

Zaya gave Arhoon a cool stare that tried, as best it could, to say *I'm not talking about the frantic midnight jungle smash & grab in front of the seven-year-old.* "I know enough about how it's made to know that it could be cheaper than it is. So production or distribution is being throttled in some way. That's all I've got."

"Good." Arhoon was, in a way she'd never seen him, far away. He wasn't a person who spent much time in his head, at least not when he was around her; but that was where he was, staring at something in the middle distance only he could see. "You asked me for twelve slabs to save your life and I laughed you off. I said I couldn't do it, and I couldn't. But I didn't really ask what I could do. I didn't really think about it."

"You don't owe me anything. You've always helped us out. I've never been able to do anything for you like you've done for us."

Arhoon snorted. "Feeding you up on overpriced gin and snacks to sponge it up with."

"How you could have been a better human is between you and the Great Pogona or whatever dragon god you pray to. But you vouched for us with the Standards Board, and you stood with us in a way that made us legitimate in the eyes of the 'stream. And the snacks kept us from going hungry, some nights. So don't snort it off either, it meant something."

"That's kind, Zaya."

"You're being weird, Arhoon. I don't know how to talk to you this way, especially in front of my kids."

"I'm sorry."

"Do what you need to do," said Zaya. "You're not hurting me. I just want to be clear that you're being weird, because I don't know why and I don't like surprises."

They crossed the southern border of Lilac Precinct into Coral Precinct; painted friezes of reefs began appearing on the tops of buildings, as well as the odd sculpture of a coral in high relief. The briny smell of fish began to tint the air. "All right," Arhoon said. "Let's leave it at, I'm acting this way because I think I should have done more. For you and Kiriki then, for you and your family now. And I think I understand what I can do. I can put some money into yliaster production, I just need to know who to talk to. But, before I do that, I can make it cheaper."

Vanako chuckled. "Good luck with that. I know a guy and a mandrill who'll come to your house late at night if you do it."

"My house is a modest, dare I say cozy, corner of the House of Pogona, a lush estate in the heart of Argent Precinct. My family would surely breathe a sigh of relief if I died at the hand of a small-time drug pusher and his monkey in a sordid home invasion type scenario, but he'd still have to get past the snipers and four to six vengeful Mastiff Drakes bred for poor impulse control."

"Sure," said Vanako. "Don't let me talk you out of anything."

"How are you going to make it cheaper?" Zaya asked.

"My position in the peerage allows me to declaim on the floor of the House of the Moon," said Arhoon. "Those transcripts are made public to the city, and there are a few reporters there to cover the proceedings. I've done a little research. In five minutes, I can elucidate exactly what the supply chain looks like. And I can do it right before the *Gong* goes to print. Just in time to file."

"What," Zaya said, stopping in the street, "does the supply chain look like?"

"Like shady people handing dodgy brown paper sacks to each other while the stewards of the public trust look the other way. At some point it forks and about ten percent of the sacks go to people like your old chum Tjaroon Copperhead. Guess where the other ninety go?"

"I know where they go."

"I declaimed on the floor of the House of the Moon once," said Arhoon. "It was an erotic poem about the comptroller. My younger self would be gutted to learn his future self would burn even five of his precious minutes under the sun on laying out a pattern of *commerce*. However interdicted." He leaned his head back and drew a long breath through his nose, as though the air were some substance he anticipated getting wildly high on. "But fuck that guy. I've read his poem, and it wasn't even funny."

"There's a child in your company, Arhoon."

"I've heard worse stuff than that in the living room," said Jaliki.

"All the more reason to limit your exposure in the wild," Zaya said to Jaliki. "If you let stuff like that build up in your brain, you become boring and unfocused. Watch, this guy's about to say he's *not* boring."

"Actually," said Arhoon, "I've been thinking for years now that I owe the old comptroller an apology. That poem was harassment. I wasn't kidding when I said it wasn't funny."

His concern seemed genuine enough that Zaya allowed him a few seconds to rest with it. "Arhoon," she said, "I don't even know what to think. I mean, break the whole thing open, please. I'm all for speaking the truth and screwing over terrible people. Just keep my family out of it."

"Of course."

"Thank you."

They turned a corner. Down the road, the first colorful tents of the market appeared.

"What I'm trying to figure out," Zaya said, "is… why did you do this? And how?"

"*How* is a combination of consummately subtle interrogations in the most exclusive clubs of the Yemari peerage, and paying private investigators—"

"Private investigators are real?" said Jaliki. "I thought they were just in books."

"A lot of things are real for rich people that are fiction for the rest of us," said Zaya.

"Precisely," said Arhoon. "As to *why*…" His face clouded over. "I've said what I feel about what I owe you. Things I should have done."

"I'm not your charity case," said Zaya.

"Says the woman who pulls in orphans and strays to live in her literal house." He smoothed his hair back with a palm. "I'm not here to argue about what I should have done. It can't be changed. I just want to be a little better. It's weird to you because 'better' is weird for me. You'll get over it. Or I'll lapse back to form. I don't have any fish to buy."

It took Zaya a moment to understand where that had come from. They'd entered the Coral Precinct fish market; bream, pomfret, and conger stared at her from a charm-cooled icebox. "All right," she said. "We'll talk more about this later, yeah? Maybe after you get drummed out of House Pogona for, I don't know, conduct unbecoming?"

Arhoon chuckled. "If that were a thing, I'd have been thrown on the dole long ago. The night after I thrash you in the Shadowrun, all right? Tjaliraan's? Co-pilots are invited, but they can't drink gin until they've grown some body hair."

"You drink your gin," said Vanako, "I'll be sipping on a tall glass of victory."

Arhoon grinned at her. "I know. Take care."

And he slipped off down an alley between the stand selling fresh squid and the cart selling grilled squid and was gone.

"He's kind of cool," said Vanako. "You should invite him over."

"He's a peer of House Pogona, Vani, I don't think he'll want to eat at our place." As soon as she said it, she regretted putting it in Jaliki's ears—or her own, for that matter. "Strike that, fuck it. We'll have him over. But not after the race. I'm not turning down a free meal at Tjaliraan's."

"Completely."

Zaya could feel Jaliki practically vibrating with questions. "Hey," she said, putting a hand on his shoulders. "Go find where Kaizeki's is set up today. OK?" He bounced twice from his ankles, nodding, then took off, dodging among the fish-buyers like an eel through rocks. The ker bounded halfheartedly behind him, running for a few steps, then walking for a few. Zaya felt a small spur of sympathy nag at her heart for the thing. She let it linger, for once. It felt like, for once, she could afford it.

CHAPTER 26

DEFENSE. WHY ANY VISITOR not directly impacted by Yemari colonial rule should have any interest in this, I have no (Peep, O Reader, my intelligence! How dare you even consider learning about things that don't immediately interest me, your omniscient spirit guide, your veritable nanny of the mind! —Ed.) (You know what, I deserve this. —SA)

Yemareir has had a few good centuries of peace, if you don't count the colonial bullshit and, you know, day-to-day violence of a state engaged in the continuing extraction of resources from its people and surroundings. The last attempt at an invasion by sea was about 550 years ago, and it was a massacre. Because, naturally, dragons. The warships of Old Mlinivoun were floating pyres, loaded with enough napalm and naphtha to burn down all the shore precincts... if they'd ever gotten in range. The smell of cooked ships and sailors hung in the air for weeks, or so one hears.

And of course it's just as well that they never reached the shore; but there's an argument that we've been haunted by the ease of that defeat. That the Mrineen of Yemareir looked out on their glorious ancestors, burning on the bay in this attempt to take a thing they claimed as their own, and saw their future.

... so, hey, catch a show by the Yemareir Air Guard if you can! Barrel rolls, loop-de- (You can stop now. —Ed.) (Oh, thank AURYN. —SA)

SEE ALSO: Beaches; Law Enforcement; History, Military.

—From "A Visitor's Handbook for Yemareir," by Shenireen Agama

***

REAL ESTATE WAS CHEAP in Olive Precinct: The starting line was on the roof of a capacious old bathhouse, whose windows still leaked mineral-soaked steam even though it no longer saw paying clientele, the local Ililuë mélange (a unit smaller than an amalgam and much smaller than a conurbation) having decided that free access was conducive to the good health of the general public. Kirono circled Bandit, checking its feathers for spots where the wax was thin. Cerminir, a snoring Enwë swaddled to her chest, was feeding Bandit the last few gulps of kumis, which she'd decided on as a more salubrious alternative to Old Cheesefeet's cloudberry moonshine. Bandit didn't share this view, but it had learned not to turn its nose up at Cerminir when Enwë was sleeping. Cerminir could get loud when she got frustrated, and nothing hit the most sensitive frequencies of Bandit's audible range quite like the squalls of a baby who wanted to be asleep and wasn't. A trio of Ililuë entered the bathhouse, and the smell of steam washed over them. Vanako yawned. She'd been up late the night before, Zaya knew, talking with Tuuro te-Kaneva under a streetlamp outside the building. Zaya would have pulled her in earlier, but under the circumstances it didn't seem right.

"Just don't fall asleep when it gets dark," Zaya said. "That's when we're going to need you the most. Every spare scrap of sensation is gold when the lights go out."

"As if I could possibly," said Vanako. "My stomach's so knotted up, you'll be lucky if I don't puke all over Bandit."

I will do a barrel roll, said Bandit.

"You wouldn't dare," said Vanako. "I'm too cute to toss."

I clean those feathers with my tongue.

"You eat three-day-old fish."

I eat it with my mouth. I don't roll in it and then lick it off my feathers.

"Whatever. My stomach will do what it needs to to protect my body."

Unless it thinks your body can bounce off a twenty-foot fall to hard cobblestones without a problem, it'll keep your breakfast inside you.

"Unexpected level of passion about feather cleanliness," said Vanako. "I feel like we're bonding here."

"'Streamers!" announced a functionary of some sort. "May I have your attention please? The Standards Board has an adjustment of protocol to announce!"

Zaya drew a breath and held it, her ribs vibrating with the surging of her heart.

"Effective immediately, the Standards Board will no longer require a psionic damper as a condition of a valid placement in any race. Dampers will no longer be distributed by the Board. 'Streamers, to wyrmback for the Omari Shadowrun!"

Cerminir turned to Zaya and snapped her arms up in victory, jostling a sleepy grunt from Enwë. Kirono just caught her eye and smiled. Some kind of two-voiced yodel threaded its way up from the crowd around the bathhouse: Definitely Taavi and Gilthiniel. Vanako sighed as if she'd just been handed the world's worst long division problem. "Great," she said. "Watch all the eager beavers try to get in on our shit now."

"They haven't changed the entry fee," said Zaya.

"I bet that's next," said Vanako. "You and your friends on the Standards Board already have it in the bag. You love the idea of packing the stream with people who remind you of you."

Zaya looked over at her daughter, hoping to divine what the hell she was getting at with that, but Vanako had already snapped her goggles on. Zaya was starting to understand why Kiriki had never liked purple; it really did clash with the green of the lenses. "You just don't want to race against Tuuro," she said.

"Correction: Whenever Tuuro is in the mood for a face full of road dust and dragon farts, I will face him on the course of his choosing." Vanako snapped her jacket straight and looked at Zaya. "Wow, purple hair sure does look like shit through green goggles."

"At least we match," said Zaya. "Kiriki and I always matched. I think that's what I've been missing this whole time."

"Hair compatibility. Can't believe we didn't figure this out sooner." Vanako stepped over to Bandit's flank and made a stirrup out of her hands. "Time to kill it, veraamaka navo. You first."

***

"Wʏʀᴍs, ғɪɴᴅ ʏᴏᴜʀ ᴍᴀʀᴋs!" came the call, but one wyrm was looking for something else: Monsoon muscled past a Kayalim-piloted Dawn Wyrm to get next to Bandit at the starting line. Zaya stared ahead, trying not to look like she was ignoring Shanhoon.

"Shearwater!" he roared. "I know you know I'm here!"

She waved once without turning her head.

"Cheating wasn't good enough for you, was it?" he said. "You have to make sure everyone else can cheat too."

She turned to him then, a serene, close-lipped smile coming to her face as naturally as breath to her chest. "I suppose you'd know what that's like," she said, not quite too quietly to carry over the distance between the wyrms.

"It won't matter," he shouted. "Not in this race. Why you chose the Shadowrun to make your move, I'll never know. Melanic Shrikes have actual sonar, Shearwater. No matter what you and your big brain do to that washed-up Dawn, you're still working with the monkey eyes your mother cursed you with."

This time, she did leave the words just a hair too quiet, so he would have to beg her for them.

"Speak up!" he said. His face was red and twisted behind the shear-field protecting it. "Or are your lungs too weak from losing too many races in a row?"

Zaya shrugged and turned to face the starting line.

"Hey, Krait!" Vanako shouted from behind her. "You really can't guess what she said?"

"If anything she said or did made enough sense for me to guess it," said Shanhoon, "she'd be working for me instead of trying to beat me in a race where she is one thousand percent doomfucked."

"She said 'You'll know,'" Vanako shouted, and the announcer shouted "To the sky!"

***

In Olive Precinct they flew down tight byways and rounded sharp switchbacks, terrifying animals, delighting children, and widening the eyes of the languid lotus-eaters who'd come north to sample the botanically altered states of consciousness that were, by and large, their sole association with their Ililuë trip-sitters, who looked on the stinking polychrome tumult of the wyrms with serene smiles of appreciation. Zaya was content to trail the pack this far, stopping Vanako when she tried to seize an easy opportunity to overtake. There were two other Kayalim teams ahead of them, fluid flyers but still raw in technique. Zaya showed Vanako the inefficiencies in their wingbeats, the subtle tells of early fatigue that would worsen as the air began to thin. *Let them have this,* she thought; *let them taste how sweet it is take an early lead, and how bitter it is to lose it.* She wasn't sure whether she'd let the thought through to Vanako, but she felt a pulse of understanding.

The border of Jade Precinct came as the wyrms' northward path began to slope up, and Olive's close streets soon gave way to Jade's meandering suburbs, odd parks and patches of green merging into full yards, some behind walls. The roadways widened and the pack spread out, ranks shifting as the wyrms who'd worked so hard to hold their place in Olive began to lose the strength of their wings. Zaya could feel Vanako begin to appreciate the decision to wait: It was easier to use an advantage in endurance here, where there was room to overtake. One of the Kayalim teams was a crop-haired couple; the other was two men whose streaming hair matched the azure blue of their goggles and their Dawn's shoulder-feathers; one of them called "veraamaka navo!" as they passed.

There were no walls where Jade Precinct ended and the wild began, only a sparse line of guard towers end-capping the roads, and an abrupt dissolution of city into forest. The guards at the towers sent a few arrows in the general direction of the passing 'streamers—it was tradition—but they didn't really mean it.

The old mine road grew out of Jade Precinct like a cilium, unpaved and long untrod, but packed so hard by centuries of traffic that the wilderness was still at pains to reclaim it. The wyrms, of course, had no appreciation for the blessed flatness of the road, only hate for the branches that had greedily overgrown it. Soon the pack had condensed more tightly than it ever did in city limits, stringing along the mine road nearly single file. For all that, though, wyrms were flagging with the thinning air and the steady gain in altitude, which had only steepened as trees began shrinking and the slope began to change from foothills into mountainside proper, the road changing from packed dirt to hewn-out stone.

"Remember," said Zaya, "when you were soaked and smelling like a brewery last night because you'd spent half an hour you'll never get back trying to coax this dumb cargo parrot into drinking ten gallons of dark beer because Cerminir insisted?"

I vaguely recollect the incident of which you speak.

"Well, this is why we listen to Cerminir even when we hate to. Bandit, time to close your eyes."

Neither Bandit nor Vanako had liked this idea, but Zaya had insisted: They'd done it twice on the Mule, and whether or not it gave them an advantage, it made a much safer race to have one pair of eyes going in that was already dark-adapted. They'd practiced maneuvering with Bandit blindfolded and Zaya steering, and both wyrm and daughter had grudgingly admitted that it worked—but Bandit still closed its eyes reluctantly as Zaya took over the steering.

The elephant-eater Ranger fell back almost as Zaya spoke the words, huffing audibly and straining. Zaya showed Vanako an image of the course before them, a composite of her own view and Bandit's memory: There was Kshalain Honu on her Peregrine Gyrdrake, Yaulë on the massive Ranger Wyrm Carnaug, Lerikaan Boomslang on Time's Warped Arrow, and vying for the top spot, Arhoon Pogona on Ice and Shanhoon Krait on Monsoon. Arrow and Carnaug were visibly flagging, and there was still a good stretch of road before the mine mouth opened.

"This is why we didn't waste the energy on overtaking these kids in the street," said Zaya. "The Shadowrun is short, and a lot of it is tight, so 'streamers plan to get in front early, use the open areas to gain ground, and lean on the course to protect their lead. They don't get that it's an endurance game. You can use a tight course to keep your lead if you can react to someone coming up behind you, but that doesn't really work when you're too exhausted to maneuver. Which is why we can pass an elephant-eater Ranger on an overgrown wagon-trail without really working at it—because Bandit is running on a hundred cross-desert trips of fourteen-hour days carrying a load at high altitudes, and ten gallons of oatmeal stout."

Vanako had no real response to that, so Zaya just assumed she was appropriately impressed by her mother's cleverness and insight. Just to make sure, she pulled Bandit up to arc over Carnaug and Arrow, entering the mouth of the Omari silver mine just behind Kshalain Honu.

It didn't take long for the light from the mine-mouth to fade immediately to black. Zaya told Bandit to open its eyes.

"Shit," Vanako said in appreciation. It was as though the walls had begun to emit the faintest grey light—just enough to see a few contours and know where the walls were—the walls, and the other wyrms. The gyrdrake had slowed to a crawl; Monsoon was far ahead, cruising down the shaft as though it were lit with torches. "Why don't they just light a light? Why don't we?"

"There are things down here that learned a while ago that light means food," said Zaya.

"Things that can pull down a wyrm?"

Zaya let her silence answer for her.

They began to see faint blazes on the walls every few dozen feet—this shaft was a teal square, but they passed shafts with yellow diamonds, purple crescents, and similar designs. They didn't shed enough light to see by, but they did at least stay at a constant height above the ground. When they passed through a large junction whose cross-shaft was marked by three orange circles, Zaya pulled them around Honu's Gyrdrake, and they began gaining ground on Monsoon and Ice.

No new shaft sprang off the teal square shaft, but they began seeing another blaze mixed in: three red arrows, the first longer than the second, which was longer than the third. The arrow blaze grew bigger each time they saw it. Zaya could hear Vanako noticing the change in the air: It was less stale, less still, the sounds of the wyrms' wings shunting off somewhere rather than reflecting back on them over and over from the shaft walls. Vanako's curiosity spoke for itself; she didn't need to voice it. "Here it comes," Zaya said in response, as the floor and walls dropped away and a soft blue light sprang from below.

Vanako gasped. Zaya grinned. Together, they banked Monsoon through a vast spherical cavern as smooth-sided as a soap bubble and as vast as the Emerald Dunes, over a glass-still sea surrounding a city.

It was not as big as Yemareir, but some of the buildings were as tall as Yemareir's. They were not the architecture of the season-city that was the bones of Yemareir, nor the Mlin structures of the early colonies or the hybrid designs enabled by Kayalim use of elephants and apes in construction; some of the designs were organic-looking, some simply nonorthogonal, leaning heavily on obtuse angles. The doors were not tall enough for humans.

Is this where the things that think of lights as dinner bells come from? Vanako wondered.

"Some of them live there," said Zaya. "But they're all wrong for the sizes of the buildings. They're latecomers, like us. Look, though."

She pointed with her mind, focusing Vanako's attention on a scrap of her visual field where there was an obelisk—full, on a second look, of portals, which could be seen by the brighter yellow light that came from within, gesturing at winding passages. It did not look anything like anything Vanako had ever seen, but its purpose was clear.

A broodspire.

"Can you believe it?"

What even broods there? Breeds? What wyrms even f—

"Maybe someone knows," said Zaya. "Not me. And not our ill-tempered lad's Melanic Shrike, that's for sure, although he'd probably tell you it was."

They were most of the way across the cavern now. Something tickled Vanako's periphery. *Mom,* she said, *there's something in the broodspire.*

"I suppose there is."

Did you ever see something in the broodspire?

"As far as I know, no one ever has."

What is it?

"Nothing my life is going to get any happier or longer wondering about."

They pulled past Arhoon Pogona, wasting the energy to arc out of Ice's range even though Zaya knew he wouldn't use the Swordwing's tail or talons against them. Arhoon called out a good-natured "Fuck youuuuuuuu!" that echoed faintly from the cavern's spherical walls. They were gaining on Monsoon; their high flight in a wide sky had activated some memory of long travels and strong wingbeats, and it seemed that Bandit was trying to compress an afternoon's travel into a few minutes. The vanishingly faint glow of a new main shaft, blazed with four diagonal white lines, caught Zaya's eye.

I think it might be climbing out *of the broodspire.*

"All the more reason to focus on getting out of this cave."

There are 'streamers just coming into the cave.

Any number of thoughts crossed Zaya's mind: *We can't help them,* and *it's probably nothing,* and *we have a race to win,* and *we knew what we were getting into when we signed up for this,* and they definitely weren't all true because they definitely couldn't all be true, but they somehow added up to true, or at least what sums she could do on the back of a feathered lizard in a sphere of vast, dark air under a mountain said they did. She couldn't untangle the ideas now, so she just let them splash over Vanako's mind, and maybe that was a better, swifter message than a string of words anyway.

They were nearly breathing down Monsoon's neck now—close enough that they could see Shanhoon's face, lit up by the sudden, piercing yellow light of a ball he held in one gloved hand. There was no manic glee on it, no triumph, just the surly scowl of business he'd rather not be doing. He threw the light and it flew farther and faster than it should have, landing at the base of Bandit's right wing—where it stuck like a wad of snot, flattened and webbed out, quivering.

"Cheater!" Zaya's voice barked out, and the cavern threw it back.

"Die mad about it," Shanhoon said, barely loud enough for them to hear. "Really."

Zaya urged Bandit forward, bringing the glow close enough to gleam from Monsoon's glossy black feathers. She'd given up on maneuvers; she wanted to plow past or maybe through the black wyrm, to beat it to the new shaft on sheer force of rage. Shanhoon was too good a flyer to allow it—but only barely, and the Bandit and Monsoon spat and raked, picking feathers off each other's wings.

From the city, something howled, and harsh wings rasped against the air.

Mom, Vanako said. *What is that.*

Whatever it was, it was a swift flyer and a huge one; Zaya could feel it filling the air behind them, its pursuit creating a front of stale, stinking air that served, almost, as a tailwind. Bandit lunged ahead to try to overtake Monsoon and took a stinking scratch on the wing from the black wyrm's tail-spikes for its trouble.

"It's the thing that's going to pick its teeth with the bones of Shanhoon Krait!" cried Zaya, and the two wyrms sped, one after the other, into the tunnel with the white-line blaze.

The tunnel shook with the impact of something huge crashing into the cave wall. Zaya didn't have time to draw breath for a sigh of relief before something filled the shaft—some uncountable number of whips or tentacles or pseudopods, blacker than Monsoon's scales, shot through with filaments in all colors like some strange, elaborate blown glass. Monsoon screamed, and so did Vanako, and Zaya's heart froze as she felt the ribbon of burning pain slash across her daughter's flank—and then her mind filled with the crackle of electricity at the counterstrike, faster than she could have imagined possible, mind and hand moving snake-quick as Vanako lashed out with her saddle-knife and the full, fierce power of her psionics.

Monsoon was limping forward, yipping and snarling with pain, its legs and wings covered with black and rainbow filaments—but they were stretching, thinning, snapping as the wyrm's wings hauled it forward. She could feel the pressure of the same tentacles around Bandit's hindquarters, but the needling pain in Vanako's side wasn't mirrored in the wyrm's mind. Zaya whispered silent thanks to Kirono for whatever he'd put in today's feather-wax.

Bandit surged forward, snapping the last of the pseudopods, and swooped around Monsoon. Vanako's mind yearned immediately backward.

"Monsoon's getting away," Zaya said. "Those tentacles aren't holding it. They don't need us."

What if they did?

Zaya did not speak back, and what she did not say said everything. A star of searing light winked ahead of them.

Mom?

What followed would have been a question, had they been speaking, but mind to mind it was an image: The wyrms behind them, behind Monsoon, flowing into the spherical cavern like a school of fish, unaware of the harsh-winged behemoth and its light-seeking and its stinging tentacles and its hunger for... whatever it hungered for, that it thought it might find in the blood of wyrms or humans.

Mom, they don't even know.

"It's not our fault."

Vanako didn't reply. She didn't have to.

Whispering every oath in every language she knew, Zaya landed Bandit in the tunnel. With the hideous, slow, awkward scrabbling of claws on stone, she turned it around.

***

BY THE TIME BANDIT was airborne again, a faint disk of blue light was opening up on at the end of the shaft, like the sun after an eclipse; the dark thing from the cave-city had begun to peel itself off away from the cavern wall. It had discovered the other wyrms in the 'stream.

They sped past Shanhoon, who shouted some question they could not hear. "What did you do?" Zaya asked Vanako as Bandit gained speed.

You're gonna have to be more specific.

"To the thing. When it tried to hurt you. You hit it back."

It didn't try to hurt me.

"Shit." Zaya had actually forgotten.

Don't worry about it. I just did the obvious thing. Hurt it a little, pair it with a spike of empathy to make it feel worse than it is. Haven't you ever done that?

"My dads were junkies, not dealers. If there was something dangerous and we couldn't put a dragon between us and it, we ran like hell."

Just amp up the pain factor. The thing clearly has zero distress tolerance, I could barely even get a hold on its mind and it still flinched. If you could call it a mind. I don't know if the knife even penetrated.

"Are you going to be OK? How bad are you hurt?" The pain was too strange, too foreign; Zaya couldn't tell how Vanako was holding up.

If you don't beat that thing back into whatever hole it lives in, a lot of 'streamers and dragons are going to die.

"If you fall out of the saddle, Minshoon is going to make me wish I was dead."

I'll be fine. Iron grip back here.

The blue disk flickered with yellow, once, then again—some dragon, using its breath weapon. They flew into the blue, from tight shaft into yawning space, and descended on the dark with mind and fire burning like a solar flare before them.

***

THE DOGFIGHT UNDER THE Mountain: A moil of blurry confusion in the blue half-light, seared at intervals into scythe-sharp images by wyrm-flame.

Lerikaan Boomslang and her Moonturn Moultwyrm, full summer green on its plumage at last, descending on the great black hulk in a fire-swathed stoop. Ajiroon Ora and Kshalain Honu on their Peregrine Gyrdrakes, darting between tentacles in a vain search for a vulnerable spot to burn; Yaulë on Carnaug the elephant-eater, wrapped in black tentacles on one doomed approach to what appeared, as best anyone could then deduce or later recollect, to be the cave-demon's head...

... until Arhoon Pogona cut him free, searing the black beast in slashing passes joined by punishing turns. His stupid giant sword flashed blue and yellow in tandem with the Swordwing's silver feathers whenever a wyrm's fire breath leapt forth. Since he was never much more than a wing's breadth away from the thing that every other wyrm in the cave was trying frantically to kill, that was basically always.

Zaya and Vanako and Bandit traded flanks with Arhoon and Ice, bathing it in fire and slashing it with talons, weaving in and out of the dark rainbow-threaded lashes that seemed to arise at will from any point on the creature's surface. Again and again those lashes hit Bandit, plucked at it, fell away. More than once, Zaya braced to slash a pseudopod flashing black in the corner of her eye, only to watch it turn away and strike Bandit's flank or wing. The cave-demon had learned too much from Vanako's counterstrike; it was afraid to touch humans. It didn't realize how unlikely that counterstrike had been, how vulnerable the wyrms' riders really were.

But the wyrms moved so fast, and the air around the demon was so thick with tentacles, it could only be a matter of time before it learned.

Zaya never saw it coming; she only felt the impact of an arm-thick whip in the small of her back, knocking her forward so her face landed in the feathers of Bandit's shoulders. The pain didn't hit for a moment, but when she tried to brace her arms to push her back up, they ignored her—and then the spasms hit, mercifully clenching her arms and legs around Bandit's ribs. She heard Vanako scream and felt her limbs move again, but now with an intention that wasn't Zaya's own. Vanako was using her own mind to make Zaya's body hold on. She tried to communicate with her daughter: *You can't pilot me and Bandit at the same time. You'll lose your own body.*

I'm not piloting Bandit. It knows what to do. I'm just keeping you hanging on.

There was a shrillness in those words, a tremor. *What's going on?* Zaya asked.

Mom, it's got Bandit. I don't know how much longer we can stay in the air.

Have Bandit burn with all it's got.

It did. Zaya realized she had felt that expansion and compression of the wyrm's lungs, felt that heat—but dimly, as though from across a cold, empty room. The demon's tentacle was still on her back, she realized, still doing whatever it did to make her feel this way. It was short-lived in small doses, at least—Vanako still had a stinging rash, but otherwise seemed recovered—but she could feel the electric cold starting to creep into Bandit, as smaller cilia burrowed under feathers to find skin.

It's OK, Vani, Zaya said. *Here's what we're going to do.*

She never knew what she was going to say after that. Thinking back on it later, she felt she must have had some idea, something more than merely a faith in herself or something higher that if she just said she had a plan, then one would come. But if she had, the mingled scream from Ice and Arhoon shivered it apart like a sand castle in a hurricane.

Zaya felt heat, again, and the tentacle on her back slid off like an eel, and Bandit dropped like a stone. She felt herself and Vanako reach for its wings at the same time. They divided the work among themselves instantly, effortlessly; they unpicked the confusion that the demon poison had threaded into Bandit's muscle fibers and made its wings move in spite of it. The uncontrolled fall turned into a glide, and then Bandit put somee of its own effort into pumping its wings and they began to gain altitude again.

Oh, shit, Vani said. *Oh no.*

Zaya pushed herself up in time to see the demon, strange black flesh now spotted with milky clouds where wyrm-flame had hit it, dip nose-down and begin to plummet to the dark water. It had wrapped Arhoon and Ice in black tentacles like a sundew.

Arhoon's sword fell from nerveless fingers. Zaya watched it fall; it sliced into the black water point-first, with barely a splash.

Lerikaan Boomslang and Time's Warped Arrow chased the demon down to the water, bathing it in flame. It didn't seem to matter. Its tentacles remained wrapped; Ice's wings fluttered like flags, moved only by the passing air. Lerikaan screamed when she pulled Arrow out of the dive, and the water swallowed demon, wyrm, and rider with the same calm as it had Arhoon's sword, the water almost stepping aside to admit them.

CHAPTER 27

DRAGONS, RARE. TOO MANY to mention, much less describe. Quantitatively inclined readers may notice, at some point, that the common dragons have maybe four or five broodspires each, which raises the question of why they're so much more common than the rare wyrms, which have at least one each. The answer is many-angled, but a few big factors are:

1. Clutch size and breeding frequency. Common wyrms have a short breeding cycle and lay lots of eggs. Argent Swordwings, for example, have a thirty-seven-year breeding cycle and lay small clutches of which, often, only one or none will hatch.

2. Affinity for people. Irascible Craw Wyrms seem rarer than they are because they generally fly off to the jungle as fast as their stubby wings can carry them.

3. Cussedness. The legendary Cinereal Vore Wyrms of Ashen Precinct have a short breeding cycle, but most of the hatchlings eat each other within a few months. If you don't get along with other dragons, that tends to shorten your lifespan when you live in a city full of dragons. A lesson for humans!

SEE ALSO: Dragon; Dragons, Common.

—From "A Visitor's Handbook for Yemareir," by Shenireen Agama

***

THERE COULDN'T HAVE BEEN silence in the spherical cave, but there might as well have been. The cavern's walls echoed, but the sheer vastness of the dark air seemed to swallow noise. Wyrms circled as if on thermals, although of course there were none. What else was there to do?

The wound from the tentacle itched and crackled and froze on Zaya's back; every muscle in her body ached from the spasms, and from what Vanako had done to fight them. She wanted nothing more than to land Bandit on the shores of that night-city and close her eyes, curled up in the crook of its flank as she had when she was sleeping in the stables. Her mind had not grasped the fact of Arhoon's goneness; every time a wyrm circling the chamber caught the corner of her eye, she looked for him.

Soon, someone would peel off to limp back to the finish line, and the race for second place would begin. By now, Shanhoon Krait had claimed first. If it was her, if she streaked for the exit now, no one could beat her. It's what Arhoon would want: For her not to be broke, at least, for this maybe not to be the last race. As it was, without a victory, Taavi and Gilthiniel would have to delay university for a year or more. Without the second-prize money, who knew how much longer that could go?

But her friend was here, dead in the dark water.

She filled her lungs, and imagined filling the chamber with her voice. *Help me, Vani,* she said, and trusted that her daughter would know what she meant.

"*Whose life has gone to the storm-boiled seas?*" she screamed into the silence, and felt pain like a punch to the chest as Vanako helped her push the words out as loud as her body could make them.

The words of the funeral haka hung in the chamber. *Are there even any fucking Kayalim in here?* Zaya thought. *Is nobody going to pick it up?*

But when Vanako called "*Arhoon Pogona!*" there was another voice that chimed in, not quite late enough to be an echo.

"*Whose flesh feeds the spirits that glint in the water? Whose bones go to decorate the coral?*" she cried.

This time the answer came from all around.

Kaalo and Zinji had known the battlefield haka, shortened from the full funeral version for when time pressed. They had not taught it to Zaya; but not many of these poor 'streamers circling in the dark could know the difference between the real battlefield haka and her truncation, where she just dropped most of the lines where the response was anything other than Arhoon's name, and saved one line for last.

In the full version, "*Let us show these streets the shape of our love for the storm-lost!*" appears about a quarter of the way through; the shape their love takes is the haka itself. But that wasn't what Zaya needed from the 'streamers of the Shadowrun, not today. Today, she saved the line for last, and instead of waiting for the response—"*We will shatter the air and shake the streets to show it!*"—Zaya turned Bandit to fly through the tunnel with the white-line blaze, out into the light.

She did not take them over Umber Precinct, whose people would spare Bandit but, no doubt, pelt the rest. Instead, she hooked west to glide over the bay.

***

THE FIGHT HAD TAKEN minutes, not hours. Sunset was in the future, but not far. Shanhoon would have been at the finish line, now, long enough to wonder what might have happened. He would have his ground crew, his entourage, the crowd, but without the furor and bustle and sulphur stench of the also-rans, the atmosphere would be more funereal than festive.

Well, that was right. She took them down the coast, then back up, giving the sun time to crouch below the waves. She let Bandit loose a mourning scream, and the rest of the line did the same. Through Vanako's eyes she saw the occasional flare of flame go up in memory of Arhoon. Wild Dawns on the hunt flew alongside the procession, sizing them up, then peeled away.

It wasn't long before a new set of wyrms came, with riders, from the heart of the city.

When they couldn't get Swordwings, the police preferred Rangers:, less nimble than some of the common wyrms, but with the instincts and endurance to take a chase through to the end. There were more of them than there were 'streamers. They formed a line parallel to the 'streamers' procession, placing themselves between it and the city. Their white uniforms gleamed pink and orange in the dusk. One of them yelled something, but it was drowned out by the waves. Zaya ignored them; the 'streamers did the same. Whoever it was who'd yelled, yelled something else. The police Rangers swelled their gut-sacs, preparing for a burn.

Zaya *reached* out for the mind of the leader's wyrm. The distance was well beyond her usual range; but with Vanako's mind amplifying her own, it was easy.

???

You know some of you'll die if you attack us, Zaya said. *We don't want to hurt you. It's not worth it.*

My rider said ready to burn. The symbol for "rider" in the wyrm's mind was some combination of master, mother, friend, and feared punisher.

What can he do?

He can do the pain-slap on my back. It was a quick double tap on the shoulder; when the wyrm had been small, it had meant pain was coming. The association was trained so deeply, it was almost as painful as the real thing.

The pain-slap can't hurt you. Gently, carefully, she explained. *Just go. Your kind are on the veldt. They'll take you in.*

Silently, the Ranger turned. The leader shouted in ugly surprise; the other wyrms and riders turned to watch as he dwindled in their sight, headed east for the veldt. One Ranger turned to follow him. Soon the rest were gone.

***

*M*om, V*anako said.*

Her mind's awe-touched voice should have lifted Zaya's heart; but something about it brought the weight of Arhoon's death down on her, as though she'd been buried in cold sand. The pain where she'd been lashed by the demon came burning back, and the soreness of her chest was like a band around her lungs. "We should go," Zaya said, and made ready to turn Bandit southeast, toward Rust Precinct and the stables.

Not yet, Vanako said, and an image of the finish line resolved in Zaya's mind.

"What's the point? Shanhoon's already won."

Kemreen and the house are there. And the 'stream needs to know. You can't just let him have his victory party without telling them what it cost. If you do it tomorrow, it won't be the same.

"You want me to talk to Jenirain Gila in this condition?"

I'll talk to her if you want.

Zaya would have argued more, but there was no point. Vanako was right. She tried to summon up the energy to shout "Let's go home," but the open sky and the muttering of the waves would swallow it. So she hooked Bandit around to shore without a word. Vanako's mind's eye threw another image into hers: A line of wyrms, peeling off the shoreline one by one, to follow.

***

THE 'STREAMERS OF THE Omari Shadowrun entered the streets of the city to the applause of the residents of Cobalt Precinct, who had no idea what was going on except that they'd been treated to a performance. They took Scrimshander's Way to Eggshell Precinct, where police barked at them and a few citizens threw rocks and bottles, and turned north into Jade Precinct and then to Olive, where the finish line stood.

Shanhoon and Monsoon had long made themselves scarce, but a crowd was still there. That seemed odd—maybe it was people like Minshoon, worried about the fates of the 'streamers? Zaya drew another mourning scream from Bandit; Vanako's eyes showed Zaya the gap in the line behind them, made by Lerikaan Boomslang hanging back to make space for the wyrm that was not there.

It was not until Zaya glided to the finish and the crowd erupted into confused but enthusiastic applause that she realized what had happened.

"Did you know?" said Zaya to Vanako.

Lucky guess.

A sylphlike Mrineen woman came with the winner's laurels in her hands and a satchel of cash looped over one shoulder. A crowd, mostly of bright-haired Kayalim, broke the flimsy fence around the finish line and began to flood toward Bandit. "Zayaaaaaaa!" cried Minshoon, his face ecstatic.

Really, Vanako said. *I don't know much about Umber Precinct, but those are the kind of people who come through. At least when it comes to violence. And they only had one target. Are you really surprised that they brought him down?*

"Think he's alive?" said Zaya, swinging a leg over Bandit's back to dismount.

We're lucky, but not that lucky.

She saw Cerminir with Enwë on her shoulders, Kirono with Eäril on his; Kemreen, Thelendil, Taavi, Gilthiniel, Jaliki. They hadn't known Arhoon. They'd remember him as an occasional benefactor, an occasional friend of hers and Kiriki's. Jaliki would remember him as the strange man with the sword by the fountain.

Was that actually all he'd been? If Kiriki were here, she'd know. Kiriki could share memories of him that Zaya had forgotten, list things they'd never do with him again. Kiriki could help her build the monument to him in her mind. What dinky, rickety tribute could Zaya make on her own?

No, said Vanako. *Nothing you build is ever fragile, and nothing you build is ever small.*

Zaya let the air pour into her lungs, wrapped her goggles around her wrist, and slid down Bandit's flank to greet the crowd.

CHAPTER 28

GOVERNMENT. *THIS IS COMPLICATED but not difficult. Each person lives in a precinct. If they own property in that precinct, they can vote. Their vote elects an alderwight, who votes on citywide matters in the House of the Stars. The House of the Stars is coequal with an unelected body, the House of the Moon, in which every peer of every noble House of Yemareir above the rank of grandee can vote.*

The House of the Stars appoints a Reeve, and the House of the Moon appoints a Vizier. The Reeve and the Vizier run the city administration and oversee the precinct administrations out of Argent Precinct. The Reeve is supposed to be more powerful, but since the Vizier represents the interests of the noble Houses, this is only sometimes true in practice.

The House of the Sun is theoretically where the gods live. It is occasionally also a governmental body represented by the Church of the Wyrm Immanent, but it gets decommissioned by the other Houses every so often until the people ask for it back.

Thankfully, the people seem to have lost interest. Unfortunately, until those of us who aren't owners get the vote, the whole thing remains complete bullshit.

(NB: The opinions of Dr. Agama do not represent those of Treadsong Books, Ltd. —Ed.) (I think you've made that super clear by now. —SA)

SEE ALSO: Argent Precinct; Law Enforcement; Peerage.

—From "A Visitor's Handbook for Yemareir," by Shenireen Agama

***

THE NEW MURAL WENT up outside House Shearwater the day after the race.

Two days after, Arhoon Pogona's funeral was held in Argent Precinct. Shanhoon Krait sent a letter lamenting how sorely missed she'd been. There had been, of course, no invitation.

In three days, House Shearwater woke up to a pair of massive spits being set up over piles of wood blocking Laurel Street, a freshly killed young rhino still leaking blood into the street by each. The carcasses were up and roasting before midmorning. When she tried to pay the men roasting them, they shook their heads. "We got them for free," they said.

"Rhinos are dangerous game," she said. "You could have sold them for a lot in the market."

"Don't try to change our minds, veraamaka navo."

"I'm not," she said. "I'm just telling you I know what this gift is worth."

***

MORE MATERIAL CAME IN throughout the day: A few aluminum tubs of bay oysters enspelled with cold charms, vats of beer and arrack and grape wine, torches, a juke band and a huapango band, a troupe of fire-jugglers, a trickling-in of Ililuë who wandered the street with no particular purpose other than offering botanicals to the food and entertainment crews.

Zaya didn't leave the house. She couldn't remember the last time she'd stayed in. She rocked and fed Enwë, kept Jaliki and Eäril from killing each other in a dispute over the newest Wing Windtwister book, crushed Taavi at hearts and lost badly to Gilthiniel, criticized Minshoon's cooking (matoke with some kind of vegetable he'd boiled into pulp) and then went back for seconds, listened to Kirono lecture about some topic in the physics of materials that he thought, incorrectly, he had simplified to the level of someone who hadn't spent her entire life studying the subject. She didn't kick the ker, but only because she'd have had to go out of her way to do it.

She took *two* naps, one on the couch.

When she woke up, Jaliki had wormed his way into the crook of her arm and fallen asleep with his head on her shoulder. By the time she woke up, her shoulder joint was screamingly sore, but somehow the smell of his cropped hair smelled her so much of his long-fled baby smell that she could not bear to wake him.

Thelendil found her like that, awake and visibly in pain, writhing under Jaliki's skull in very gradual, tiny motions. "I keep being surprised that you two look nothing alike," he said quietly.

"I didn't bear him."

"That's why I'm surprised that I'm surprised."

"He's got Kiriki's face."

"He does."

There was a catch in his voice when he said it. Zaya looked at him for a long time. "You want to talk about it?"

"I don't know."

"Did you and Jaliki talk about it?"

"No. It didn't feel right, not without talking to you first."

"You can say anything true to my son. Any of my children. We don't punish truth in this house." She looked for a long time at his unhappy face. "You don't want to say it. You want me to say it."

Thelendil's face darkened; he turned away.

"What?"

"When you say it like that, it sounds craven."

"It's not craven to be scared to talk about this with a child."

"You're taking it well."

"I'm stuck here. I don't have a choice."

He shot an exasperated jet of air through his nose, like an annoyed wyrm, and looked away.

"All right," said Zaya. "Here's why I'm 'taking it well,' and why I'm leaving it to you to say to him. I don't care." She gave Thelendil a beat to respond; he didn't take it. "I don't need him to know who sired him. I don't need him to not know. It's nothing to do with me. If I tell him for you, what does that teach him? That I care about what body he came from? I don't. That I should speak for a grown man who can speak for himself? Not doing it, don't feel bad about it."

"If you don't care who made him," Thelendil said, "maybe you care how it happened."

Something cold and electric ran from her tailbone up her spine to the base of her neck and lodged there, vibrating.

Cerminir had taken them to Cildinior Amalgam for what she called "a proper wedding." Kaalo and Zinji hadn't had the money, and their families had shunned the relationship in any case; but the Ililuë of Cildinior Amalgam were perfectly willing to throw a party for their long-lost daughter's newfound sisters. Thelendil was one of a small cohort around their age, and they had hit it off immediately. She and Kiriki had spent ample time with him, together and alone—as they had with Cerminir, as they had with any number of others. Of course it could have happened.

And Kiriki had been in a rush to conceive after the wedding.

But she'd been in a rush before as well. It had taken Zaya so long to earn Kiriki's trust, after the beach, where she'd met her and almost lost her in the same space of seconds; but, once earned, that trust had been complete, and Kiriki had lost no time in making plans to build on it. And the way she'd talked about the baby—after the wedding as well as before—there'd been nothing furtive in it, nothing worried.

Had there?

Zaya looked at Thelendil's face again. It was bearded, lined, and scarred in ways it had not been when they met; but the hurt in those bright eyes, the trembling of his jaw, they were a boy's. The counting of days, the weighing of memories, seemed suddenly like pointless chores. Her dead wife had slept with him, or she hadn't slept with him. She would never do anything else wrong or make anything else right, and this man she might have slept with was here, too late, wanting to be what no one had ever asked him to be, and Zaya wasn't sure if this bone-deep knowledge that she couldn't teach him to do it came because she didn't know how, or because life was just too fucking short.

"If you want to talk about this any more," she said, with a gentleness that amazed her, "you're going to have to learn to say things for yourself, because I'm not going to say them for you."

Thelendil left without a word.

Jaliki's breath had grown faster, shallower. He waited a minute before opening his eyes to admit he was awake.

*****

Vanako went down to Laurel Street while the sun was beginning to think about setting and the huapango band was still tuning their violins. She'd caught sight of Tuuro striking a conversation with Zayeni, and that could not be allowed to continue. Taavi and Gilthiniel followed soon after, unable to stomach the thought that Vanako and Zayeni might create drama and they might miss it. Violin and guitar sang out, a man's voice cut the evening air with the ringing high note that began "Kuuro," and Zaya slipped out quietly, alone.

Eyes were on the door to House Shearwater, and she was swiftly buttonholed by Elekko and Zaava, a couple who both worked in Eggshell Precinct in city administration. That conversation ran to kids and schools, as it always did—they had children close in age to Jaliki and Eäril—but then they were joined by Zishi, an aging bachelor who made a point of patronizing all the traditional Kay-alim music and drama that he could, and of distributing drinks and smokes to anyone who partook. From there, the neighbors and the conversations began to run together: Congratulations on her victory, the first won by a Kayalim team since Kiriki died; and unfocused inquiries into the dogfight with the black hulk in the Omari Shadowrun, a topic no one could stand to skip and everyone seemed pleased to drop; and inquiries about Zaya's own plans, now that immediate financial peril was behind her. Each such question seemed to carry the hope that she would remain in the 'stream or the hope that she would quit, and when the question came up it was time to deflect it with something noncommittal and move on to the next neighbor, or stranger, or the next song that would not not be danced to.

Then the juke band cut into the middle of one of the huapango band's songs with an ululating shout of "*Eka vakē!*" Zaya shouted "*Iriara takena!*" just like everybody else, then faced the band and with a stomp on the ground and a slap on the tops of her thighs. The instruments trailed off as the call-and-response began:

***

WHO RETURNS TO US from the storm-boiled seas?
    Veraamaka navo!
    Who rises unscratched from shattered spars and shredded sails?
    Veraamaka navo!
    A woman of ours has crafted distinction for herself!
    A woman of ours has shown us one of the million roads to golden deeds!
    Gold is in the reach of the least of us!
    Behind everything some further thing is found—the wind behind the wave, the sinew behind the spear!
    Behind our efforts, what shall be found?
    Our efforts!
    Behind our efforts, what shall be found?
    Our efforts!
    This we write in the wind!
    In the wind, we write it!

***

IT WAS NOT UNTIL the haka's last syllables rang through the streets that she heard the echo of a familiar voice—as though she had purposely shouted it a shred of a second late, to catch Zaya's ear. Zaya turned to her left and there she was: Taller and slimmer than Zaya, with the eyes like cups of chocolate and the jawline that could cut rubies, the only woman who'd ever worn the cropped Kayalim hairstyle well. The only Kayalim Grandee of House Amphisbaena—or, no, Arhoon had corrected her just weeks ago, when he was living: she was Baronet of Ahjanshoun now. Kaalo and Zinji's younger daughter.

Ziyuki.

Words fled. Ziyuki spoke first, as always. "Is there somewhere we can talk?"

Zaya drew a deep breath, tried to calm her racing heart, and said "Here's fine."

"It's too crowded, and too loud."

"It's where I'm safe, Baronet."

"What am I going to do to you?" Ziyuki said. "If I laid a finger on you, these fine people would murder me. As they should. We can't talk here, Zaya, and we need to talk."

They found a stoop toward the end of the street, one of the entrances to Zayeni's apartment building. Somehow Ziyuki had gotten hold of a pair of drinks in banana-leaf cups; she handed one to Zaya. She considered sniffing at it, just to be contrary, then shrugged and knocked it back. It was a bad decision—the drink was some kind of gin-and-mint thing, mostly gin—but she kept her cough back and looked Ziyuki straight in the eyes as she tried to keep her spine from collapsing like a wet noodle. She took in the sweat drying on her little sister's skin, the way the Kayalim clothes hung awkwardly on her—the fabric was stiff, as if new-bought and not yet washed. "What are you here for?" Zaya asked.

"Why did you do that stunt in Umber Precinct?"

"To win the Shadowrun."

Ziyuki blinked twice; then the wheels started turning. If Zaya ever worried about some shapeshifter ever trying to get close to her in a Ziyuki suit, all she needed to do was say something out of place and wait for the blink and the wheels. "That makes sense. I didn't think of that."

"Great. Good talk."

"Is that the only reason?"

"Who's asking?"

Ziyuki sighed and took a long pull on her banana-leaf cup. "For the present, let's stipulate that it's because you're my brood-sister and I care about your goals and objectives in life."

"That was very convincing."

"It's not just about the Shadowrun. You're righteously pissed off at the city, and you got a whole Precinct to agree with you to the point of shooting down a dragon. A peer of House Krait had to scuttle for his life like a bushpig."

"Was Monsoon OK, though?" Zaya asked.

"Don't pretend you don't know. If they'd hurt Monsoon, you wouldn't be such a smug shit about it all."

Zaya conceded a chuckle and took a sip of too-much-gin-and-mint. "Hell, maybe you are my sister."

"That's the nicest thing you've said to me since Papa Kaalo died."

"It's the nicest thing I've said to you since you abandoned our family."

"Now you're trying to distract me by starting a fight."

"How could I be trying to distract you, Your Splendiferousness, without having the first clue what in all the corners of all the chambers of this great green Earth you're driving at?"

"All right. Do you know why yliaster is banned in Yemareir?"

"Yes, my dumb cop fuckbuddy had much to say on the topic."

"You can't talk about this head-on," said Ziyuki. "I'm talking about you inciting a class war in a rogue precinct and all you've got is dad jokes and deflections. Why?"

"Asks the woman who got me drunk on purpose." Zaya raised her cup of gin-and-mint and took another sip. "You think I'm inciting a class war?"

"Are you trying to convince me you aren't?"

Zaya laughed softly and shook her head—a mistake; the stairs reared and lurched under her. "When your generals are in real wars," she said, "do they sit on stoops to drink and talk tactics with the enemy generals?"

Ziyuki breathed out through her nose, then knocked back the rest of the drink. "All right. That's all I needed to know. Good talk."

She stood to go, and Zaya's traitor heart was suddenly overflowing with words that needed saying. "Hold on just a second!" she shouted, feeling the slur in her voice. "You want to talk dad jokes and deflections? I asked you a direct question. Why are you here?"

"For information," Ziyuki said icily, not sitting back down. "To get it and to share it. Yliaster is banned in Yemareir for a very good reason. You know exactly what it is, thanks to your associate in the Azure Precinct police, who deserves better from you than 'dumb cop fuckbuddy' even if you are drunk. You think it's a bad ban because of your own personal tragedy... which I took steps to avert, as directly as I could, out of the coffers of House Amphisbaena, which has no reason, institutional or otherwise, to give a sack of dog farts about your dead wife's son. Some stray you picked up got you in hot water with a thug, you couldn't crime your way out of it, and I paid him off so the whole thing would go away... because I'm the world's best estranged aunt, but even more so because I know you when you've got the bit in your teeth. Once you knew there was a cure, you were going to make a very intimate and horrible problem between Jaliki and the twenty-three-dimensional larva that wants to eat his soul into something that was somehow the fault of the city that fed and housed us when our feckless dads were on the dole. That even now turns a blind eye to your juvenile insistence on riding flame-breathing killer lizards through the streets for prize money. You can't hurt Jaliki's ker. So you're going to take your leftover pain about Jaliki to something you can hurt. Even though you have no reason to hurt any more. Because I paid for it. But now *I can't pay for it.*"

It felt as though Zaya's body had dematerialized for a second, just long enough for all the alcohol to fall out of her bloodstream and onto the steps of the stoop. "What?"

"The Brimstone Slipstream Standards Board," Ziyuki said, "the 'governing body' of an *illegal and dangerous underground sports league,* is blundering around asking questions about the source of some House Krait antinoötic prototype they've apparently been using without knowing it. This is such a bad look for the ministries of trade and border protection, to say nothing of the police, that everyone who's been gently persuaded to look the other way now has their eyes firmly fixed on *exactly where they were supposed to be.* Black market supply is about to tighten like a..." Ziyuki looked at her own fist, white-knuckle tight, and relaxed it. "And I can't be anywhere near any of it. I can't help Jaliki any more, Zaya."

"Horseshit. If you can't buy the treatment directly, give us the cash and we will. You know we won't spend it on booze and bad bets."

"I could channel the payment through that slug Tjaroon," Ziyuki said tightly. "That relationship is over. I can't just replace it with a payoff to my brood-family."

"The Slayer's crusty-ass spear, Ziyuki, what happened to the self-righteous beaker of twat juice giving me lectures about how I should sit back and be grateful that the House of the Moon set aside a ration of grits and bad water for me when I was a kid? Is the Baronet of Ahjanshoun seriously filling out expense reports?"

"The Baronet of Ahjanshoun was born Kayalim," Ziyuki said, "and the House of the Moon takes pains to remind her of it every day."

Zaya drained her cup, then closed her eyes against the itching tears that flooded them. She crushed the banana leaf in her hand, felt the dregs of the gin dribble down her palm. "No more psionic dampers, at least."

Ziyuki sat down beside her. "Please," she said. "The industrial yliaster trade is about to become legal. Only the consumer trade is interdicted. House Krait and House Taipan are going to have a great year." She pressed her fingertips to her forehead. "Of course, they see the potential in anti-kerostatic applications as well. Eventually they'll figure out how to create a solution that'll work to treat kids like Jaliki but can't be used in goety—"

"How long until they can do it cheaply enough to make a profit off the poorest person in the city?"

"You're not the poorest—"

"I'm not asking about me," said Zaya. "You know you're killing my son. But it's not just about my son."

"Zaya, I know I seem powerful from where you're sitting—"

"I made myself a thief," said Zaya. "I fetched and carried for a criminal. The police hate me, and they're everywhere. And that wasn't even for Jaliki. That was for the kid I thought I could save. I don't know what your world is like, so I guess I should listen when you try to tell me. But all I see is a woman draped in gold jewelry whining about how heavy it is."

"If I start funneling money to you to spend on black-market yliaster," Ziyuki said in a voice low enough that the juke band nearly drowned it, "I will be discovered, I will be stripped of my rank and House, and you and I will both be held accountable for making House Amphisbaena whole. It will destroy me, you, and your family. I know this because I have been told it, in almost exactly the words I just spoke, by individuals within House Amphisbaena who anticipated exactly this conversation between you and me."

Zaya shrugged. "Sure, Ziyuki. Whatever. I guess all I'm saying is, if you're not going to give any of that gold away, you'd better get strong enough to wear it all yourself."

"What does that even mean?"

Zaya mushed the gin-soaked pulp of the banana leaf in her hand, squeezing out a drop of green juice. "It means do some squats. Maybe a bicep curl or two. What do you think it means? It means *grow a spine, you coward.*"

She stared straight ahead as Ziyuki got up; she did not look one inch to the right or left as her brood-sister, peer of House Amphisbaena and Baronet of Ahjanshoun, the most powerful person she knew, walked away.

She closed her eyes and let the harmonica and the smell of roast rhino wash over her.

This was her fault. Ziyuki had been right. This was what was always going to happen if she got the bit in her teeth. If she asked questions without ready answers, if she started poking into shrubs and turning over rocks, if she pointed out the strange bulges in people's pockets. She'd made the black market yliaster trade riskier than it was worth, and now it was gone and Jaliki was going to die.

She felt the solidity of a body set down next to her, felt a head on her shoulder. The long hair roughened with cheap bleach and dye, the bony shoulder, the smell of beer on her breath: "Hi, Vani."

"I saw you hanging out with Ziyuki-*cha*," Vanako said. "Want to talk about it?"

"Deal's off with House Amphisbaena. Just like you said."

She felt Vanako swallow. "Shit. What are we going to do?"

"I don't know, my breath." The endearment reminded Zaya to breathe; she filled her lungs with the warm night air, roast meat and alcohol and jasmine and the fug of summer heat still hanging on. "But whatever it is, it's not going to be small."

Epilogue

There were any number of people Zaya would never have expected to see at her door while she was still nursing a gin-and-mint hangover, but of those still living, Jenirain Gila was possibly the least expected.

"You look as shit as your street," said Jenirain.

"Who told you where I live?"

"I'm the Standards Board. We know things. Your street looks like a shark attack victim, by the way, if there were sharks that ate cities. I won't be long."

"Entire mountains have worn away to sand in the time you've been here," Zaya said. "I know this because it happened inside my skull."

Jenirain held up a knife sheathed in poor leather, gripping it by the blade; the hilt, poking toward Zaya, was cracked wood. "Someone from House Pogona gave this to us. They found it in Arhoon's apartment and recognized it as a 'streamer's saddle-knife, figured we might want it. I don't know how he got it, but I recognized it."

"That makes one of us."

Jenirain frowned. "It's Kiriki's. I'd recognize it anywhere."

"Jenirain," said Zaya. "Kiriki's saddle-knife is a piece of slag on the cobblestones in Ashen Precinct." *Unless it's in the gut of some Vore Wyrm,* she almost said, but the words choked her.

"That's what I thought." Jenirain flipped the knife around and drew it carefully. "I've only ever seen one blade with an inlay like this. Just have a look."

Zaya was ready to push her out of the doorframe, but the flat of the blade stopped her. "What in the eight gullets of Tiamat." Jenirain gave her a self-satisfied look; Zaya curled her lip. "It's not Kiriki's. She had a nice hilt, a nice sheath. This one is garbage. But… yeah, I recognize the blade." She ran a fingertip over the pearly purple inlay, the circle-and-line designs. "The decoration is different, hers had a winged snake on it. And it's made wrong. There's space between the inlay and the blade." She dug a short fingernail in and snagged at it to emphasize the point.

"So a first draft."

"I guess?"

"What's with your dog?"

Zaya looked back to see the ker, which had moved into the kitchen, as far away as it could get from the door while still seeing what was happening there. "It's not my dog. Can I have that?" Zaya took the knife without asking, then walked casually up to the ker.

First it backed away. Then, when it could not, it growled at Zaya, baring teeth and raising hackles. Then, when Zaya didn't give it space, it disappeared.

"I say again, what's with your dog?" said Jenirain.

"It's a persistence hunting demon that wants to eat my son. And it doesn't like this knife. Can I keep this knife?"

"I don't have anyone else to give it to."

Zaya nodded. Jenirain stayed in the doorway.

"OK," Zaya said at last. "Thanks, you can go."

"Am I going to run into your pet demon in the hallway?"

"Probably not," said Zaya, "It doesn't want to eat you anyway. When it's not eating little kids, it likes old bread and bacon."

"I heard about Jaliki a while back," said Jenirain, "but I'd forgotten. I'm so sorry, Zaya."

"Not as sorry as my brain, which is trying to crawl out of my left eye socket." She made herself look Jenirain in the eye. "Thank you."

Jenirain nodded and left without a word.

Zaya took the knife over to the couch. The ker had reappeared, curled up in the far corner of the common space. She slashed the knife through the air a few times in its general direction and it disappeared again. Even with the shitty grip, the balance was the same as Kiriki's had been.

She looked at the half-separated inlay, the circles and lines whose like, she now realized, she'd seen on Arhoon. The same style, if maybe not the same design. Some kind of House thing, some sorcerous pattern? Or just a design he'd thought was cool? But if he'd liked it, why was the knife he'd given to Kiriki different?

"My breath," she finally said, "what is this?"

Before you go,

A quick word from your humble author. If you enjoyed this book, I'd love it if you'd leave an honest review on the platform or platforms of your choice! Reviews are gold for authors; they encourage readers to buy our books and platforms to promote them.

The next book in the Streets of Flame series is called *Heatstroke Heartbeat*, and it's available for preorder now from your platform of choice:

https://books2read.com/heatstroke-heartbeat

And if you'd like to hear from me when it's available to order, sign up for my newsletter here:

https://www.cobblerandbard.com/mailing-list/

Whether you join or not, thank you for reading! Turn the page to sample a first draft chapter of *Heatstroke Heartbeat*—

Matt

Here follows an excerpt from the next book in the Brimstone Slip-stream series, *Heatstroke Heartbeat!*

CHAPTER 1

No matter how fast she pedaled, the slipstream of the bike didn't dry the blood on Zaya's dress. Maybe the sweat had kept it wet; the night was seasonably hot, the wind—when there was wind—blowing in from the east, bringing the wet of the cloud forest and the heat of the veldt to mingle in the streets. Embers of pain burned in her thighs, heralds of stiff stilt-walking tomorrow; she didn't realize until she dismounted, practically hurling the piece-of-shit bike across the street, that her forearms ached from squeezing the handlebars like a stewing hen's neck.

Stepping toward the compound made the world slow down. Neither wheels nor wings were here to make her fly now. The fug of the night was edged with harissa, mutton fat, and some syrup-sweet alcohol; the aroma sent a blade of thirst through Zaya's throat, and the taste-memory of shaved ice with lemon-cloudberry syrup followed like a lance to the chest. A thickly built shape stepped from the shadows by the gate, a scimitar jutting proudly from a sword belt. Zaya's mind *reached* for other minds and found them: A pangolin rooting through trash for ants, a dozing fennec, a brace of idly watching shearwaters—and a human, holding unnaturally still. Zaya seized the shearwaters and the fennec and fixed her eyes on the human, whom she still could barely see, and walked directly toward them until she could.

"Slow down, ma'am," said the other human, the one with the scimitar.

"Yeah, no," said Zaya, keeping her eyes fixed on the hidden person. She brought the fennec over with the scent-image of barbecue and had it look in the same direction she was looking. "Stop hiding, it's not working."

The hidden person didn't move. "Are you supposed to be here?" said Scimitar. "Because no one told me anyone was supposed to be here."

Zaya had the shearwaters land on her shoulders. They, she, and the fennec all stared into the shadows where the hidden person lurked.

They sighed through their nose and stepped out into the streetlamp-light. The lurker turned out to be a short, slight Mrineen woman, with a faintly glowing knotwork face tattoo of the kind you occasionally saw on some Mrineen who wanted to show how strongly they identified with their forebears who knapped flint and interfered with herd animals in the hills and hinterlands of Mrineendom a million years ago. Lurking in shadows while sporting a glowing face tattoo is the kind of thing you need magic to do, so there was that. Face Tattoo cast a quick glance up to her partner. "No appointment," she said, "but she's expected."

"Since when?"

"There's birds on her shoulders."

"I had leeches on my balls once," said Scimitar, "but it didn't get me in the boss' house at midnight."

"They're not there to scrape out her earwax, dipshit," said Face Tattoo. "She's telling us who she is."

Zaya felt a mind probing at hers. She lashed out with lightning and harsh static, and Face Tattoo flinched and hissed as if she'd been burned. The hiss faded to a grin, though. "All right, Shearwater-cha. The birds can clean out your ears for now, but they don't come inside. I'm getting a friend to verify you're who you seem to be saying you are, and then you and my employer can have the conversation."

"What conversation?" said Scimitar.

"If you don't know, I don't believe I'm authorized to enlighten you."

"She's got blood on her dress," said Scimitar. "Are you sure we ought to let her in?"

Zaya felt a familiar consciousness skitter into her mental field of view. She looked to the gate; a mandrill was staring at her. It looked at the lurker, who didn't look back, then left.

"She's the article," Face Tattoo said to Scimitar. She looked Zaya up and down, eyes lingering on the blood. "My colleague's right, though. You're in a touch of disarray. What happened?"

She didn't wait for an answer as she dug around pockets for a key and began opening the gate. Zaya felt Face Tattoo's mind just outside her own, though, watching. "Someone close to me is very badly hurt," Zaya said.

"Interesting," said Face Tattoo. "What do you expect himself to do about it?"

"If I give you the right answer, will you let me in?"

"Just making conversation," Face Tattoo said, palm out in conciliation. "I let in who the monkey says I let in. Even weeping women with blood all over themselves."

"I'm not weeping."

Face Tattoo chuffed a quick chuckle. Zaya swept past her, sending the fennec and the shearwaters on their way, and through the gate. It began to creak closed, but she felt the lurker follow.

The courtyard was small but well designed: A little pond with a fountain, a pair of benches, a banana tree. It was only a few steps to the front door of the house. Face Tattoo stepped in front of her to unlock the door, and they both stepped into a cramped, close waiting room. "You get the white glove treatment," Face Tattoo said. "Precious few guests who can pull me away from the door and back here into the *vestibule*." She pronounced the word with a deliberate twist. "Most people get the monkey. You know why, though, right? It's not because you're special. It's because you're dangerous."

Zaya looked down at her hands, still aching from squeezing the handlebars. What were they any good for? They couldn't keep their grip on what mattered most.

"You're really in no state, are you?" Face Tattoo said. Her voice was brash and jeering when she said it, but her mind was close enough in that Zaya could feel a thread of real concern. It wasn't all for Zaya; Face Tattoo wasn't sure how this would leave her with her boss, bringing in a woman who was obviously distraught, who perhaps couldn't execute, or follow through on, whatever transaction she was here for. "My name's Tanishain."

"Zaya." Zaya made herself look at Tanishain, tried to erase some of the ruin from her face. From close up she could see a dusting of fine stubble on her jawline. "Sorry about outside. It's been a rough night."

"Forgive me, Zaya, if I say I've seen women come in from rougher."

"Sure. I suppose I'm just unusually fragile."

"I doubt that. And, look, the mystery and the intensity got you in the door, didn't it? Showed us you're serious. But unless that blood's the blood of the last person beneath this sun who ever loved you... I mean, look, boss man's going to want to get down to brass tacks. Intensity's good for brass tacks. Mystery, though—"

"Tanishain," Zaya said, with a voice as clear as she could make it, "you're not going to regret bringing me in the door. I don't know whether Tjaroon and I are going to part ways with a deal or not. That was never going to be up to you. But you're not going to present your boss with a blithering sack of snot and regrets who can't hold up her end of a dessert tab." Cold pierced her again: Lemon and cloudberry syrup over shaved ice. "And you were right. I do have people waiting on me at home, and I plan on coming back to them." The words felt hollow, but she said them lightly, naturally, with no special emphasis. "You've got nothing to worry about." She glanced at the pale form at the top of the stairs. "Though I guess I should have just been talking to the monkey." Tanishain's face twitched a bit; that had stung. "Relay. Right? I used to do that once in a while. Much more useful for you, though; that's smart. Anything else I need to send along?"

Tanishain laughed softly. "Good spot. He wants to know what you're here for."

Zaya didn't try to keep the catch out of her throat. "My son. He said he could help out with my son."

"That's right."

"How long?"

"Five years."

"Not enough."

Tanishain looked off to the side a moment. "It'll have to be enough. And it'll be enough, he says. Things are changing."

Zaya closed her eyes against the sting of tears, then made herself speak before she could think too hard about it. "Fine. And what do I have to do?"

The mandrill stood and deftly opened the door at the top of the stairs. Tanishain jerked her head up toward it. "That one doesn't go through me, love."

Zaya stood and walked over to the stairs. Her legs, still so much slower than wings or wheels, made the journey an infinity. She thought the mandrill had disappeared into the room, but when she looked up, she saw a pair of flashing eyes and the ghost of a snout, watching to see what she would do.

She closed her eyes briefly, bit her lip, and placed one foot on the lowest stair.

ABOUT THE AUTHOR

Matt Weber is the author of the Streets of Flame series, *The Dandelion Knight*, *Reverie Syndrome*, and *Verso & Other Stories*, as well as short fiction in *Nature*, *Cosmos*, and *Kaleidotrope*. By day, he has worked in a number of data-related professions in academia, digital health, fintech, and government. He lives in New Jersey under a pile of writhing juvenile D&D addicts.

Bluesky: @mattweber.bsky.social
Newsletter: https://www.cobblerandbard.com/mailing-list

www.ingramcontent.com/pod-product-compliance
Lightning Source LLC
Chambersburg PA
CBHW050845210726
48290CB00004B/1088